LINDA HOWARD

says that whether she's reading them or writing them, books have long played a profound role in her life. She cut her teeth on Margaret Mitchell and from then on continued to read widely and eagerly. In recent years her interest has settled on romance fiction, because she's "easily bored by murder, mayhem and politics." After twenty-one years of penning stories for her own enjoyment, Ms. Howard finally worked up the courage to submit a novel for publication—and met with success! Happily, the Alabama author has been steadily publishing ever since, and has made numerous appearances on the *New York Times* bestseller list.

ALLISON LEIGH

There is a saying that you can never be too rich or too thin. Allison doesn't believe that, but she does believe that you can never have enough bookshelves or enough books! When her stories find a way into the hearts—and onto the bookshelves—of others, Allison says she feels she's done something right. Making her home in Arizona with her family, she enjoys hearing from her readers at: Allison@allisonleigh.com or P.O. Box 40772, Mesa, AZ 85274-0772.

LINDA HOWARD

HOWARD

ALLISON LEIGH

On His Terms

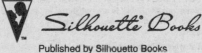
Silhouette Books

Published by Silhouette Books

America's Publisher of Contemporary Romance

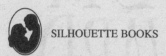

SILHOUETTE BOOKS

ON HIS TERMS

Copyright © 2003 by Harlequin Books S.A.

ISBN 0-373-21804-4

The publisher acknowledges the copyright holders of the individual works as follows:

LOVING EVANGELINE
Copyright © 1994 by Linda Howington

ONE MORE CHANCE
Copyright © 2003 by Allison Lee Davidson

Visit Silhouette at www.eHarlequin.com

Printed in U.S.A.

CONTENTS

LOVING EVANGELINE
by Linda Howard

Chapter 1

Davis Priesen didn't think of himself as a coward, but he would rather have had surgery without anesthesia than face Robert Cannon and tell him what he had to tell him. It wasn't that the majority stockholder, CEO and president of Cannon Group would hold him responsible for the bad news; Cannon had never been known to shoot the messenger. But those icy green eyes would become even colder, even more remote, and Davis knew from experience that he would feel the frigid touch of fear along his spine. Cannon had a reputation for scrupulous fairness, but also for unmatched ruthlessness when someone tried to screw him. Davis couldn't think of anyone he respected more than Robert Cannon, but that didn't relieve his dread.

Other men in Cannon's position, with his power,

insulated themselves behind layers of assistants. It was a measure of his own control and personal remoteness that only Cannon's personal assistant guarded the gates to his inner sanctum. Felice Koury had been Cannon's PA for eight years and ran his office with the precision of a Swiss watch. She was a tall, lean, ageless woman with iron-gray hair and the smooth complexion of a twenty-year-old. Davis knew that her youngest child was in his mid-twenties, putting Felice at least in her mid-forties, but it was impossible to guess her age from her appearance. She was cool under fire, frighteningly efficient and had never shown a hint of nervousness around her boss. Davis wished he had a little of that last ability.

He had called beforehand to make certain Cannon could see him, so Felice wasn't surprised when he entered her office. "Good morning, Mr. Priesen." She reached immediately for the phone and punched a button. "Mr. Priesen is here, sir." She replaced the receiver and stood. "He'll see you now." With the smooth efficiency that always intimidated him, she was at the door of the inner office before he could reach it, opening it for him, then firmly closing it when he was inside. There was nothing subservient in Felice's attention; rather, he felt as if she controlled even his entrance into Cannon's office. Which, of course, she did.

Cannon's office was huge, luxurious and exquisitely decorated. It was a tribute to his taste that the effect was relaxing, rather than overwhelming, even though original oil paintings hung on the walls and a two-hundred-year-old Persian rug was underfoot. To the right was a large sitting area, complete with entertainment center, though Davis doubted that Cannon ever used the large-screen television or VCR for anything other than business. Six Palladian windows marched along the wall, framing the matchless views of New York City as if they were six paintings. The windows were works of art in themselves, beautifully fashioned panes of cut glass that took the light streaming through them and splintered it into diamonds.

Cannon's massive desk was another antique, a masterpiece of carved black wood that supposedly had belonged to the eighteenth-century Romanovs. He looked very at home behind it.

He was a tall, lean man, with the elegant grace and power of a panther. There was something pantherish about his coloring, too, with his sleek black hair and pale green eyes. One might even think of Robert Cannon as indolent. One would be dangerously mistaken.

He rose to his feet to shake hands, his long, well-shaped fingers gripping Davis's with surprising strength. Davis was always taken aback by the steeliness of that grip.

On some occasions Cannon had invited him to the sitting area and asked if he would like coffee. This was not one of those occasions. Cannon hadn't reached his position by misreading people, and his eyes narrowed as he examined the tension in Davis's face. "I would say it's good to see you, Davis," he remarked, "but I don't think you're here to tell me something I'm going to like."

His voice had been easy, almost casual, but Davis felt his tension go up another ten notches. "No, sir."

"Is it your fault?"

"No, sir." Then, scrupulously honest, he admitted, "Though I probably should have caught it sooner."

"Then relax and sit down," Robert said gently as he reseated himself. "If it isn't your fault, you're safe. Now, tell me what the problem is."

Davis nervously took a seat, but relaxing was out of the question. He perched on the edge of a soft leather chair. "Someone in Huntsville is selling our software for the space station," he blurted.

Cannon was never a restless man, but now he became even more still, and those green eyes took on the glacial look that Davis dreaded. "Do you have proof?" he asked.

"Yes, sir."

"Do you know who?"

"I think so, sir."

"Fill me in." With those abrupt words, Cannon leaned back, his gaze focused on Davis like a pale green laser.

Davis did, stumbling several times as he tried to explain how he had become suspicious and done a bit of investigating on his own to verify his suspicions before he accused anyone. Cannon listened in silence, and Davis wiped the sweat from his brow as he described the results of his sleuthing. The Cannon

Group company, PowerNet, located in Huntsville, Alabama, was currently working on highly classified software developed for NASA. That software was definitely showing up in the hands of a company affiliated with another country. This wasn't just industrial espionage, which would have been enough; this was treason.

His suspicions had centered on Landon Mercer, the company manager. Mercer had divorced the year before, and his style of living had gone noticeably upward. His salary was very good, but not good enough to support a family and live the way he had been living. Davis had discreetly hired an investigation service that had discovered large deposits into Mercer's bank account. After following him for several weeks, they had reported that he regularly visited a marina in Guntersville, a small town nearby, situated on Guntersville Lake, an impoundment of the Tennessee river.

The owner/operator of the marina was a woman named Evie Shaw; the investigators hadn't yet been able to find out anything substantive from her bank accounts or spending habits, which could mean only that she was smarter than Mercer. On at least two occasions, however, Mercer had rented a motorboat at the marina, and shortly after he had left in the boat, Evie Shaw had closed the marina, gotten into her own boat and followed him. They had returned separately, some fifteen minutes apart. It looked as if they were meeting somewhere on the big lake, where they would find it very easy both to conceal their actions, and to see and hear anyone approaching them. It was much safer than trying to conduct clandestine business in the busy marina; in fact, the popularity of the marina made it all the odder that she would close it down in the middle of the day.

When Davis had finished and sat nervously cracking his knuckles, Cannon's face was hard and expressionless. "Thank you, Davis," he said calmly. "I'll notify the FBI and take it from here. Good work."

Davis flushed as he got to his feet. "I'm sorry I didn't catch it sooner."

"Security isn't your area. Someone was falling down on the job. I'll take care of that, too. We're lucky that you're as sharp as you are." Robert made a mental note to both increase Davis's salary, which was already healthy, and begin grooming him for more responsibility and power. He had shown a sharpness and initiative that shouldn't go unrewarded. "I'm sure the FBI will want to speak with you, so stay available for the rest of the day."

"Yes, sir."

As soon as Davis had left, Robert used his private line to call the FBI. The bureau maintained a huge force in the city, and he had had occasion to work with them before. He was put through immediately to the supervisory agent. His control was such that none of his rage was revealed in his voice as he requested that the two best agents come to his office as soon as possible. His influence was such that no questions were asked; he was simply given the quiet assurance that two agents would be there within the half hour.

That done, he sat back and considered all the options open to him. He didn't allow his cold fury to cloud his thinking. Uncontrolled emotion was not only useless, it was stupid, and Robert never allowed himself to do anything stupid. He took it personally that someone at one of his companies was selling classified computer programs; it was a blemish on his own reputation. He had nothing but contempt for someone who would sell out his own country merely for the money involved, and he would stop at nothing to halt the theft and put the perpetrator behind bars. Within fifteen minutes, he had formulated his plan of action.

The two agents arrived in twenty minutes. When Felice buzzed him, he told her to send them in, and that he wanted no interruptions of any kind until the gentlemen had left. A perfect secretary to the bone, she asked no questions.

She ushered the two conservatively dressed men into his office and firmly closed the door behind them. Robert stood to welcome them, but all the while he was assessing them with his cool, unreadable gaze. The younger man, about thirty, was immediately recognizable as a midlevel civil servant, but there was also a certain self-assurance in the man's eyes that Robert approved of. The older man, perhaps in his early fifties, had light brown hair that had gone mostly gray. He was not quite of average height, and was stocky of build. The blue eyes, be-

hind metal-framed glasses, were tired, but nevertheless sparkled with intelligence and authority. No ju-
nior agent, this.

The older man held out his hand to Robert. "Mr.
Cannon?" At Robert's nod, he said, "I'm William
Brent, senior agent with the Federal Bureau of Investigation. This is Lee Murray, special agent assigned to counterespionage."

"Counterespionage," Robert murmured, his eyes
cool. The presence of these two particular agents meant
that the FBI had already been investigating PowerNet.
"Good guess, gentlemen. Please sit down."

"It wasn't much of a guess," Agent Brent replied
ruefully, as they took the offered seats. "A corpo-
ration such as yours, which handles so many government contracts, is unfortunately a prime target for
espionage. I'm also aware that you have some experience in that area yourself, so it followed that you
might need our particular talents, so to speak."

He was good, Robert thought. Just the type of person to inspire trust. They wanted to know if he knew
anything, but they weren't going to tip their own
hand if he didn't mention PowerNet. That little cha-
rade was a screen of innocence, behind which they
could exhibit surprise and consternation if he informed them that he had discovered a leak at the
company, or hide their own knowledge if he didn't
mention the matter.

He didn't let them get away with it. "I see you've
picked up some disquieting information yourselves,"

he said remotely. "I'm interested in knowing why you didn't contact me immediately."

William Brent grimaced. He had heard that nothing got by Robert Cannon, but still, he hadn't expected the man to be so acute.

Cannon was looking at him with a slight, cool lift of his eyebrow that invited explanations, an expression most people found difficult to resist.

Brent managed to control the inclination to rush into speech, mingling explanation with apology; he was astonished that the impulse even existed. It made him study Robert Cannon even more closely. He already knew a lot about the man, as he had made it his business to find out. Cannon came from a cultured, moneyed background, but had made himself much wealthier with his own astute business sense, and his reputation was impeccable. He also had a lot of friends in both the State and Justice departments, powerful men in their own right, who held him in the greatest respect. "Look, here," one of those men had said. "If something crooked is going on with any of the Cannon Group companies, I'd take it as a personal favor if you'd let Robert Cannon know about it before you do anything."

"I can't do that," Brent had replied. "It would compromise the investigation."

"Not at all," the man had said. "I would trust Cannon with the country's most sensitive intelligence. As a matter of fact, I already have, on several occasions. He's done some…favors for us."

"It's possible he could be in on it," Brent had

warned, still resisting the idea of briefing a civilian outsider on the situation developing down in Alabama.

But the other man had shaken his head. "No. Not Robert Cannon."

After learning something about the nature and magnitude of the "favors" Cannon had done, and the dangers involved, Brent had reluctantly agreed to apprise Cannon of the situation before they put any plans into operation. Cannon had derailed that by calling first; and they hadn't been certain if he already knew, or not. The plan had been to keep quiet until they found out why he had called. It hadn't worked. He'd seen through them immediately.

Brent was used to reading men, but he couldn't read Cannon. His persona was that of a wealthy, cultured, sophisticated man, and Brent supposed he was all that, but nevertheless, it was only the first layer. The other layers, whatever they were, were so well hidden that he only sensed their existence, and even that was due only to his own access to privileged information. Watching Cannon's leanly handsome face, he couldn't catch so much as a flicker of expression; there were only those remote eyes watching him with unlimited patience.

Making a swift decision, William Brent leaned forward. "Mr. Cannon, I'm going to tell you a lot more than I had originally planned. We have a definite problem at one of your companies, a software company down in Alabama—"

"Suppose I tell you what I know?" Robert interrupted in an even tone. "Then you can tell me if you have anything to add."

With calm, precise sentences, he recounted what Davis Priesen had told him. The two agents shared one startled, involuntary glance that revealed they hadn't discovered as much as Davis had, which upped that young man's stock with Robert even more.

When he had finished, William Brent cleared his throat and leaned forward. "Congratulations. You're a bit ahead of us. This will help us considerably in our investigation—"

"I'm flying down there tomorrow morning," Robert said.

Brent looked disapproving. "Mr. Cannon, I appreciate your desire to help, but this is best handled by the bureau."

"You misunderstand. I don't intend to *help*. This is my company, my problem. I'll take care of it myself. I'm merely apprising you of the situation and my intentions. I don't have to take the time to set up a cover and get inside the operation, because I own it. I will, of course, keep you informed."

Brent was already shaking his head. "No, it's out of the question."

"Who better? I not only have access to everything, my presence wouldn't be as alarming as that of federal investigators." He paused, then said gently, "I'm not a rank amateur."

"I'm aware of that, Mr. Cannon."

"Then I suggest you talk this over with your superiors." He glanced at his watch. "In the meantime, I have arrangements to make."

He had no doubt that when Brent took this to his superiors, he would be surprised and chagrined to be told to back off and let Robert Cannon handle this problem on his own. They would provide every assistance, of course, and have backup in place if he needed it, but Agent Brent would find that Robert was calling the shots.

He spent the rest of the day clearing his calendar. Felice made the open-ended flight arrangements and his hotel reservation in Huntsville. Just before leaving that night, he checked his watch and took a chance. Though it was eight o'clock in New York, it was only six in Montana, and the long summer daylight hours meant ranch work went on for much longer than during the winter.

To his delight, the phone was picked up on the third ring and his sister's lazy drawl came over the line. "Duncans' Madhouse, Madelyn speaking."

Robert chuckled. He could hear in the background the din his two young nephews were making. "Had a busy day, honey?"

"Robert!" Pleasure warmed her voice. "You might say that. Would you be interested in having your nephews for a prolonged visit?"

"Not until they're housebroken. I won't be at home, anyway."

"Where are you off to this time?"

"Huntsville, Alabama."

She paused. "It's hot down there."

"I'm aware of that."

"You might even *sweat*," she warned him. "Think how upset you'd be."

His firm mouth twitched at the amusement in her voice. "That's a chance I'll have to take."

"It must be serious, then. Trouble?"

"A few glitches."

"Take care."

"I will. If it looks as though I'll be down there for any length of time, I'll call you and give you my number."

"All right. Love you."

"Love you, too." He smiled a bit as he hung up. It was typical of Madelyn that she hadn't asked questions but had immediately sensed the seriousness of the situation awaiting him in Alabama. In six words she had given him her blessing, her support and her love. Though she was actually only his stepsister, the affection and understanding between them were as strong as if they had been connected by blood.

Next he called the woman he had been escorting rather regularly lately, Valentina Lawrence. The relationship hadn't progressed far enough that he would expect her to wait until his return, so the easiest thing for both of them was if he made it clear that she was free to see anyone she wished. It was a pity; Valentina was too popular to remain unattached for long, and he suspected he would be in Alabama for several weeks.

She was just the sort of woman Robert had always been most attracted to: the thoroughbred racehorse type—tall, lean, small-breasted. Her makeup was always impeccable and understated, her clothing both stylish and tasteful. She had a genuinely pleasant personality, and enjoyed the theater and opera as much as he did. She would have been a wonderful companion, if this problem hadn't interfered.

It had been several months since he had ended his last relationship, and he was feeling restless. He much preferred living with a woman to living alone, though he was perfectly content with his own company. He deeply enjoyed women, both mentally and physically, and he normally preferred the steadiness of a long-term relationship. He didn't do one-nighters and disdained those who were so stupid. He refrained from making love to a woman until she had committed herself to a relationship with him.

Valentina accepted the news of his prolonged absence with grace; after all, they weren't lovers and had no claim on each other. He could hear the gentle regret in her voice, but she didn't ask him to call when he returned.

That final piece of business concluded, he sat for several minutes, frowning as he allowed himself to think about the relationship that hadn't quite developed into intimacy, and how long it would be before he had time to attend to the sexual part of his life again. He wasn't pleased at the prospect of a long wait.

He wasn't casual about sex in any way. His intense sexuality was always under strict control; with the difference between a man's strength and a woman's, a man who *wasn't* in control could easily brutalize a woman, something that disgusted him. He tempered both his sexual appetite and his steely strength, reining them in with the icy power of his intellect. He never pressured a woman, though he always made it clear when he was attracted, so she would know where she stood. But he let his lady set the pace, let the intimacy progress at her speed. He respected a woman's natural caution about opening her tender, vulnerable body to a much bigger, stronger male. When it came to sex, he treated women gently and took his time so they could become fully aroused. Such control was no hardship; he could spend hours caressing soft, feminine skin and intriguing curves. Lingering over the lovemaking helped satisfy his own hunger, while intensifying his partner's.

There was nothing like making love that first time with a new partner, he mused. Never again was the experience so intense and hungry. He always tried to make it special for his lady, to make *her* feel special. He never stinted on the little details that made a woman feel treasured: romantic dinners for two, candlelight, champagne, thoughtful gifts, his complete attention. When the time finally came to retire to the bedroom, he would use all of his skill and control to satisfy her again and again before he allowed release for himself.

Thinking about what the problem in Alabama was causing him to miss made him irritated.

He was roused by a knock on his door. He looked up as Felice stuck her head in. "You should have gone home," he reproved. "You didn't have to stay."

"A messenger brought this envelope for you," she said, approaching to place it on his desk. She ignored his comment. No matter how late, she seldom left before he did.

"Go home," he said calmly. "That's an order. I'll call you tomorrow."

"Do you need anything before I go? A fresh pot of coffee?"

"No, I won't be staying much longer myself."

"Then have a good trip." She smiled and left the room. He could hear her in the outer office gathering together her possessions and locking everything up for the night.

He doubted that anything about the trip would be good. He was in a vengeful mood and out for blood.

He noticed that the manila envelope had no return address. He opened it and slid several pages out. There was one grainy, photostated picture, a recap of the situation and what they already knew about it, and a brief message from Agent Brent, identifying the woman in the picture and informing Robert that the bureau would cooperate with him in all matters, which was only what he had expected.

He picked up the reproduced photograph and studied it. It was of very poor quality, but pictured a woman standing on a dock, with motorboats in the background. So this was Evie Shaw. She was wearing sunglasses, so it was difficult to tell much about her, other than she had blondish, untidy hair and

seemed to be rather hefty. No Mata Hari there, he
thought, his fastidious taste offended by her poor
choice of clothes and her general hayseed appearance. She looked more like a female mud wrestler,
a coarse hick who was selling out her country for
greed.

Briskly he returned the papers to the envelope. He
looked forward to bringing both Landon Mercer and
Evie Shaw to justice.

Chapter 2

It was a typically hot, sultry Southern summer day. The sky overhead was a deep, rich blue, dotted with fat white clouds that lazily sailed along on a breeze so slight it barely rippled the lake's surface. Gulls wheeled overhead and boats bobbed hypnotically in their slips. A few diehard fishermen and skiers dotted the water, ignoring the heat, but most of the fishermen who had gone out that morning had returned before noon. The air was heavy and humid, intensifying the odors of the lake and the surrounding lush, green mountains.

Evangeline Shaw looked out over her domain from the big plate-glass windows at the rear of the main marina building. Everyone on earth needed his own kingdom, and hers was this sprawling skeletal maze of docks and boat slips. Nothing within these few square acres escaped her attention. Five years ago, when she had taken over, it had been run-down and barely paying expenses. A sizable bank loan had been required to give it the infusion of capital it had needed, but within a year she had had it spruced up, expanded and bringing in more money than it ever had before. Of course, it took more money to run it, but now the marina was making a nice profit. With any luck she would have the bank loan paid off in another three years. Then the marina would be completely hers, free and clear of debt, and she would be able to expand even more, as well as diversify her holdings. She only hoped business would hold up; the fishing trade had slacked off a lot, due to the Tennessee Valley Authority's "weed management" program that had managed to kill most of the water plants that had harbored and protected the fish.

But she had been careful, and she hadn't overextended. Her debt was manageable, unlike that of others who had thought the fishing boom would last forever and had gone deeply into debt to expand. Her domain was secure.

Old Virgil Dodd had been with her most of the morning, sitting in the rocking chair behind the counter and entertaining her and her customers with tales of his growing-up days, back in the 1900s. The old man was as tough as shoe leather, but almost a century weighed on his inceasingly frail shoulders, and Evie was afraid that another couple of years, three at the most, would be too much for him. She had known him all her life; he had been *old* all her life, changing little, as enduring as the river and the mountains. But she knew all too well how fleeting and uncertain human life was, and she treasured the mornings that Virgil spent with her. He enjoyed them, too; he no longer went out fishing, as he had for the first eighty years of his life, but at the marina he was still close to the boats, where he could hear the slap of the water against the docks and smell the lake.

They were alone now, just the two of them, and Virgil had launched into another tale from his youth. Evie perched on a tall stool, occasionally glancing out the windows to see if anyone had pulled up to the gas pump on the dock, but giving most of her attention to Virgil.

The side door opened, and a tall, lean man stepped inside. He stood for a moment before removing his sunglasses, helping his eyes adjust to the relative dimness, then moved toward her with a silent, pantherish stroll.

Evie gave him only a swift glance before turning her attention back to Virgil, but it was enough to make her defenses rise. She didn't know who he was, but she recognized immediately *what* he was; he was not only a stranger, he was an outsider. There were a lot of Northerners who had retired to Guntersville, charmed by the mild winters, the slow pace, low cost of living and natural beauty of the lake, but he wasn't one of them. He was far too young to be retired, for one thing. His accent would be fast and hard, his clothes expensive and his attitude disdainful. Evie had met his kind before. She hadn't been impressed then, either.

But it wasn't just that. It was the other quality she had caught that made her want to put a wall at her back.

He was dangerous.

Though she smiled at Virgil, instinctively she analyzed the stranger. She had grown up with bad boys, daredevils and hell-raisers; the South produced them in abundance. This man was something different, something…more. He didn't embrace danger as much as he *was* danger. It was a different mind-set, a will and temperament that brooked no opposition, a force of character that had glittered in those startlingly pale eyes.

She didn't know how or why, but she sensed that he was a threat to her.

"Excuse me," he said, and the deepness of his voice ran over her like velvet. A strange little quiver tightened her belly and ran up her spine. The words were courteous, but the iron will behind them told her that he expected her to immediately attend to him.

She gave him another quick, dismissive glance. "I'll be with you in a minute," she said, her tone merely polite, then she turned back to Virgil with real warmth. "What happened then, Virgil?"

No hint of emotion showed on Robert's face, though he was a bit startled by the woman's lack of response. That was unusual. He wasn't accustomed to being ignored by anyone, and certainly not by a

woman. Women had always been acutely aware of
him, responding to the intense masculinity he kept
under ruthless control. He wasn't vain, but his effect
on women was something he largely took for
granted. He couldn't remember ever wanting a
woman and not having her, eventually.

But he was willing to wait and use the opportunity
to watch this woman. Her appearance had thrown
him a little off balance, also something unusual for
him. He still hadn't adjusted his expectations to the
reality.

This was Evie Shaw, no doubt about it. She sat on
a stool behind the counter, all her attention on an old
man who sat in a rocking chair, his aged voice glee-
ful as he continued to recount some tall tale from his
long-ago youth. Robert's eyes narrowed fractionally
as he studied her.

She wasn't the thick-bodied hayseed he had expected. Or rather, she wasn't thick-bodied; he re-
served judgment on the hayseed part. The unflatter-
ing image he'd formed must have been caused by the
combination of bad photography and poorly fitting
clothes. He had walked in looking for a woman who
was coarse and ill-bred, but that wasn't what he'd
found.

Instead, she…glowed.

It was an unsettling illusion, perhaps produced by
the brilliant sunlight streaming in through the big
windows, haloing her sunny hair and lighting the
tawny depths of her hazel eyes. The light caressed
her golden skin, which was as smooth and unblem-

ished as a porcelain doll's. Illusion or not, the woman was luminous.

Her voice had been surprisingly deep and a little raspy, bringing up memories of old Bogie and Bacall movies and making Robert's spine prickle. Her accent was lazy and liquid, as melodious as a murmuring creek or the wind in the trees, a voice that made him think of tangled sheets and long, hot nights.

Watching her, he felt something inside him go still.

The old man leaned forward, folding his gnarled hands over the crook of his walking cane. His faded blue eyes were full of laughter and the memories of good times. "Well, we'd tried ever way we knowed to get John H. away from that still, but he weren't budging. He kept an old shotgun loaded with rat shot, so we were afeard to venture too close. He knowed it was just a bunch of young'uns aggravating him, but *we* didn't know he knowed. Ever time he grabbed that shotgun, we'd run like jackrabbits, then we'd come sneakin' back...."

Robert forced himself to look around as he tuned out the rest of Virgil's tale. Ramshackle though the building was, the business seemed to be prospering, if the amount of tackle on hand and the number of occupied boat slips were any indication. A pegboard behind the counter held the ignition keys to the rental boats, each key neatly labeled and numbered. He wondered how she kept track of who had which boat.

Virgil was well into his tale, slapping his knee and

chortling. Evie Shaw threw back her head with a shout of pure enjoyment, her laughter as deep as her speaking voice. Robert was suddenly aware of how accustomed he had become to carefully controlled social laughter, how shrill and shallow it was compared to her unabashed mirth, with nothing forced or held back.

He tried to resist the compulsion to stare at her, but, to his surprise, it was like resisting the need to breathe. He could manage it for a little while, but it was a losing battle from the start. With a mixture of fury and curiosity, he gave in to the temptation and let his gaze greedily drink her in.

He watched her with an impassive expression, his self-control so absolute that neither his posture nor his face betrayed any hint of his thoughts. Unfortunately, that self-control didn't extend to those thoughts as his attention focused on Evie Shaw with such intensity that he was no longer aware of his surroundings, that he no longer heard Virgil's cracked voice continuing with his tale.

She wasn't anything like the women he had always found most attractive. She was also a traitor, or at least was involved in industrial espionage. He had every intention of breaking her, of bringing her to justice. Yet he couldn't take his eyes off her, couldn't control his wayward thoughts, couldn't still the sudden hard thumping in his chest. He had been sweating in the suffocating heat, but suddenly the heat inside him was so blistering that it made the outer temperature seem cool in comparison. His skin felt too tight, his clothing too restrictive. A familiar heaviness in his loins made the last two sensations all too real, rather than products of his imagination.

The women he had wanted in the past, for all the differences in their characters, had shared a certain sense of style, of sophistication. They had all looked—and been—expensive. He hadn't minded, and had enjoyed spoiling them more. They had all been well dressed, perfumed, exquisitely turned out. His sister Madelyn had disparagingly referred to a couple of them as mannequins, but Madelyn herself was a clotheshorse of the highest order, so he had been amused rather than irritated by the comment.

Evie Shaw, in contrast, evidently paid no attention to her clothes. She wore an oversize T-shirt that she had knotted at the waist, a pair of jeans so ancient that they were threadbare and almost colorless, and equally old docksiders. Her hair, a sun-streaked blond that ranged in color from light brown to the palest flax, and included several different shades of gold, was pulled back and confined in an untidy braid that was as thick as his wrist and hung halfway down her back. Her makeup was minimal and probably a waste of time in this humidity, but with her complexion, she didn't really need it.

Damn it, how could she glow like that? It wasn't the sheen of perspiration, but the odd impression that light was attracted to her, as if she forever stood in a subtle spotlight. Her skin was lightly tanned, a creamy golden hue, and it looked like warm, living satin. Even her eyes were the golden brown hazel of dark topaz.

He had always preferred tall, lean women; as tall as he was himself, he had felt better matched with them on the dance floor and in bed. Evie Shaw was no more than five-four, if that. Nor was she lean; rather, the word that came to mind was *luscious,* followed immediately by *delicious.* Caught off guard by the violence of his reaction, he wondered savagely if he wanted to make love to her or eat her, and the swift mental answer to his own question was a flat, unequivocal "yes." To both choices.

She was a symphony of curves, not quite full-figured, but sleek and rounded, the absolute essence of femaleness. No slim, boyish hips there, but a definite flare from her waist, and she had firm, round buttocks. He had always adored the delicacy of small breasts but now found himself entranced by the soft globes that shaped the front of the annoyingly loose T-shirt. They weren't big, heavy breasts, though they had a slight bounce that riveted his attention whenever she moved; they weren't exactly voluptuous, but were just full enough to be maddeningly tempting. Their soft, warm weight would fill his hands, hands that he tightened into fists in an effort to resist the urge to reach out and touch her.

Everything about her was shaped for a man's delight, but he wasn't delighted by his reaction. If *he* could respond to her like this, maybe Mercer was her pawn rather than the other way around. It was a possibility he couldn't ignore.

Not only was she nothing like the women he had previously desired, he was furious with himself for wanting her. He was down here to gather evidence that would send her to prison, and he couldn't let lust make him lose sight of that. This woman was wading hip-deep in the sewer of espionage, and he shouldn't feel anything for her except disgust. Instead he was struggling with a physical desire so intense that it was all he could do to simply stand there, rather than act. He didn't want to court her, seduce her; he wanted to grab her and carry her away. His lair was a hideously expensive Manhattan penthouse, but the primitive instinct was the same one that had impelled men to the same action back when their lairs were caves. He wanted her, and there was nothing civilized or gentle about it. The urge made a mockery of both his intellect and his self-control.

He wanted to ignore the attraction, but he couldn't; it was too strong, the challenge too great. Evie Shaw was not just ignoring him, she was totally oblivious to the pure male intent that was surging through him. He might as well have been a post for all the attention she was paying to him, and every aggressive cell in his body was on alert. By God, he *would* have her.

The door behind him opened, and he turned, grateful for the interruption. A young woman, clad in shorts, sandals and a T-shirt, smiled at him and murmured, ''Hello,'' as she approached. Both the smile and the look lingered for just a moment before she turned her attention to the two people behind the counter. "Have you enjoyed your visit, PawPaw? Who all has been in today?"

"Had a good time," Virgil said, slowly getting to his feet with a lot of help from the cane. "Burt Mardis spent some time with us, and both of the Gibbs boys came by. Have you got the young'uns rounded up?"

"They're in the car with the groceries." She turned to Evie. "I hate to run, but it's so hot I want to get the food put up before it spoils."

"Everything I can, I put off until night," Evie said. "Including buying groceries. Bye, Virgil. You take care of that knee, all right? And come back soon."

"The knee feels better already," he assured her. "Getting old ain't no fun, but it's better than dying." He winked and steadily made his way down the aisle, using the cane but otherwise not making much allowance for his noticeable limp.

"See you later, Evie," the young woman said as she turned to go. She gave Robert another smile in passing.

When the old man and young woman had left and the door had closed behind them, Robert leaned negligently against the counter and said in a mild tone, "I assume she's his granddaughter."

Evie shook her head and turned away to check the gas pumps again. She was too aware of being alone with him, which was ridiculous; she was alone with male customers several times a day and had never felt the least hint of uneasiness—until now. She had felt a subtle alarm the second he had walked in the door. He hadn't said or done anything untoward, but still, she couldn't shake that feeling of wariness. "Great-granddaughter. He lives with her. I apologize for making you wait, but I'll have other customers, while Virgil is ninety-three, and he may not be around much longer."

"I understand," he said calmly, not wanting to antagonize her. He held out his hand, a gesture calculated to force her to look at him, truly acknowledge him, *touch* him. "I'm Robert Cannon."

She put her hand in his, just slowly enough to let him know that she was reluctant to shake hands with him and did it only to be polite. Her fingers were slim and cool and gripped his with surprising strength. "Evie Shaw," she said. He made certain his own grip was firm, but not enough to hurt, and promptly released her. The contact was brief, impersonal…and not enough.

Immediately she turned away and said briskly, "What is it you need, Mr. Cannon?"

He came up with several graphic ideas but didn't give voice to them. Instead he thoughtfully eyed her slim back, rapidly adjusting his impressions. He had thought her oblivious to him, but she was too studiously ignoring him for that; no, quite the contrary, she was very aware of him, and very on edge. In a flash, all of his plans changed.

He had entered the marina wanting only to look around a little, get an idea of the security and layout of the place, maybe buy a fishing license or map, but all of that had changed in the past few minutes. Rather than shadow Mercer, he now intended to stick to Evie Shaw like glue.

Why was she so wary of him? She had been, right from the beginning, even before he had introduced himself. The only explanation that came to mind was that she had already known who he was, had somehow recognized him, and she could only have done that if she had been briefed. If so, this operation was more sophisticated than he had expected. It wouldn't be beyond his capabilities, but it would certainly be more of a challenge. With one of his lightning-fast decisions, he changed the base of his investigation from Huntsville to Guntersville. Before the fall of the Soviet Union, he had, on a couple of memorable occasions, found himself attracted to female operatives; taking them to bed had been a risk, but a delightful one. Danger certainly added to the excitement. Bedding Evie Shaw, he suspected, would be an event he would never forget.

"First, I need information," he said, irritated because she still wasn't looking at him, but not a hint of it sounded in his voice. He needed to lull her suspicions, make her comfortable with him. Gentling women had never been difficult for him before, and he didn't expect it to be now. As far as anyone outside a few government officials knew, he was nothing more than a very wealthy businessman; if she was as smart as he now suspected her to be, she would soon see the benefits in becoming close to him, not only for what he could give her but for the information she could get from him. A summer fling would be perfect for her needs, and he intended to give her just that.

"Perhaps you should go to the Visitors' Center," she suggested.

"Perhaps," he murmured. "But I was told that you can help me."

"Maybe." Her tone was reluctant. She certainly wasn't committing herself to anything. "What kind of information do you need?"

"I'm taking a long vacation here, for the rest of the summer," he said. "My second reason for coming here is to rent a boat slip, but I also want someone to show me around the lake. I was told that you know the area as well as anyone."

She faced him, her gaze hooded. "That's true, but I don't guide. I can help you with the boat, but that's all."

She had thrown up a wall as soon as she had seen him, and she had no intention of being cooperative about anything. He gave her a gentle smile, one that had been soothing nervous women for years. "I understand. You don't know me."

He saw the involuntary reaction to that smile in the way her pupils flared. Now she looked uncertain. "It isn't that. I don't know a lot of my customers."

"I believe the going rate for guides is a hundred a day, plus expenses. I'm willing to pay twice that."

"It isn't a matter of money, Mr. Cannon. I don't have the time."

Pushing her now wouldn't accomplish anything,

and he had a lot to get in place before he could really pursue her. He had made certain she wouldn't forget him, which was enough for a first meeting. "Can you recommend a guide, then?" he asked, and saw her relax a little.

She reeled off several names, which he committed to memory, for he fully intended to learn the river. Then she said, "Would you like to look at the boat slips that are available now?"

"Yes, of course." It would give him a chance to inspect her security arrangements, too.

She picked up a portable phone and clipped it to a belt loop, then came out from behind the counter. Robert fell into step slightly behind her, his heavy-lidded gaze wandering over her curvy hips and heart-shaped bottom, clearly outlined by the snug jeans. Her sun-streaked head barely reached the top of his shoulder. His blood throbbed warmly through his veins as he thought of cupping her bottom in his hands. It was an effort to wrench his attention away from the image that thought provoked.

"Do you just leave the store unattended?" he asked as they walked down the dock. The sunlight was blinding as it reflected off the water, and he slipped his sunglasses into place again. The heat was incredible, like a sauna.

"I can see from the docks if anyone drives up," she replied.

"How many others work here?"

She gave him a curious glance, as if wondering why he would ask. "I have a mechanic, and a boy who works mornings for me during the summer, then shifts to afternoons during the school year.''

"How many hours a day are you open?"

"From six in the morning until eight at night."

"That's a long day."

"It isn't so bad. During the winter, I'm only open from eight until five."

Four of the docks were covered, and most of the slips were occupied. A variety of crafts bobbed in the placid water: houseboats, cabin cruisers, pontoon boats, ski boats, sailboats. The four covered docks were on the left, and the entrance to them was blocked by a locked gate. To the right were two un-covered docks, for use by general traffic. The rental boats were in the first row of boat slips on the se-cured dock closest to the marina building.

Evie unlocked the padlock that secured the gate, and they stepped onto the floating dock, which bobbed gently on the water. Silently she led him down the rows of boats, indicating which of the empty slips were available. Finally she asked, "What size boat do you have?"

He made another instant decision. "I intend to buy a small one. A speedboat, not a cabin cruiser. Can you recommend a good dealership in the area?"

She gave him another of those hooded looks, but merely said in a brisk tone, "There are several boat dealerships in town. It won't be hard to find what you want." Then she turned and started back toward the marina office, her steps sure and graceful on the bobbing dock.

Again Robert followed her, enjoying the view just as much as he had before. She probably thought she was rid of him, but there was no way that would happen. Anger and anticipation mingled, forming a volatile aggression that made him feel more alert, more on edge, than he ever had before. She would pay for stealing from him, in more ways than one.

"Will you have dinner with me tonight?" he asked, using a totally unaggressive tone. She halted so abruptly that he bumped into her. He could have prevented the contact, but deliberately let his body collide with hers. She staggered off balance, and he grabbed her waist to steady her, easing her back against him before she regained control. He felt the shiver that ran through her as he savored the heat and feel of her under his hands, against his thighs and loins and belly. "Sorry," he said with light amusement. "I didn't realize having dinner with me was such a frightening concept."

She should have done a number of things. If reluctant, she should have moved away from the subtle sexuality of his embrace. If compliant, she should have turned to face him. She should have hastened to assure him that his invitation hadn't frightened her at all, then accepted to prove that it hadn't. She did none of those things. She stood stock-still, as if paralyzed by his hands clasping her waist. Silence thickened between them, growing taut. She shivered again, a delicately sensual movement that made his hands tighten on her, made his male flesh quiver and rise. Why didn't she move, why didn't she say something?

"Evie?" he murmured.

"No," she said abruptly, her voice raspier than usual. She wrenched away from him. "I'm sorry, but I can't go out to dinner with you."

Then a boat idled into the marina, and he watched her golden head turn, her face light with a smile as she recognized her customer. Sharp fury flared through him at how easily she smiled at others, but would scarcely even glance at him.

She lifted her left arm to wave, and with shock Robert focused on that slim hand.

She was wearing a wedding ring.

Chapter 3

Evie tried to concentrate on the ledgers that lay open on her desk, but she couldn't keep her mind on posting the day's income and expenses. A dark, lean face kept forming in her mind's eye, blotting out the figures. Every time she thought of those pale, predatory eyes, the bottom would drop out of her stomach and her heart would begin hammering. Fear. Though he had been polite, Robert Cannon could no more hide his true nature than could a panther. In some way she could only sense, without being able to tell the exact nature of it, he was a threat to her.

Her instincts were primitive; she wanted to barricade herself against him, wall him out. She had fought too long to put her life on an even keel to let this dark stranger disrupt what she had built. Her life was placid, deliberately so, and she resented this interruption in the even fabric of days she had fashioned about herself.

She looked up at the small photograph that sat on the top shelf of her old-fashioned rolltop desk. It wasn't one of her wedding photos; she had never looked at any of those. This photo was one that had been taken the summer before their senior year in high school; a group of kids had gotten together and spent the whole day on the water, skiing, goofing off, going back on shore to cook out. Becky Walls had brought her mother's camera and taken photos of all of them that golden summer day. Matt had been chasing Evie with an ice cube, trying to drop it down her blouse, but when he finally caught her, she had struggled and made him drop it. Matt's hands had been on her waist, and they had been laughing. Becky had called, "Hey, Matt!" and snapped the photo when they both automatically looked over at her.

Matt. Tall, just outgrowing the gangliness of adolescence and putting on some of the weight that came with maturity. That shock of dark hair falling over his brow, crooked grin flashing, bright blue eyes twinkling. He'd always been laughing. Evie didn't spare any looks for the girl she had been then, but she saw the way Matt had held her, the link between them that had been obvious even in that happy-go-lucky moment. She looked down at the slim gold band on her left hand. *Matt.*

In all the years since, there hadn't been anyone. She hadn't wanted anyone, had been neither interested nor tempted. There were people she loved, of course, but in a romantic sense her emotional isolation had been so complete that she had been totally unaware if any man had been attracted to her...until Robert Cannon had walked into her marina and looked at her with eyes like green ice. Though his expression had been impassive, she had felt his attention focus on her like a laser, had felt the heated sexual quality of it. That, and something else. Something even more dangerous.

He had left immediately after looking at the boat slips, but he would be back. She knew that without question. Evie sighed as she got up and walked to the French doors. She could see starlight twinkling on the water and stepped out onto the deck. The warm night air wrapped around her, humid, fragrant. Her little house sat right on the riverfront, with steps leading down from the deck to her private dock and boathouse. She sat in one of the patio chairs and propped her feet on the railing, calmed by the peacefulness of the river.

The summer nights weren't quiet, what with the constant chirp of insects, frogs and night birds, the splash of fish jumping, the rustle of the trees, the low murmur of the river itself, but there was a serenity in the noise. There was no moon, so the stars were plainly visible in the black bowl of the sky, the fragile, twinkling light reflected in millions of tiny diamonds on the water. The main river channel curved through the lake not sixty feet from her dock, the current ruffling the surface into waves.

Her nearest neighbors were a quarter of a mile away, out of sight around a small promontory. The only houses she could see from her deck were on the other side of the lake, well over a mile away. Guntersville Lake, formed when the TVA had dammed the Tennessee River back in the thirties, was both long and wide, irregularly shaped, curving back and forth, with hundreds of inlets. Numerous small, tree-covered islands dotted the lake.

She had lived here all her life. Here was home, family, friends, a network of roots almost two hundred years old that spread both wide and deep. She knew the pace of the seasons, the pulse of the river. She had never wanted to be anywhere else. The fabric of life here was her fortress. Now, however, her fortress was being threatened by two different enemies, and she would have to fight to protect herself.

The first threat was one that made her furious. Landon Mercer was up to no good. She didn't know the man well, but she had a certain instinct about people that was seldom wrong. There was a slickness to his character that had put her off from the start, when he had first begun renting one of her boats, but she hadn't actually become suspicious of him for a couple of months. It had been a lot of little things that had gradually alerted her, like the way he always carefully looked around before leaving the dock; it would have made sense if he'd been looking at the river traffic, but instead he'd looked at the parking lot and the highway. And there was always a mixture of triumph and relief in his expression when he returned, as if he'd done something he shouldn't have and gotten away with it.

His clothes were wrong, somehow. He made an effort to dress casually, the way he thought a fisherman would dress, but never quite got it right. He carried a rod and reel and one small tackle box, but from what Evie could tell, he never used them. He certainly never came back with any fish, and the same lure had been tied onto the line every time he went out. She knew it was the same one, because it was missing the back set of treble hooks. No, Mercer wasn't fishing. So why carry the tackle? The only logical explanation was that he was using it as a disguise; if anyone saw him, they wouldn't think anything about it.

But because Evie was alert to anything that threatened her domain, she wondered why he would need a disguise. Was he seeing a married woman? She dismissed that possibility. Boats were noisy and obvious; using them wasn't a good way to sneak around. If his lover's house was isolated, a car would be better, because then Mercer wouldn't have to worry about the vagaries of the weather. If the house had neighbors within sight, then a boat would attract attention when it pulled up to the dock; river people tended to notice strange boats. Nor was an assignation in the middle of the lake a good idea, given the river traffic.

Drugs, maybe. Maybe the little tackle box was full of cocaine, instead of tackle. If he had a system set up, selling in the middle of the river would be safe;

the water patrol couldn't sneak up on him, and if they did approach, all he had to do was drop the evidence over the side. His most dangerous time would be before he got out on the water, while he could be caught carrying the stuff. That was why he never examined the parking lot when he returned; the evidence was gone. For all intents and purposes, he had just been enjoying a little fishing.

She had no hard evidence. Twice she had tried to follow him, but had lost him in the multitude of coves and islands. But if he was using one of her boats to either sell or transfer drugs, he was jeopardizing her business. Not only could the boat be confiscated, the publicity would be terrible for the marina. Boat owners would pull out of the slips they rented from her; there were enough marinas in the Guntersville area that they could always find another place to house their boats.

Both times Mercer had headed toward the same area, the island-dotted area around the Marshall County Park, where it was easy to lose sight of a boat. Evie knew every inch of the river; eventually she would be able to narrow down the choices and find him. She didn't have any grandiose scheme to apprehend him, assuming he *was* doing something illegal. She didn't even intend to get all that close to him; she carried a pair of powerful binoculars with her in the boat. All she wanted to do was satisfy her suspicions; if she was correct, then she would turn the matter over to the sheriff and let him work it out with the water patrol. That way, she would have protected both her reputation and the marina. She might still lose the boat, but she didn't think the sheriff would confiscate it if she were the one who put him onto Mercer to begin with. All she wanted was to be certain in her own mind before she accused a man of something as serious as drug dealing.

The problem with following Mercer was that she never knew when to expect him; if she had customers in the marina, she couldn't just drop everything and hop in a boat.

But she would handle that as the opportunity presented itself. Robert Cannon was something else entirely.

She didn't want to handle him. She didn't want anything to do with him—this man with his cold, intense eyes and clipped speech, this stranger, this Yankee. He made her feel like a rabbit facing a cobra: terrified, but fascinated at the same time. He tried to hide his ruthlessness behind smooth, cosmopolitan manners, but Evie had no doubts about the real nature of the man.

He wanted her. He intended to have her. And he wouldn't care if he destroyed her in the taking.

She touched her wedding ring, turning it on her finger. Why couldn't Matt have lived? So many years had passed without him, and she had survived, had gotten on with her life, but his death had irrevocably changed her. She was stronger, yes, but also set apart, isolated from other men who might have wanted to claim her. Other men had respected that distance; *he* wouldn't.

Robert Cannon was a complication she couldn't afford. At the very least, he would distract her at a time when she needed to be alert. At the worst, he would breach her defenses and take what he wanted, then leave without any thought for the emotional devastation he left behind. Evie shuddered at the thought. She had survived once; she wasn't sure she could do it again.

Today, when he had put his hands on her waist and pulled her against his lean, hard body, she had been both shocked and virtually paralyzed by the exquisite pleasure of the contact. It had been so many years since she had felt that kind of joy that she had forgotten how enthralling, how potent, it was to feel hard male flesh against her. She had been startled by the heated strength of his hands and the subtle muskiness of his scent. She had been swamped by the sensations, by her memories. But her memories were old ones, of two young people who no longer existed. The hands holding her had been Matt's; the eager, yearning kisses had been from Matt's lips. Time had dulled those memories, the precious ones, but the image of Robert Cannon was sharp, almost painful, in its freshness.

The safest thing would be to ignore him, but that was the one thing she was sure he wouldn't allow.

Robert strolled into the offices of PowerNet the next morning and introduced himself to the receptionist, a plump, astute woman in her thirties who immediately made a phone call and then personally escorted him to Landon Mercer's office. He was in a savage mood, had been since he'd seen the wedding ring on Evie Shaw's hand, but he gave the receptionist a gentle smile and thanked her, making her blush. He never took out his temper on innocents; in fact, his self-control was so great that the vast majority of his employees didn't know he even *had* a temper. The few who knew otherwise had learned it the hard way.

Landon Mercer, however, was no innocent. He came swiftly out of his office to meet Robert halfway, heartily greeting him. "Mr. Cannon, what a surprise! No one let us know you were in Huntsville. We're honored!"

"Hardly that," Robert murmured as he shook hands with Mercer, deliberately modifying his grip to use very little strength. His mood deteriorated even further to find that Mercer was tall and good-looking, with thick blond hair and a very European sense of style. Expertly Robert assessed the cost of the Italian silk suit Mercer was wearing, and mentally he raised his eyebrows. The man had expensive tastes.

"Come in, come in," Mercer urged, inviting Robert into his office. "Would you like coffee?"

"Please." The acceptance of hospitality, Robert had found, often made subordinates relax a little. Landon Mercer would be edgy at his sudden appearance, anyway; it wouldn't hurt to calm him down.

Mercer turned to his secretary, who was making

herself very busy. "Trish, would you bring in two coffees, please?"

"Of course. How do you take yours, Mr. Cannon?"

"Black."

They went on into Mercer's office, and Robert took one of the comfortable visitors' chairs, rather than automatically taking Mercer's big chair behind the desk to show his authority. "I apologize for just dropping in on you without warning," he said calmly. "I'm in the area on vacation and thought I'd take the opportunity to see the operation, since I've never personally been down here."

"We're pleased to have you anytime," Mercer replied, still in that hearty tone of voice. "Vacation, you say? Strange place to take a vacation, especially in the middle of summer. The heat is murderous, as I'm sure you've noticed."

"Not so strange." Robert could almost hear Mercer's furiously churning, suspicious thoughts. Why was Robert here? Why now? Were they on to Mercer? If they were, why hadn't he been arrested? Robert didn't mind Mercer being suspicious; in fact, he was counting on it.

There was a light knock on the door; then Trish entered with two cups of steaming coffee. She passed Robert's to him first, then gave the other cup to Mercer. "Thank you," Robert said. Mercer didn't bother with the courtesy.

"About your vacation?" Mercer prompted, when Trish had closed the door behind her.

Robert leaned back in the chair and indolently crossed his legs. He could feel Mercer sharply studying him and knew what he would see: a lean, elegantly dressed man with cool, slightly bored eyes, certainly nothing to alarm him, despite this unexpected visit. "I have a house on the lake in Guntersville," he said in a lazy, slightly remote tone. It was a lie, but Mercer wouldn't know that. "I bought it and some land several years ago. I've never been down here before, but I've let several of my executives use the place, and they've all returned with the usual exaggerated fishing stories. Even allowing for that, they've all been enthusiastic about coming back, so I thought I'd try out the fishing for myself."

"I've heard it's a good lake," Mercer said politely, but the mental wheels were whirling faster than before.

"We'll see." Robert allowed himself a slight smile. "It seems like a nice, quiet place. Just what the doctor ordered."

"Doctor?"

"High blood pressure. Stress." Robert shrugged. "I feel fine, but the doctor insisted that I needed a long vacation, and this seemed like the perfect place to avoid stress."

"That's for sure," Mercer said. Suspicion still lingered in his eyes, but now it was tempered with relief at the plausible explanation for Robert's presence.

"I don't know how long I'll stay," Robert continued in an indifferent tone. "I won't be dropping in on you constantly, though. I'm supposed to forget about work for a while."

"We'll be glad to see you anytime, but you really should listen to your doctor," Mercer urged. "Since you're here, would you like a tour of the place? There isn't much to see, of course, just a lot of programmers and their computers."

Robert glanced at his watch, as if he had somewhere else to go. "I believe I have time, if it wouldn't be too much trouble."

"No, not at all." Mercer was already on his feet, anxious to complete the tour and send Robert on his way.

Even if he hadn't already known about Mercer, Robert thought, he would have disliked him; there was a slickness to him that was immediately off-putting. Mercer tried to disguise it with a glib, hearty attitude, but the man thought he was smarter than everyone else, and the contempt slipped through every so often. Did he treat Evie with the same attitude? Or was she, despite her relative lack of sophistication, cool and discerning enough that Mercer watched his step with her?

They were probably lovers, he thought, even though she was married. When had marital vows ever prevented anyone from straying, if they were so inclined? And why would a woman involved in espionage hesitate at cheating on her husband? Odd that her marital status hadn't been included in the information he'd received on her, but then, why would it be, unless her husband was also involved?

Evidently he wasn't, but nevertheless, as soon as Robert had returned to his hotel room in Huntsville the afternoon before, he had called his own investigative people and asked for information concerning the man. He was coldly furious; he had never, under any circumstances, allowed himself to become involved with a married woman, and he wasn't going to lower his standards now. But neither had he ever wanted another woman as violently as he wanted Evie Shaw, and knowing that he had to deprive himself made his temper very precarious.

Mercer was all smooth bonhomie as he escorted Robert through the offices, pointing out the various features and explaining the work in progress. Robert made use of the tour to gather information. Calling on his ability to totally concentrate on one thing at a time, he pushed Evie Shaw out of his mind and ruthlessly focused on the business at hand. PowerNet was housed in a long, one-story brick building. The company offices were in front, while the real work, the programming, was done in the back, with computer geniuses working their peculiar magic. Robert quietly noted the security setup and approved; there were surveillance cameras, and motion and thermal alarms. Access to the classified material could be gained only by a coded magnetic card, and the bearer still had to have the necessary security clearance. No paperwork or computer disks were allowed to leave the building. All work was logged in and placed in a secure vault when the programmers left for the day.

For Robert, the security measures made things

simple; the only way the system could have been breached without detection was by someone in a position of authority, someone who had access to the vault: Landon Mercer.

He made a point of checking his watch several times during the tour, and as soon as it was completed, he said, "I've enjoyed this very much, but I'm supposed to meet with a contractor to do a few repairs on the house. Perhaps we could get together for a round of golf sometime."

"Of course, anytime," Mercer said. "Just call."

Robert allowed himself a brief smile. "I'll do that."

He was satisfied with the visit; his intention hadn't been to do any actual snooping but rather to let Mercer know he was in town and to see for himself the security measures at PowerNet. He had the security layout from the original specs, of course, but it was always best to check out the details and make certain nothing had been changed. He might have to slip into the building at night, but that wasn't his primary plan, merely a possibility. Catching Mercer on-site with classified data didn't prove anything; the trick was to catch him passing it to someone else. Let his presence make Mercer nervous. Nervous people made mistakes.

An envelope from his personal investigators was waiting for him at the desk when he returned to the hotel. Robert stepped into the empty elevator and opened the envelope as the car began moving upward. He quickly scanned the single sheet. The information was brief. Matt Shaw, Evie's husband, had been killed in a car accident the day after their wedding, twelve years before.

He calmly slid the sheet back into the envelope, but a savage elation was rushing through him. She was a widow! She was available. And, though she didn't know it yet, she was his for the taking.

Once in his hotel room, he picked up the phone and began making calls, sliding the chess pieces of intrigue into place.

Chapter 4

Evie stuck her head out the door. "Jason!" she bellowed at her fourteen-year-old nephew. "Stop horsing around. *Now!*"

"Aw, okay," he grudgingly replied, and Evie pulled her head back inside, though she kept an eye on him, anyway. She adored the kid but never forgot that he *was* just a kid, with an attention span that leaped around like a flea and all the ungovernable energy and awkwardness that went with early adolescence. Her niece, Paige, was content to sit inside with her, in the air-conditioning, but a couple of Jason's buddies had come by, and now they were out on the docks, clowning around. Evie expected any or all of the boys to fall into the water at any time.

"They're so jerky," Paige said with all the disdain a thirteen-year-old could muster, which was plenty.

Evie smiled at her. "They'll improve with age."

"They'd better," Paige said ominously. She pulled her long, coltish legs up into the rocking chair and returned to the young-adult romance she was reading. She was a beautiful girl, Evie thought, studying the delicate lines of the young face, which still wore some of the innocence of childhood. Paige had dark hair, like her father, and a classic bone structure that would only improve with age. Jason was more outgoing than his sister, but then, Jason was more outgoing than just about everyone.

A boat idled into the marina and pulled up to the gas pumps. Evie went outside to take care of her customers, two young couples who had already spent too much time on the water, judging by their sunburns. After they had paid and left, she checked on Jason and his friends again, but for the time being they were ambling along one of the docks and refraining from any rough horseplay. Knowing teenage boys as she did, she didn't expect that state of affairs to last long.

The day was another scorcher. She glanced up at the white sun in the cloudless sky; no chance of rain to cool things off. Though she had been outside for only a few minutes, she could already feel her hair sticking to the back of her neck as she opened the door to the office and stepped inside. How could the boys stand even being outside in this heat, much less doing anything as strenuous as their energetic clowning around?

She paused as she entered, momentarily blinded

by the transition from bright sunlight into relative
dimness. Paige was chatting with someone, her eager
tone unusual in a girl who was normally quiet except
with family members. Evie could see a man standing
in front of the counter, but it was another minute
before her vision cleared enough for her to make out
his lean height and the width of his shoulders. She
still couldn't see his features clearly, but nevertheless
a tiny alarm of recognition tingled through her, and
she drew a controlled breath. "Mr. Cannon."

"Hello." His pale green gaze slipped downward,
leisurely examined her legs, which were exposed today, because the heat had been so oppressive that
she had worn shorts. The once-over made her feel
uncomfortable, and she slipped behind the counter to
ring up the gas sale and put the money in the cash
drawer.

"What may I do for you?" she asked, without
looking at him. She was aware of Paige watching
them with open interest, alerted perhaps by the difference in Evie's manner from the way she usually
treated customers.

He ignored the distance in her tone. "I've brought
my boat." He paused. "You *do* still have an available slip?"

"Of course." Business was business, Evie
thought. She opened a drawer and pulled out a rental
agreement. "If you'll complete this, I'll show you to
your slip. When you were here the other day, did
you see any particular location that you'd like?"

He glanced down at the sheet in his hand. "No,

any one of them will do,'' he absently replied as he rapidly read the agreement. It was straightforward and simple, stating the rental fee and outlining the rules. At the bottom of the sheet was a place for two signatures, his and hers. ''Is there an extra copy?'' he asked, the businessman in him balking at signing something without keeping a record of it.

She shrugged and pulled out an extra copy of the rental agreement, took the one he held from his hands and slipped a sheet of carbon paper between the two sheets. Briskly she stapled them together and handed them back to him. Controlling a smile, Robert swiftly filled out the form, giving his name and address and how long he intended to rent the slip. Then he signed at the bottom, returned the forms to her and pulled out his wallet. The small sign taped to the counter stated that the marina accepted all major credit cards, so he removed one and laid it on the counter.

She still didn't look at him as she prepared a credit-card slip. Robert watched her with well-hidden greed. In the three days since he'd first met her, he had decided that she couldn't possibly have been as lovely as he had first thought or have such an impact on his senses. He had been wrong. From the moment he had entered the marina and watched her through the plate-glass window as she pumped gas, tension had twisted his guts until he could barely breathe. She was still as sleek and golden and sensual as a pagan goddess, and he wanted her.

He had accomplished a lot in those three days. In addition to making the first chess move with Mercer, he had bought a boat, a car and a house on the river. It had taken two days for the dealership to rig the boat, but he had taken possession of the house faster than that, having moved in the afternoon before. The Realtor still hadn't recovered from his blitzing style of decision making. But Robert wasn't accustomed to being thwarted; in record time the utilities had been turned on, the paperwork completed, a cleaning service from Huntsville dragooned into giving the place a thorough cleaning, and new furniture both selected and delivered. He had also put another plan into progress, one that would force Evie Shaw and Landon Mercer into a trap.

Silently Evie handed him the credit-card slip to sign. He scrawled his signature and returned it to her just as shouts from outside made her whirl.

Robert glanced out the window and saw several teenage boys roughhousing on the docks. "Excuse me," Evie said, and went over to open the door.

"They're going to get it now," Paige piped up with obvious satisfaction, getting to her knees in the rocking chair.

Just as Evie reached the door, Jason laughingly pushed one of his buddies, who immediately returned the shove, with interest. Jason had already turned away, and the motion propelled him forward; his sneakers skidded on a wet spot perilously close to the edge of the dock. His gangly arms began windmilling comically as he tried to reverse direction, but his feet shot out from under him and he flew into the air, over the water.

"Jason!"

He was too close to the dock. Evie saw it even as she raced through the door, her heart in her mouth. She heard the sickening crack as his head hit the edge of the dock. His thin body went limp in midair, and a half second later he hit the water, immediately slipping beneath the surface.

One of the boys yelled, his young voice cracking. Evie caught only a glimpse of their bewildered, suddenly terrified faces as she fought her way through the thick, overheated air. The dock looked so far away, and she didn't seem to be making any progress, even though she could feel her feet thudding on the wood. Frantically she searched the spot where Jason had gone under, but there was nothing, nothing....

She hit the water in a long, flat dive, stroking strongly for where she had last seen him. She was dimly aware of a distant splashing, but she ignored it, all her attention on reaching Jason in time. Don't let it be too late. Dear God, don't let it be too late. She could still hear the sodden *thunk* of his head hitting the dock. He could already be dead, or paralyzed. No. Not Jason. She refused to lose him; she couldn't lose him. She couldn't go through that again.

She took a deep breath and dived, pushing her way through the water, her desperately searching hands reaching out. Visibility in the river wasn't good; she would have to locate him mostly by touch. She reached the muddy bottom and clawed her way along it. He had to be here! There was the dark pillar of the dock, telling her that she wasn't too far away from where he had gone in.

Her lungs began to ache, but she refused to surface. That would use precious seconds, seconds that Jason didn't have.

Maybe the wave motion had washed him *under* the dock.

Fiercely she kicked, propelling herself into the darker water under the dock. Her groping hands swept the water in front of her. *Nothing.*

Her lungs were burning. The need to inhale was almost impossible to resist. Grimly she fought the impulse as she forced her way down to feel along the bottom again.

Something brushed her hand.

She grabbed, and clutched fabric. Her other hand, groping blindly, caught an arm. Using the last of her strength, she tugged her limp burden out of the shadow of the docks and feebly kicked upward. Progress was frustratingly, agonizingly slow; her lungs were demanding air, her vision fading. Dear God, had she found Jason only to drown with him, because she lacked the strength to get them to the surface?

Then strong hands caught her, gripping her ribs with bruising force, and she was propelled upward in a mighty rush. Her head broke the surface, and she inhaled convulsively, choking and gasping.

"I have you," a deep, calm voice said in her ear. "I have both of you. Just relax against me."

She could hardly do anything else. She was supported by an arm as unyielding as iron as he stroked the short distance to the dock. The boys were on their knees, reaching eager hands down toward him. "Just hold him," she heard Cannon order. "Don't try to pull him out of the water. Let me do it. And one of you go call 911."

"I already have," Evie heard Paige say, the girl's voice wavery and thin.

"Good girl." His tone changed to brisk command, the words close by her ear. "Evie. I want you to hang on to the edge of the dock. Can you do that?"

She was still gasping, unable to talk, so she nodded.

"Let go of Jason. The boys are holding him, so he'll be okay. Do it now."

She obeyed, and he placed her hands on the edge of the dock. Grimly she clung to the wood as he heaved himself out of the water. She pushed her streaming hair out of her eyes with one hand as he knelt down and slipped both hands under Jason's arms. "He might have a spinal-cord injury," she croaked.

"I know." Robert's face was grim. "But he isn't breathing. If we don't get him up here and do CPR, he won't make it."

She swallowed hard and nodded again. As gently as possible, Robert lifted Jason out of the water, the muscles in his arms and shoulders cording under the wet shirt. Evie took one agonized look at Jason's still, blue face, and then she hauled herself out of the water, using strength she hadn't known she still possessed. She collapsed on the dock beside Jason, then struggled to her knees. "Jason!"

Robert felt for a pulse in the boy's neck and located a faint throb. Relieved, he said, "He has a heartbeat," then bent over the sprawled, limp body, pinching the boy's nostrils shut and using his other hand to press on his chin, forcing his mouth open. He placed his own mouth on the chill blue lips and carefully, forcefully, blew his breath outward. The thin chest rose. Robert lifted his mouth, and the air sighed out of the boy, his chest falling again.

Evie reached out, then forced herself to draw back. She couldn't do anything that Robert wasn't already doing, and she was still so weak and shaky that she couldn't do it nearly as well. She felt as if she were choking on her pain and desperation, on the overwhelming need to do *something,* anything. Her ears were buzzing. She would rather die herself than helplessly watch someone else she loved slowly die before her eyes.

Robert repeated the process again and again, silently counting. Fiercely he focused on what he was doing, ignoring the terrified kids grouped around them, not letting himself think about Evie's silence, her stillness. The kid's chest was rising with each breath forced into him, meaning oxygen was getting into his lungs. His heart was beating; if he didn't have a serious head or spinal injury, he should be okay, if he would just start breathing on his own. The seconds ticked by. One minute. Two. Then

abruptly the boy's chest heaved, and he began choking. Quickly Robert drew back.

Jason suddenly convulsed, rolling to his side and
knocking against Evie as he choked and gagged. She
lurched sideways, off balance, unable to catch herself. Robert's hand shot out across Jason to steady
her, the lean fingers catching her arm and preventing
her from going into the water a second time. With
effortless strength, he dragged her across Jason's
legs, pulling her to him.

Water streamed from Jason's nostrils and open
mouth. He gulped and coughed again, then abruptly
vomited up a quantity of river water.

"Thank God," Robert said quietly. "No paraly-
sis."

"No." Evie pulled loose from his grip. Tears
burned her eyes as she crouched once again by Jason's side. Gently she touched the boy, soothing him,
and noticed that the back of his head was red with
blood. "You'll be okay, honey," she murmured as
she examined the cut. "Nothing that a few stitches
won't fix." She glanced up and saw Paige's white,
tear-streaked face. "Paige, get a towel for me, please.
And be careful! Don't run."

Paige gulped and headed back toward the marina.
She didn't exactly run, but it was close.

Jason's coughing fit subsided, and he lay exhausted on his side, gulping in air. Evie stroked his
arm, repeating that he was going to be all right.

Paige returned with the towel, and gently Evie
pressed it to the deep cut, stanching the flow of

blood. "A-aunt Evie?" Jason croaked, his voice so hoarse it was almost soundless.

"I'm here."

"Can I sit up?" he asked, beginning to be embarrassed by the attention.

"I don't know," she replied neutrally. "Can you?"

Slowly, cautiously, he eased himself into a sitting position, but he was weak, and Robert knelt down to support him, shifting so that one strong thigh was behind Jason's back. "My head hurts," Jason groaned.

"I imagine so," Robert said in a calm, almost genial voice. "You hit it on the edge of the dock." Sirens wailed, swiftly coming closer. Jason's eyes flickered as he realized a further fuss was going to be made.

Gingerly he reached back and touched his head. Wincing, he let his hand fall to his side. "Mom's going to be peed off," he said glumly.

"Mom isn't the only one," Evie replied. "But we'll settle that between ourselves later."

He looked abashed. He tried to move away from Robert's support but didn't quite make it. Then the paramedics were there, hurrying down the dock, carrying their tackle boxes of medical equipment. Robert drew back and pulled Evie with him, giving the paramedics room to work. Paige sidled over and slipped her arms around Evie's waist, burrowing close and hiding her face against Evie's wet shirt in a child's instinctive bid for reassurance. It was a simple thing for Robert to put his arms around both of them, and Evie was too tired, too numb, to resist. She stood docilely in his embrace. His strength enfolded her; his heat comforted her. He had saved Jason's life, and maybe even her own, because she wasn't certain she could have gotten Jason to the surface without his help. If so, she would simply have drowned with him rather than let him go and try to save her own life at the expense of his.

Jason was quickly checked; then the paramedics began preparations to transport him to the hospital. "That cut will have to be stitched," one of them said to Evie. "He probably has a concussion, too, so I wouldn't be surprised if they keep him overnight, at least."

Evie stirred in Robert's embrace. "I have to call Rebecca," she said. "And I want to ride with him to the hospital."

"I'll drive you," he said, releasing her. "You'll need a way back."

"Rebecca can bring me," she said as she hurried to the office, Robert and Paige both following her inside. She reached for the phone, then halted, rubbing her forehead. "No, she'll stay with Jason. Never mind. I can drive myself."

"Of course you can," he said gently. "But you won't, because I'm driving you."

She gave him a distracted look as she dialed her sister's number. "That isn't necessary—Becky. Listen, Jason slipped on the dock and cut his head. He's going to be okay, but he needs stitches, and the paramedics are taking him to the hospital. They're leaving now. I'll meet you there. Yes, I'm bringing Paige with me. Okay. Bye.''

She hung up, then lifted the receiver and dialed another number. ''Craig, this is Evie. Can you take over the marina for a couple of hours? Jason's had an accident, and I'm going with him to the hospital. No, he'll be okay. Five minutes? Great. I'm leaving now.''

Then, moving swiftly, she got her purse from under the counter and fished out her keys. Like lightning, Robert caught her hand and calmly removed the keys from her grasp. ''You're too shaky,'' he said in a gentle, implacable tone. ''You came close to drowning yourself. Don't fight me on this, Evie.''

It was obvious that she lacked the strength to physically fight him for the keys. Frustrated, she gave in rather than waste more time. ''All right.''

She drove a sturdy, serviceable four-wheel-drive pickup, handy for pulling boats up a launch ramp. Paige raced ahead to scramble inside, as if afraid she would be left behind if she didn't beat them to the vehicle. Evie was only grateful that the child automatically slid to the middle of the seat, positioning herself between Evie and Robert and hastily buckling herself in.

''It's a straight shift,'' she blurted unnecessarily as she buckled her own seat belt.

He gave her a gentle smile as he started the engine. ''I can manage.''

Of course, he did more than manage. He shifted

gears with the smooth expertise of someone who knew exactly what he was doing. Evie's heart gave a little thump as she tried to imagine Robert Cannon being awkward at anything.

She forced herself to watch the road, rather than him, as she gave directions to the hospital. She didn't want to look at him, didn't want to feel that primal pull deep inside her. He was dripping wet, of course, his black hair plastered to his head and his white silk shirt clinging to his muscled torso like a second skin. His leanness was deceptive; the wet shirt revealed the width of his shoulders and chest, and the smooth, steely muscles of his abdomen and back. She thought the image of him, the outline of his body, was probably branded on her mind for all eternity, as was everything else that had happened in the last fifteen minutes. Only fifteen minutes? It felt like a lifetime.

He drove fast, pulling into the hospital parking lot right behind the ambulance. The hospital was small but new, and he couldn't fault the staff's response. Jason was whisked into an examining room beforc Evie could reach his side to speak to him.

Firmly Robert took her arm and ushered both her and Paige to seats in the waiting area. "Sit here," he said, and though his voice was mild, that implacable tone was in it again. "I'll get coffee for us. How about you, sweetheart?" he asked Paige. "Do you want a soft drink?"

Dumbly Paige nodded, then shook her head. "May I have coffee, too, Aunt Evie?" she whispered. "I'm cold. Or maybe hot chocolate."

Evie nodded her agreement, and Robert strode to the vending machines. She put her arm around Paige and gathered her close, knowing that the girl had suffered a shock at seeing her brother almost die. "Don't worry, honey. Jason will be home by tomorrow, probably, griping about his headache and driving you up the wall."

Paige sniffed back tears. "I know. I'll get mad at him then, but right now I just want him to be okay."

"He will be. I promise."

Robert returned with three cups, one filled with hot chocolate and the other two with coffee. Evie and Paige took theirs from him, and he settled into the chair on Evie's other side. When she sipped the hot brew, she found that he had liberally dosed it with sugar. She glanced at him and found him watching her, gauging her reaction. "Drink it," he said softly. "You're a little shocky, too."

Because he was right, she obeyed without argument, folding her cold fingers around the cup in an effort to warm them. Her wet clothes were uncomfortably chilly here in the air-conditioned hospital, and she barely restrained a shiver. He should be cold, too, she thought, but knew that he wasn't. His arm touched hers, and she felt heat radiating through his wet clothing.

As slight as it was, he felt the shiver that raced through her. "I'll get a blanket for you," he said, rising to his feet.

She watched him approach the desk and speak to the nurse. He was courteous, restrained, but in about thirty seconds he was returning with a blanket in his hands. He had an air of natural command, she thought. One look into those icy green eyes and people scurried to do his bidding.

He bent over her to tuck the blanket around her, and she let him. Just as he finished, the emergency room doors swung open and her sister, Rebecca, hurried inside, looking tense and scared. Seeing Evie and Paige, she changed her direction to join them. "What's happening?" she demanded.

"He's in the treatment room now," Robert answered for Evie, his deep voice as soothing as when he'd talked to Paige. "He'll have a few stitches in the back of his head, and a bad headache. They'll probably keep him overnight, but his injuries are relatively minor."

Rebecca turned her shrewd brown eyes on him and bluntly demanded, "Who are you?"

"This is Robert Cannon," Evie said, making an effort to appear calm as she made the introductions. "He dragged both Jason and me out of the water. Mr. Cannon, this is my sister, Rebecca Wood."

Rebecca took in Robert's wet clothes, then looked at Evie, seeing the strain on her sister's pale face. "I'll see about Jason first," she said in her usual decisive manner. "Then I want to know exactly what happened." She turned and marched toward a nurse, identified herself and was directed to the treatment room where Jason was located.

Robert sat down beside Evie. "What branch of the

military was your sister in?'' he asked, provoking a nervous giggle from Paige.

"I think it's called motherhood," Evie replied. "She began practicing on me at an early age."

"She's older, I presume."

"Five years."

"So you've always been 'baby sister' to her."

"I don't mind."

"I'm sure you don't. Drink your coffee," he admonished, lifting the cup himself and holding it to her lips.

Evie drank, then gave him a wry glance. "You aren't bad at the mother-hen routine yourself."

He allowed himself a slight smile. "I take care of my own." The words were a subtle threat—and a warning, if she were astute enough to hear it.

She didn't make the obvious retort, that she wasn't "his"; instead she withdrew, sinking back in her chair and staring straight ahead. Jason's close call had brought too many old memories to the surface, making it difficult for her to deal with anything just now, much less Robert Cannon. Right now, what she wanted most of all was to crawl into bed and pull the covers over her head, shutting out the world until she felt capable of facing it again. Maybe by the time night came, certainly by tomorrow, she would be all right. Then she would worry about the way he had taken over and about the gentle possessiveness that she couldn't fight. With Cannon, Evie was beginning to link gentleness with an implacable force of will that let nothing stand in his way. He would be tender and protective, but he would not be thwarted.

They sat in silence until Rebecca came out of the treatment room to rejoin them. "They're keeping him overnight," she said. "He has a slight concussion, a big shaved spot on the back of his head and ten stitches. He also won't say exactly what happened, other than mumbling that he fell. What's he trying to hide from me?"

Evie hesitated, trying to decide exactly what to tell Rebecca, and that gave Paige enough time to pipe up. "Scott and Jeff and Patrick came by the marina, and they were all acting silly out on the docks. Aunt Evie yelled at Jason to settle down, but they didn't. Jason pushed Patrick, and Patrick pushed him back, and Jason slipped and fell, and hit his head on the dock, then went into the water. Aunt Evie went in after him, and she was under forever and ever, and Mr. Cannon tried to find both of them. Then Aunt Evie came up, and she had Jason, and Mr. Cannon pulled them to the dock. Jason wasn't breathing, Mom, and Aunt Evie nearly drowned, too. Mr. Cannon had to do that artificial breathing stuff on Jason, and then Jason started coughing and puking, and the paramedics came. I called 911," she finished in a rush.

Rebecca looked a bit bemused at this flood of words from her quiet child but heard the fear still lurking under the loquaciousness. She sat down beside Paige and hugged her. "You did exactly right," she praised, and Paige gave a little sigh of relief.

Rebecca examined Evie's pale, drawn face. "He's all right," she said reassuringly. "At least for now. As soon as he's recovered, I'm going to kill him. Better yet, I think I'll ground him for the rest of the summer. *Then* I'll kill him."

Evie managed a smile. "If he lives through all that, I want a turn at him."

"It's a deal. Now, I want you to go home and get out of those wet clothes. You look worse than Jason does."

The smile, this time, was easier. "Gee, thanks." But she knew that Rebecca's sharp eyes had seen below the surface and recognized the strain that she was under.

"I'll see to her," Robert said, standing and urging Evie to her feet. She wanted to protest, she really did, but she was so tired, her nerves so strained, that it was too much effort. So she managed to say good-bye to Rebecca and Paige, and tell them to kiss Jason for her; then she gave in and let him usher her out of the building and across the parking lot to the truck. She had left the blanket behind, but the searing afternoon heat washed over her like a glow, and she shivered with delight.

Robert's arm tightened around her waist. "Are you still cold?"

"No, I'm fine," she murmured. "The heat feels good."

He opened the truck door and lifted her onto the seat. The strength in his hands and arms, the ease with which he picked her up, made her shiver again.

She closed her eyes and let her head rest against the window, as much from a desire to shut him out as from an almost overpowering fatigue.

"You can't go to sleep," he said as he got in on the driver's side, amusement lacing his tone. "You have to give me directions to your house."

She forced herself to open her eyes and sit up, and gave him calm, coherent directions. It didn't take long to get anywhere in Guntersville, and less than fifteen minutes later he stopped the truck in her driveway. She fumbled with the door but was so clumsy that he was there before she managed it, opening it and supporting her with a firm hand under her elbow. She got out, reluctant to let him inside her house but accepting the inevitable. Best just to go shower and change as fast as she could, and get it over with.

He entered right behind her. "Have a seat," she invited automatically as she headed toward her bedroom. "I'll be out in about fifteen minutes."

"I'm still too wet to sit down," he said. "But take your time. I'll go out on the deck, if that's okay with you."

"Of course," she said, giving him a polite smile without really looking at him, and escaped into the privacy of her bedroom.

Robert eyed the closed door thoughtfully. She was so wary of him that she wouldn't even look at him if she could help it. It wasn't a response he was accustomed to from a woman, though God knew she had reason to be wary, given his assumption that she knew of his connection to PowerNet. She couldn't have acted any more guilty if he had caught her redhanded. He could opt for patience and let time disarm her, but he already had plans in motion that would force the issue, so he decided to allay her suspicions in another manner, by making a definite, concerted effort to seduce her. He had planned to seduce her, anyway; he would simply intensify the pressure.

He heard the shower start running. He couldn't have asked for a better opportunity to look around, and he took advantage of it. The house was probably forty years old, he thought, but had been remodeled so the interior was open and more modern, with exposed beams and gleaming hardwood floors. She had a green thumb; indoor plants of all sizes occupied every available flat surface. He could see into the kitchen from where he stood in the living room, and beyond that was the deck, with double French doors opening onto it. A dock led from the deck down to a boathouse.

Her furnishings were neat and comfortable, but certainly not luxurious. Without haste, he went over to the big, old-fashioned rolltop desk and methodically searched it, unearthing nothing of any great interest, not that he had expected to find anything. It wasn't likely she would have been fool enough to leave him in the room with an unlocked desk if the desk contained anything incriminating. He looked through her bank statement but found no unusually large deposits, at least at this particular bank or on this particular statement.

There was a small, framed photograph on the desk.
He picked it up and examined the two people pictured. Evie, defintiely—a very young Evie, but already glowing with seductiveness. The boy, for he
was nothing more than that, was probably her husband, dead now for twelve years. Robert studied the
boy's face more closely, seeing laughter and happiness and yes, devotion. But had the boy any idea how
to handle the sensual treasure that the girl in his arms
represented? Of course not; what teenage boy would?
Still, Robert felt an unexpected and unpleasant
twinge of jealousy for this long-dead boy, for the
riches that had so briefly been his. Evie had loved
him, enough that she still wore his wedding ring after
all these years.

He heard the shower shut off and replaced the photograph, then quietly walked out onto the deck. She
had a nice place here, nothing extravagant, but cozy
and homey. There was plenty of privacy, too, with
no houses visible except for those on the far side of
the lake. The water was very blue, reflecting both the
green of the mountains and the deep blue bowl of
the sky. The afternoon was slipping away, and the
sun was lower now, but still white and searing. Soon
it would begin to turn bronze, and the lush scents of
the heavy greenery would grow stronger. By the time
purple twilight brought a respite from the heat, the
air would be redolent with honeysuckle and roses,
pine and fresh-cut grass. Time was slower here; people didn't rush from one occupation to another. He
had actually seen people sitting on their front

porches, reading newspapers or shelling peas, occasionally waving to passersby. Of course, people from New York and other large cities would say that the locals here had nothing to rush *to,* but from what he'd seen they stayed busy enough; they just didn't get in any great hurry.

He heard Evie come to the open French door. "I'm ready," she said.

He turned and looked at her. Her newly washed hair was still wet, but she had braided it and pinned the braids up so they wouldn't get her shirt damp. She had exchanged the shorts for jeans, and had on a pink T-shirt that made her golden skin glow. But her cheeks were still a bit pale, and her expression was strained.

"You have a nice place," he said.

"Thanks. I inherited it from my in-laws."

Though he knew the answer, now was the time to ask for information; it would be odd if he didn't. "You're married?" he asked.

"Widowed." She turned and retreated into the house, and Robert followed her.

"Ah. I'm sorry. How long has it been?"

"Twelve years."

"I saw the picture on the desk. Is that your husband?"

"Yes, that's Matt." She stopped and looked toward the photograph, and an ineffable sadness darkened her eyes. "We were just kids." Then she seemed to gather herself and walked briskly to the door. "I need to get back to the marina."

Loving Evangeline

"My house is about five miles from here," he said. "It won't take long for me to shower and change."

She carried a towel out to the truck and dried the seat before she got inside. She didn't even bother protesting his continued possession of her keys; it would be pointless, though she was now obviously calm enough to drive safely.

His clothes had dried enough that they were merely damp now, rather than dripping wet, but she knew they had to be uncomfortable. Hers certainly had been. Her conscience twinged. He had not only saved Jason's life but likely hers, as well, and had put himself to a great deal of trouble to see that she was taken care of. No matter how he alarmed her, she knew that she would never forget his quick actions or his cool decisiveness.

"Thank you," she said softly, staring straight ahead. "Jason and I probably wouldn't have made it without you."

"The likelihood was unnerving," he said, his tone cool and even. "You'd pushed yourself so far that you couldn't have gotten him out of the water. Didn't it occur to you to let go of him and come up for another breath?"

"No." The single word was flat. "I couldn't have done that."

He glanced at her profile, saw the deepening strain in her expression and deftly changed the subject. "Will your sister really ground him for the rest of the summer?"

Evie was startled into a laugh, a rusty little sound that went right to his gut. "I'd say he'll be lucky if that's all she does. It isn't that he was fooling around, but that I'd already told him to stop and he disobeyed me."

"So he broke a cardinal rule?"

"Just about."

Robert intended to have a few words with the young man himself, about acting responsibly and the possible consequences of reckless actions, but he didn't mention it to Evie. She was obviously very protective of her niece and nephew, and though she couldn't say that it wasn't any of his business, she wouldn't like it. His conversation with Jason would be private.

When he stopped in the driveway of his new house, Evie looked around with interest. "This place has been on the market for almost a year," she said.

"Then I'm lucky no one beat me to it, aren't I?" He got out and walked around the truck to open the door for her. Though she hadn't waited for him to perform the service at the hospital, that had been an emergency; nor would she have waited when they had reached her house, if she had been able to get the door open in time. He'd had the strong impression then that she had wanted to bolt inside and lock him out. Now, however, she waited with the natural air of a queen, as if he were only doing what he should. She might be dressed in jeans, sneakers and a T-shirt, but that didn't lessen her femininity one whit; she *expected* that male act of servitude. Robert had always preferred to treat women with the small courtesies but hadn't insisted on them when his partner had protested. He was both amused and charmed by Evie's rather regal, very Southern attitude.

He mused about this subtle signal as he ushered her into the house. Though she was still very wary of him, obviously on some level her resistance had weakened. Anticipation tightened his muscles, but he deliberately resisted it. Now was not the time. Not quite yet.

"Make yourself at home while I shower," he invited, smiling faintly as he walked toward his bedroom, which was down the hallway to the right. He had no doubt that she would do exactly as he had done, take full advantage of the opportunity to do a quick search.

Evie stood in the middle of the living room after he had gone, too tense to "make herself at home." She looked around, trying to distract herself. The house was sprawling and modern, one story of brick and redwood, easily three times the size of her own. A huge rock fireplace dominated the left wall, the chimney soaring upward to the cathedral ceiling. Twin white ceiling fans stirred a gentle breeze. The furniture was chic but comfortable-looking, sized to fit a man of his height.

The living room was separated from the dining room by a waist-high planter in which luxurious ferns flourished. Huge double windows revealed a deck, furnished with comfortable chairs, an umbrella table and even more plants. Hesitantly she walked into the dining room for a better view. The kitchen opened up to the right, an immaculate oasis gleaming with the most modern appliances available. Even the coffeemaker looked as if the user would need a degree in engineering to work the thing. There was a breakfast nook on the far side of the kitchen, occupied by a smallish table with a white ceramic tile top. She could see him sitting there in the mornings, reading a newspaper and drinking coffee. Double French doors, far more ornate and stylish than her own, led from the breakfast nook onto the deck. She would have liked to explore further but felt too constrained here on his territory. Instead she retreated to the living room once more.

Robert took his time showering and dressing. Let her look around all she wanted; the fact that she wouldn't find anything alarming would help allay her suspicions. She would begin to relax, which was exactly what he wanted.

A lot of men, maybe most of them, would have made a move while they had been at her house; she had been more off-balance, vulnerable. He had even had the opportunity, had he chosen to take it, of walking in on her while she was unclothed. But he had elected to wait, knowing she would be more at ease now that the most provocative and dangerous circumstances were past. He hadn't made a pass at her then, so she wouldn't be expecting him to do so now. And since she wouldn't be mentally prepared to handle an advance, her response would be honest, unguarded.

Finally he stopped dawdling and returned to the living room. To his surprise, she was still standing almost exactly where he had left her, and little of the strain had faded from her face. She turned to watch him. Her lovely golden brown eyes were still dark with some inner distress that went far deeper than the episode with Jason, traumatic as that had been.

Robert paused while still several feet from her,

studying those somber eyes. Then he simply moved forward with a graceful speed that gave her no time to evade him, and took her in his arms. He heard her instinctive intake of breath, saw the alarm widening her eyes as she lifted her head to protest, a protest that was smothered when his mouth covered hers.

She jerked in his arms, and he gently controlled the action, pulling her even more firmly against him. He took care not to hurt her but deepened the insistent pressure of his mouth until he felt her own mouth yield and open. The sweetness of her lips sent an electrical thrill along his nerves, tightening his muscles and swelling his sex. He took her mouth with his tongue, holding her still for the imitative sexual possession, repeating the motion again and again, until she shivered and softened in his arms, her lips beginning to cling to his.

Her tentative response made his head swim, and to his surprise he had to struggle to maintain his control. But she felt perfect in his arms, damn her, all those soft, luscious curves molding to the hard, muscled planes of his body. Her mouth was sweeter than any he had ever tasted before, and the simple act of kissing her was arousing him to an unbelievable degree.

He didn't want to stop. He hadn't planned to do more than kiss her, but he hadn't expected the intensity of his own response. His mouth crushed fiercely down on hers, demanding even more. He heard the soft, helpless sound she made in her throat; then her arms lifted around his neck, and she pressed full length against him. Pure, primitive male triumph roared through him at this evidence of her own arousal. He could feel her breasts, round and firm, the nipples hard against his chest, and he slipped his hand under her shirt to cup one of them, his thumb rubbing across the peaked nipple through the thin lace of her bra. Her body arched, her hips pressing hard against his...and then suddenly she was fighting, panicked, trying to squirm free.

He let her go, though every cell in his body was screaming for more. "Easy," he managed to say, but the word was low and rough and his breath was uneven. He tried for a more controlled reassurance. "I won't hurt you, sweetheart."

Evie had backed away from him, her face pale but her lips swollen and red from his kisses. She forced herself to stop retreating, to stand her ground and face him. The sensual pull of his masculinity was almost overwhelming, tempting her to go back into those arms, to yield to that fierce domination. She felt a sense of doom; he was far more dangerous to her than she had first suspected.

"Yes, you will," she whispered. Her teeth were chattering. "Why are you doing this? What do you want from me?"

Chapter 5

She looked ready to bolt. To soothe her, he moved back a few paces and let his hands relax at his sides. His eyes gleamed with faint irony. "You're a lovely woman, sweetheart. Surely you aren't surprised that I'm attracted to you? As for what I want from you, I was holding you closely enough that the answer to that question should have been obvious."

She didn't respond to his gentle teasing. Instead her somber gaze remained locked on his face, trying to probe beneath that smooth, urbane sophistication. He was very cosmopolitan, beyond a doubt, but he used that slick surface as a shield to hide the real man, the man who had kissed her with such ruthless passion. There were many hidden layers to him, his motives complex and unfathomable. Yes, he was attracted to her, as she was to him. It would be foolish to deny her own participation, and Evie wasn't a foolish woman. But she always had the feeling that he was studying her, manipulating her in some subtle manner. From the very first she had sensed his determination to force himself into her life, and he was doing exactly that with a calm force of will that refused to be denied. Whatever his motive, it was something that went beyond the physical.

"I don't have casual sex," she said.

He almost smiled. It was merely an expression in those pale eyes, rather than an actual movement of his mouth. "My dear, I promise you there wouldn't be anything *casual* about it." He paused. "Are you involved with someone else?"

She shook her head. "No."

He wasn't surprised that she had denied any involvement with Mercer. "Then we don't have a problem, do we? You can't say that you aren't attracted to me, too."

She lifted her chin, and his pale eyes gleamed at that proud motion. "That velvet glove covers an iron fist, doesn't it?" she commented neutrally. "No, I can't say that I'm not attracted to you."

Her perception disturbed him, a reaction that he didn't allow to surface. "I can be determined when I want something...or someone."

She made an abrupt motion, as if tiring of the verbal jousting. "I phrased it wrong. I don't have affairs, either."

"A wise decision, but in this case too restrictive." He approached her now, and she didn't retreat.

Gently he cupped her face with one long-fingered hand, his fingers stroking over the velvety texture of her cheek. God, she was lovely, not classically beautiful, but glowing with an intensely female seductiveness that made him think her name was very apt indeed. So must Eve have been, glorious in her nudity. No wonder Adam had been so easily led, a weakness he wouldn't allow himself, though he intended to fully enjoy Evie's sensuality. Her sweet, warm scent wafted up to him. "I won't force you," he murmured. "But I will have you."

"If you won't use force, how do you intend to go about it?" she asked.

His eyebrows lifted. "You think I should warn you?"

"Yes."

"An interesting notion, but one I'm going to leave untried." He rubbed his thumb over her lower lip. "For now, sweetheart, we'd better get back to the marina. You have a business to run, and I have a boat to get into a slip."

He let his hand drop as he spoke, and Evie turned from him with relief, as if she had been released from a force field. Her face tingled where he had touched her, and she remembered the electric sensation when he had put his hand on her breast. His boldness spoke of vast experience and self-confidence with women, something that put her at a disadvantage.

They were both silent on the drive back to the marina. She was vaguely surprised to see how late it was, the sun dipping low even for these long summer days. The sultry heat hadn't abated, though there was a hint of purple on the horizon that gave the promise of a cooling rain shower.

Robert's speedboat, a sleek, dark eighteen-footer, was still where he had left it, hitched to a black Jeep Renegade. Thank heavens it hadn't been blocking the launch ramps, or Craig would have had a mess on his hands. She hurried into the marina office, and Craig looked up from the sports magazine he was reading. "Is everything okay?" he asked, getting to his feet. "The kids said that Jason nearly drowned."

"He has a concussion, but he'll go home tomorrow," she said. "Thanks for coming in. I'm sorry for wrecking your day."

"No problem," he said cheerfully. He was seventeen, a tall, muscular, dark-haired kid who would be a senior when the new school year started. He had been working part-time for her for almost two years and was so steady that she had no qualms about leaving him in charge. "Say, what about that new boat outside?"

"It's mine," Robert said, stepping inside. "I'll be renting a slip here." He held out his hand. "I'm Robert Cannon."

Craig took his hand with a firm grip. "Craig Foster. Glad to meet you, Mr. Cannon. You must be the guy who pulled Evie and Jason out of the water. The kids said it was a tall Yankee."

"I'm the guy," Robert affirmed, amusement in his eyes.

"Thought so. Want me to help you get the boat into a slip?"

"I can do it," Evie said. "I've taken enough time out of your day."

"You pay me for it," Craig replied, grinning. "I might as well, since I'm already here. Mom won't be expecting me back until supper, anyway." He and Robert left, chatting companionably.

Kids seemed to like Robert, Evie thought, watching them from the window. Even shy Paige had been at ease with him. He didn't treat kids as equals—he was the adult, his was the authority—but at the same time he didn't dismiss them. Authority and responsibility sat easily on those broad shoulders, she mused. He was obviously accustomed to command.

For her own sake, her own protection, she had to hold him at bay, and she didn't know if she could. Today, with a few kisses and frightening ease, he had shown her that he could arouse her beyond her own control. She could love him, and that was the most terrifying prospect of all. He was a strong man, in mind and soul as well as body, a man worthy of love. He would steal her heart if she weren't careful, if she didn't keep her guard up at all times.

She turned away from the window. Twelve years ago, love had almost destroyed her, leaving only a forlorn heap of ashes from which she had laboriously rebuilt a controlled, protected life. She couldn't do that again; she didn't have the strength to once more live through that hell and emerge victorious. She had already lost too many people to believe that love, or life, lasted forever. She couldn't do anything about the people she already loved, the ones already in her heart: her family, old Virgil, a very few close friends, but she hadn't allowed anyone new to stake a claim on her emotions. She had already paid out too much in pain and had precious little reserve of spirit left. She had almost lost Jason today, and the pain had been overwhelming. Rebecca knew, had realized that if Evie hadn't been able to find Jason, she would now be mourning a sister as well as a son. That was the real basis for her sister's fury with Jason.

And Evie knew that Robert Cannon planned to force his way into her life. He would be here for the summer, he'd said; he wouldn't be looking for anything more than a pleasant affair, companionship during the long, lazy weeks. If she fell in love with him, that would make the affair sweeter. But at the end of summer he would go back to his real life, and Evie would have to continue here, with one more wound on a heart that had barely survived the last blow. Emotionally, she couldn't afford him.

There were always a hundred and one things to be doing around the marina, but suddenly she couldn't think of a single one. She felt oddly disoriented, as if the world had been turned upside down. Maybe it had.

She called the hospital and was put through to Jason's room. Her sister answered the phone on the first ring. "He's grouchy and has a throbbing headache," Rebecca cheerfully announced when Evie asked his condition. "I have to wake him every couple of hours tonight, but if he does okay, then he can go home in the morning. Paul left just a few minutes ago to take Paige to his mother's, then he's coming back here. How about you? Nerves settled down yet?''

''Not quite,'' Evie said truthfully, though Jason's close call wasn't all that had unsettled her. ''But I'm over the shakes.''

''Are you at home, I hope?''

''You know better than that.''

''You should have taken it easy for the rest of the day,'' Rebecca scolded. ''I had hopes that Mr. Cannon would take you in hand. He seems good at giving orders.''

''World-class champion,'' Evie agreed. ''I'll come by to see Jason after the marina closes. Do you want me to bring you anything? A pillow, a book, a hamburger?''

''No, I don't need anything. Don't come here. Jason's okay, and you need to go home and rest. I mean it, Evie.''

''I'm okay, too,'' Evie calmly replied. ''And I want to see Jason, even if just for a few minutes—'' She cried out in surprise as the phone was plucked from her hand. She whirled as Robert lifted the receiver to his ear.

''Mrs. Wood? Robert Cannon. I'll see that she goes straight home. Yes, she's still a little wobbly.''

''I am not,'' Evie said, narrowing her eyes at him. He reached out and gently stroked her cheek. Deliberately she stepped back, out of his reach.

"I'll take care of her," he firmly assured Rebecca, never moving his gaze from Evie's face. "On second thought, I'll take her out to dinner before I take her home. I think so, too. Goodbye."

As he hung up, Evie said in a cold voice, "I despise being treated as if I'm a helpless idiot."

"Hardly that," he murmured.

She didn't relent. "I suppose you thought that I would feel safe and protected, to have you take over and make my decisions for me. I don't. I feel insulted."

Robert lifted an inquisitive brow, hiding his true reaction. He had indeed hoped to provoke exactly that response from her and felt an uneasy surprise that she had so easily gone straight to the truth of the matter. She was proving to be uncomfortably astute. "What I think," he said carefully, "is that you were in more danger than you want your sister to know, and that you're still shaky. If you go to the hospital again, you'll have to put up a front to keep from scaring both her and Jason, and that will put even more strain on you."

"What *I* think," she replied, standing with her fists clenched at her sides, "is that I'm in far more danger from you than I ever was from the water." Her golden brown eyes were cool and unwaveringly level.

Again he felt a twinge of discomfort at her insight. Still, he was certain he could soften her stand, and his tone turned gently cajoling. "Even if I offer you a truce for tonight? No kisses, not even any hand-holding. Just dinner, then I'll see you safely home, and you can get a good night's rest."

"No, thank you. I won't have dinner with you, and I can get home by myself."

He gave her a considering look. "In that case, the offer of a truce is null and void."

His tone was so calm that she listened to it first, rather than to the actual words. She hesitated only a split second, but that was enough for him to have her in his arms again, and again she felt overcome by his steely, deceptive strength. His body was unyielding, his grip careful but unbreakable. The male muskiness of his clean, warm skin made her head swim. She had the dizzy impression that his mouth was lowering to hers and quickly ducked her head to rest it against his chest. It was disconcerting to hear a quiet chuckle over her head.

"Such a cowardly act, from one who isn't," he murmured, the words rich with amusement. "But I don't mind simply holding you. It has its own compensations."

She *was* a coward, though, Evie thought. She was terrified of him, not in a physical way, but emotional fear was just as weighty a burden to carry. She was handling him all wrong; he wouldn't be accustomed to rejection, so every time she turned him down it made him just that much more determined to have his way. If she had played up to him from the beginning, gushed over him, he would have been bored and left her alone. Hindsight, though, despite its acuity, was depressingly useless.

His hand moved soothingly over her back, subtly urging her closer. It was so easy to let him take more of her weight, so easy to give in to the strain and fatigue she had been successfully fighting until now. She resisted the urge to put her arms around him, to feel the heated vibrancy of his body under her hands, but she could hear the strong, steady thumping of his heartbeat beneath her ear, feel the rise and fall of his chest as he breathed, and that was enough to work its own seduction. The forces of life were strong in him, luring women to that intense strength. She was no different from all those countless, nameless others.

"Robert," she whispered. "Don't." A cowardly, shameless, useless plea.

That hand stroked up to her shoulder blades, rubbed the sensitive tendons that ran from her neck to her shoulders, massaged her tender nape. "Evie," he whispered in return. "Don't what?" He continued without waiting for a reply. "Is Evie your real name, or is it a nickname for Eve? Or possibly Evelyn? No matter, it suits you."

Her eyes drifted shut as his warmth and strength continued to work their black magic on her nerves, her will. Oh God, it would be so foolishly easy just to give in to him. His skill was nothing short of diabolical. "Neither. It's short for Evangeline."

"Ah." The short sigh was one of approval. He truly hadn't known her full name; none of the reports he had seen had called her anything except Evie. "Evangeline. Feminine, spiritual, sensual...sad."

Evie didn't respond outwardly to that analysis of her name, but the last word shook her. Sad...yes. So sad that for several long, bleak years she couldn't have said if the sun ever shone or not, because with her heart she had seen only gray. She could see the sunshine now; the relentless current of life as a whole had swept her out of the darkness, but there was never a day when she didn't realize how closely the shadows lurked. They were always there, a permanent counterpoint to life. If there was light, there had to be darkness; joy was balanced by pain, intimacy by loneliness. No one sailed through life untouched.

He was subtly rocking her with his body, a barely perceptible swaying that nevertheless urged her deeper and deeper into his embrace. He was aroused again; there was no mistaking that. She thought she should move away, but somehow in the past few minutes that had ceased to be an option. She was so tired, and the gentle motion of his body was soothing, like the swaying of a boat at anchor. The ancient rhythms were difficult to resist, linked as they were to instincts aeons beyond her control.

After several minutes he murmured, "Are you going to sleep?"

"I could," she replied, not opening her eyes. Beyond the danger, there was deep comfort in his embrace.

"It's almost six-thirty. Under the circumstances, I'm sure your customers would understand if you closed a little early."

"An hour and a half isn't a 'little' early. No, I'll stay until eight, as usual."

"Then so will I." He stifled his surge of annoyance. He himself let very few things interfere with his work—in actuality, only Madelyn and her family—but he didn't like the idea of Evie pushing herself into exhaustion at the marina.

"It isn't necessary."

"I rather believe it is," he replied thoughtfully.

"I still won't go out to dinner with you."

"Fair enough. I'll bring dinner to you. Do you have any preferences?"

She shook her head. "I'm not very hungry. I was going to have a sandwich when I got home."

"Leave it all to me."

She said against his chest, "You take charge very naturally. I suppose this is normal behavior for you."

"I'm decisive, yes."

"Don't forget autocratic."

"I'm sure you'll remind me if I forget."

She heard the undertone of amusement in his voice. Damn him, why couldn't he be nasty in his bullying, rather than relentlessly, gently cosseting? She never allowed herself to rely on anyone, though Rebecca had been trying to take care of her for years, but Robert simply ignored her resistance.

"I realize I'm rushing you," he murmured into her hair. "Today is only the second time we've met. I'll back off, sweetheart, and give you time to get to know me better and feel more comfortable around me. Okay?"

Her head moved up and down. She didn't want to agree to have anything to do with him, but right now she would grasp at any offer to cool down the situation. He had knocked her off balance, and she still hadn't regained it. Yes, she needed time, a lot of it.

Robert cupped her chin in his hand and forced her to lift her head away from the shelter of his chest. His pale green eyes were glittering with intensity. "But I won't go away," he warned.

Evie slept heavily that night, exhausted by the stress of the day. When she woke at dawn at the far-off roar of an early fisherman's outboard motor, she didn't rise immediately as was her habit but lay watching the pearly light spread across the sky.

For twelve years she had kept herself safe inside her carefully constructed fortress, but Robert was storming the walls. *Had* stormed them, if she was honest with herself. He was already in the inner court, though he hadn't yet managed to breach the defenses of the keep. Since Matt's death, she hadn't really *seen* any man, but Robert had forced her to see him. She was attracted to him, mentally as well as physically; it was only with effort that she had kept her emotions still safely locked away. She didn't want to love him and knew she risked doing exactly that if she continued to see him.

But she *would* see him, time and again. He had warned her—or was it a promise?—that he wasn't going to leave her alone, and he wasn't a man who could be easily distracted from his purpose.

He would kiss her, hold her, caress her. Eventually, she knew, all of her caution would vanish under the sheer force of physical desire, and she wouldn't be able to stop him—or herself.

She closed her eyes and relived the way he had kissed her the afternoon before, the way he had tasted, the calm expertise with which he had deepened the kiss. She thought of his lean fingers on her breast, and her nipples throbbed. For the first time since Matt, she wondered about making love in relation to herself. She thought of the feel of Robert's hard weight pressing down on her, of his hands and mouth moving over her bare skin, of his muscled thighs spreading hers apart as he positioned himself to take her. The appeal of her fantasy was strong enough to make her entire body clench with desire. Yes, she wanted him, as much as she feared the pain he would leave behind when he walked out of her life.

A prudent woman would immediately see a doctor about birth control, and Evie was a prudent woman. She could protect herself in that way, at least.

Chapter 6

Evie slid two food-filled plates onto the table, one in front of Rebecca and the other in front of her own seat, then refilled their coffee cups. "Thanks." Rebecca sighed, picking up her fork. Her eyes were dark-circled after the long, sleepless night spent with Jason in the hospital.

Evie sat down. After making a doctor's appointment for the next day, she had called the hospital to check on Jason. He was fine, but Rebecca had some definitely frayed edges. Not only had she been awake all night to keep watch on him and wake him regularly, evidently Jason had become as fractious and ill-tempered as he'd been as a baby whenever he was ill. He had complained about everything, griping about being woken every hour, even though both the doctor and Rebecca had explained the reason for it.

In short, his mother's wrath was about to come down hard on his sore head.

So Evie had gone up to the hospital to take care of the myriad details involved in releasing Jason. Then she'd followed them home, helped get the restless teenager settled, pushed Rebecca into a chair and set about making breakfast for them all. She knew her way around Rebecca's kitchen as well as she did her own, so the work went smoothly, and in no time at all they were digging into scrambled eggs, bacon and toast. Jason was enthroned on the couch with a tray on his lap and the television blaring.

The coffee revived Rebecca enough that her big-sister instincts kicked in. She gave Evie a shrewd look over the rim of her cup. "Where did you have dinner last night?"

"At the marina. Sandwiches," Evie clarified.

Rebecca sat back, looking disgruntled. "He said he would take you out to dinner, then make sure you got home okay."

"I didn't want to go out."

"Really," Rebecca grumbled, "I'd thought the man was made of stronger stuff than that."

If he'd been any stronger, Evie thought wryly, she would have slept in *his* bed last night. "I was too tired to go out, so he brought sandwiches there. It was kind of him to do everything he did yesterday."

"Especially hauling both you and my brat out of the river," Rebecca said judiciously as she demolished a slice of bacon. "I need to thank him again for you. I'm reserving judgment on the wisdom of saving Jason.''

Evie chuckled at Rebecca's sardonic statement. A sharp turn of phrase was a family trait that she shared with her sister, and even Paige had been exhibiting it for some time now.

"However," Rebecca continued in the same tone, "I know a man on the hunt when I see one, so don't try to throw me off the subject by telling me how *kind* he was. Kindness was the last thing on his mind."

Evie looked down at her eggs. "I know."

"Are you going to give him a chance, or are you going to look straight through him, like all the others?"

"What others?" Evie asked, puzzled.

"See what I mean? They were invisible to you. You've never even noticed all the guys who would have liked to go out with you."

"No one's ever asked me out."

"Why would they, when you never notice them? But I'll bet Robert asked you out, didn't he?"

"No." He'd *told* her that she was going out to dinner with him, and he had told her that he intended to make love to her, but he'd never actually asked her out.

Rebecca looked disbelieving. "You're pulling my leg."

"I am not. But he'll probably ask the next time he comes to the marina, if that's any consolation to you."

"The real question," her sister said shrewdly, "is if you'll go with him."

"I don't know." Evie propped her elbows on the table, the coffee cup cradled in her palms as she sipped the hot liquid. "He excites me, Becky, but he scares me, too. I don't want to get involved with anyone, and I'm afraid I wouldn't be able to stop myself with him."

"This is bad?" asked her sister with some exasperation. "Honey, it's been twelve years. Maybe it's time you became interested in men again."

"Maybe," Evie said in qualified agreement, though privately she didn't think so at all. "But Robert Cannon isn't the safest choice I could make, not by a long shot. There's something about him... I don't know. I just get the feeling that he's coming on to me for another reason besides the obvious. There's a hidden agenda there somewhere. And he puts up a good front, but he's *not* a gentleman."

"Good. A gentleman would probably take you at your word and never bother you again, after a hundred or so refusals. I have to admit, though, he struck me as being both gentle and protective."

"Possessive," Evie corrected. "And ruthless." No, he wasn't a gentleman. That cold force of will in his green diamond eyes was the look of an adventurer with a predator's heart. A hollow look of fear entered her own eyes.

Rebecca leaned forward and touched Evie's arm. "I know," she said gently. And she did, because Rebecca had been there and seen it all. "I don't want to push you into doing something you'll regret, but you never know what's going to happen. If Robert Cannon is someone you could love, can you afford to pass up that chance?''

Evie sighed. Rebecca's arguments to the contrary, could she afford to *take* that chance? And was she going to have the choice?

To her relief, Robert wasn't at the marina when she arrived to relieve Craig. Huge, black-bellied clouds were threatening overhead, and a brisk, cool wind began to blow, signaling one of the tempestuous thunderstorms so common during summer. Both pleasure-boaters and fishermen began coming in off the lake, and for an hour she didn't have a moment's rest. Lightning forked downward over the mountains, a slash of white against the purplish black background. Thunder boomed, echoing over the water, and the storm broke with blinding sheets of rain blowing across the lake.

With all of the fishermen who had put in at the marina safely off the water and the other boats snugly in their slips, Evie gladly retreated to the office where she could watch the storm from behind the protection of the thick, Plexiglass windows. She hadn't quite escaped all the rain, though, and she shivered as she rubbed a towel over her bare arms. The temperature had dropped twenty degrees in about ten minutes; the break from the heat was welcome, but the abrupt contrast was always chilling.

She loved the energy and drama of thunderstorms,

and settled contentedly into her rocking chair to watch this one play out against the background of lake and mountains. Listening to the rain was unutterably soothing. Inevitably she became drowsy and got up to turn on the small television she kept to entertain Paige and Jason. A small logo at the bottom of the television screen announced "T'storm watch."

"I'm watching, I'm watching," she told the television, and returned to the rocking chair.

Eventually the violence of the storm dissipated, but the welcome rain continued, settling down to a steady soaker, the kind farmers loved. The marina was deserted, except for the mechanic, Burt Mardis, who was contentedly working on an outboard motor in the big metal building where he did all the repairs. She could see him occasionally through the open door as he moved back and forth. There wouldn't be any more business until the weather cleared, which it showed no signs of doing. At the top of the hour the local television meteorologist broke in on the normal programming to show the progression of the line of thunderstorms that were marching across the state, as well as the solid area of rain they had left behind, stretching all the way back into Mississippi. Rain was predicted well into the night, tapering off shortly before midnight.

It looked like a long, lazy afternoon ahead of her. She always kept a book there for such times and pulled it out now, but so much time had lapsed since she had started the thing that she didn't remember much about it, so she had to start over. Actually, this was the third time she had started over; she would have to carry it home if she ever hoped to finish it.

But she was already fighting drowsiness and after ten minutes she knew that reading was going to tip the scales in favor of sleep. Regretfully she put the book aside and looked around for some chores to do. Craig, however, had cleaned up that morning; the floors were freshly swept and mopped, the merchandise impeccably straight on the shelves or hanging on pegboard hooks.

She yawned and desperately turned the television channel to rock music videos. That should jar her awake.

When Robert walked in half an hour later, she was standing in front of the television, watching with a sort of amazed disbelief. Turning to him, she said in bemusement, ''I wonder why bird-legged, sunken-chested musicians feel compelled to show their bodies to the audience?''

He was startled into a deep chuckle. He almost never laughed aloud, his amusement normally expressed, at most, by a twinkle in his eyes. This was twice, though, that Evie had charmed him into laughter. No one would ever suspect her of espionage, he thought suddenly, perhaps because of that very charm. It would be almost impossible for anyuone who knew her at all to think ill of her. Even he, who was well aware of her activities, couldn't keep himself from wanting her with a violence that both angered him and made him uneasy, because he couldn't control it.

He pushed those thoughts away as he walked toward her. If he let himself think about it now he would become enraged all over again, and Evie was so astute that he might not be able to hide it from her. When he reached her, though, and encircled her with his arms, forgetting about the other was laughably easy.

She blinked up at him, startled. Automatically she put her hands against his chest in a defensive movement. "You said you were going to back off and give me time," she accused.

"I am," Robert replied, lifting her left hand and pressing his warm, open mouth to the tender flesh on the inside of her wrist. Her pulse fluttered and raced beneath his lips. The scent of her skin was fresh and elusively, lightly fragrant, teasing him far more than if she had dabbed herself with perfume, no matter how expensive. He touched the tip of his tongue to the delicate blue veins that traced just under her skin and felt the throb of her blood beneath his touch.

Evie trembled at the subtle caress, her knees weakening. He felt that betraying quiver and gathered her more firmly against him, then lightly bit the pad at the base of her thumb. She swallowed a gasp; dear God, she hadn't known that could be so erotic.

"Will you go out to dinner with me tonight?" he murmured as his lips traveled on to her palm. Again his tongue flicked out, tasting her. Her hand trembled at the sensation.

"No, I can't." The instinctive denial was out before she could stop it, the habits of a dozen years firmly ingrained. Stunned, she realized that she *had* wanted to accept, much as a moth yearned toward the flame.

"Do you have another date?"

"No. It—it's difficult." He had no idea how difficult. She took a deep breath. "I haven't dated since my husband died."

Robert lifted his head, a slight frown drawing the black wings of his eyebrows together. "What did you say?"

She flushed and tugged her hand free. She started to wipe her palm against her jeans but instead tightly closed her fingers to hold the feel of his kiss. "I haven't gone out with anyone since Matt died."

He was silent, digesting this information, weighing it for truth. It was difficult to believe of anyone, but especially of a woman who looked like Evie. It was possible, of course, that she wasn't having an affair with Mercer after all, but to have lived like a nun for twelve years just didn't seem feasible. Still, he wasn't about to infuriate her by suggesting she was a liar.

Instead he gently stroked the underside of her jaw with the back of one finger and was immediately absorbed with the velvety texture of her skin. "Why is that?" he murmured a bit absently. "I know all the men down here can't be blind."

She bit her lip. "It was my choice. I...wasn't interested, and it didn't seem fair to waste a man's time under those circumstances."

"Reasonable, for a while. But twelve years?"

Restlessly she tried to pull away from him, but he stilled the movement, tightening the arm that remained around her. They were pressed firmly together from waist to knees, his muscled thighs hard and warm against hers. A man's strength was wonderful, she thought, inviting a woman to relax against him. Until Robert had taken her in his arms, she hadn't realized how very much she needed to be held. But not by just any man; only by him. In that moment Evie knew for certain that she had lost the battle. There was no use trying to evade him; not only would he refuse to let her get away with it, but she didn't *want* to get away with it, not any longer. For better or worse, and with dizzying speed, she had gotten herself involved with Robert Cannon. Dear God, she didn't know if she had the strength to do this, but she knew she had to try.

She didn't try to explain those twelve years. Instead she said, to his chest, "All right. I'll go out with you. Now what?"

"For starters, you could raise your head."

Slowly she did, mentally bracing herself as she met his crystalline eyes. She had expected to see amusement in them, but it was triumph glittering there rather than mirth. She shivered, more from sudden alarm than from the coolness brought by the steady rain.

"Cold?" he asked softly, rubbing his warm hands up the length of her arms.

"No. Afraid," she admitted, with painful candor. "Of you, of getting involved with you." Her eyes were deep and mysterious with shadows as she looked up at this man who had so inexplicably forced himself into her life. If he insisted on establishing some kind of romantic relationship with her, he should know up front how she felt about a few things. "I'm not good at games, Robert. Don't kiss me unless it's for real. Don't come around unless you mean to stay."

"Do you mean marriage?" he asked coolly, his expressive eyebrows lifting.

Her cheeks burned at his tone. Of course it was ridiculous to think of marriage; that wasn't at all what she had meant. At least, not the legality of marriage, the institution itself. Mentally she shied from the notion, unable to even think of it. "Of course not! I never want to get married again. But the stability, the emotional security, what I had with Matt…well, I won't settle for anything less than that, so if you're looking for a summer affair, I'm not your woman."

His mouth twisted as an unreadable expression crossed his face. "Oh, but you are. You just haven't admitted it to yourself yet."

She shivered again, but her gaze didn't waver. "I want emotional commitment. Under those terms, if you're still willing to get involved with me, I'll go out with you. I'm not comfortable with you, but I expect that will change as we get to know each other. And I don't want to sleep with you. That would just be too risky." He probably thought she meant physically, but for her the emotional risk was by far more dangerous.

He studied her face for a long moment before saying calmly, ''All right, we'll take our time and get to know each other. But I *do* want to make love with you, and I'm not going to take a vow of chastity.'' He cupped her face in his hands, and the glitter in his eyes became more pronounced as his head began to slowly descend. ''All you have to do to stop me, at any time,'' he whispered as his mouth touched hers, ''is say no.''

Her breath sighed out of her, as soft as a night breeze. The freedom to enjoy him was glorious; it felt as if she had long been frozen and was now thawing, growing warm with life again. For the first time her mouth opened welcomingly beneath his, and he took it with a calm mastery that liquefied her bones. He could give lessons in kissing, she thought hazily. His tongue probed and stroked, enticing her into a like response, so that their tongues touched and curled and petted. It was surprisingly sweet, and totally erotic.

It seemed as if he kissed her like that for a long time, simply holding her face between his palms, her body still pressed full against his. The play of his lips and tongue was both lulling and arousing. Her anxiety faded even as warmth slowly spread through her breasts and loins, making her feel as soft as butter. Her left hand was closed around his right wrist, but her right hand was leisurely stroking his back, feeling the firm, hard layers of muscle, the hollow of his spine, instinctively learning some of the details of how he was made.

The television played on unnoticed. No one came to the door on this rainy day; they stood alone in the office, oblivious to the music and the steady patter of the rain, hearing only each other's breathing and the soft, unconscious sounds of pleasure. Like a morning glory opening its shy face to the sun, Evie slowly bloomed in his arms, her golden sensuality growing in confidence. He was painfully aroused but held himself under strict control, ignoring his own condition so that she didn't feel pressured. She felt...safe, free to relax, and let herself feel the new sensations, explore the limits of her own desire. It was very different from the way it had been with Matt. She had been a girl then, and now she was a woman, with a woman's deeper and richer passion.

Though he had kissed her before, she had been distracted by the dangerous desire she felt for this man. Now, having given in, she could concentrate on the little details. She reveled in his taste, as the coolness of his lips rapidly became warm, then hard and hot. She measured the broadness of his shoulders, her palms smoothing over the curve of the joint and feeling the hardness of his solid bones covered by pads of muscle. She touched his hair, feeling it thick and silky and cool, warmer underneath, where it lay close to his skull. She felt the rasp of his five o'clock stubble against her cheeks. She inhaled the clean, musky scent of his maleness, a faint odor of soap, the fresh smell of rain on his clothes and skin.

"God." Abruptly he drew away, letting his head fall back as he drew in a deep breath. Her response had been hesitant at first, but then she had come alive in his arms, and he felt singed, as if he had been holding the sweetest of fires. His own response to her shook him with its violence. It was difficult to think of anything but taking her, and only their present location kept him from trying. "I'm the one calling a halt this time, sweetheart. We either have to stop or find a more private place."

She felt bereft, suddenly deprived of his touch. Her heart was pounding, and her skin felt as if it glowed with heat. Still, he was right. This wasn't the place for making out like teenagers. "There isn't a more private place," she said as she reached out to turn the television from rock to a country video station. The music abruptly changed from rap to a hauntingly passionate love song, and that was even more jarring to her nerves. She punched the Off button, and in the sudden quiet the rain sounded heavier than before. She looked out the window at the gray curtain that veiled the lake, obscuring the far bank.

"No one will be using their boats for the rest of the day," Robert said. "Why don't you close early and we'll go to Huntsville for dinner."

She considered how his questions and suggestions sounded like statements and demands. Had no one before her ever said no to this man? "I can't close early."

"The rain is supposed to last halfway through the night," he said reasonably.

"But that won't stop people from coming in to buy tackle. Granted, there probably won't be many, maybe not any, but the sign says that I'm open until eight."

And she would be, he thought, exasperated by the difficulty of courting a woman who refused to make time for him. He had certainly never had that problem before. In fact, he couldn't say that he'd ever had a problem with a woman at all—until Evie. Getting close to her presented him with as many obstacles as a mine field. Ruefully he thought that if he was going to spend any time with her, most of it would obviously be here at the marina.

Rather than become angry, which would only make her more obstinate, he said, "Could Craig swap shifts with you occasionally, if we give him advance notice?"

A tiny smile lifted the corners of her mouth, telling him that he was learning. "I suppose he could. He's generally accommodating."

"Tomorrow?"

This time she almost laughed aloud. "I can't tomorrow." She had an appointment with her doctor at ten in the morning. Though she had told Robert that she didn't want to sleep with him, he had said only that he would stop if she told him to. The "if" told her that she should be prudent, because his physical effect on her was potent. Of course, she wasn't going to tell Robert that she was arranging birth control; he would consider it a green light to making love.

He sighed. "The day after tomorrow?"

"I'll ask him."

"Thank you," he said with faint irony.

Robert received two phone calls the next morning. He was out on the deck, reading a sheaf of papers that Felice had faxed to him; it was remarkably easy, he'd found, to keep abreast of things by way of phone, computer and fax. The first call was from Madelyn. "How are things in Alabama?"

"Hot," he replied. He was wearing only gym shorts. The rain of the day before had made everything seem even more green and lush, the scents more intense, but it hadn't done anything to ease the heat. If anything, the heat was worse. The morning sun burned on his bare chest and legs. Luckily, with his olive complexion, he didn't have to worry about sunburn.

"The weather is perfect here, about seventy-five degrees. Why don't you fly up for the weekend?"

"I can't," he said, and realized how much he sounded like Evie. "I don't know how long I'll be down here, but I can't leave until everything is tied up."

"The invitation stands," Madelyn said in her lazy drawl. A funny pang went through him as he realized how similar Madelyn's accent was to Evie's. "If you do happen to find a couple of days free, we'd love to see you."

"I'll try to get up there before I go back to New York," he promised.

"Try really hard. We haven't seen you since spring. Take care."

The phone rang again almost immediately. This time it was the man he had hired to keep watch on Landon Mercer. "He had a visitor last night. We followed the visitor when he left, and we're working on identifying him. There hasn't been anything of interest on the phones."

"All right. Keep watching and listening. Has he spotted his tail yet?"

"No, sir."

"Anything in his house?" Robert was briefly thankful that he was a civilian and didn't have to follow the same tortuous rules and procedures that cops did, though it could have been sticky if his men had been caught breaking and entering. They hadn't seized any evidence, merely looked for it. Information was power.

"Clean as a whistle. Too clean. There's not even a bank statement lying around. We found out that he has a safety deposit box, so he might keep his paperwork in it, but we haven't been able to get into it yet. I'm working on getting a copy of his bank statement."

"Keep me informed," Robert said, and hung up. In a few days Mercer would start feeling a slight squeeze. He wouldn't think much of it at first, but soon it would become suffocating. Robert's plans for Evie, both personal and financial, were moving along nicely, too.

Chapter 7

Robert didn't intend to see Evie at all that day. He was an expert strategist in the eternal battle between men and women; after his determined pursuit of her, she would be expecting him to either call or come to the marina, and the lack of any contact with him would knock her slightly off balance, further weakening her defenses. He had often thought that seduction was similar to chess, in that the one who could keep the other guessing was the one in control of the game.

He was in control of the seduction. His instincts in that part of the game were infallible. It might take him a few weeks of gentling, but Evie would end up in his bed. Not long after that, he would have this entire mess cleaned up; Mercer and Evie would be arrested, and he would go back to New York.

Damn.

That was the problem, of course. He didn't want Evie in jail. He had been furious when he had come down here, determined to put both her and her lover away for a very long time. But that was before he had met her, before he had held her and tasted the heady sweetness of her. Before he had seen the underlying sadness in those golden brown eyes, and wondered if he would cause that expression to deepen. The thought made him uneasy.

Was she even guilty? At first he had been convinced that she was; now, even after such a short acquaintance, he was no longer certain. No criminal was untouched by his deeds. There was always a mark left behind, perhaps in a certain coldness in the eye, a lack of moral concern in certain matters. He hadn't been able to find any such mark in Evie. He had often thought that those who dealt in espionage, in the betrayal of their own country, were some of the coldest people ever born. They lacked the depth of emotion that others had. That lack of feeling wasn't evident in Evie; if anything, he would say that she felt far too much.

She hadn't hesitated at all in going into the river after Jason. That in itself wasn't unusual; any number of strangers would have done the same thing, much less a relative. But, knowing that every second counted, she had stayed down far too long herself in the effort to find the boy. He knew as surely as he knew the sun was in the sky that she would not have been able to make it back to the surface without his help...and that she had been willing to die rather than release Jason and save herself. Even now, the memory made his bones turn cold.

He had gone inside to work at the computer, but now he got up and restlessly walked out onto the deck, where the burning sun could dispel his sudden chill.

Only a person of deep emotion was capable of that kind of sacrifice.

He braced his hands on the top railing and stared out at the river. It wasn't green today, but rather a rich blue, reflecting the deep blue of the cloudless sky. There was little, if any, breeze, and the water's surface was calm. It lapped gently against the dock and the bank with a sound that tugged at something deep within him. All life had originated in the sea; perhaps it was an echo of that ancient time that made people respond so to water. But this river, peaceful as it was now, had almost taken Evie's life.

He shivered from another chill. He couldn't remember, he thought absently, when he had been so enraged...or so afraid. He had ruthlessly controlled both emotions, allowing no hint of them to surface, but they had roiled deep within him. It hadn't been an intellectual anger, but rather a gut-level rage at fate, at chance, which had seemed to be snatching Evie out of his grasp before he could...what? Have her indicted? He snorted mirthlessly at that idea. The thought hadn't entered his mind. No, he had been furious that he wouldn't be able to hold her, make love to her, that the endless stretch of his days wouldn't have her in them.

Was Evie the type of person who could betray her country? He was beginning to doubt his own information.

Indecision wasn't normally part of Robert's makeup, and he was impatient with himself now. He couldn't allow his doubts about Evie's guilt to alter his plans. If she was innocent, then she wouldn't be harmed. She would have some uncomfortable moments, she would be worried, but in the end he would take care of the situation, and she would be okay.

Thinking about her made him edgy. He glanced at his watch; it was a little after noon. She should be at the marina now, and he should already have heard from the tail that he had assigned to follow her every move.

Right on cue, the phone rang, and he stepped inside to pick it up.

"She went to Huntsville this morning," a quiet female voice reported. "Her destination was an office building. The elevator closed before I could get on it with her, so I don't know where she went. I waited, and she returned to the lobby after an hour and twenty-three minutes. She drove straight home, changed clothes and then went to the marina. Mercer was in his office at PowerNet the entire time, and they didn't talk on the phone. There was no contact between them at all."

"What kind of tenants are in the office building?"

"I made a list. There are two insurance firms, a

real estate office, four medical doctors, four lawyers, three dentists, an office temp company and two computer programming firms.''

Damn, Robert thought bleakly. Aloud he said, ''Find out where she went. Concentrate first on the two programming firms.''

''Yes, sir.''

He swore as he hung up. Why couldn't she have spent the morning shopping, or paying bills?

He wanted to see her. He wanted to shake her until her teeth rattled. He wanted to whisk her away to some secluded place and keep her locked up there until he had this mess settled. He wanted to ride her until she wept with submission. The violence of all those longings was alien to him, but he couldn't deny it. She had definitely gotten under his skin in a way no other woman had ever done.

Temper and frustration merged, and with a muttered curse he gave in. After swiftly dressing, he left the house and climbed in the black Jeep. Damn it, he wanted to see her, so he would.

Virgil was visiting with Evie again that day. His knee was better, he said, and indeed, he was walking with less effort. The day had been fairly busy, with customers in and out on a regular basis, and Virgil had passed the time with several old friends and casual acquaintances.

She was busy ringing up a fisherman's purchase of gas, a soft drink and a pack of crackers when the door opened. Without looking, she knew Robert had entered. Her skin tingled, and she felt an instant of panic. She had hoped, foolishly, that she wouldn't see him that day, that her frazzled nerves would have a chance to recover somewhat before she actually went out with him the next night. On the other hand, she thought wryly, time and distance probably wouldn't help at all. Even if he wasn't there personally, he was in her mind, dominating both her thoughts and dreams.

Her customer taken care of, she allowed herself to look at him as he genially introduced himself to Virgil, who remembered him, of course. Very little got by that old man.

Robert was wearing jeans and a loose, white cotton shirt. A khaki baseball cap covered his black hair, and a pair of expensive sunglasses dangled from one hand. Her blood raced through her veins in excitement; even in such casual dress, there was something elegant and dangerous about him. The jeans were soft and faded with age, and he was as at home in them as he was in his silk shirts.

Then he was touching her on the arm, and it was like being burned with a tiny spark of electricity. "I'm going to take the boat out for a while, run the river and learn something about it."

So he wasn't going to be hanging around the marina all day. She was both relieved and disappointed. "Have you hired a guide?"

"No, but the river channel's marked, isn't it?"

"Yes, there shouldn't be any problem, unless you

want to explore out of the channel. I'll give you a map.''

''Okay.'' Thoughtfully Robert looked at Virgil. ''Would you like to show me around the lake, Mr. Dodd? That is, if you don't have plans for the afternoon.''

Virgil cackled, his faded eyes suddenly gleaming with enthusiasm. ''Plans?'' he snorted. ''I'm ninety-three years old! Who in tarnation makes plans at my age? I could stop breathin' any minute now.''

Amusement danced in Robert's eyes, making them look like pale green diamonds. ''I'm willing to take the chance if you are, but I warn you, a corpse in the boat would be a real inconvenience.''

Virgil hauled himself out of the rocking chair. ''Tell you what, son. For the chance to park myself in a boat again, I'll try real hard not to put you to the trouble of havin' to call the coroner.''

''It's a deal.'' Robert winked at Evie as he turned away.

Evie shook her head as she smiled at Virgil. She knew better than to try talking him out of going. Besides, he deserved to enjoy an hour or so on the river he loved, and she had faith that Robert would be as skillful at handling a boat as he was at everything else he did. How had he guessed, on such short acquaintance, that Virgil would dearly love getting out on the water again?

''Both of you be careful,'' she admonished. ''Virgil, don't forget your cap.''

''I won't, I won't,'' he said testily. ''Think I'm

fool enough to go out without somethin' on my head?''

"I'll bring the boat around to the dock," Robert said, and she was grateful to him for sparing Virgil the longer walk to the boat slip. He reached the door, stopped and came back to her. "I forgot something."

"What?"

He cupped her chin in one hand, leaned down and calmly kissed her. It wasn't a passionate kiss; it was almost leisurely. Still, when he lifted his head, her heart was pounding and her thoughts scattered. "That," he murmured.

She heard Virgil's cracked laughter and became aware of the interested gazes of the two customers who were browsing among the hooks and spinner baits. Her cheeks burned with a blush, and she turned away to fiddle with some papers until she could regain her composure.

Virgil patted her on the arm. Though stooped under the weight of nine decades, he was still taller than she, and he grinned at her. "Heard tell that young feller made hisself useful the other day, when Becky's boy fell in."

She cleared her throat. "Yes. If he hadn't been there, Jason and I both would probably have drowned."

"Fast mover, is he?"

She found herself blushing again and waved Virgil off with shooing motions. Why on earth had Robert kissed her in public? She would never have thought that he was given to public displays of affection;

there was something too contained about him. But he had certainly done just that!

She watched out the window as he idled the sleek black boat around to the dock, the powerful motor rumbling like thunder. The sunglasses were in place on the high-bridged nose, giving him a remote, lethal air. She had seen soldiers with that exact expression, and she wondered at it. With a start, she realized how little she knew about Robert Cannon. What did he do for a living? She knew he had to have some money to be able to afford that house, a new boat and the new Jeep. Where was he from? Did he have family, had he been married before, was he married *now,* did he have children? A chill went through her as she thought of all she didn't know about him.

And yet, in a way, she knew the man. He was cool and complicated, a private man who kept a subtle but permanent distance between himself and everyone else. The distance wasn't physical, God knows; he was the most physical, *sensual* man she'd ever met. Emotionally, though, he always held something back, keeping the inner man untouched. Probably most people thought of him as very controlled and unemotional; Evie agreed with the controlled part, but there was a ferocity lurking beneath the control that alarmed her even as it called to her own inner fire. He was ruthless, he was autocratic…and he had seen, almost at a glance, how much an old man would love to take a boat ride on his beloved river once more.

Her breath caught, and there was a pain in her

chest. Panic filled her as she watched Virgil hobble out to the dock as Robert brought the boat alongside. Robert held out a strong hand, and Virgil gripped it and stepped aboard the craft. There was a wide smile on his face as he settled onto the seat. Robert handed him a life jacket, and obediently Virgil slipped it on, though Evie was fairly certain he'd never worn one before in his life.

The panic that almost suffocated her was comprised of equal parts terror and tenderness. She *couldn't* feel this much for him, not so soon. You had to know someone for that, and she had just been thinking how little she knew about him. She was fascinated by him, that was all. It was understandable. He was the first man in her life since Matt's death, twelve long, desolate years ago. He had brought passion alive in her again, with his skillful kisses and determined pursuit.

She had never felt so violently attracted to a man before.

With Matt...they had grown up together, they'd been in the same class in school, from first grade through graduation. She had known Matt as well as she knew herself; they'd been like two halves of a whole. The love had grown gradually between them, pure and steady, like a candle flame. Robert...Robert was an inferno, and the heat between them could leave her in ashes.

Robert and Virgil had been gone for over an hour when Landon Mercer strolled into the marina. "Hi, doll,'' he said jovially. ''How's the prettiest woman in this part of the state?''

Evie's expression was impassive as she glanced at him. Unfortunately, business had slowed down and she was there alone. She always preferred to have company around when she had to deal with him. Of course, being alone meant that she would have the opportunity to follow him again. Her thoughts began to hum. ''Hello, Mr. Mercer.''

''Landon,'' he said, as he always did. He leaned against the counter in a negligent pose, one designed to show off his physique. Mercer was a good-looking man, she admitted, but he left her cold.

''Do you want to rent a boat today?'' she asked, turning to check which ones were available, though she knew without looking. She had quickly discovered that the best way to deflect his attention was to appear oblivious to it.

''Sure do. It's been a while since I've done any fishing, so I decided to play hooky from work this afternoon.'' He laughed at his own pun.

Evie managed a polite smile. He had brought in a small tackle box and one rod and reel, the same rig he always carried. The same lure was tied to the line.

''Do you want any particular boat?''

''No, any of them will do.'' He leaned closer. ''When I get back, why don't we go out to dinner tonight? Not anywhere here. We'll go someplace nice, maybe in Birmingham.''

''Thanks, but I'm busy tonight,'' she replied, her tone conveying no interest at all. Unfortunately, he was so taken with his own charm that he was oblivious to her lack of response to him.

"Tomorrow night, then. It's Saturday night. We can even go to Atlanta for some real fun, since we wouldn't have to be back for work."

"The marina's open seven days a week."

"Oh. Okay, we'll go to Birmingham."

"No, thank you, Mr. Mercer. I'm busy tomorrow night, too."

"C'mon, how busy can you be? Whatever it is, you can put it off."

Her teeth were on edge. She barely managed to be polite as she said, "I have a date tomorrow night."

"Now I'm jealous. Who's the lucky man?"

"No one you know." She took an ignition key from the pegboard and slid it across the counter to him. "There you go. Number five, the one at the end of the dock."

He took out his wallet and extracted a couple of twenties. "I'll have it back in two hours." He picked up the ignition key.

"Fine." She mustered a smile. "Have a good time. Hope you catch a lot."

"I never do, but it's fun to try," he said breezily as he picked up his tackle and went out the door.

Evie put the money into the cash drawer and locked it, all the while eyeing Mercer as he walked down the dock. He was looking around, studying the parking lot and the traffic on the street out front, as well as on the bisecting causeway.

Swiftly she picked up the phone and buzzed Burt

in the maintenance building. He picked up just as Mercer was getting into the boat.

"Burt, I'm taking the boat out for a while," Evie said swiftly. "I'm locking the store, but keep an eye on the gas pumps while I'm gone."

"Sure," he said, as unquestioning as ever. Burt Mardis didn't have a curious bone in his body.

Mercer was idling away from the dock. Evie jammed a ball cap on her head, grabbed her sunglasses and hurried from the building. She locked the door behind her, then sprinted for her own boat.

He was beyond the wave breakers by the time she reached her boat, and she heard the roar as he opened up the throttle. She all but threw herself into the boat and turned the key in the ignition. The motor coughed to life with a satisfying roar. Her boat was faster than any of the rentals, but on the water, and at speed, it was difficult to distinguish one vessel from another.

She had to idle away from the marina, because a fast takeoff would make waves large enough to violently rock the boats in their slips, possibly damaging them. Swearing at every lost second, she waited until she was past the wave breakers before pushing the throttle forward. The motor roared, and the front end of the boat lifted in the air as the vessel shot forward. It planed off almost immediately, the nose dropping into the running position.

She scanned the water for Mercer; unfortunately, he had gained enough distance that she couldn't positively identify him, and there were three boats speeding away from her, small specks that bobbed slightly as they cut through the waves. Which one was Mercer?

The sun wasn't far past its apex, and the glare turned the lake into a mirror. Hot air hit her, pulling tendrils of hair loose around her face. The scent of the river filled her head and lungs, and a quiet exultation spread through her. This was a part of her life that she loved—the wind in her face, the sense of speed, the feel of the boat as it glided over calm water and bumped over waves. Though there were other boats on the lake, and houses visible all along the shoreline, when she was speeding across the water it was like being alone with God. She would have been perfectly content, if only she knew what Mercer was up to.

After a minute one boat slowed and turned toward another marina. As she neared, she could tell that it held two passengers.

That left two. The throttle was full forward, and she was gaining on one, while the other, probably a speedy bass boat, was pulling away. Since her boat was faster than the rental, the one she was overtaking had to be Mercer. Cautiously she throttled back, enough to stay at a pace with him but not so close that he would see and identify her. Just about everyone on the water would be wearing a ball cap and sunglasses, and her hair was pulled back in a braid rather than flying loose, so she felt fairly confident that he wouldn't recognize her.

He was heading toward the same area, where there

were a lot of small islands dotting the lake. She wouldn't be able to get very close, because once he cut his speed he would be able to hear other boats. Her best bet, she thought, was to stop some distance away and pretend to be fishing.

The boat ahead slowed and cut between two islands. Evie kept her speed steady and cruised on past. There was a distance of over two hundred yards between them, but she could tell that now he was idling closer to the bank of the island on the right.

She turned in the opposite direction, away from him. A barge was coming downriver, heavily loaded and settled deep into the water, pushing out a wave as it plowed forward. If she let the barge come between her and Mercer, it would block his activities for almost half a minute, plenty long enough for her to lose him. But if she moved inside the barge's path, it would put her closer to him than she wanted to be.

There was no help for it. She tucked her long braid inside her shirt to hide that identifying detail and turned the boat to angle back across the river ahead of the barge.

"Guntersville Lake's easy to learn," Virgil stated. "'Course, I was fishin' the river back before the TVA built the dam, so I knowed the lay of the land before the water backed up and covered it. Not many of us around now remembers the way it used to be. River used to flood a lot. So Roosevelt's boys decided we needed us a dam, so there wouldn't be no more floods. Well, hell, 'course there ain't, 'cause now the land that flooded ever now an' then is permanently under water. The government calls it flood control. They throwed around words like eminent domain, but what they did is take people's land, turn them off their farms, and put a lot of good land under water.''

"The TVA brought electricity to the Tennessee River Valley, didn't it?'' Robert asked. He was holding the boat to around twenty miles an hour, not much more than idling speed to the powerful motor behind them, but the slow speed made conversation possible. They had to raise their voices, but they could hear each other.

Virgil snorted. "Sure it did. Glad to have it, too. But nobody ever thought the TVA built that dam to make our lives easier. Hell, we knew what was goin' on. It was the Depression, and Roosevelt would have built the second Tower of Babel to make jobs for folks, for all the good it did to the economy. It took the war to kick-start things again.''

"Did you fight in the war?''

"Too old for that one.'' Virgil cackled with glee. "Imagine that! Over fifty years ago, they said I was too old! But I was in the first one. Lied about my age to get in. Not that they checked too close, 'cause they needed men could hit the broad side of a barn with a rifle slug. During the second one, I volunteered to help train the younger fellers with their rifles, but that was all stateside. Suited me. My wife weren't none too pleased with me, anyway, leavin' her to handle five young'uns on her own. She'd have been mad as hell if I'd gone overseas. Our oldest boy, John Edward, was seventeen when it all started, and he joined the navy. It fretted her enough that he was gone. He made it back fine, though. Imagine that. The boy went through a war in the Pacific without a scratch, then come home and died two years later with the pneumonia. Life's got a lotta strange turns in it. Don't guess I'll see too many more of them, but then, I didn't plan on hangin' around this long to begin with.''

The old man lapsed into silence, perhaps remembering all the people who had come and gone through his life. After a minute he roused himself. ''Got a lot of creeks emptyin' into the lake. We passed Short Creek a ways back. This here's Town Creek.''

Robert had studied maps of the lake, so when Virgil identified the creeks he was able to pinpoint their location. Since the river channel was marked, staying in safely deep water was no problem. It was when he ventured out of the river channel that Virgil's expertise came in handy, because he knew where it was shallow, where the hidden stump rows were lurking just under the surface, ready to tear the bottom out of a boat if the driver wasn't careful. For several more minutes, Virgil devoted himself to his appointed task, pointing out quirks of the lake.

Then he said, ''I've lost a lot of folks over the years. My own mama and pa, of course, and all my brothers and sisters. There were sixteen of us, and I'm the only one left. Got a piss pot full of nieces and nephews, though, and all of their kids, and their kids' kids. My wife passed on in sixty-four. Lord, it don't seem like it's been that long. I've lost three of my own kids. Parents ought not to outlive their kids. It ain't right. And all my friends that I growed up with, they're long gone.

"Yep, I've had to bury many a loved one, so I get right protective of the ones I got left." Faded blue eyes were suddenly piercing as he turned them on Robert. "Evie's a special woman. She's had enough sorrow in her young life, so if you don't mean to do right by her, it would be a kindness if you'd leave her alone and haul your ass back up north."

Robert's face was impassive. "Evie's related to you?" he asked neutrally, ignoring Virgil's rather combative statement. He wasn't about to get into an argument with a ninety-three-year-old man.

Virgil snorted. "Not by blood. But I've knowed her all her life, watched her grow up, and there's not a finer woman in this town. Now, I watch television, so I know times have changed from when I was young enough to court a woman. Back then we had enough respect for womenfolk not to do nothing to cause them harm. But, like I said, times have changed. I know young folks now get serious about things without tyin' the knot proper, and that ain't what I'm talkin' about. Thing is, if you're just lookin' for a good time, then find some other woman. Evie ain't like that."

Robert had to struggle with several conflicting emotions. Foremost was his cold, instinctive anger at

Virgil's scolding interference. In neither his business nor his personal life was he accustomed to being taken to task. Right after that, though, was amusement. He was thirty-six and, moreover, an extremely wealthy man who wielded a great deal of power in both financial and political circles. He almost smiled at Virgil lumping him in with "young folks."

What took most of his attention, though, was this second warning that Evie wasn't a good-time girl. Evie herself had issued the first warning: *Don't kiss me unless it's for real.* After Virgil's little speech, the underlying meaning of those warnings was clear, though the reason wasn't.

"I don't usually discuss my relationships," he finally said in a faintly distant tone, just enough to signal his displeasure. "But my interest in Evie isn't casual." *In any way.* "What did you mean, she's had enough sorrow in her life?" Because that had been the basis of the talk: *Don't hurt her.*

"I mean, life ain't been easy on her. Grief comes to everybody, if they live long enough. Some folks, though, it hits harder than others. Losin' Matt the way she did, the day after they got married...well, it changed her. There ain't no sunshine in her eyes now, the way there used to be. She never looked at another man since Matt died, until you. So don't disappoint her, is what I'm sayin'."

Robert was knocked off balance by the surge of jealousy that seared through him. Jealousy? He'd never been jealous in his life, especially where a woman was concerned. Either his women were faithful to him or the relationship ended. Period. How could he be jealous of a boy who had been dead for a dozen years? But Evie still wore Matt Shaw's wedding ring on her finger and had evidently remained faithful to him even after all this time. Forget Mercer; that had obviously been an error. An understandable one, but still an error. He was both glad that she wasn't involved with Mercer, at least on that level, and furious that she was determined to waste herself on a memory. *I don't want to sleep with you,* she'd said. She was still trying to be faithful to a dead husband.

"What kind of person was Matt?" he asked. He didn't want to know, didn't want to talk about the boy, but he felt compelled to find out.

"He was a fine boy. Would have been a good man, if he'd had the chance. Good-natured, honest. Kindhearted, too. Can't say that about too many folks, but Matt didn't have a mean bone in his body. He never dated anybody but Evie, and it was the same with her. They planned to marry each other from the time they started high school together. Never saw two kids love each other the way they did. It was a shame that they didn't have no more time together than what they had. She didn't even have his child to keep part of him alive. Damn shame. She needed somthing to live for, back then."

Robert had had enough. He couldn't listen to much more about how wonderful Matt Shaw had been, and how much Evie had loved him, without losing his temper. He couldn't remember the last time he had lost control, but there was a deep-seated fury in him now that was surging forward. He didn't try to analyze his anger; he simply and ruthlessly contained it, shoving it down as he turned the boat downriver and headed back toward the marina. He eased the throttle forward so the noise would make conversation impossible.

Fifteen minutes later they were idling up to the docks. At the sound of the motor, a man wearing grease-covered coveralls came out of the maintenance building and walked out on the dock. He nodded a greeting to Robert and said to Virgil, "Come in outta the sun and keep me company for a while. Evie closed the office and took her boat out for a while." As he talked, he extended a muscular arm to steady Virgil as he climbed out of the boat onto the dock.

"When was this?" Robert asked sharply.

The mechanic shrugged. "An hour, maybe. I didn't pay no attention to the time."

She had refused to close the marina early one rainy late afternoon, when there had been no customers, but now she had closed it not long after lunch on a beautiful, sunny, *busy* day. Robert's eyes narrowed. He looked at the parking lot. He knew the make, model and color of Mercer's car, and there it sat.

Damn her. She had left to meet with the traitorous bastard.

Chapter 8

Robert was standing on the dock when Evie eased her boat into its regular slip. He was wearing those extra dark sunglasses that completely hid his eyes, but she didn't need to see them to know that they were icy with rage. Maybe it was the way he moved, very deliberately, every action contained, that alerted her to his mood. An uncontrollable shiver ran over her, despite the heat. There was something far more alarming about that cold, ruthless control than if he had been violent. Again she had the thought that he was the most dangerous man she'd ever seen. But what had put him in such a menacing mood?

She tied off and leapt up onto the dock. "Did Virgil enjoy himself?" she asked as she stepped around Robert, heading toward the office. He wasn't the only one who had self-control. Right now she had other concerns besides dealing with his temper. She could hear the roar of a boat coming closer; that might or might not be Mercer, but she wasn't taking any more chances. When Mercer returned to the marina, she intended to be inside the office building, doing business as usual.

"Just a minute," Robert said, his tone clipped, and reached for her.

Evie evaded his grasp. "Later," she said, and hurried up the dock.

He was right behind her when she unlocked the door, but he didn't have a chance to say anything. Virgil had seen her boat and was slowly making his way across the lot. Robert eyed the old man's progress; he wouldn't have time to get any answers out of her before Virgil was there, so it would be better to wait, as she'd said, until later. Once more he controlled his anger and frustration, but the fury in him remained hot. If anything, he was becoming even angrier.

Virgil reached the doorway and gave a sigh of pleasure as the cool air-conditioning washed over him. "Got spoiled in my old age," he griped. "The heat didn't used to bother me none."

"No point in letting it bother you back then," Evie pointed out, smiling at him. "There wasn't any air-conditioning, so we all had to put up with it."

The old man eased into the rocking chair. "Spoiled," he repeated contentedly.

She went over to a vending machine and fed in the change for three soft drinks. She kept the ma-

chine's temperatre set low enough to form ice crys-
tals in the drinks, to the delight of her customers.
She popped the tops off the bottles and thrust one
into Robert's hands, then gave another to Virgil. The
third she drank herself, turning up the bottle for a
long, cold swallow of the crisp, biting liquid.

She saw Robert eye the hourglass bottle in his
hand with a less-than-thrilled expression; then he,
too, took a drink. His tastes were probably too sophisticated to run to soft drinks, she thought, but if
he was going to live here for the summer, he should
do as the natives did. One of the front lines of defense against the heat was to consume cola every day
as coolant for the insides.

A boat was idling in past the wave breakers. A
quick glance told Evie that it was the rental boat.
Mercer had seen her, she knew, but she didn't think
he had recognized her. Wearing the universal ball
cap and sunglasses, with her hair tucked in, she could
have been anyone. It was doubtful that he had even
been able to tell she was a woman.

Robert hitched one hip onto the counter, a sock-
less, docksider-clad foot swinging as he nursed the
soft drink. His expression didn't give anything away,
but she had the strong impression that he
was…waiting. Until they could talk? No. It was more
immediate than that.

She watched Mercer tie up the boat and walk jaun-
tily along the dock, tackle box in one hand and useless tackle in the other. Then the door opened and
he breezed in, all ego and self-satisfaction. "Nothing

today, doll,'' he said in his obnoxious, too-hearty manner. "Maybe I'd have better luck if you went along. What do you say?''

"I'm not much for fishing,'' she lied without compunction, causing Virgil to almost choke on his drink.

Robert's back, as he sat on the counter, had been half-turned toward Mercer. Now he shifted around to face the other man. "Hello, Landon,'' he said coolly. "I'd like to go fishing with you the next time you take the afternoon off.''

Evie was startled to hear Robert call Mercer by his first name, and a mental alarm began clanging. *How did Robert know the man?*

But if she was startled, the effect on Mercer was electric. He froze in place, his face draining of color as he gaped at Robert. "M-Mr. Cannon,'' he stuttered. "I—uh, how—w-what are you doing here?''

The black slashes of Robert's eyebrows rose in that sardonic way of his. Mercer was totally aghast at having run into him, Evie saw, and the tension in her relaxed. Whatever the connection, Robert wasn't in league with Mercer, or the other man wouldn't have been so taken aback at his presence.

The most obvious answer to Mercer's question would have been that he kept his boat here; that wasn't, however, what Robert said. Instead he looked deliberately at Evie and said, "The place has a certain attraction.''

She felt silly, but she couldn't stop the color from

heating her face. Mercer looked even more aghast, for some reason.

"Oh," he mumbled. "Yeah, sure." With an effort, he regained a bit of control and managed a sickly smile. "It's getting late. I should be going. Call me when you're free, Mr. Cannon, and we'll get in that game of golf we talked about."

"Or some fishing," Robert suggested, his voice like silk.

"Uh...yeah. Yes, we'll do that. Anytime." Mercer tossed the boat keys onto the counter and hastily left.

"Wonder what set his britches on fire," Virgil mused.

"Perhaps it was his bad luck in taking an afternoon off from work to go fishing and running into his employer at the marina," Robert suggested, his eyes hooded.

Virgil leaned back in the rocker, wheezing with laughter. "Well, I'll be! He works for you, eh? Bet that ruined his fun for the day."

"I'm certain it did."

Evie stood motionless, absorbing all the nuances of the brief scene with Mercer, and also the silkiness of Robert's murmured reply. He had taken a great deal of pleasure in watching Mercer squirm. He had also made that remark about her being the reason for his presence for the same reason: to make Mercer squirm. After all, what man would feel comfortable to find out he had just come on to the boss's woman...in front of the boss? This was in addition to being caught playing hooky from work.

Mercer probably didn't realize it, but it had been plain to Evie that Robert disliked him. He had been perfectly cordial, but the dislike had been there, underlying every word. She was enormously relieved. For a horrible moment she had been afraid that Robert was involved with whatever crooked deal Mercer had going on, but Mercer's manner certainly hadn't been that of someone who had met a friend. She was worried, though, to find that Mercer worked for Robert. Just as she didn't want his dirty waves to touch the marina, she also didn't want him to somehow harm Robert.

She hadn't been successful in finding out any more about what Mercer was up to; he had idled a twisting path around several of the islands, finally stopping for a moment on the back side of one of the larger ones. She hadn't been able to see what, if anything, he was doing. If she had had a trolling motor, she would have been able to get much closer without him hearing her, but her boat wasn't equipped with one. Then Mercer had started his motor again and resumed his weaving in and out of the islands. She had watched him as best she could, but there was no way to keep him in sight all the time. When he had finally left the islands, it had taken all the speed her boat was capable of to outpace him and reach the marina far enough in advance that he wouldn't see her.

So she still had nothing but suspicion. While she was wondering whether or not to confide in Robert when she had nothing of substance to tell him, Virgil's great-granddaughter came in. This time she was carrying a wide-eyed, eleven-month-old girl on her hip, and was followed by two towheaded boys, ages four and six. "PawPaw, PawPaw," both boys yelled. They ran toward the rocking chair, climbing up on Virgil's lap with a naturalness that suggested they had been doing it all their lives.

"Well, how'd it go?" Virgil asked, gathering both small bodies against him. "Did the dentist give you a sucker?"

"Yep," said the oldest one, pulling a bright red lollipop from his pocket. "Mom says it's okay, because it's sugarless. You want it?" His expression said that he was disappointed by the sugarless state of the candy.

"It's tempting," Virgil allowed, "but you keep it."

Evie smiled as she watched Virgil with his great-great-grandchildren, then turned back to their mother. "Sherry, this is Robert Cannon. He and Virgil have been out running the river today. Robert, Virgil's great-granddaughter, Sherry Ferguson."

"Pleased to meet you," Sherry said with her friendly smile. She obviously remembered Robert from the first time he had come to the marina. She shifted the baby onto her other hip and held out her hand.

Robert reached to shake Sherry's hand, and the baby evidently thought he was reaching for her; with a gurgle of pleasure she released her grip on Sherry's blouse and lunged forward, both dimpled little arms outstretched. Sherry made a startled grab for the child, but Robert was faster, scooping the baby into his arms almost before she had left the safety of her mother's.

"Allison Rose!" Sherry gasped, staring at the baby. "I'm sorry," she apologized to Robert as she reached to retrieve her child. "I don't know what got into her. She's never gone to a stranger like that before."

Allison Rose wouldn't have any of it; she shrieked and turned away from her mother's hands, clinging to Robert's shirt with all her might.

"She's all right," Robert said, his wonderful deep voice now holding a soothing tone to calm both mother and daughter. One powerful hand steadied the baby's back as his eyes smiled at Sherry. "I've always had a way with women."

That was nothing less than the truth, Evie thought, her blood moving in a slow throb through her veins as she watched him cradle the baby as comfortably as if he had a dozen of his own. Was there anything the man couldn't do? Sherry was all but melting under that smiling look, and tiny Allison was in heaven.

Perched on his arm, Allison looked around with a beatific expression, as if she were a queen surveying her subjects. Robert bent his head to brush his nose against the soft blond curls and reflected that girls were different from boys even at this young age. He had rocked Madelyn's two boys when they were infants and played with them as toddlers, but they hadn't been quite as soft as the baby girl in his arms, and her scent was indefinably sweeter. He found himself

enchanted by the tiny sandals on her feet and the ruffled sundress she wore. The feel of her chubby, dimpled arms clinging to him was strangely satisfying.

Oh God, Evie thought. Her chest was so tight she
could barely breathe. She had to turn away to hide
the shattered look in her eyes. Why couldn't he have
been uncomfortable with babies? Why did he have
to cradle Allison so tenderly and close his eyes with
delight at her sweet baby scent? The emotion swelling in her was so overwhelming that she couldn't
think, couldn't function.

For the rest of her life she would remember the
exact moment when she fell in love with Robert Cannon.

She busied herself fiddling with papers, though
she couldn't have said what those papers were. As
if from a distance, she could hear Sherry asking
about Virgil's excursion on the river, could hear the
enthusiasm in Virgil's reply and Robert's comments. The calm, soothing tone was still there, she
noticed. How could Sherry fail to be reassured about
the safety of the outing when his utter placidity and
self-confidence said that he had taken every care
without appearing to fuss over Virgil's safety?

He did it deliberately, she realized as she listened
to them talk. She felt oddly detached, not really hearing words, but rather the way things were said, the
underlying emotion. Robert was a master at reading
people, then using his voice and manner with uncanny accuracy to manipulate them into the response
he desired. It was almost as if he were a puppeteer,

pulling everyone's strings so subtly that they never noticed they were being directed by his will.

And if he manipulated *them,* then it followed that he manipulated *her.*

There was a dull roaring in her ears, as if she might faint. Evie flatly refused to do something that silly and concentrated on breathing deeply. As she sucked in the first breath, she discovered that it was the first time she had done so for some time, judging by the acute relief in her lungs. She had simply stopped breathing, probably about the time Robert had rubbed his face against Allison's curls. No wonder she had felt faint.

Emotionally she had been groping for solid ground, had felt her fingers finally brush against something to which she had thought she could hold. Now she felt as if that lifeline had been jerked away from her and she was lost again, swirling away. Had anything Robert said to her been the truth, or had every word been a subtle manipulation, designed to...what? Get her into his bed? Was the thrill, for him, in the chase? The problem was that he could just as easily be sincere. How was she to tell the difference?

The answer, she thought painfully, was that she couldn't. Only time would tell if she could depend on him, entrust her heart to him, and she doubted that the time was there. He'd said he was here for the rest of the summer, and summer was half-over. He would be here another six, maybe seven, weeks.

"Evie." Her name was spoken quietly, almost in her ear. She felt his heat against her back, smelled the fresh, clean sweat on his body. His hand touched her arm. "Sherry and Virgil are leaving."

She turned, summoning both a smile and self-control. No one else had noticed her preoccupation, she saw, but Robert had, another disturbing example of his acute perception. Allison had been enticed, with one of the red suckers as bait, back into Sherry's arms, where she was engrossed with turning the cellophane-wrapped candy around and around, trying to find access. Finally she simply popped it into her mouth, cellophane and all. Virgil was standing, and the boys were already at the door, shouting that they wanted a Blizzard before they went home, while Sherry insisted that she wasn't driving all the way to Boaz to get one, at which Virgil added that he wouldn't mind having a Blizzard, himself. That, of course, settled the issue.

Evie added her voice to all the rowdy commotion, telling them goodbye, telling Virgil to take care. The boys raced out the door and headed toward the docks. Sherry stepped out and said, "Y'all get back here, *now!*" in a tone that stopped them in their tracks and brought them, pouting, back to her. It took another few minutes to get everyone settled in the station wagon, and through it all Evie was acutely aware of Robert standing very close behind her, his hand on the small of her back. Neither Sherry nor Virgil would have missed the body language, much less the touch, that stated his claim on her.

The silence after their departure was almost deafening. She closed the door and tried to slide past him, but his hands closed on her waist, and, with a dizzy whirl, she found herself plunked down on the counter with him standing between her legs to prevent her from getting down. She stared at the center of his chest, refusing to look up at him. She didn't want this, didn't want to confront him when she was still reeling from the jolting realization that she loved him and could trust him even less than she had thought.

"Damn it," he said very softly. Then, "Look at me."

"Why?"

"Because I don't want to talk to the top of your head."

"I can hear you just fine the way I am."

He hissed a curse just under his breath and caught her face between his hands, tilting it up. He was careful not to hurt her, but there was no resisting the easy strength of that grip. She tried to concentrate on his nose, but the pale green glitter of his eyes dominated his face, drawing her attention. There was no way *not* to see the cold fury there.

"Where did you go?"

The question was deceptively calm, almost idle. If she hadn't been able to see his eyes, if she hadn't been able to feel the roiling anger in him, she might have been fooled. "I had an errand to run."

"Ah." His hands tightened on her face. "Were you meeting Landon Mercer?" he asked abruptly. "Are you having an affair with him?"

She stared at him, stupefied. For several moments she was unable to formulate a single thought, her mind a total blank. How on earth had he managed to link her to Mercer? He had been gone when she had left, and she and Mercer had not come back at the same time. But she *had* left because of Mercer, even though she hadn't been with him. She could feel her cheeks heating and knew that she looked guilty, but she still couldn't seem to manage a coherent reply. Then the last question sank in, and she snapped, "No, I'm not having an affair with him! I *detest* the man!"

Robert's lips were thin. "Then why did you sneak off to meet with him?"

"I didn't sneak anywhere," she flared. "And I did *not* meet him!"

"But you closed the office in the middle of a busy day," he said relentlessly. "When you wouldn't close it a little early on a rainy afternoon when there weren't any customers at all."

"I told you, I had an errand."

"So you went in a boat?"

"I live on the water," she pointed out, light brown eyes glowing more golden by the second. "I can cross the lake faster than I can drive to my house. Sometimes, if the weather is good and I'm in the mood, I use the boat, anyway, rather than driving."

The dangerous look hadn't faded from his eyes. "Are you saying that you went home?"

Very deliberately she caught his wrists and removed his hands from her face. "I had an errand," she repeated. "I didn't meet Mercer. I'm not having an affair with him. And what in hell makes you think you have the right to interrogate me?'' The last sentence was shouted as she tried to shove him away.

He didn't move, not an inch. "This," he said in a stifled tone, then moved forward as he bent his head to her.

She caught her breath at the heat of his mouth, the ravaging pressure. His movement had forced her thighs even wider, and he settled his hips in the notch. Evie quivered at the hard thrust of his sex against the vulnerable softness of her private body, alarmed by the contact even through several layers of cloth. The passion in him was as overwhelming as his anger had been, buffeting her, bending her under his will. His arms were painfully tight, and she tried to push him away once more, with the same result. "Stop it," he muttered against her mouth, and one arm dropped to encircle her bottom and pull her closer against him, rubbing her against the ridge beneath his jeans.

Unexpected, acute, the pleasure that shot through her loins made her cry out, the sound muffled by his lips. He repeated the motion, rocking his pelvis against her in a fury of jealousy and desire. The jolt was even stronger, and she arched in his arms, her hands lifting to cling to his shoulders. The transition from anger to desire was so swift that she couldn't control it, and the current of pleasure leaped within her. Every move he made increased the sensation, pushed her higher, as if she were being forced up a mountain and the purpose, once she reached the peak, was to hurl her over. The dizzying, panicked sensation was the same, and she clutched at him as the only anchor.

It had never been like this with Matt, she thought dimly. Their youthful passion had been shy, untutored, sweet but hesitant. Robert was a man who knew exactly what he was doing.

Though he hadn't touched them, her breasts were throbbing, the nipples tightly drawn and aching. She arched again, a soft, frantic sound in her throat as she tried to ease the ache by rubbing them against his chest. He knew, and whispered, "Easy," just as his hand closed over one firm, jutting mound.

She whimpered at the heat, the delicious pressure. She knew she should stop him, but putting an end to this ecstasy was the last thing she wanted to do. Her body was pliant, voluptuous with need, glowing with heat. He put his hand under her shirt and deftly opened the front snap of her bra. The cups slid apart, and then his fingers were on her naked flesh. He stroked the satin curves, then circled the tight nipples until she writhed in an agony of unfulfillment. "Is this what you want?" he murmured, and lightly pinched the distended tips. She moaned as a river of heat ran through her, gathering moisture to deposit between her thighs.

He bent her backward over his arm, the position thrusting her breasts upward. Her shirt was pulled up to completely bare them, she realized, wondering when that had happened. She saw her nipples, as red as berries; then his mouth closed over one, and her eyes closed as her head fell back.

He was going to take her right here, on the counter. She felt his determination, his own rampant desire. Panic surged through her, combating the heat that undermined her own will and common sense. He would take her here, where anyone could walk in and see them. He would take her without any thought for birth control. And she, besides risking her reputation and the chance of pregnancy, would lose the last bit of protection she retained for her heart.

His mouth was tugging at her nipple, drawing strongly on it before moving to the other one. And his hands were working at the waistband of her jeans, unsnapping and unzipping.

Desperately she wedged her arms between their bodies and stiffened them. "No," she said. The word was hoarse, barely audible. "Robert, no! Stop it!"

He froze, his muscled body taut as he held himself motionless for a long moment. Then, very slowly, he lifted his hands from her and moved back, one step, then two. His breathing was fast and audible.

Evie couldn't look at him as she slid from the counter and hastily fumbled her clothing back into presentable shape, fastening her bra, smoothing her shirt down, snapping and zipping her jeans. Her own breath was coming light and fast.

"Don't look so scared," he said calmly. "I gave you my word that I'd stop, and I did."

No, the problem wasn't with his willpower, she thought wildly, but with hers. Had they been anywhere else but in the marina, she didn't know if she could have made herself say no.

"Nothing to say?" he asked a moment later, when she remained silent.

She cleared her throat. "Not yet."

"All right." He still sounded far too calm and in control. "We'll talk tomorrow. I'll pick you up at seven o'clock."

"Seven," she echoed as he left.

Robert was on the secure mobile phone in the Jeep by the time he had pulled out of the marina's parking lot. "Did you follow him from the time he left work?" he asked as soon as the phone was answered.

"Yes, sir, we did. We saw your Jeep at the marina and pulled back."

"Damn. I was out in my boat. He rented a boat and met someone out on the lake, possibly Evie, because she left the marina in her boat, too. Was he carrying anything when he left work?"

"Not that we could tell, but he could easily have had a disk in his coat pocket."

"He didn't fish in his suit. Where did he change clothes?"

"At his house. He was there for not quite five minutes, then came out carrying a tackle box and a fishing rod."

"If he had a disk at all, it would have been in the tackle box."

"Yes, sir. We didn't have a chance to get to it."

"I know. It wasn't your fault. First thing, though, I'm going to have a secure phone put in the boat.

That way, if I'm out on the water, you can get in touch with me.''

''Good idea. We went through his house again while we had the chance. Nothing.''

''Damn. Okay, continue to watch him. And send someone out to Evie's house tonight.''

''The matter we discussed?''

''Yes,'' Robert replied. It was time for the pressure to begin.

Chapter 9

The next morning was awful. Evie hadn't slept well—had scarcely slept at all. She had set the alarm for four-thirty, and when it went off she had been asleep for less than two hours. Dreaming about Robert was one thing, but she had been wide-awake and hadn't been able to get him out of her mind. Her thoughts had darted from the seething passion of his lovemaking, incomplete as it had been, to the unease she felt every time she thought of how he so skillfully manipulated people. She tried to analyze what he did and couldn't find any time when he had been malicious, but that didn't reassure her.

Sometime after midnight, lying in the darkness and staring at the ceiling, she realized what it was that so bothered her. It was as if Robert allowed people to see and know only a part of him; the other part, probably the closest to being the real man, was standing back, inviolate, carefully watching and analyzing, gauging reactions, deciding which subtle pressures to apply to gain the results he wanted. Everyone was shut away from that inner man, the razor-sharp intelligence functioning almost like a computer, isolated in a sterile environment. What was most upsetting was to realize that this was how he wanted it, that he had deliberately fashioned that inner isolation and wasn't about to invite anyone inside.

What place could she hope to have in his life? He desired her; he would be perfectly willing to make her the center of his attention for a time, in order to gain what he wanted: a carnal relationship. But unless she could break through into that fiercely guarded inner core, she would never reach his emotions. He would be fine, but she would break her heart battering against his defenses.

She, better than others, knew how important emotional barriers were. She had propped herself up with her own defenses for many years, until she had slowly healed to the point where she could stand on her own. How could she condemn him for staying within his own fortress? She didn't know if she should even try to get inside.

The thing was, she didn't know if she had a choice any longer. For better or worse, this afternoon he had slipped through her defenses. Such a little thing: playing with a baby. But it was the little things, rather than the watershed events, on which love was built. She had softened toward him when he had saved her and Jason's lives, but her heart had remained her own. Today she had fallen in love; it wasn't something she could back away from and ignore. It might be impossible to breach Robert's defenses and reach his heart, but she had to try.

Finally she drifted into sleep, but the alarm too soon urged her out of bed. Heavy-eyed, she put on the coffee and showered while it was brewing. Then, as she absently munched on a bowl of cereal and poured in the caffeine, a dull cramp knotted her lower belly. "Damn it," she muttered. Just what she needed; she was going out with Robert for the first time that night, and her period was starting. She had thought she had another couple of days before it was due. She made a mental note that in a few days she should begin taking the birth-control pills the doctor had just prescribed.

Normally her period didn't bother her, but the timing of this one, added to lack of sleep, made her cranky as she left the house in the predawn darkness and climbed into the truck.

The sturdy pickup, usually so reliable despite its high mileage, made some unfamiliar noises as she drove along the dark, deserted side road. "Don't you dare break down on me now," she warned it. She was just getting on a firm financial footing; a major repair job right now was just what she didn't need.

She reached U.S. 431 and turned onto it. The truck shuddered and began making loud clanging noises. Startled, she slowed and swept the gauges with a quick glance. The temperature was fine, the oil— Oh

God, the oil gauge was red-lining. She slammed on the brakes and started to veer toward the shoulder, and that was when the engine blew. There were more clanging and grinding noises, and smoke boiled up around the hood, obscuring her vision. She steered the truck off the highway, fighting the heavy wheel as, deprived of power, the vehicle lurched to a halt.

Evie got out and stood looking at the smoking corpse as it pinged and rattled, the sounds of mechanical death. Her language was usually mild, but there were some occasions that called for swear words, and this was one of them. She used every curse word she had ever heard, stringing them together in rather innovative ways. That didn't bring life back to the motor, and it didn't make her bank account any healthier, but it relieved some of her frustration. When she ran out of new ways to say things, she stopped, took a deep breath and looked up and down the highway. Dawn was lightening the sky, and traffic was picking up; maybe someone she knew would come by and she wouldn't have to walk the full two miles to a pay phone. With a sigh she got the pistol out from under the truck seat, slipped it into her purse, then locked the truck—though obviously anyone who stole it would have to haul it away—and began walking.

It was less than a minute when another pickup rolled to a stop beside her. She glanced around and saw the boat hitched up behind. Two men were in the truck, and the one on the passenger side rolled down his window. "Havin' trouble?" Then he said, a bit uncertainly, "Miss Evie?"

With relief she recognized Russ McElroy and Jim Haynes, two area fisherman whom she had known casually for several years. "Hi, Russ. Jim. The motor in my truck just blew."

Russ opened the door and hopped out. "Come on, we'll give you a ride to the marina. You don't need to be out by yourself like this. There's too much meanness goin' on these days."

Gratefully she climbed into the cab of the truck and slid to the middle of the seat. Russ got back in and closed the door, and Jim eased the rig onto the highway. "You got a good mechanic?" Jim asked.

"I thought I'd have Burt, the mechanic at the marina, take a look at it. He's good with motors."

Jim nodded. "Yeah, I know Burt Mardis. He's real good. But if he can't get to it, there's another guy, owns a shop just off Blount, who's just as good. His name's Roy Simms. Just look it up in the phone book, Simms' Automotive Repair."

"Thanks, I'll remember that."

Jim and Russ launched into a discussion of other good mechanics in the area, and soon they reached the marina. She thanked them, and Russ got out again to let her out. They probably hadn't intended to put in at her marina, but since they were there they decided they might as well. As she unlocked the gate that blocked the launch ramp, Jim began to maneuver the truck so he could back the boat into the water. Next she unlocked the office and turned on the lights. Just as Jim and Russ were idling away from the dock, Burt drove up, and she went to tell him about the demise of her truck.

It wasn't long after dawn when the phone rang. Robert opened one eye and examined the golden rose of the sky as he reached for the receiver. "Yes."

"The truck didn't make it into town. It blew just as she reached the highway. She caught a ride to the marina."

Robert sat up in bed. He could feel the fine hairs on the back of his neck prickling with mingled anger and alarm. "Damn it, she hitchhiked?"

"Yeah, I was a little worried about that, so I followed to make certain she didn't have any trouble. No problem. It was a couple of fishermen who picked her up. I guess she knew them."

That wasn't much better. Guntersville wasn't exactly a hotbed of crime, but anything could happen to a woman alone. Neither did it soothe him that she had been followed, that help was right behind if she'd needed it. The situation shouldn't have arisen in the first place. "Why was the timing off?"

"The hole in the oil line must have been bigger than West thought. Probably there's a big oil puddle in her driveway. She would have seen it if it hadn't still been dark when she left the house."

In a very calm, remote voice Robert said, "If anything had happened to her because of his mistake, I wouldn't have liked it."

There was a pause on the other end of the line. Then, "I understand. It won't happen again."

Having made his point, Robert didn't belabor it. He moved on. "Be careful when you're in the house tonight. I don't want her to notice anything out of place."

"She won't. I'll see to it myself."

After hanging up the phone, Robert lay back down and hooked his hands behind his head as he watched the sun peek over the mountains. The day before had made him more uncertain than ever of Evie's connection with Mercer. He was fairly certain she had rendezvoused with Mercer out on the water, but either she hadn't told Mercer of his presence, or she had been unaware of his own connection with PowerNet. This appeared to be an efficient espionage ring, to have escaped notice and capture for as long as they had; given that, Evie should have known of him. At the very least, Mercer should have notified her of his presence. What reason could they have had for keeping her in the dark about his identity, unless her participation was very peripheral and no one had thought she needed to know?

The other possibility was that Evie had indeed recognized his name, or been notified, but for reasons of her own had chosen not to pass on the information that he had leased a slip at her marina and appeared to have formed an intense personal interest in her.

Either way, it followed that Evie wasn't on good terms with the others in the espionage ring. On the one hand, it gave him a weakness he could exploit. On the other, her life could be in danger.

Evie made arrangements to have a wrecker tow the truck to the marina. That accomplished, Burt stuck his head under the hood to begin the examination. Next he lay down on a dolly and rolled underneath for another view. When he emerged, he wasn't optimistic about rebuilding the motor. "Too much damage," he said. "You'd be better off just buying another motor."

She had been expecting that, and she had already been mentally juggling her finances. The payment on the bank loan for the marina would be late this month, and then she would have to put off other payments to make the one on the loan. She could get by without transportation for a few days by using the boat to go back and forth from home to the marina. If she absolutely needed to go somewhere, she could borrow Becky's car, though she didn't like to.

"I'll call around and try to find one," she said. "Will you have time to put it in for me?"

"Sure," Burt said easily. "It's a little slow right now, anyway."

By the time Craig arrived to relieve her, it was all arranged. She had located an engine, and Burt would begin work putting it in as soon as it arrived. Depending on how much marina work came in, she might be driving home the next afternoon.

In Evie's experience, things didn't generally work

that well. She wouldn't be surprised if Burt was suddenly flooded with a lot of boats needing attention.

The trip across the lake was enjoyable, despite her worries. The water was green, the surrounding mountains a misty blue, and fat, fluffy clouds drifted lazily across the sky, offering an occasional brief respite from the blazing sun. Gulls wheeled lazily over the water, and an eagle soared high in the distance. It was the kind of day when being inside was almost intolerable.

With that thought in mind, once she arrived home she put her financial worries on hold and got out the lawn mower to give her yard a trimming. She glared at the big black oil stain on the driveway where the truck had been parked. If it had been daylight when she'd left this morning, if she hadn't swapped shifts with Craig, she would have seen the oil and not have driven the truck; the motor would still be intact, and the repair bill would be much smaller.

Just simple bad timing.

The yard work finished, she went inside to cool off and tackle the housework, which was minimal. By three o'clock she was back outside, sitting on the dock with her feet in the water and a sweat-dewed glass of ice tea beside her. Fretting about the truck wouldn't accomplish anything. She would handle this just as she had handled every other money crisis that had arisen over the years, by strict economizing until all bills were paid. She couldn't do anything more than that, since it wasn't likely a good fairy would drop the money into her lap. Though there might be the possibility of taking a part-time job in the mornings at one of the fast-food restaurants serving breakfast. Forty dollars a week was a hundred and sixty dollars a month, enough to pay the power bill, with a little left over for the gas bill. But for now all she wanted was to sit on the dock with her feet in the water and gaze at the mountains, feeling contentment spread through her.

That was how Robert found her. He came around the side of the house and paused when he saw her sitting on the weathered dock, her eyes closed, face lifted to the sun. The long, thick, golden braid had been pulled forward over one shoulder, revealing the enticing, delicate furrow of her nape. She was wearing faded denim shorts and a white chemise top, hardly a sophisticated outfit, but his pulse began to throb as he studied the graceful curve of her shoulders, the delectable roundness of her slender arms, the shapeliness of her legs. Her skin glowed with a warm, pale gold luminescence, like a succulent peach. His eyes, his entire body, burned as he stared at her. His mouth was literally watering, and he had to swallow. He had never felt such urgent lust for any other woman. What he wanted was to simply throw himself on her and have her right here, right now, without thought or finesse.

She was unaware of his presence until the dock vibrated when he stepped onto it. There was no alarm in her eyes as she turned her head to see who had come visiting, only lazy curiosity followed by a warm look of welcome. Even the average five-year-old in a large city was more wary than the people around here, he thought as he sat down beside her and began taking off his shoes.

"Hi," she said, a sort of smiling serenity in that one word, which was drawled so that it took twice as long for her to say than it did for him.

He found himself smiling back, actually smiling, his mouth curved into a tender line as his heart pounded inside his chest. He had wanted her from the moment he'd first seen her; he'd been, several times, unexpectedly charmed by her. Both reactions were acute at this moment, but even more, he was enchanted.

He had whirled across countless dance floors with countless beautiful women in his arms, women who could afford to pamper themselves and wear the most expensive gowns and jewelry, women whom he had genuinely liked. He had made love to those women gently, slowly, in luxurious surroundings. He had taken women when the added fillip of danger made each encounter more intense. But never had he felt more enthralled than he was right now, sitting beside Evie on a weathered old dock, with a blazing afternoon sun, almost brutal in its clarity, bathing everything in pure light. Sweat trickled down his back and chest from the steamy heat, and his entire body pulsed with life. Even his fingertips throbbed. It took all of his formidable self-control to prevent himself from pushing her down on the dock and spreading her legs for his entry.

And yet, for all the intensity of his desire, he was

oddly content to wait. He would have her. For now he was caught in the enchantment of her slow smile, in the luminous sheen of her skin, in her warm, female scent that no perfume could match. Simply to sit beside her was to be seduced, and he was more than willing.

Having removed his shoes, he rolled up the legs of his khaki pants and stuck his feet into the water. The water was tepid, but refreshing in contrast to the heat of his skin. It made him feel almost comfortable.

"It isn't seven o'clock yet," she pointed out, but she was smiling.

"I wanted to make sure you hadn't chickened out."

"Not yet. Give me a couple of hours."

Despite the teasing, he was certain she wouldn't have stood him up. She might be nervous, even a little reluctant, but she had agreed, and she would keep her word. Her lack of enthusiasm in going out with him might have been insulting if he hadn't known how potent her physical reaction to him was. Whatever reasons she had for being wary of him, her body was oblivious to them.

She lazily moved her feet back and forth, watching the water swirl around her ankles. After a minute of wondering about the advisability of bringing up the subject that had been bothering her so much, she decided to do so, anyway. "Robert, have you ever let anyone really get close to you? Has anyone ever truly known you?"

She felt his stillness, just for a split second. Then

he said in a light tone, "I've been trying to get close to you from the moment I first saw you."

She turned her head and found him watching her, his ice-green eyes cool and unreadable. "That was a nice evasion, but you just demonstrated what I meant."

"I did? What was that?" he murmured indulgently, leaning forward to press his lips to her bare shoulder.

She didn't let that burning little caress distract her. "How you deflect personal questions without answering them. How you keep everyone at arm's length. How you watch and manipulate and never give away anything of your real thoughts or feelings."

He looked amused. "You're accusing *me* of being difficult to get to know, when you're as open as the Sphinx?"

"We both have our defenses," she admitted readily.

"Suppose I turn your questions around?" he said, watching her intently. "Have you ever let anyone get close to you and really get to know you?"

A pang went through her. "Of course. My family...and Matt."

She lapsed into silence then, and Robert saw the sadness move over her face, like a cloud passing over the sun. Matt again! What had been so special about an eighteen-year-old boy that twelve years later just the mention of his name could make her grieve? He didn't like himself for the way he felt, violently jealous and resentful of a dead boy. But at least Matt's memory had diverted Evie from her uncomfortable line of questioning.

She seemed content to sit in silence now, dabbling her feet in the water and watching the sunlight change patterns as it moved lower in the sky. Robert left her to her thoughts, suddenly preoccupied with his own.

Her perception was disturbing. She had, unfortunately, been dead on the money. He had always felt it necessary to keep a large part of himself private; the persona he presented to the world, that of a wealthy, urbane businessman, was not false. It was merely a small part of the whole, the part that he chose to display. It worked very well; it was perfect for doing business, for courting and seducing the women he wanted, and was an entrée into those parts of the world where his business was not quite what it seemed.

None of his closest associates suspected that he was anything other than the cool, controlled executive. They didn't know about his taste for adventure, or the way he relished danger. They didn't know about the extremely risky favors he had done, out of sheer patriotism, for various government departments and agencies. They didn't know about all the ongoing, specialized training he did to keep himself in shape and his skills sharp. They didn't know about his volcanic temper, because he kept it under ruthless control. Robert knew himself well, knew his own lethal capabilities. It had always seemed better to keep the intense aspects of his personality to himself, to never unleash the sheer battering force of which he was capable. If that meant no one ever really *knew* him, he was content with that. There was a certain safety in it.

No woman had ever reached the seething core of his emotions, had ever made him lose control. He never wanted to truly love a woman in the romantic sense, to find himself open to her, vulnerable to her. He planned to marry someday, and his wife would be supremely happy. He would treat her with every care and consideration, pleasing her in bed and cosseting her out of it. She would never want for anything. He would be a tender, affectionate husband and father. And she would never know that she had never truly reached him, that his heart remained whole, in his isolated core.

Madelyn, of course, knew that there were fiercely guarded depths to him, but she had never probed. She had known herself to be loved, and that was enough for her. His sister was a formidable person in her own right, her lazy manner masking an almost frightening determination, as her husband had discovered to his great surprise.

But how could Evie, on such short acquaintance, so clearly see what others never did? It made him feel exposed, and he didn't like it one damn bit. He would have to be more careful around her.

The sun was shining full on his back now, and his spine was prickling with sweat. Deciding that the silence had gone on long enough, he asked in an idle tone, ''Where's your truck?''

''I'm having a new motor put in it,'' she replied. ''I might have it back by tomorrow afternoon, but until then I'm using the boat to get to the marina and back.''

He waited, but there was no additional explanation. Surprised, he realized that she wasn't going to tell him about the motor blowing, wasn't going to broadcast her troubles in any way. He was accustomed to people bringing their problems to him for deft handling. He had also thought it possible that Evie would ask him for a loan to cover the repairs. They hadn't discussed his financial status, but she had seen the new boat, the new Jeep, the house on the waterfront, and she was far from stupid; she had to know he had money. He wouldn't have given her a loan, of course, because that would have defeated his subtle maneuvering to put financial pressure on her, but still, he wouldn't have been surprised if she'd asked. Instead, she hadn't even planned to tell him that her truck had broken down.

''If you need to go anywhere, call me,'' he finally offered.

''Thanks, but I don't have any errands that can't be put off until I get the truck back.''

''There's no need to put them off,'' he insisted gently. ''Just call me.''

She smiled and let the subject drop, but he knew she wouldn't call. Even if he installed himself at the marina until her truck was repaired, she wouldn't tell him if she needed anything.

He took her hand and gently stroked her fingers. "You haven't asked me where we're going tonight."

She gave him a surprised look. "I hadn't thought about it." That was the truth. Where they went was inconsequential; the fact that she would be with *him* was what had occupied her mind.

"That isn't very flattering," he said with a faint smile.

"I didn't say I hadn't thought about going out with you. It's just that the *where* never entered my mind."

The sophisticated socialites he normally squired about New York and the world's other major cities would never have made such an artless confession. Or rather, if they had, it would have been in an intimately flirtatious manner. Evie wasn't flirting. She had simply stated the truth and let him take it as he would. He wanted to kiss her for it but refrained for now. She would be more relaxed if she didn't have to deal with a seduction attempt every time she saw him.

Then she turned to him, brown eyes grave and steady. "I answered your question," she said. "Now answer mine."

"Ah." So she had been delayed but not diverted. Swiftly he decided on an answer that would satisfy her but not leave him open. It had the advantage of being the truth, as far as it went. "I'm a private person," he said quietly. "I don't blurt out my life story to anyone who asks. You don't either, so you should understand that.''

Those golden brown eyes studied him for another long moment; then, with a sigh, she turned away. He sensed that his answer hadn't satisfied her, but that she wasn't going to ask again. The sensation of being given up on wasn't a pleasant one, but he didn't want her to keep prying, either.

He checked his watch. There were a few calls he had to make before picking her up for the evening, not to mention showering and changing clothes. He kissed her shoulder again and got to his feet. "I have to leave or I'll be late to an appointment. Don't stay out much longer or you'll get a sunburn. Your shoulders are already hot.''

"All right. I'll see you at seven.'' She remained sitting on the dock, and Robert looked down at her streaked tawny head with stifled frustration. Just when he thought he was finally making serious progress with her, she mentally retreated again, like a turtle withdrawing into its shell. But this afternoon's mood was an odd blend of contentment, melancholy and resignation. Maybe she was worried about the truck; maybe she was nervous about their first date, though why she should be, when he'd already had her half-naked, was beyond his comprehension.

The truth was that she was as opaque to him as he was to others. He had always had the ability to read people, but Evie's mind was either closed to him or she reacted in a totally unexpected way. He couldn't predict what she would do or tell what she was thinking, and it was slowly driving him mad. He forced himself to walk away, rather than stand there waiting for her to look up at him. What would that accomplish? It was likely that she would figure out why he was waiting and look up just to get it over with, so he would go. Little mind games were only for the insecure, and Robert didn't have an insecure bone in his body. Nevertheless, he was reluctant to leave her. The only time he wasn't worried about what she was doing was when he was with her.

As he climbed into the Jeep, he wryly reflected that it was a sad state of affairs when he was so obsessed with a woman he couldn't trust out of his sight.

Evie remained where she was until long after the sound of the Jeep's engine had faded in the distance. Robert had stonewalled her questions, and sadly she realized that he simply wasn't going to allow her to get close to him. She supposed she could make a pest of herself and keep yammering at him, but that would only make him close up more. No, if she wanted a relationship with him, she would have to content herself with the litte he was comfortable in giving. She had known Matt to the bone and loved him as deeply. How ironic it was that now she had fallen in love with a man who allowed her to touch only the surface.

Finally she pulled her feet out of the water and stood. This had been a day of fretting, though she had tried not to. She would be better off getting ready for her big date. She had the feeling she would need every bit of preparation she could manage.

Chapter 10

A woman couldn't have asked for a more perfect escort, she realized about halfway through the evening. For all his sophistication, or perhaps because of it, there was something very old-fashioned in the courtesy and protectiveness with which he treated her. Everything was arranged for *her* pleasure, *her* comfort, and she herself was old-fashioned enough, Southern enough, to accept it as the way things should be. Robert Cannon was courting her, so of course he should make certain she was pleased by the evening.

His attention was solely on her. He didn't eye other women, though she noticed other women watching him. He held her chair for her whenever she got up or sat down, poured wine for her and asked the maitre d' to turn up the thermostat when he noticed her shivering. It was a matter of his own presence that his request was instantly honored. Whenever they walked, his hand rested warmly on the small of her back in a protective, possessive touch.

In no time, he had put her at ease. It was only natural that she had been nervous about the evening; after all, she hadn't been on a date in twelve years, and there was a great deal of difference between eighteen and thirty. Back then a date had been a hamburger and a movie, or just getting together with a bunch of friends at the skating rink. She wasn't at all certain what one did on a date with a man who was used to the most cosmopolitan of entertainments.

As she watched his dark, lean face, she realized how truly sophisticated he was. He had brought her to a very nice restaurant in Huntsville, but she was well aware that it didn't compare to the sort of establishments available in New York or Paris or New Orleans. Not by even a hint, though, did he indicate that the standards were less than those to which he was accustomed. Others, worldly but less sophisticated—and certainly less polite—would have subtly tried to impress by describing the *truly* good restaurants where they'd eaten. Not Robert. She doubted that he even thought of it, for he had the true sophisticate's knack of being at home in any surrounding. He didn't rate or compare; he simply enjoyed. He would have been as happy eating barbecue with his fingers as he was dining with gold flatware and blotting his mouth with a starched linen napkin.

Oh, God. Not only did he play with babies, he was totally comfortable in her world. Just one more thing to love.

He waved his fingers in front of her face. "You've been watching me and smiling for about five minutes," he said with amusement coloring his tone. "Ordinarily I'd be flattered, but somehow it makes me uneasy."

Her mouth quirked as she picked up her fork. "It shouldn't, because actually it was flattering. I was thinking how comfortable you are down here, despite how different things are."

He shrugged and said gently, "The differences are mostly good ones, though I admit I wasn't prepared for the heat. Somehow, ninety degrees in New York is different from ninety degrees here."

Her brows lifted delicately. "Ninety degrees isn't all that hot."

He chuckled and again wondered briefly at her ability to amuse him. It wasn't anything overt, just the subtle differences in her outlook and the way she phrased it. "That's the difference, one of attitude. Though, of course, it gets hotter than that occasionally, to a New Yorker ninety degrees is *hot*. To you, it's a nice day."

"Not exactly. Ninety degrees is hot to us, too. It's just that, compared to a hundred degrees, it isn't bad."

"Like I said, attitude." He sipped his wine. "I like New York for what it is. I like it down here for the same reason. In New York there's an air of excitement and energy, the opera and ballet and museums. Here, you have clean air, no overcrowding, no traffic jams. No one seems to hurry. People smile at strangers." His eyes lingered on her face, and when he continued his voice was a little deeper. "Though I admit I've been disappointed that I haven't heard you say 'y'all' at all. In fact, I've heard it very few times since I've been here."

She hid her smile. "Why would I say it to you? Y'all is plural. You're singular."

"Is it? That minor detail had escaped me."

"That you're singular?" She paused, aware that she was trespassing into his private life and that he might well shut down as he had that afternoon. "Have you ever been married?"

He sipped his wine again, and his eyes glittered at her over the rim of the glass. "No," he replied easily. "I was engaged once, when I was in college, but we both realized in time that getting married—particularly to each other—would have been a stupid thing to do."

"How old are you?"

"Thirty-six. To satisfy any other pertinent questions you may have, my sexual interest is exclusively in women. I've never done drugs, and I don't have any communicable diseases. My parents are dead, but I have a sister, Madelyn, who lives in Montana with her husband and two sons. There are a few distant cousins, but we don't keep in touch."

She regarded him calmly. He was totally relaxed, telling her that he didn't regard those details of his life as being particularly revealing. They were simply facts. She listened, though, because such minutiae made up the skeleton of his life. "Becky and I have relatives scattered all over the state," she said. "One of my uncles has a huge farm down around Montgomery, and every June we get together there for a family reunion. We aren't a close family, but we're friendly, and it's a way to stay in touch. If it wasn't for the reunion, Jason and Paige would never know Becky's side of the family, only their father's, so we make an effort to go every year."

"Your parents are dead?" He knew they were, for that had been in the supplementary report he had received.

"Yes." The golden glow in her eyes dimmed. "Becky is the only immediate family I have. When Mom died, I lived with Becky and Paul until Matt and I married." Her voice faltered, just a little, at the end.

"What about afterward?" he asked gently.

"Then I lived with Matt's parents." The words were soft, almost soundless. "Where I live now. It was their house. The marina was theirs, too. Matt was their only child, and when they died, they left everything to me."

Robert was pierced by another arrow of jealousy. She was still living in the house where Matt had grown up; there was no way she could walk into that house without being reminded of him at every turn. "Have you ever thought of moving? Of buying a more modern house?"

She shook her head. "Home is important to me. I lost my home when Mom died, and though Becky and Paul made me welcome, I was always aware that it was their home and not mine. Matt and I were going to live in a trailer, at first, but after he died I couldn't.... Anyway, his parents asked me to live with them, and they needed me as much as I needed company. Maybe because they needed me, I felt comfortable there, more like it really was my own home. And now," she said simply, "it is."

He regarded her thoughtfully. He had never felt that sort of attachment for a place, never felt the tug of roots. There had been a large country estate in Connecticut, when he was growing up, but it had simply been the place where he lived. Now his penthouse served the same emotionless function. Evie wouldn't like it, though it was spacious and impeccably decorated. Still, he was comfortable there, and the security was excellent.

The restaurant featured a live band, and they were really very good. In keeping with the image of the place, they played old standards, meant for real dancing rather than solitary gyrations. He held out his hand to Evie. "Would you like to dance?"

A glowing smile touched her face as she placed her hand in his, but then she hesitated, and a look of uncertainty replaced the pleasure. "It's been so long," she said honestly, "that I don't know if I can."

"Trust me," he said, soothing her worries. "I

won't let you come to grief. It's like riding a bicycle.''

She went into his arms. She was stiff at first, but after several turns she relaxed and let the pleasure of the music and the movement sweep through her. Robert was an expert dancer, but then, she hadn't expected anything else. He held her closely enough that she felt secure, but not so close as to touch intimately. More of those exquisite manners, she thought.

As the music continued, she realized that he didn't have to be blatant. Dancing was its own seduction. There was the tender way he clasped her hand, the warm firmness of his other hand on her back. His breath brushed her hair; the clean scent of his skin teased her nostrils. This close, she could see the closely shaven stubble of his beard, dark against his olive skin. Occasionally her breasts brushed against his chest or arm, or their thighs slid together. It was stylized, unconsummated lovemaking, and she wasn't immune to it.

They left at midnight. During the forty-minute drive back to Guntersville, Evie sat silently beside him as he competently handled the black Renegade. They didn't speak until he pulled into her driveway and turned off the ignition, flooding the sudden darkness with silence. As their eyes adjusted, they could see the river stretching, soundless and glistening, behind her house.

''Tomorrow night?'' he asked, turning toward her and draping one arm over the steering wheel.

She shook her head. ''I can't. I haven't arranged

for Craig to take over my shift, so he'll open the marina in the morning as usual. I wouldn't, anyway. That isn't the deal we made.''

He sighed. ''All right, we'll compromise. How about swapping shifts with him once a week? Would that be acceptable to your strange scruples? He works for you, rather than the other way around, you know.''

''He's also a friend, and he does a lot of favors for me. I won't take advantage of him.'' The coolness in her voice told him that he had offended her.

He got out and walked around to open the door for her. As he lifted her to the ground, he said with a touch of whimsy, ''Will you try to make a little time for me, anyway?''

''I'll talk to Craig about it,'' she replied noncommittally.

''Please.''

She extracted her house key from her purse, and Robert deftly lifted it out of her fingers. He unlocked the door, reached inside to turn on a light, then stepped back. ''Thank you,'' she said.

He delayed her with his hand on her arm as she started to go inside. ''Good night, sweetheart,'' he murmured, and placed his mouth over hers.

The kiss was slow and warm and relatively undemanding. He didn't touch her, except for his hand on her arm and his lips moving over hers. Unconsciously she sighed with pleasure, opening her mouth to the warmth of his breath and the leisurely penetration of his tongue.

When he lifted his head, her breasts were tingling, her body was warm, and she was breathing faster than normal. It gratified her to notice that his breath, too, was a little rough. "I'll see you tomorrow," he said. Then he kissed her again and walked back to the Jeep.

She closed the door, locked it and leaned against it until she heard the sound of the Jeep fade in the distance. Her chest felt tight, her heart swollen and tender. She wanted to weep, and she wanted to sing.

Instead, she kicked off her shoes and walked into the kitchen to get a drink of water. Her left foot landed solidly in something wet and cold, and she jumped in alarm. Quickly she turned on the kitchen light and stared in dismay at the puddle around the bottom of the refrigerator. Even more ominously, there was no faint humming sound coming from the appliance. She jerked the door open, but no little light came on. The interior remained dark.

"Oh no, not now," she moaned. What a time for the refrigerator to die! She simply couldn't afford to get it repaired now. She supposed she could buy a new one on credit, but she hated to add another payment to the monthly load. The refrigerator had been elderly, but why couldn't it have lasted another year? By then she would have paid off a couple of debts and had more ready cash. Another six months would have made a difference.

There was nothing, however, that she could do about the refrigerator at nearly one in the morning. She was drooping with fatigue, but she mopped up the water and put down towels to catch any additional leaks.

When she finally got into bed, she couldn't sleep. That part-time job she had thought about during the afternoon now looked like a necessity, rather than an option. Her lower abdomen was dully aching. The evening with Robert, about which she had been so nervous, had turned out to be the best part of the day.

At seven o'clock she was on the phone to Becky. While Becky was calling around to her friends, Evie began systematically calling in response to every Refrigerator For Sale ad in the paper. As she had suspected, even at that early hour there were a number of calls that weren't answered. One, which had seemed the most promising, had sold the refrigerator as soon as the ad appeared.

By nine o'clock, she and Becky had located a good refrigerator for sale. At a hundred dollars, it was more than she could readily afford, but considerably less than a new one would cost. Becky came to get her, and they drove out together to look at it.

"It's ten years old, so it probably has another five to seven years," the woman said cheerfully as she showed them into the kitchen. "There isn't anything wrong with it, but we're building a new house, and I wanted a big side-by-side refrigerator. We were getting one, anyway, but last week I found just what I wanted, on sale at that, so I didn't wait. As soon as

I get this one sold, I can have the new one delivered.''

"It's sold," Evie said.

"How are you going to get it home?" asked Becky practically. "Until your truck is fixed, you don't have any way to haul it." Having stated the problem, she set about trying to solve it, running down the list of everyone she knew who owned a pickup truck and might be available.

Evie's own list was formidable. After all, she knew a lot of fishermen. Half an hour later, Sonny, a friend who worked second shift and had his mornings free, was on his way.

Time was running short for Evie by the time they got the refrigerator to her house. She called Craig to let him know what was going on and that she might be a few minutes late. "No sweat," was his easygoing reply.

Sonny hooked up the ice maker while Evie and Becky hurriedly transferred what food had survived from the old refrigerator into the new one. The frozen stuff was okay, and since she hadn't opened the door, most of the food in the other compartment was still cool and salvageable. She threw away the eggs and milk, just to be on the safe side.

"Do you want me to haul off the old one?" Sonny asked.

"No, you need to go to work. Let's just push it out onto the deck, and I'll take care of getting rid of it when I get my truck back. Thanks, Sonny. I don't know what I'd have done without you today."

"Anytime," he said genially, and bent his muscles to the job of getting the old refrigerator outside.

After that was accomplished and Sonny had left, Becky grinned at her sister. "I know you're in a hurry to get to the marina, so I'll call you tonight. I can't wait to hear all the juicy details about your evening with Robert."

Evie blew a wisp of hair out of her face. "It was fine," she said, smiling because she knew the answer would disappoint Becky. "I was worried for nothing. He was a perfect gentleman all night long."

"Well, damn," muttered her once-protective big sister.

With Murphy's Law in full effect, when Evie arrived at the marina she found that the afternoon before had indeed brought Burt several repair jobs on boats that had to be done before he could get to her truck. Because the people who used the marina were her livelihood, she didn't protest the delay. Financially, it would be better for her if even more repair jobs came in. Enough of them would pay for fixing her truck.

Craig met her at the dock, took one look at her and said, with his tongue firmly planted in his cheek, "Boss, you need to stop all this carousing and get a good night's sleep."

"That bad, huh?"

"Not really. Dark circles are in this month."

"If one more thing tears up," she said direly, "I'm going to shoot it."

He put his brawny young arm around her shoulders. "Aw, everything will be okay. Chin up, boss. You're just tired. If you want to take a nap, I'll hang around for another couple of hours. I've got a date tonight, but I'm free this afternoon."

She smiled at him, touched by his offer. "No, I'm fine. You go on home, and I'll see about getting a morning job to help pay for all this stuff that's going kablooey."

"What stuff?" asked a deep voice behind them. She and Craig turned. A boat had been idling outside, and the noise had masked the sound of Robert's arrival. Unlike her, he looked well rested. His expression didn't give anything away, but she sensed that he didn't like Craig putting his arm around her.

"My refrigerator died last night," she replied. "I spent the morning locating a good used one and getting it home."

That seemed to give him pause, for some reason. Then he gave her a considering look and said, "You didn't get much sleep, did you?"

"A few hours. I'll sleep like a log tonight, though."

Craig said, "If you're sure you don't want me to stay for a while...?"

"I'm sure. I'll see you tomorrow."

"Okay." He took off, whistling. Robert turned to watch him go, a tall, well-built boy who gave the promise of being an outstanding man.

"You don't have any reason to be jealous of Craig," Evie said coolly as she brushed by him, heading toward the office and the promise of air-conditioning.

Robert's eyebrows climbed as he followed her. When they were inside, he murmured, "I don't recall saying anything."

"You didn't, but it was plain what what you were thinking."

He was taken aback. God, her perception was expanding into mind reading. He didn't like the feeling of transparency.

"I've known Craig since he was a child. There's absolutely nothing sexual in our relationship."

"Maybe not from your perspective," he said calmly, "but I was a teenage boy once myself."

"I don't want to hear about raging hormones. If all you can do is criticize, then leave. I'm too tired to deal with it right now."

"So you are." He took her in his arms and tucked her head into the hollow of his shoulder. With one hand he stroked her sun-warmed hair, which was restricted into its usual braid. The night before, she had worn it in an elegant twist. One day soon—or rather, one night—he was going to see it down and spread across his pillow.

Gently he swayed, rocking her. The support of his hard, warm body was so delicious that Evie felt her eyes drifting shut. When she realized that she actually was dozing off, she forced herself to lift her head and step away. "Enough of that or I'll be asleep in your arms."

"You'll sleep there eventually," he said. "But in different surroundings."

Her heart gave a great thump. What he so effort-lessly did to her simply wasn't fair. Unbidden, she thought of the one night she had slept in Matt's arms, the sweetness that had so shortly been overlaid with bitterness and regret when his life had ended the next day. Sleeping with Robert wouldn't be anything like that long-ago night....

He saw the sadness darken her eyes again, and he felt like swearing savagely. Every time he thought he was making progress, he slammed into Matt Shaw's ghost, standing like an ethereal wall between Evie and any other man. As unlikely—as damned *ridiculous*—as it seemed, he couldn't doubt that she'd been entirely chaste during her widowhood. Her connection with Landon Mercer, whatever else it was, certainly wasn't physical.

Her relationship with *him*, on the other hand, certainly would be.

"Did you come by for any particular reason?" she asked.

"Just to see you for a moment. Would you like to get a quick bite to eat tonight before you go home?"

"I don't think so. I'm so tired I just want to go home and get some sleep."

"All right." Gently he touched her cheek. "I'll see you tomorrow, then. Take care going across the lake tonight."

"I will. The days are so long, I'll be home before it gets dark."

"Take care, anyway." He leaned over and kissed her, then left.

As soon as he was out of her sight, his black brows pulled together in a frown. Last night's ploy hadn't worked all that well because of something he simply hadn't considered, and he was impatient with himself. He'd been born into money and had made even more, so the option of buying a second-hand refrigerator hadn't occurred to him. He had no idea what she'd paid for it, but he assumed that it was considerably less than a new one, even the cheapest model, would have cost. Though a little more financial pressure had been brought to bear on her, it hadn't been as much as he'd planned.

Mercer was beginning to find the financial waters a little choppy these days, too. It wasn't anything for him to worry about…yet. Soon he would find himself in a pinch with a growing need for ready cash. The next time he made a move, Robert would be ready for him. The net was slowly closing.

He estimated another two weeks, three at the most. He could make things move faster, but he was oddly reluctant to bring everything to a close just yet. If Mercer tried to make another sale, of course he would have to act, but until then, he intended to use the time to complete Evie's seduction.

That was, if he could keep her mind off her dead husband. Robert's jealous fury was banked, but glowing hotly under the restraint. It was ironic that he, of all people, should be jealous. It wasn't an emotion that he'd ever felt before, and he'd been coolly contemptuous of those who allowed someone to become that important to them. But he had never wanted a woman so violently, nor found himself up against such a formidable rival. That, too, was a new experience for him. If a woman had been interested in another man, he had simply moved on, on the theory that battling for her affections was too much trouble and complicated what was, for him, a fairly simple issue.

But then he'd met Evangeline. Her name whispered through his mind, as musical and elegant as the wind sighing in the trees. Evangeline. A poetic name, associated with undying love.

He couldn't accept that she was Matt Shaw's forever, that he might never have her.

Damn it, what was this appeal that teenage boys had for her? He had wanted to punch Craig in the jaw for daring to touch her, but his own sense of fair play had restrained him. Craig looked to be as strong as a young ox, but Robert knew his own capabilities. He could easily have killed the boy without meaning to.

Because Matt had died so young, was Evie's taste forever frozen at that age? The idea was distasteful. He was disgusted with himself for even thinking it. He had no basis for the ugly speculation; he knew very well that there was nothing sexual between Evie and Craig. It was his own jealousy that had spurred the thought.

He had to have her. Soon.

Chapter 11

Evie slept soundly for ten hours that night, from nine until seven the following morning. She woke feeling much better, though she was groggy from sleeping so hard. She stumbled through the house toward the kitchen, keeping her fingers crossed that nothing else had gone on the fritz during the night, especially the coffeemaker. Everything seemed to be in working order, though, so she put on a pot of coffee and headed back toward the bathroom while it was brewing.

Fifteen minutes later, semidressed and with hair and teeth brushed, she was contentedly curled in a chair on the deck, sipping her first cup of coffee. She closed her eyes as the morning sun bathed her with soothing heat. It was a perfect morning, clear and still and fragrant. The birds were singing madly, and the temperature was still comfortable, probably in the high seventies.

She heard tires singing on the road, the particular note that meant four-wheel drive, and a few seconds later Robert pulled into her driveway. Though she couldn't see either the driveway or the road from the deck, and though she knew any number of people who had four-wheel-drive vehicles, she had no doubt of her visitor's identity. Her blood had started moving faster, her skin tingled, and a subtle heat that had nothing to do with either the sun or the coffee had begun spreading through her body.

How many women had loved him? Instinct told her that she was far from the first. Poor creatures. They, like her, had been unable to resist that gentle, ruthless charm. She knew just as certainly that he had never loved any of them in return.

Through the open patio door she heard the knock at the front. "Robert?" she called. "I'm on the deck."

His footsteps in the grass were silent as he walked around, but in fifteen seconds he was coming up the three shallow steps onto the deck. He stopped, his eyes kindling as he stared at her.

Surprised, she curled a little tighter in the chair. "What have I done now?"

His expression relaxed as he moved to take the chair beside her. "You mistake the matter. That was lust, not anger."

"Ah." She used the cup to hide her face as she took another sip. "That should tell you something."

"Should it?"

"That I see anger from you more often than I do lust." Her heart was pounding even harder. My God, she was *flirting.* She was stunned by the realization. She had never in her life engaged in suggestive banter with a man, especially not to discuss his lust for her. She didn't think she had ever even flirted with Matt; somehow things had always seemed settled between them, and they hadn't gone through that dizzying, intense stage of courtship before commitment. They had grown up committed to each other.

"Again you mistake the matter," Robert said idly.

"In what way?"

"The lust is always there, Evangeline."

The quiet, almost casual, statement left her breathless. This time she took refuge in good manners, unwinding her legs to stand up as she said, "Would you like a cup of coffee?"

"I'll get it," he said, stopping her with a hand on her shoulder. His touch lingered, his fingertips lightly caressing the curve of the joint. "You look as contented as a cat. Just tell me where the cups are."

"In the cabinet directly over the coffeemaker. I don't have any cream, only skim milk—"

"It doesn't matter. I drink it black, like you. While I'm in there, would you like a refill?"

Silently she handed him her cup, and he disappeared into the house.

As Robert got a cup from the cabinet, he noticed that his hand was shaking slightly. He was both amused and amazed at the force of his reaction to her, though he had gotten used to being at least semi-aroused whenever he was in her company. But when he had first seen her this morning...well, he had wanted to see her with her hair down, and now he had gotten his wish.

He just hadn't expected the potency of his response, hadn't expected that thick, tawny-gold, streaky mantle flowing halfway down her back, the sunlight glinting along the strands like precious metal. Only the ends curled, frothing in delight at having been released from the confines of her habitual braid. One lock hung over her shoulder and breast, the curl wrapping around her nipple as perfectly as if it had been created to do just that. It had taken only a glance for him to tell that she wasn't wearing a bra under the pale peach camisole top with the tiny tucks down the front that she probably thought disguised her braless state.

He should have become accustomed by now to the luminosity of her skin. He hadn't. Every time he saw her anew, he was struck by the way she seemed to glow. This morning the effect had been particularly acute. She had been curled in the chair like a cat, sleepy and slightly tousled, her shapely legs and delicate feet bare, the bright sunlight somehow lighting her from within.

He wanted to pick her up and carry her back into the dim coolness of her bedroom, strip her naked and sate himself on the golden pearl of her flesh. But he remembered, with an unpleasant jolt, that this was the house where Matt had grown up. He didn't want to take her here, where the memories of the boy abounded.

"Robert?" Her tone was questioning at his long delay.

"I'm just reading your coffee cups," he called back, and heard her chuckle in reply.

He chose the cup that said, "I'm forty-nine percent sweet. It's the other fifty-one percent you have to worry about," and poured coffee into it, then refilled her cup. He carried both of them out onto the deck and carefully gave hers to her, not wanting even a drop of the hot liquid to spill on her bare legs.

"That's quite a collection of cups."

"Isn't it? Jason and Paige are the culprits. Every birthday, every Christmas, they give me a cup as a gag gift. It's become tradition. They put so much time and effort into picking the cup that it's gotten to where unwrapping it is the highlight of the occasion. They don't let Becky or Paul see it beforehand, so it's always a surprise to them, too."

"Some of them are rather suggestive."

She grinned. "Paige's doing. She's an expert at finding them."

He raised his eyebrows. "That delicate, innocent child?"

"That precocious, inventive child. Don't let the shyness fool you."

"She didn't seem shy to me. She started talking to me right away when I first met her."

"Blame your own charm. She isn't that open with most people. But considering the way Sherry's baby took to you," she said judiciously, "it seems that little girls have an affinity for you."

"That's all well and good," he replied, watching her calmly over the rim of his cup, "but what about the grown-up ones?"

"I'll bring you a big stick tomorrow so you can keep them beat off." Very calmly he leaned over to place his cup on the deck, then took her cup from her hand and put it beside his. She eyed him warily. "What are you doing?"

"This." With one swift, deft movement, he scooped her out of her chair, and settled down in his again with her on his lap. She sat stunned, stiffly erect, her eyes big with surprise. He retrieved her cup and placed it in her hands, then shifted her so she was off balance and had to relax against his chest.

"Robert," she said in a weak protest.

"Evangeline." His voice lingered over the long *i*.

She couldn't think of anything else to say. She sat there wrapped by his strength, his warmth, his scent. She could feel the steady thumping of his heart. She had known that he was tall, but even now, with her sitting on his lap, her head wasn't as high as his. She felt physically overwhelmed and remarkably safe. Not from him, but from the rest of the world.

His thighs were hard under her, and something else was, too.

"Finish your coffee," he said, and unthinkingly she raised the cup to her lips.

They sat there in peaceful silence as the heat grew and the traffic on the river increased. When their cups

were empty, he set them aside, then caught her face
in his hand and turned it up for his slow, deep kiss.

Like a flower turning toward the sun, she shifted
toward him, fitting herself more firmly against him.
The taste of coffee was in his mouth and hers. His
tongue gently explored, and she trembled, her arms
lifting to encircle his neck. How long he drank from
her mouth she didn't know; time was measured only
by the heavy pulse of her blood, throbbing through
every inch of her body.

His hand brushed across her breast, pushing her
hair aside, then returned to firmly cup the soft
mound. Evie stiffened slightly, but he soothed her
with a deep murmur, not really a word, only a calming sound. He had had his hands and his mouth on
her breasts before, but he could sense that she was
still uncertain about allowing the caress. He petted
her, gently circling her nipples with one fingertip until they stood temptingly erect, stroking the lush
curves with tender care. He wanted her to relax, but
instead the tension in her changed, became more
finely charged, and he knew that he was arousing her
instead.

Deliberately he unbuttoned the first three buttons
of the camisole and slid his hand inside. With a
sharply indrawn breath, she turned her face into his
neck, but she didn't say the one word that would stop
him. Her satiny flesh was cool to his touch, the small
nipples puckered and tight. He played with them,
rubbing them between his fingers, lightly pinching as
he watched her with acute attention to learn exactly

what she liked. Slowly her breasts grew warm from his touch, the paleness taking on a pinkish glow.

Evie held herself very still, barely breathing, her eyes closed as she tried to deal with the delicate, exquisite pleasure sweeping through her. She knew she was playing with fire, but she couldn't seem to make herself stop. What if he carried her inside? She would have to call a halt then, because she was still having her period, and she was neither sophisticated nor experienced enough to either let him proceed or tell him, without embarrassment, why he couldn't.

"Shall I stop?" he asked, the sound very low.

She swallowed. "I think you should." But she didn't lift her face, and that wasn't the agreed signal. He shifted her, lifted her, and the shocking heat of his mouth closed over the distended nipple of her exposed breast. She cried out, her nipple prickling at the sensation, and fire shot straight through to her loins.

Then, incredibly, his mouth left her body and he was sitting her up on his lap. "We have to stop," he was saying with gentle regret. "I don't think you're ready to give me the go-ahead, and I don't want to push my self-control much further."

Evie bent her head, struggling with a mixture of relief and chagrin as she fumbled with her buttons, restoring her clothing to order. He was right, of course. She didn't want their intimacy to go any further than it already had, though she intended to be prepared if it did.

She managed to smile at him as she scrambled out

of his lap and bent down to get the coffee cups. "Thank you," she said, and carried the cups inside.

Robert rubbed his hand over his eyes. God, that had been closer than he'd let on, at least for him. Would she have let him make love to her, after all? Somehow he didn't think so; he could still sense reluctance in her. In a few more minutes she would have said no, and the way he felt now, the strain might well have killed him. Even if she had said yes, he didn't want to make love to her in this house, so it was just as well he'd had the sense to stop.

They spent the morning together without a repeat of the scene on the deck. He'd already had enough frustration for one day, he decided. When it was time for her to cross the lake to work, he kissed her goodbye and left.

The wind blowing in her face helped clear Evie's mind as she sped across the water. What did he do for most of the day? she wondered. He'd said that he was on vacation, but a person, especially a man like Robert, could take only so much relaxation.

To her relief, Burt had made real progress on the marina jobs and thought he would be able to get started on her truck that afternoon. The prospect of having a vehicle to drive home the next day made her cheerful. Perhaps the run of bad luck was over.

She called the local fast-food restaurants to ask about a part-time job in the mornings, but with school out for the summer, none of them needed any help, all of the part-time jobs being filled by teenagers. Call again after school starts, she was told.

"Well, that was a dead end," she muttered to herself as she hung up from the last call. It looked as if the pendulum of luck hadn't swung back her way, after all.

On the other hand, she had the knack of existing on practically nothing when she had to. Over the next few days Evie cut operating expenses where she could and her personal expenses to the bone. She ate oatmeal or cold cereal for breakfast, and allowed herself one sandwich for lunch and one for supper. There were no snacks, no soft drinks, nothing extra. She turned off the air-conditioning at home, making do with the ceiling fans and drinking a lot of ice water. She was pragmatic enough that she didn't feel particularly deprived by these cost-cutting measures. It was simply something that had to be done, so she did it and didn't think much about it one way or the other.

For one thing, Robert occupied a great deal of her thoughts. If he didn't drop by the house in the morning, he came by the marina in the afternoon. He often kissed her, whenever they were alone, but he didn't pressure her for sex. The more he refrained, the more confused she became about whether she wanted to make love with him or not. She had never bemoaned her lack of practical experience before, but now she did; she needed every bit of help she could muster in handling her feelings for him. With every passing day she wanted him more physically, but caution kept warning her away from letting him become more important to her than he already was. She loved him, but somehow, if she didn't make love with him, some small part of her heart remained hers. If he claimed her body, he would claim all of her, and she would have no reserve to fall back on when the end came.

Still, she was acutely aware of how gradually and skillfully he was undermining her resolve. Every day she became more accustomed to his kisses, to the touch of those lean hands, until he had only to look at her and her breasts would tighten in anticipation. Frightened of the consequences if her willpower faltered, she began taking the birth-control pills on schedule, and as she did so, she wondered if she wasn't actually weakening her own position, for knowing that she was protected might make her less inclined to say no. She was well and truly caught on the horns of that particular dilemma, afraid not to take the pills and afraid of what would happen if she did. In the end, the deciding factor had been that she would rather gamble with her own well-being than that of a helpless baby.

When the next weekend came, Robert once again asked her to swap shifts with Craig so they could have an evening out. Remembering with pleasure the first time she'd had dinner with him, and the dancing afterward, she quickly agreed.

When he picked her up the next night, a slow fire lit the green of his eyes as he looked her up and down. Evie felt a very female gratification at his response. She knew she was looking particularly good, her hair and makeup just as she had wanted, and her dress was very flattering. It was the only cocktail dress she owned, purchased three years before, when the chamber of commerce had organized a party for the local businessmen and women to meet some manufacturing representatives who were thinking about locating in Guntersville.

The deal had fallen through, but the cocktail dress was still smashing. It was teal green, a shade that did wonders for her complexion. There was a full, flirty skirt that swirled just above her knees, a sweetheart bodice supported by thin straps, and it was very low-cut in the back. She had pinned up her hair in a loose twist, with several tendrils left around her ears. Simple gold hoop earrings and her wedding band were the only jewelry she wore, but she had never liked a lot of jewelry weighing her down, so she was satisfied.

Robert was wearing an impeccable black suit with a snowy white silk shirt, but with the heat so oppressive, she wondered how he could stand it. Not that he looked hot; on the contrary, he was as cool and imperturbable as ever, except for the expression in his eyes.

"You're lovely," he said, touching her cheek and watching her bloom at the compliment.

"Thank you." She accepted his verbal appreciation with serene dignity as he drew her outside and locked the door behind them.

He helped her into the Jeep, and as he got in on the other side he said, "I think you'll like the club we're going go. It's quiet, has good food and a wonderful patio for dancing.''

''Is it in Huntsville?''

''No, it's here. It's a private club.''

She didn't ask how, if it were private, he had managed to get reservations for them. Robert didn't make a show of being wealthy and influential, but he obviously was, given the quality of his clothing, the things he'd bought. Any local bigwig worth his salt would be more than willing to extend an invitation for Robert to join his club.

There was no place in Guntersville that couldn't be gotten to rather quickly. Robert turned the Jeep off of the highway onto a small private road that wound toward the river and soon was parking in a paved lot. The club was a sprawling one-story cedar-and-rock affair, with manicured grounds and a soothing atmosphere. She had seen it before only from the water which glistened just beyond the club. It was only seven-thirty, still daylight, but already the parking lot was crowded.

Robert's hand was firm and very warm on Evie's bare back as he ushered her inside, where they were met by a smiling, very correct maitre d'. They were seated in a small horseshoe booth, upholstered in buttery soft leather.

They ordered their meals, and Robert requested champagne. Evie didn't know anything about wines, period, but his choice brought a spark to the waiter's eyes.

The only time she had tasted champagne had been

at her wedding, and that had been an inexpensive brand. The pale gold wine that Robert poured into her glass had nothing in common with that long-ago liquid except its wetness. The taste was dry and delicious, the bubbles dancing in her mouth and exploding with flavor. She was careful to only sip it, not knowing what effect it would have on her.

As before, the evening was wonderful, so wonderful that it was half-over before Evie realized that Robert was herding her toward some swiftly nearing conclusion as implacably as a stallion herded the mare he had chosen to breed, keeping after her, blocking all retreat, until she was cornered. Robert was unfailingly gentle and courteous, but nevertheless relentless. She could see it in those pale eyes, in which a fire smoldered. He intended to have her before the evening was finished.

It was evident in the way he touched her almost constantly, small touches that looked casual but were not. They were seductive touches, light caresses that both gentled her and accustomed her to his hand on her body, while at the same time patiently beginning the process of arousing her.

When they danced, his fingertips moved over her bare back, leaving a trail of heat behind and making her shiver in response. His body moved against hers in rhythm with the music, with her heartbeat, until it seemed as if the music flowed through her. And when they returned to their booth, he was close beside her. Several times she shifted uncomfortably, putting more distance between them, but he was inexorable; he would move closer, so that she could feel the heat of his body, smell the faint, spicy scent of his cologne and the muskiness of his skin. He would lightly stroke her arm, or trace the line of her jaw with one long finger, or rub his thumb over the curve of her collarbone. His leg would slide along hers, and then she would feel the hard curve of his arm behind her back, the firm clasp of his hand at her waist. With every move he made her more aware of him and at the same time broadcast his possession of her to any male in the vicinity who might be thinking of poaching.

Evie was both alarmed and excited, and therefore couldn't get her thoughts in order. She managed to retain an outward calm, but inside she was quietly panicking. Robert had always presented the image of an urbane, eminently civilized man, but from the beginning she had seen beneath the cosmopolitan surface to a far more primitive man, a man of swift and ruthless passion. Now she saw that she had underestimated that volatile streak. He meant to take her to bed with him that very night, and she didn't know if she could stop him.

She didn't even know if she *wanted* to stop him. Was it the champagne, or the fever of desire he had been expertly feeding, not just tonight, but from the moment he'd first kissed her? Her usually clear thought processes kept getting tangled by the slowly increasing heat and hunger of her own body. She tried to think why she should say no, why he was so dangerous for her, but all she could bring to mind was his mouth on her breasts, the way it felt when he touched her.

Physically...oh God, physically he had destroyed all the years of control, of peaceful solitude. She had wanted no man since Matt—until Robert—and she had never wanted Matt this much. Matt had died on the verge of manhood and was forever frozen in her memory as a laughing, wonderful boy. Robert was a man, in the purest sense of the word. He knew the power of the flesh. He knew that, in the taking of her body, he would also be forging a claim, a possession as old as time. His experience far exceeded hers, and he wanted all of her. She would never be able to hold herself, her inner self, inviolate against his taking. A small voice in her cried out in abject fear, and she struggled toward control.

But he seemed to sense whenever that clear inner voice would gather itself, whenever she would panic as she realized anew what he was doing, and with a warm, lingering touch and the brush of his hard body against her soft curves, he would fan the flames of physical desire to overcome the voice of sanity. He was too good at seduction; even though she recognized it, she couldn't stop it. She had the bitter realization that he could have had her any time he'd wanted, that her will was proving no match for his expertise. He had held back only for some reason of his own, and now he had decided that he wasn't waiting any longer.

He asked her to dance again, and helplessly she went into his arms. She felt too warm, her skin too

sensitive. She could feel the fabric of her dress sliding over her body, rasping her nipples, caressing her
belly and thighs. Whenever he touched her, her entire
body seemed to clench. They moved across the dance
floor on the patio, and he held her close while his
powerful legs slid against hers, sometimes thrusting
his thigh between hers, and she began to throb with
a hollow ache between her legs. In the distance, heat
flashes lit the sky over the mountains with flickers
of purple and gold. There was a sullen rumble of
thunder, and the air was humid and still, waiting.

She felt weak, physically weak. She hadn't known
that desire robbed the muscles of power. She melted
against him, flowed against him, until she felt as if
only his arm around her was holding her up.

He brushed his hard mouth over the fragile skin
at her temple, his warm breath stirring her hair,
touching her ear. "Shall we go home?"

A last, small vestige of caution cried, "No!" but
she was so caught in his sensual web that she could
only nod her head, and the cry remained unvoiced.
She leaned against him as he walked her out to the
Jeep.

Not even on the way home did he ease the relentless pressure. After he had shifted gears, he put
his right hand on her thigh, sliding it up under her
skirt, and the heat of his palm on her naked flesh
almost made her moan aloud. She didn't even realize
where he was taking her until he parked in front of
his house, rather than hers.

"This isn't—" she blurted.

"No," he said quietly. "It isn't. Come inside, Evie."

She could say no. Even now, she could say no. She could insist that he take her home. But even if she did, she suspected, the outcome would be the same. All she would be changing was the location.

He held out his hand. The intent behind it was ruthless. She could feel the heavy arousal and hunger that tightened his lean, powerful frame. He was going to take her.

She put her hand in his.

Even though she sensed his savage satisfaction at her tacit surrender, he remained gentle. If he had not, perhaps her common sense would have won after all. But he was too experienced to make that mistake, and she found herself standing in his moonlit bedroom with his big bed looming behind her. She looked out the French doors to the lake, a black mirror reflecting the cool, pale moon. Another low rumble of thunder reached her ears, and she knew that the heat flashes were continuing, bright bursts of light that teased with their promise of rain but never delivered.

Robert put his hands on her waist and turned her to him. Her heart thudded painfully against her ribs as he bent his head and his mouth claimed hers. His kisses were slow, so slow, and devastatingly thorough. His tongue probed, and his mouth drank deeply from hers as his hands leisurely moved over her body, unzipping, loosening, removing. The bodice of her dress fell to her waist, and beyond. He paused a moment to caress her smooth back, the inward curve of her waist; then he gently removed the dress and tossed it aside.

She stood before him wearing only high heels and panties. He caught her to him for more kisses, his tongue stroking deeply within. His hands moved over her breasts, molding them under his lean fingers. Desperately Evie clung to his broad, muscled shoulders, trying to steady her spinning senses. His silk shirt slid across her tightly budded nipples, making her whimper. He murmured soothingly as he unbuttoned his shirt and shrugged out of it, dropping it, too, to the floor. Then her naked breasts were pressed full against his bare chest, nestled into the curly black hair, and she heard herself make a low, hungry sound.

"Easy, darling," he whispered. He kicked out of his shoes and unfastened his pants, letting them drop. His thick sex extended the front of his short, snug boxers. She arched against him, blindly thrusting her pelvis forward to nestle that rigid length. His breath hissed inward, and his control cracked. Fiercely he crushed her to him, his arms tightening until pain made her cry out, the sound stifled against his shoulder.

He lowered her to the bed, the sheets cool against her heated flesh. In a swift movement he divested himself of his shorts. Evie's eyes flared as she saw him totally naked, aroused, the muscles in his body taut with desire and the strain of control. His leanness was dangerously deceptive, for it was all steely muscle, the graceful strength of a panther rather than the bulk of a lion. He lowered himself beside her, one arm cradling her head, while his other hand efficiently removed her shoes and panties. Her total nudity was suddenly startling; she made a brief movement to cover herself, a movement that he halted by catching her wrists and pinning them on each side of her head. Then, very deliberately, he mounted her.

Evie couldn't catch her breath. He was heavier, much heavier, than she had imagined. The sensations were alarming, jarring through her consciousness, coming too swiftly on waves of pleasure that both panicked and beguiled. She was violently aware of his muscled thighs pushing between hers, holding them apart, of his furry, ridged abdomen rubbing against her much softer belly, of the hard press of his chest on her breasts. Between her legs, on her bare loins, she could feel the insistent push of his naked sex against her. Her own sex felt swollen and hot, throbbing in rhythm to her own heartbeat.

He loomed over her in the darkness, much bigger, much stronger. The moonlight was sufficient for her to see the pale glitter of his eyes, the hard planes of his face. His expression was stamped with savage male triumph.

Then he released her wrists and cupped her jaw in one hard, hot hand, turning her face up to him. He held her for the deep thrust of his tongue, the blatant domination of his mouth. Helplessly she responded, caught in the heated madness.

He suckled her breasts, lingering over them and

making her writhe with pleasure, and all the while she could feel that hard length impatiently nudging her softest flesh.

The moment came too soon, and not fast enough. He braced himself over her on one arm and reached between their bodies with the other. She felt his lean fingers on her sex, gently parting the folds, finding and stroking her soft, wet entrance. Her hips strained instinctively upward. Her entire body was throbbing. "Robert," she whispered. The single word was taut with strain.

He guided his rigid shaft to her, leaning over and into her as he tightened his buttocks and increased the pressure against the tender opening, forcing it to widen and admit him.

Evie stiffened, her breath quickening. The pressure swiftly became burning pain, real pain. He rocked against her, forcing himself fractionally deeper with every controlled thrust. Her fists knotted the sheet beneath her. She turned her head away, closing her eyes against the hot tears that seeped out beneath her lashes.

He froze as realization hit him.

He turned her head so that she faced him. Her eyes flew open, brilliant with tears in the silver moonlight, and then she couldn't look away. His chest was heaving with the force of his breathing, the sound loud in the quiet, still bedroom. There was nothing of the urbane sophisticate in the man who leaned over her, his face hard with desire. For a split second she saw straight into his soul, into the frighteningly intense, primitive core of him. He held her, forced her to look at him, and with a guttural, explosive sound of control breaking, thrust hard into the depths of her silky body, forcing his way past the barrier of her virginity. She cried out, her body arching under the deep lash of pain. Beyond the pain was the stunning shock of invasion, worse than she had imagined, her delicate inner tissues shivering as they tried to adjust to and accommodate the hard bulk of the intruder.

A rough, deep growl sounded in his throat as he gripped her hips, pulling her more tightly into his possession.

He rode her hard, thrusting heavily, his hips hammering and recoiling as he imprinted his physical brand on her flesh. He had never before been less than gentle with a woman, but with Evie he was ferocious in his need. He couldn't be gentle, not with his head and heart reeling, his entire body exploding with savage pleasure. She was hot and tight, silky, wet…and his. No one else's. Ever. *His.*

He shuddered, gasping, convulsing, and she felt the hot wash of his seed deep inside her. Then he slowly collapsed, shaking in every muscle, blindly groping for support. His heavy weight settled over her, pressing her into the mattress.

Dazed, Evie lay beneath him. She felt shattered, unable to form a coherent thought.

And then she found that it wasn't over.

Chapter 12

Slowly Robert surfaced from the depths of pure physical sensation, his mind sluggishly beginning to function once more. The power of what he had experienced left him shaken, with a sense of being outside himself, not quite connected. He was intensely aware of his own body in a way he never had been before. He could feel the warmth of his blood pumping through his veins with the heavy, slowly calming beats of his heart. He could feel the harsh bellowing of his lungs decreasing to a more normal pace, feel the intense sexual satisfaction relaxing his muscles, feel the hot, delicious clasp of Evie's body as he remained firmly inside her, satisfied but not yet sated. She was naked beneath him, just the way he had wanted.

Then, with an abrupt shift, the sluggishness was

gone from his brain and reality settled in with ruthless clarity. Robert tensed, appalled at himself. He had lost control, something that had never happened before. Gentleness on his part had never been more needed, and instead he had taken her like a marauder, intent only on his own pleasure, on the conquest and possession of her silky flesh.

She lay motionless beneath him, holding herself in a sort of desperate stillness, as if to avoid attracting his attention again. His heart squeezed painfully. Robert shoved aside the matter of her virginity—he would know the answer to that puzzle later—and concentrated instead on the task of reassuring her. His mind was racing. If he let her escape him now, he would have a hell of a time getting anywhere near her again, and he couldn't blame her for being wary. Wary, hell. She would probably be downright scared, and with good reason.

He had shown her the relentless drive of passion but none of the pleasure. She had known nothing but pain, and the scale was dangerously tilted; unless he could balance the pain with pleasure, he was afraid he would lose her. It was the first time Robert had felt that sort of fear, but a sensation of panic seized him and mixed with his determination. A part of his brain remained blindingly clear. He knew exactly how to bring a woman to climax in a variety of ways: fast or slow, using his mouth or hands or body. He could gently take her to ecstasy with his mouth, and that way would perhaps be the kindest, but his instinct rejected it. He had to do it fast, before she recovered enough to begin fighting—God, he couldn't bear that—and he had to do it the same way that had caused her the pain to begin with. He wanted her to find pleasure in his body rather than dread the thrust that brought their flesh together.

He was still hard, and once more he began moving, slowly, within her. She tensed, and her hands flattened against his chest as if she would try to shove him off. "No," he said harshly, forestalling her resistance. "I won't stop. I know I'm hurting you now, but before I'm finished I'm going to make you like having me inside you."

She stared up at him, her eyes darkened with distress. But she didn't say anything, and he gathered her close, adjusting their positions so she would have the maximum sensation. He could feel her thighs quivering alongside his hips.

He took a deep breath and gentled his voice, wanting to reassure her. "I can make it good for you," he promised, brushing her soft mouth with kisses and feeling it tremble beneath his. "Will you trust me, Evangeline? Will you?"

Still she didn't say anything, hadn't spoken a word since whispering his name at the beginning. Robert hesitated for half a heartbeat, then lifted her hands and put them around his neck. After a moment her fingers shifted slightly to press against him, and relief shuddered through him at that small gesture of permission.

Evie closed her eyes again, gathering herself to once more endure this painful use of her body. At the moment, that was the limit of her capability; she couldn't act, couldn't think, could only endure. She wanted to curl herself into a protective ball and weep in shock and pain and disappointment, but she couldn't do that, either. She was helpless, her body penetrated; she was dependent on his mercy, and he seemed to have none.

At first there was only more pain. But then, abruptly, the twisting thrust of his hips made her arch off the bed with something that wasn't pain, but was just as sharp. There was no warning, no gradual lessening of pain and buildup of pleasure, only that jolt of sensation that made her cry out. He did it again, and with a strangled moan she discovered that her body was even less under her control than she had thought.

She had been cold, but now she was suffused with heat, great waves of it, rolling up from her toes until she felt as if her entire body glowed. It concentrated between her legs, increasing with each inward thrust. Her hands slid from his neck to his shoulders, clinging now, her nails biting into the hard layer of muscle. He was gripping her buttocks, lifting her up to meet him, moving her, rocking her subtly back and forth, and each tiny movement set off new explosions of pleasure within her. She had the sensation of being relentlessly driven up an internal mountain toward some point she couldn't see, but now she was straining to reach it. He pushed her further with each hard recoil of his hips until she was panting and desperate, sobbing as she arched tightly into him. And then he forced her over the edge, and Evie screamed as her senses shattered.

She shuddered and bucked, trying to meld into his flesh, as devastated by the paroxysms of pleasure as she had been by the pain that went before. Robert held himself still and deep, gritting his teeth, but the frantic milking of her internal muscles was more than he could stand, and with a groan he gave himself over, pulsing with release. Somehow he forced himself not to thrust, to let her take her pleasure and not intrude with his, and that only intensified the sensation. From a distance he heard himself groan again as he dissolved, collapsing heavily in her arms.

If Evie had been dazed before, she was even more so now. She lay limply beneath him, drifting in and out of a haze. The demands he'd made on her body, the roller-coaster succession of pain and shock and ecstasy, had left her with neither mind nor body functioning. Perhaps she dozed; she knew she dreamed, flickering images that faded too swiftly to grasp as she surfaced into foggy consciousness once more. She felt him separate himself from her, knew he was trying to be careful, but couldn't prevent a moan at the pain of his withdrawal. She didn't open her eyes as he paused, then murmured softly, a soothing sound that also held a note of apology, and completed the motion. She felt instantly bereft, cold in the air-conditioned darkness. She would have curled protectively on her side, but her limbs were too heavy. The next moment the dark fog closed about her again.

A light snapped on, blindingly bright against her

eyelids. She flinched away from it, but he stilled her with a touch. The mattress shifted as he sat down beside her and firmly parted her thighs. Evie made a faint sound of protest and tried to struggle upward, but again the effort was too much.

"Shh," he whispered, a mere rustle of reassurance. "Let me make you more comfortable, sweetheart. You'll sleep better."

A cool wet cloth touched her between her legs. Deftly, tenderly, he cleaned away the evidence of their lovemaking, then dried her with a soft towel. Evie gave a soft sigh of pleasure. He returned the washcloth and towel to the bathroom, and when he came back to turn out the lamp and slide into bed beside her, she was asleep. She didn't rouse even when he turned her into his arms, cradling her protectively against him.

Evie woke in the still, dark silence before dawn. The moon had long since set, and even the stars seemed to have given up their twinkling efforts. The darkness that pressed against the patio doors was more complete than at any other time of night, in the last moments before being dispelled by the first graying that heralded the approach of the sun. She was still sleepy, exhausted by the tumultuous night in Robert's arms. It was as if her body was no longer hers, the way he called forth and controlled her responses. He had seduced her past caring about fear, about pain, so that her body arched eagerly into his possessive thrusts.

Robert lay beside her, his breathing slow and deep. One arm was curled under her head, the other lay heavily across her waist. His heat enveloped her, welcome in the cool night. The strangeness of his presence beside her made her breath catch.

She didn't want to think about the night that had just passed, or the things that had happened between them. She was too tired, too off balance, to handle the riot of impressions and thoughts that whirled in her brain, but she was also too tired to fend them off. She gave up the effort and instead tried to make sense of what she was feeling.

She had never thought that giving herself to the man she loved would prove so traumatic, but it had. The physical pain, oddly, was the least of it, the most understandable. She had known that, under his urbane manner, Robert had the soul of a conqueror. She had also known that he had been sexually frustrated from the time they'd met. It would have made her very uneasy if, under those circumstances, his control *hadn't* wavered. She hadn't expected such a complete collapse, but then, to be perfectly fair, he hadn't expected everything that had happened, either.

She should have told him that she was a virgin, she knew, but the telling would have required an explanation that she simply hadn't been able to give. Talking about Matt, reliving those brief hours of their marriage, was too painful. Her throat tightened with dread, knowing that Robert would demand that explanation soon. She had hoped—foolishly—that he wouldn't be able to tell, that her first time would provide no more than a momentary discomfort that she could easily disguise or ignore. She felt like weeping and laughing at the same time. Had she told him, that might well have been the extent of her pain. As it was, she had paid dearly for keeping her secret, only to have it known, anyway.

The two most difficult things for her to deal with, however, were mingled grief and terror. She had known that sleeping with Robert would destroy her defenses, but she hadn't known how panicked she would feel, or that giving herself to him would call up such poignant memories of Matt. She couldn't distance herself from the grief; loving Matt, and losing him the way she had, had shaped her life and her soul. He had, in effect, made her into the woman she was now.

For twelve years she had been faithful to him, and his memory had wrapped around her like an invisible shield, protecting her. But now she had given herself irrevocably to another man, in both heart and body, and there was no going back. She loved Robert with an intensity that swelled in her chest and made her breath catch. For better or worse, *he* filled her life now. She would have to let Matt go, surrender his memory so that it became only a small, indelible part of her, rather than a bulwark between her and the world. It was like losing him twice.

"Goodbye, Matt," she whispered in her mind to the image of the laughing, dark-haired boy she carried there. "I loved you…but I'm his now, and I love him, too, so much." The image stilled, then nodded gravely, and she saw a smile, a blessing, move across the young face as it faded away.

She couldn't bear it. With a low, keening sound of grief she surged out of bed, awakening Robert. He shot out a hand to catch her, but she evaded it and stood in the middle of the floor, looking wildly around the dark bedroom, her fist pressed to her mouth to stop the sobs that pressed for release.

"What's wrong?" he asked softly, every muscle in his body tense and alert. "Come back to bed, sweetheart."

"I—I have to go home." She didn't want to turn on a light, feeling unable to bear his too-discerning gaze, not now, with her emotions stripped bare. But she needed to find her clothes, get dressed.... There was a dark heap on the carpet, and she snatched it up, touch telling her that it was her dress. Oh God, her muscles protested every move she made, his lovemaking during the night echoing now in her flesh. A deep internal ache marked where he had been.

"Why?" His voice remained soft, compelling. "It's early yet. We have time."

Time for what? she wanted to ask, but she knew, anyway. If she got back into that bed, he would make love to her again. And again. Shaking with grief, caught in the transition between the old love and the new, she thought she would break into pieces if he touched her. She was irrevocably passing from one phase of her life into another, traumatic enough under any circumstances, but she had the sensation of leaving a secure fortress and plunging headlong into unknown danger. She needed to be alone to deal with what she was feeling, to get herself back.

"I have to go," she repeated in a ghostly voice, tight with suppressed tears.

He got out of bed, his naked body pale in the shadowy darkness. "All right," he said gently. "I'll take you home." She watched in bewilderment as he stripped the top sheet from the bed. His next movement was a blur, so swift that she couldn't tell what he was doing until it was too late. With two quick steps he was beside her. He swathed the sheet tightly around her, then lifted her in his arms. "Later," he added as he opened the patio doors and stepped outside with her.

The early morning was silent, as if all God's creatures were holding their breath, waiting for first light. Not even a cricket chirped. The water lapped at the bank with only a slight rustling sound, like silk petticoats. Robert sat down in one of the deck chairs and held her cradled on his lap, the sheet protecting her from the cool, damp air.

Evie tried to hold herself tight, all emotion contained. She managed for a few minutes. Robert simply held her, not saying anything, looking out over the dark water as if he, too, were waiting for the dawn. It was his silence that defeated her; if he had talked, she could have concentrated on her replies. Faced with nothing but her own thoughts, she lost the battle.

She turned her face into his neck as hot tears ran down her cheeks and her body shook with sobs.

He didn't try to hush her, didn't try to talk to her, simply held her more closely to him and gave her the comfort of his body. It was, despite her chaotic emotions, a considerable comfort. The bonds of the flesh that he had forged during the night were fresh and strong, her senses so attuned to him that it was as if his breath were hers, her jerky inhalations gradually slowing and taking on the steady rhythm of his.

When she had calmed, he used a corner of the sheet to dry her face. He didn't bother to wipe her tears from his neck.

Exhausted, empty of emotion, her eyes burning and grainy feeling, she stared out at the lake. In a tree close by, a bird gave a tentative chirp, and as if that were a signal, in the next moment hundreds of birds began singing madly, delirious with joy at the new day. In the time while she had wept, the morning had grown perceptibly lighter, the darkness fading to a dim gray that gave new mystery to details that had been hidden before. That dark hump out in the water—was that a stump, a rock or a magical sea creature that would vanish with the light?

Robert was very warm, the heat of his powerful, naked body seeping through the sheet in animal comfort. She felt the steely columns of his thighs beneath her, the solid support of his chest, the secure grasp of his arms. She rested her head against that wide, smoothly muscled shoulder and felt as if she had come home.

"I love you," she said quietly.

Foolish of her to admit it; how many other women had told him the same thing, especially after a night in his arms? It must be nothing new to him. But what would she gain by holding it back? It would allow a pretense, when he left, that he had been nothing more than a summer affair, but she couldn't fool herself with a sop to her pride. Probably she couldn't even fool him, though he would be gentleman enough to allow her the pretense.

All the same, she was glad of his self-possession. He didn't parrot the words back to her; she would have known he was lying, and she would have hated that. Nor did he act uncomfortable or nervous. He merely gave her a searching look and asked in a level tone, "Then why the tears?"

Evie sighed and returned to staring at the water. He was due some explanation, would probably insist on one, but even though she loved him, she simply couldn't strip her soul bare and blurt out everything. She had a deeply private core, and even if she remained Robert's lover for years, there would be some things she wouldn't be able to tell him, memories that brought up too much pain.

"Evie." It wasn't a prompt but a gentle, implacable demand.

Sadness haunted her eyes and trembled around her mouth. She was very familiar with it, had walked with it for twelve years, gone to bed with it at night, awakened with it on countless mornings. Sadness and a deep lonelines that neither friends nor family had been able to dispel had been her constant, invisible companions. But Robert wanted an answer. A man who had held a woman through such a bout of bitter weeping should at least know the reason for her tears.

"I realized," she finally said in a low, shaking voice, "that Matt is truly gone now."

Cradled against him as she was, she felt the way his muscled body tightened. His words, however, were still controlled. "He's been gone for a long time."

"Yes, he has." Only she knew exactly how long those twelve years had been. "But until last night, I was still his wife."

"No," he said flatly. "You weren't." He put one finger under her chin and tilted it up, forcing her to look at him. It was light enough now for her to see those pale eyes glittering. "You were never his wife. You never slept with him. I hope you aren't going to try to pretend you weren't a virgin, because I'm not a fool, and the stain on the sheet isn't because you're having your period."

Evie flinched. "No," she whispered. God, it was eerie how he had gone straight to the secret she had kept for so long.

"You married him," he continued relentlessly. "How is it that I'm the only man who's ever had you?"

Sadness still darkened her eyes, but she said, "I had a June wedding," and a wealth of grief and irony lay in those brief words.

He didn't understand, but he lifted his dark brows, inviting her to continue.

"It's impossible to book a church for a wedding in June unless you do it about a year in advance," she explained. "Matt and I picked the day when we were still juniors in high school. But there's no way to do any personal planning that far ahead of time." Evie turned her head away from him once more, toward her private solace, the water. "It was a beautiful wedding. The weather was perfect, the decorations were perfect, the cake was perfect. Everything went off without a hitch. And my period started that morning."

Robert was silent, still waiting. Evie swallowed, aching inside as she looked back at the innocent girl she had been. "I was so embarrassed that night, when I had to tell Matt that we couldn't make love. We were both miserable."

"Why didn't you—" he began, but then stopped as he realized that two teenagers wouldn't have the ease and experience of two adults.

"Exactly," Evie said, as if he had put his thoughts into words. "We had never made love, obviously. Matt didn't have any more experience than I did. What experience we had, we'd gotten together, but we'd both wanted to wait until after we were married. So there we were, two eighteen-year-olds on our wedding night, and all we could do was neck and hold hands. Matt was so miserable that we didn't even do much of that.

"But he was basically such a cheerful person that

nothing depressed him for long. He was making jokes about it the next morning, making me laugh, but we both agreed that it was something we'd *never* tell our kids when we got old.'' Her voice wavered and faded until it was almost soundless. ''He died that day.''

Gently Robert pushed a strand of hair away from her face. So she had never made love with her young husband, but for over a decade had kept herself untouched for him. With an acuteness of insight that often made people uncomfortable, he saw exactly how it had been. Traumatized by Matt's death, she had doubly mourned the fact that they had never been able to make love and had sealed herself off from other men. If her first time couldn't be with Matt, it would be with no one. She had existed ever since as an animated Sleeping Beauty whose body had kept on functioning while her emotions had been suspended.

Robert felt a deep, savage satisfaction. Despite that enormous barrier, he had succeeded where others hadn't even been able to begin. Her first time had been *his*. She was *his*.

He had always despised promiscuity but hadn't prized virginity. It had seemed to him the height of hypocrisy to demand something from a woman that he himself lacked. All of his sophisticated affairs, however, had nothing in common with the powerful, primitive sense of jealous possessiveness that had swept over him the moment he had realized that he was the only man ever to make love to Evie.

Her association with Landon Mercer, whatever it was, was certainly not romantic in any sense. Sitting there in the early dawn, with Evie cradled on his lap, Robert made a swift decision. He wouldn't stop the investigation, wouldn't warn her in any way, because the espionage had to be halted before it did irreparable harm to both the space station and national security. But when the net was tightened and all the traitorous little fish caught, he would step in and use his influence to shield Evie from prosecution. She wouldn't escape punishment, but the punishment would be his, and his alone, to mete out. The simple truth was that he couldn't bear for her to go to prison. He was astonished at himself, but there it was.

He didn't know why she was involved in something so vile. He was a very good judge of people, and he would have sworn that honor was a cornerstone of her character. Therefore, she had to be doing it for what she considered a good reason, though he couldn't imagine what that could be. It was possible she didn't realize exactly what was going on; that explanation fit better than any other, and made him all the more determined to protect her. As he had told her once, he was good at taking care of his own, and last night Evie had become his in the most basic of ways.

He was fiercely glad that nature's rhythm had interfered with her wedding night all those years ago. Poor Matt. A lot of his jealousy for the boy faded away, and a rather poignant pity took its place. Matt

Shaw had died without ever tasting the perfection of his young wife's body.

Robert remembered the moment the night before when he had removed her last garment and seen her totally naked, nothing left to his imagination any longer. To his numb surprise, his imagination had fallen short. He had seen her breasts before, but each time he had marveled at how firm and round they were, delightfully upright, the nipples small and a delectable shade of dark pink. Her body curved in to a lithe waist, then flared again to very womanly hips. Her skin, in the silver moonlight, had glowed like alabaster. Instead of being model thin, like the women he had been accustomed to, her curves had been lush and sensual. He hadn't been able to wait but had mounted her immediately.

A gentleman would have been far more considerate of her than he had been, but he had always been wryly aware that, despite what all his acquaintances thought, he was definitely *not* a gentleman. He was controlled and intelligent and not a cruel man, but that wasn't the same thing as being gentlemanly. Where Evie was concerned, though, his control went right out the window. His mouth took on a grim line as he remembered the wild rush of passion, the primitive instinct to make her his, that had blotted out all reason. Not only had he hurt her, he hadn't used a condom. He, who had never before neglected to make certain some form of protection was used, hadn't even given a thought to birth control.

She might be pregnant. He allowed the possibility

to seep into his mind just as the golden light began to seep over the ridge of mountains. To his surprise, he didn't feel any panic or disgust at his stupidity. Rather, he felt pleased—and intrigued.

He put his hand inside the sheet, resting it on her cool, flat belly. "We may be parents. I didn't wear a condom."

"It's all right." She gave him a composed look. The tears and grief were now well under control. "I went to my doctor in Huntsville and got a prescription for birth-control pills."

He felt a not altogether pleasant jolt. He should have been relieved, but instead he was strangely disappointed. Common sense prevailed however. "When?"

"Not long after meeting you," she said wryly.

Robert almost snorted at the amount of work he'd had his people doing, trying to find out what she had been doing, whom she had seen, that day in Huntsville. He would pull them off that particular job now, but he would be damned if he'd tell them what she *had* been doing.

He lifted his eyebrows at her, a sardonic look on his face. "I distinctly remember you saying that you didn't intend to sleep with me."

"I didn't. But that doesn't mean I'd leave something that important to chance, because you were determined, and I wasn't entirely sure of my willpower."

"Your willpower would have been fine," he said, "if you hadn't wanted me, too."

"I know," she admitted softly.

Dawn was well and truly upon them now, golden light spilling across the water. The roar of outboard motors broke the serene hush of the morning, and soon the river would be crowded with fishermen and pleasure boaters. Though Evie's position on his lap would keep anyone from seeing he was naked, Robert thought it best not to chance shocking the locals. After all, she ran a business here, and she might be recognized. He stood up easily, still cradling her securely in his arms, and carried her back through the open patio doors.

He had never been more content than he was at this moment. Evie probably didn't know what was really going on with Mercer and was involved only peripherally; he would be able to protect her without much problem. He had taken her to bed, and now he knew what had lain beneath her mysterious sadness. He doubted that Evie would ever completely stop thinking about Matt, but that was okay now, because Matt Shaw's ghost had been banished and she had emerged from her emotional deep freeze. She had said that she loved him, and he knew instinctively that she hadn't been mouthing the words merely to rationalize their lovemaking. If she hadn't already loved him, he would never have been able to seduce her.

Some of the women who had come before had also told him that they loved him—most of them, in fact. The declarations had never elicited more from him than a rather tender pity for their vulnerability.

Though he had liked and enjoyed all his lovers, none of them had ever managed to pierce his shell; he doubted any of them had even known the shell existed.

Evie's simple statement, though, had filled him with a satisfaction so fierce that his blood had thrummed through his veins. She hadn't expected him to respond. Now that he thought about it, she expected less from him than anyone else ever had. It was a startling realization to a man accustomed to having people come to him with their problems, expecting him to make decisions that would affect thousands of workers and millions of dollars. Evie expected nothing. How was it, then, that she gave so much?

He carried her into the bathroom and stood her on her feet, then unwrapped her from the sheet. The sight of her creamy golden flesh aroused him again, drew his hands to cup her breasts and feel the cool, silky weight of them. His thumbs rubbed across her nipples, making them tighten. Evie's eyes were wide with alarm as she stared at him.

His mouth quirked into a crooked smile. "Don't look so worried," he said as he bent down to press his lips to her forehead. "I'll restrain myself until you've had time to heal. Get in the tub, sweetheart, while I put on the coffee. A bath will relieve some of the soreness."

"Good idea," she said with absolute sincerity.

He chuckled as he left her there. The feeling of contentment was even deeper. She was *his*.

Chapter 13

How could experiencing such a night not leave an imprint on her face? Evie wondered as she got ready for work. After her leisurely soak in the soothing hot water and an equally leisurely breakfast, which Robert had cooked with the same easy competence with which he handled everything else, he had driven her home and reluctantly kissed her goodbye for the day, saying that he had some business to attend to in Huntsville but would try to get back before she closed the marina. If not, he would come to her house.

She had forced herself to do the normal things, but she felt as if her entire life had been turned upside down, as if nothing were the same. *She* wasn't the same. Robert had turned her into a woman who actively longed for his possession, despite the discomfort of her newly initiated body. She hadn't known, hadn't even suspected, that passion could be so savage and all-encompassing, that the pain would be as nothing before the need to link her body with his.

She wanted him even more now than before. He had brought up the long-buried sensuality of her nature and made it his, so that she responded to the lightest touch of his hand. When she thought of him, her body throbbed with the need to wrap her legs around him and take him inside her, to cradle his heavy weight, accept and tame the driving need of his masculinity. The scent of his skin, warm and musky, aroused her. Her memory was filled now with details that she hadn't known before, like the guttural growl of his words and the way his neck corded when he threw his head back in the arching frenzy of satisfaction.

She stared at her face in the mirror as she swiftly braided her hair. Her eyes had shadows under them, but she didn't look tired. She simply looked…like herself. If there was any change at all, it was in the expression in her eyes, as if there was a spark that had been missing before.

But if her face was the same, her body bore the signs of his lovemaking. Her breasts were pink and slightly raw from contact with his beard stubble, her nipples so sensitive from his mouth that the soft fabric of her bra rasped them. There were several small bruises on her hips, where he had gripped her during his climax, and her thighs ached. She was sore enough that every step reminded her of his posses-

Loving Evangeline

sion and awakened echoes of sensation that made her acutely aware of her body.

It was much earlier than usual when she drove to the marina, but she needed the distraction to take her mind off Robert. If she was lucky, Sherry would bring Virgil by to spend the day with her.

Craig was gassing up a boat when she arrived. When he had finished, he came in and rang up the sale, putting the money in the cash drawer. "How come you're in so early? Have a nice time last night?"

Her nerves jumped, but she managed a composed smile. "Yes, we did. We went to a private club for dinner and dancing. And I came in early…just because."

"That's a good enough reason for me." He brushed his dark hair out of his eyes and gave her an urchin's grin. "I'm glad you're going out with him. You deserve some fun, after the way you've worked to build up this place."

"Thanks for swapping shifts with me."

"You bet."

Another customer idled up to the docks, and Craig went out again. Evie picked up the morning mail and began sorting through it. The junk mail and sales papers went into the trash. The bills went to one side, to be juggled later. One letter was from a New York bank she'd never heard of, probably wanting her to apply for a credit card. She started to toss it without opening it, but on second thought decided to see what it was about. She picked up the penknife she used as a letter opener and slit the envelope.

Thirty seconds later, her brows knit in puzzlement, she let the single sheet of paper drop to the desk. Somehow this bank had gotten her confused with someone else, though she couldn't think how they had gotten her name on one of their files when she had never done business with them. The letter stated, in brisk terms, that due to a poor payment record they would be forced to foreclose on her loan unless it was paid in full within thirty days.

She would have ignored it except that the amount noted was the same as what she owed her bank for the loan against the marina. She knew that figure well, had struggled to get it down to that amount. Each payment brought it even lower. She didn't know how, but obviously her file had gotten into this other bank's computers, and they wanted her to pay fifteen thousand, two hundred and sixty-two dollars within thirty days.

Well, it was obviously something she would have to clear up before it got even more tangled. Evie called her bank, gave her name and asked for her loan officer, Tommy Fowler, who was also an old school friend.

The line clicked, and Tommy's voice said, "Hi, Evie. How're you doing?"

"Just fine. How are you and Karen doing, and the kids?"

"We're doing okay, though Karen says the kids are driving her crazy, and if school doesn't start soon she's going to get herself arrested, so she can have some peace and quiet.''

Evie chuckled. The Fowler kids were known for their frenetic energy.

"What can I help you with today?'' Tommy asked.

"There's been a really strange mix-up, and I need to know how to straighten it out. I got a letter today from a bank in New York, asking for payment in full on a loan, and it's the same amount as the one I took out from you, on the marina.''

"Is that so? Wonder what's going on. Do you have your account number handy?''

"Not with me, no. I'm at work, and all my bookkeeping is at home.''

"That's okay, I'll pull it up under your name. Just a minute.''

She could hear the tapping of computer keys as he hummed softly to himself. Then he stopped humming and silence reigned, stretching out for so long that Evie wondered if he'd left the room. Finally a few more keys were tapped, then more silence.

He fumbled with the receiver. "Evie, I—'' Reluctance was heavy in his voice.

"What's wrong? What's happened?''

"There's a problem, all right, hon. A big one. Your loan was bought by that bank.''

Evie's mind went blank. "What do you mean, bought?''

"I mean we sold off some of our loans. It's a common practice. Banks do it to reduce their debt load. Other financial institutions buy them to diversify their own debt load. According to the records, this transaction took place ten days ago.''

"Ten days! Just ten days, and already they're demanding payment in full? Tommy, can they do that?''

"Not if you've fulfilled the terms of the loan. Have you...ah...were you late with the payment?''

She knew he must have her payment record there in front of him, showing that she had been late several times, though she had never fallen a full month behind and had always gotten back on schedule. "It's late now," she said numbly. "I had an unexpected expense, and it'll be next week before I can.''

She heard him exhale heavily. "Then they're legally within their rights, though the normal procedure would be to make an effort at collecting the payment, rather than the full amount.''

"What do I do?''

"Call them. It should be fairly easy to straighten out. After all, you're a good risk. But be sure to follow up by letter, so you'll have a record in writing.''

"Okay. Thanks for the advice, Tommy.''

"You're welcome. I'm sorry about this, hon. It never would have happened if we'd still held the loan.''

"I know. I'll see what I can do.''

"Call me if there's anything I can do to help.''

"Thanks," she said again and hung up.

Her heart was pounding as she dialed the number

on the letterhead. An impersonal voice answered and nasally requested her business. Evie gave the name of the man who had signed the letter, and the connection was made before she could even say please.

The call was brief. Mr. Borowitz was as brisk as his letter had been and as impersonal as the operator. There was nothing he could do, nor did he sound interested in trying. The outstanding amount was due in full by the time limit set forth in the letter, or the loan would be foreclosed and the property forfeit.

Slowly she hung up and sat there staring out the window at the blindingly bright day. The lake was crowded with boaters, people laughing, having fun. The marina was busy, with owners cleaning their craft, others using her ramps to launch their boats, still others idling in for gas. If she didn't somehow come up with over fifteen thousand dollars within the next thirty days, she would lose it all.

She loved the marina. Because she and Matt had been playmates before they had become sweethearts, she had spent a lot of time here even as a child. She had spent hours playing on the docks, had grown up with the smell of the water in her nostrils. The rhythms of the marina were as much a part of her as her own heartbeat. She had helped Matt work here, and later, after his death, had taken over the lion's share of the work from his parents. When they had left the marina to her, she had channeled all her energy and efforts into making it prosperous, but it had been a labor of love. The marina, as much as her family, had given her a reason for going on when she had been doubtful that she wanted to even try.

This was her kingdom, her home, as much or more than the house in which she lived. She couldn't bear to lose it. Some way, any way, she would find the money to pay off the loan.

The most obvious solution was to borrow against the house. The amount of the debt would be the same, but it would be stretched out over a longer period of time, and that would actually lower the payments. She felt giddy for a moment as the shock and horror lifted from her shoulders. She would be in even better shape than before, with more free cash every month.

She called Tommy again and got the ball rolling. He agreed that a mortgage was the perfect solution. He would have to get an okay on the loan, but he didn't foresee any problems and promised to call her as soon as permission came through.

When she hung up, Evie sat with her head in her hands for a long moment. She felt as if she had just survived combat. She was shaky, but elated at her victory. If she had lost the marina… She couldn't let herself imagine it.

When she finally lifted her head and looked out the window, driven by a need to see her domain still safe and secure, still hers, her face broke into a smile. Business was good today. So good, in fact, that Craig desperately needed a hand and was probably wondering why she wasn't out there helping him. Evie

bounded to her feet, energy restored, and rushed out
to help him with the sudden glut of customers.

Robert arrived at the marina just after seven that
evening. It had been busy all day, and she was on
the dock selling gas and oil to yet another happy,
sun-roasted boater. Alerted by a sensitivity to her
lover's presence, Evie looked around and saw him
standing just outside the door, watching her. She
lifted her hand. "I'll be there in a few minutes."

He nodded and stepped inside, and she turned her
attention back to her customer.

Robert watched her through the big window as he
stepped behind the counter. He had been notified that
she had received the letter and called the bank that
he had arranged to buy her loan, and that, as instructed, they had been totally unwilling to cooperate
on the matter. Glancing down, he saw the letter lying
on top of the stack of mail, the single sheet of paper
neatly folded and stuffed back into the envelope.

She had to be uspet. He regretted the need for it,
but he had decided to see the plan through. Though
he was almost certain she didn't know exactly what
Mercer was doing, that she was more of an unwitting
accomplice than anything else, there was still the
small chance that she was involved up to her pretty
neck. Because of that, he couldn't relent in his financial pressure. If she *was* involved, she would be
forced into another sale just to raise the money to
pay the loan. If she wasn't involved, he would take
care of her money problems just as soon as he had

Mercer in jail. There were others, and he would get them, too. But Evie was his, one way or the other.

Since he had left her that morning, he had several times been struck with amazement that he wouldn't see her sent to jail, even if she was guilty. This was his country's security at stake, something he took very seriously indeed. He had risked his life more than once for the same principle. He had relished the adventure, but the underlying reason for taking those risks had been a simple, rock-solid love of country. If Evie had betrayed it, she deserved prison. But acknowledging that in no way changed his decision. He would protect her from prosecution.

The sunburned customer and his trio of friends, all young men in their early twenties, were obviously in no hurry to stop chatting with Evie. Robert scowled out the window, but he couldn't blame them. Only a dead man wouldn't respond to her curvy, glowing femininity.

He slipped the letter out of the envelope and unfolded it. There was no reason for doing so, except a meticulous attention to detail. He wanted to know exactly what it said. Swiftly he scanned the contents, satisfied with the way it had been handled. Then he read Evie's notes, hastily scribbled in the margin.

She had written down the name ''Tommy Fowler,'' with a phone number beside it. Underneath she had written ''mortgage house'' and circled that.

A smile tugged at his mouth. She was certainly a resourceful, common-sense woman. Relief welled up in him. If she was truly involved in stealing the

NASA computer programs, she wouldn't be trying to mortgage her house to pay the loan; she would simply arrange another buy. In his experience, criminals didn't think of things like honest work to pay off debts; they were leeches, living off the effort of others, and would simply steal again.

Robert returned the letter to the envelope. More than ever, he regretted the need to play out what he had begun, but he never left anything to chance, certainly not in a matter this serious. He would have to squash any attempt to mortgage the house, of course. Evie would be worried sick, but he would make it up to her afterward.

He sat down on the high stool and watched her as she finally got rid of the four admiring young men. She was dressed much as she had been the first time he'd seen her, in jeans and a T-shirt with her tawny blond hair in a thick, loose braid. His reaction, too, was almost the same: he was poleaxed with lust. The only difference was that it was more intense now, and he hadn't thought that possible. But now he knew exactly how she looked naked, knew all the delectable textures and curves of her body, and the hot, tight clasp of being sheathed deep inside her. He shivered with desire, his burning gaze locked on her as she walked up the dock. He knew the sounds she made at the peak of pleasure, knew how she clung to him, the way her legs locked convulsively around him, and how her nipples hardened to tight little raspberries. He knew the taste of her, the scent, and wanted to have it again.

She came inside, glanced at him and froze in place. He saw the shudder of awareness that rippled over her as she sensed his arousal. God, was she even more attuned to him than she had been before? The thought was unsettling.

"Come here," he said softly, and she blindly walked into his arms.

He didn't rise from the stool but pulled her between his thighs. Her arms circled his shoulders as he bent his mouth to hers. He kissed her for a long time, so hungry for her that he couldn't be gentle. Evie moved against him, her hips rolling in a languorous, wanton manner that made his heart almost stop in his chest. Kissing her when her response was reluctant had been intoxicating enough; now that she was willing, her mouth clung to his in a way that made him forget about Mercer and the stolen computer programs, about the mess she was embroiled in, even where he was, everything but the hot joy of holding her.

But she would be too sore for any more lovemaking today, and reluctantly he eased away from her mouth, trailing kisses across her temple and the curve of her jaw. He would have to restrain himself for a while yet.

"How did your day go?" he murmured, opening the door for her to tell him about the problem with the bank loan.

"It was as busy today as I've ever seen it," she replied, leaning back in the circle of his arms. Her eyes were soft and sleepy. "How about yours?"

"Tedious. I had some boring details to handle."
That was a lie. No detail was boring to him.

"I wish you had been here today, I'd have put you
to work. I think everyone who owns a boat was on
the water today." She glanced over his shoulder.
"There's another one," she said as she slipped out
his arms.

This group didn't need any gas but trooped inside
in search of some snacks and cold drinks. They had
the ruddiness of people who had been out in the sun
and wind all day, and brought with them the coconut
scent of sunscreen lotion. Once inside, they seemed
reluctant to leave the air-conditioning and milled
around looking at the fishing tackle. Evie didn't try
to hurry them, instead chatting pleasantly. They were
two couples about her age, out for a day of relaxation
on the lake. One of the women mentioned how nice
it was to have a day away from the kids, and for a
while the conversation centered on the antics of their
children. When the group finally left, it was with
friendly goodbyes.

"Alone at last," Robert said, glancing at his
watch. "It's closing time, anyway."

"Thank goodness." Evie stretched and yawned,
catching herself in midstretch with a wince that she
quickly covered, but not quickly enough. He saw that
slight hesitation. He would indeed have to exercise
self-control.

He helped her to close up, then sent her home
while he stopped for takeout. They ate dinner together, then sat out on the deck in the cooling night,

talking softly about routine things. But Evie soon became sleepy, a direct result of not sleeping much the night before. On her third yawn, Robert stood up and held out his hand. "That's it, sleepyhead. Bedtime."

She put her hand in his and let him pull her to her feet. He led her to the bedroom and gently began undressing her.

"Robert, wait," she said uneasily, trying to draw away from him. "I can't—"

"I know," he said, and kissed her forehead. "I told you I'd give you time to heal. I didn't say anything about not sleeping together, but *sleep* is the operative word."

She relaxed into his arms again, and he finished the task of undressing both of them. It was too warm in the house for him to be comfortable, but when they were both naked and lying on the bed, the ceiling fan wafted a cooling breeze over them, and he began to get drowsy, anyway. They lay nestled spoon fashion, his hard thighs under her round bottom, one hand possessively covering a breast.

He lay quietly. She was already asleep, her breathing slow and even. All his objections to staying in this house had faded when he had found that Evie had never truly been Matt's wife. He would still have preferred being in his own house; the bed was much bigger, for one thing. But Evie would be more comfortable in her own home, and that was the most important thing. He had notified his people where he would be, just as he had notified them that Evie would be staying with him the night before.

He had given her every opportunity to tell him about the bank loan, but she hadn't said a word about it. Just as she had with the blown motor in her truck, she kept her trouble to herself rather than running to him for help or even emotional support. For someone who was so open and friendly, Evie was a very solitary person, accustomed to handling everything on her own. Though he would have had to turn her down if she'd asked for help, he wanted her to confide in him, to let him far enough into her life that he knew about the problems as well as the pleasures. When they were married, he would make damn certain he knew every time she stubbed her toe.

Until that moment, he hadn't let his plans for the future progress that far, but suddenly it seemed the thing to do. He had never wanted any other woman the way he wanted Evie, and he sincerely doubted that he ever would. After this mess was settled, he intended to keep her close by, which would mean taking her to New York with him. And he knew Evie. Though she had given herself to him, she was essentially a conventional soul. She would want the security of marriage; therefore, he would marry her. Other women had wanted marriage from him, but this was the first time in his life he'd been willing to give it. He couldn't imagine ever becoming bored with Evie, which had always happened with other lovers. Even more, he couldn't imagine letting any other man have the chance to marry her.

He didn't regret the impending loss of freedom. He thought of dressing her in silk gowns and expen-

sive jewelry, of settling her in the lap of luxury—
his—so that she wouldn't have to work seven days
a week or worry about paying bills. She wouldn't
have to make do with a secondhand refrigerator or
drive around in a beat-up old truck. She wouldn't be
so tired that dark smudges lay under her eyes. He
would take her with him on his business trips, show
her Paris and London and Rome, and they would
take vacations on the ranch in Montana. Madelyn, he
suspected, would gloat because he had finally been
caught, but she would like Evie. Evie, despite that
glowing sensuality, wasn't the type of woman that
other women disliked on sight. She was friendly and
courteous and unselfconscious about her looks. He
had seen a lot of women who were far more vain
than Evie, and with a lot less reason.

Within a month, perhaps even sooner, all of this
would be behind them and they would be in New
York. He fell asleep, thinking with pleasure of having her all to himself.

As usual, Evie woke at dawn. Robert lay close
beside her, his body heat bathing her in warmth, despite the fact that the sheet had been kicked completely off the bed. He had done that, she supposed,
because he wasn't accustomed to doing without air-
conditioning. His arm was draped heavily across her
hips, and his breath stirred the hair at the back of her
neck.

She had slept with him for two nights in a row

now and wondered how she would be able to bear the desolation when he was no longer there.

She turned within the circle of that enveloping arm and rose up on one elbow. He woke immediately. "Is anything wrong?" he asked, and just for a moment there was something feral and frightening in his eyes, and an instant tension in his muscles, as if he were poised to attack.

Quickly she shook her head to reassure him. "No. I just wanted to see you."

He relaxed at her words, lying back on the pillows. His olive-toned skin was dark against the whiteness. His thick black hair was tousled, and his jaw darkened by a heavy stubble. She was entranced by his sheer, uncomplicated masculinity, not yet smoothed over with grooming and clothes that somewhat obscured his true nature. Lying there with his iron-hard body naked and relaxed, he looked like what he was, a warrior honed down and redefined by years of battle.

She put her hand on his chest, and he lay quietly, watching her from beneath lowered lids but content to let her do as she wished. She didn't whisper her love to him; she had already told him how she felt and didn't intend to badger him about it. She concentrated, instead, on learning as much as she could about him. She had spent the first eighteen years of her life gathering memories about Matt, but she would have a much shorter time with Robert, and she didn't want to waste a minute.

She bent over him, her long hair trailing across his

chest and shoulder as she planted a line of gentle kisses down his body. He smelled delicious in the morning, she thought, all warm and sleepy. The crispy curls of black hair on his chest invited her to rub her cheek against them, catlike. His nipples, tiny and brown, were almost hidden in the hair. She sought them out, tickled by the minute points that stood out when she rubbed her fingertip across them. Robert flexed restlessly on the sheet as desire tightened his muscles, then forced himself to relax again to better enjoy her attentions.

"I wonder if that's the same expression a pasha would have, lying back and letting his favorite concubine pleasure him," she murmured.

"Probably." He put his hands on her head, fingers sliding beneath the heavy fall of hair to massage her scalp. "You do pleasure me, Evangeline."

She continued her dreamy exploration, down the furry ridged abdomen toward his hips and thighs, detouring around his early morning erection. Something high on the inside of his left thigh caught her eye, and she bent closer to examine the mark. The morning sunlight clearly revealed a stylized outline of an eagle, or perhaps a phoenix, with upswept wings. The tattoo was small, not even an inch in length, but so finely made that she could see the fierceness of the raptor.

She was startled by the tattoo—not the design, but its very presence. Lightly she traced her finger over it, wondering why he had it. After all, Robert hardly seemed the type of man who would have a tattoo; he was too polished and sophisticated. But for all that sophistication, he wasn't quite civilized, and the tattoo matched that part of him. This was perhaps the only overt signal he permitted himself that he was more than what he seemed.

"How long have you had it?" she asked, looking up at him.

He was watching her with piercingly intent eyes. "Quite a while."

It was a very inexact answer, but she sensed that it was all she would get from him, at least for now. Slowly she leaned down and licked the tattoo, her tongue gently caressing the sign in his flesh that signaled the presence of the inner man.

A low, rough sound vibrated in his throat, and his entire body tightened.

"Do you want me?" she whispered, licking him again. She felt very warm, and slightly drunk with her feminine power. Desire was unfurling inside her, opening like a flower. Her breasts throbbed, and she rubbed them against his leg.

He gave a strangled laugh, almost undone by her natural sensuality. "Look a few inches to your right and tell me what you think."

She did, turning her head with slow deliberation to survey the straining, pulsing length of his sex. "I believe you do."

"The sixty-four-thousand-dollar question is, how do *you* feel?"

Evie gave him a slow, luminous smile of desire that promised him more than he thought he could

survive. "I feel...willing," she purred, crawling up
the length of his body to lie on him as she wound
her arms around his neck.

His face was strained as he rolled, placing her beneath him. "I'll be careful," he promised in a rough
whisper.

She reached up to touch his beard-roughened
cheek and opened her thighs to clasp them around
him. Her heart was in her eyes as he began slowly,
with almost agonizing care, to enter her. "I trust
you," she said, giving him her body as surely as she
had given him her heart.

Chapter 14

Landon Mercer caught himself wearing a habitually worried expression whenever he glanced into a mirror. Nothing was going right, for no particular reason that he could tell. One day he had been feeling pretty damn good about himself and the way everything was going, and the next it all began to go to hell. It was just little things at first, like that bastard Cannon showing up and nearly giving him a heart attack, though it turned out that Cannon had been the least of his worries. The big boss's reputation had been vastly overstated; he was nothing more than another lazy playboy, born into money, without any real idea of what it was like to get out and hustle for what he had.

Sometimes, though, Cannon had a cold look in his eyes that was downright spooky, as if he could see right through flesh. Mercer wouldn't soon forget the panic he'd felt when Cannon had caught him in Shaw's Marina. For one terror-stricken minute, Mercer had thought he was caught, that they'd somehow managed to find out what he was doing. But all Cannon had seemed interested in was that he'd taken off from work for the afternoon, something he'd been careful not to do again. Of all the damn luck! There were plenty of marinas in Guntersville; why had Cannon picked Shaw's? It wasn't the biggest, or the best run. In fact, for him, its major attraction was that it was small, a bit out of the way and basically a one-horse outfit. Evie Shaw didn't have time to pay attention to everything going on around her.

Of course, once Cannon had seen Evie, it was understandable why he kept hanging around. Mercer had been trying for months to get her to go out with him, but she was as standoffish as she was stacked. He just didn't have enough money, he supposed; she had latched on to Cannon fast enough.

Of course, if things had worked out, he *would* have had enough money to interest her. He wasn't stupid. He hadn't blown the payoffs; he'd invested them. The ventures he'd picked had all seemed sound. He'd stayed away from the high-interest but volatile money markets and opted for slower but more secure returns. In a few years, he'd figured, he would have enough money invested to be on easy street.

But stocks that had looked good one day went sour the next, prices going on a steady slide as other investors dumped their shares. In one terrible week the tidy little nest egg he'd built up had decreased in value to less than half of what it had been before.

He had sold out, taking a loss, and in a desperate move to recoup his money had invested it all in the money markets. The money market had promptly plummeted, almost wiping him out. He felt like King Midas in reverse; everything he touched turned to dross.

When he was contacted about another sale, he was so relieved that he almost thanked them for calling. If his bank account didn't get a cash transfusion soon, he wouldn't be able to make his car payment, or the payments on all his credit cards. Mercer was horrified at the thought of losing his beloved Mercedes. There were more expensive cars, and he intended to have them eventually, but the Mercedes was the first car he'd had that said he was *somebody*, a man on the way up. He couldn't bear to go back to being nothing.

Evie felt as if she had been split into two separate beings. Half of her was deliriously happy, overwhelmed by the intoxication of having Robert for a lover. She had never dreamed she could be so happy again, or feel so whole, but the great emptiness that had lurked in her heart for so long had been filled. Robert was both passionate and considerate, paying her so much attention that she felt as if she were the center of his universe. He never ignored her, never took anything about her for granted, always made her feel as if she were the most desirable woman he'd ever seen. Whenever they went out, his attention never wandered to other women, though she was well aware of other women looking at him.

She saw him every day, slept with him almost

every night. As she became more at ease with her own body and the passion he aroused, their love-making became more leisurely, and even more intense, until sometimes she screamed with the force of it. He was a sophisticated lover, leading her into new positions, new variations, new sensations, and he was so skilled that he didn't make her feel awkward or ignorant. He made love to her almost every night. Only once, but that once was long and complete, leaving her sated and sleepy. Then, in the morning when they woke, they would make love again, silently, drifting in that half-awake state when dreams still shadow consciousness.

His mastery of her body was so complete that thoughts of him were always with her, lurking just under the surface, ready to come to the fore and bringing desire with them. She didn't know which she enjoyed most, the intense sessions at night or the dreamy ones of early morning. It was amazing how quickly her body had learned to crave sexual pleasure with him, so that, as the afternoon hours advanced, she would become jittery with anticipation and need. He knew it, surely. She could see him watching her, as if gauging her readiness. Sometimes she had a violent desire to pin him to the floor and have her way with him, but she always restrained herself, because the buildup of desire, though maddening, was equally delicious.

She had become accustomed to containing her thoughts and emotions, guarding them behind a wall of reserve, but Robert drew her out. They had long, involved discussions about a wide variety of subjects. Sitting out on the deck at night, staring up at the stars, they would discuss astronomy and various theories, from the big bang to black holes, dark matter and the relativity of time. His intelligence and the scope of his interests were almost frightening. Without giving any indication of restlessness, his mind was always working, looking for new facts to absorb or arranging those he already had. They would trade sections of the newspaper, and debate politics and national events. They swapped childhood stories, she telling him about growing up with an older sister as bossy as Becky, he making her laugh with stories of his indomitable younger sister, Madelyn. He told her about the ranch in Montana, which he owned in partnership with Reese Duncan, Madelyn's husband, and about their two rowdy little boys.

The sense of closeness with Robert was at once seductive and terrifying. There was a powerful lure that drew her to him, creating an intimacy as much of the mind as of the body, so that she was no longer a solitary creature but half of a *couple,* her entire sense of being altering to include him. Sometimes, in the back of her mind, she wondered how she would survive if he were to leave—she had to think of it as *if* now, rather than *when*—and the thought of losing him made her almost sick with terror.

She couldn't let herself worry about that. Loving him now, in the present, demanded all her attention. She couldn't hold anything back; she was helpless to even try.

At the same time, the other part of her, the part that wasn't preoccupied with Robert, worried incessantly about the bank loan and the mortgage on the house. Tommy hadn't called her back. She had called the bank twice; the first time he said that permission simply hadn't come through yet, but he didn't think there was any problem and that she should just be patient. The second time she called, he was out of town.

She couldn't wait much longer. It had already been eleven days, leaving just nineteen until the loan had to be paid. If her bank couldn't give her a loan, she would have to find a bank that would, and if all banks moved so slowly, she could find herself running out of time. Just thinking of the possibility was enough to make her break out in a cold sweat.

She tried to think of other options, of some way to quickly raise the money in case the loan didn't go through fast enough. She could put her boat up for sale, but it wasn't worth even half the amount that she needed and might not sell in time, anyway. Asking Becky and Paul for a loan was out of the question; they had their own financial responsibilities, and supporting two teenagers was expensive.

She could sell the rental boats, which would raise enough money but deprive her of a surprisingly tidy bit of income. Of course, with the loan paid, and if she didn't have to take out another one, she would have much more available cash and would soon be able to acquire more boats for rent. The only problem with that was time—again. In her experience, people took their time buying boats. Boats, even in a town like Guntersville that was geared toward the river, weren't a necessity of life. People looked at them, thought about it, discussed it over the dinner table, checked and double-checked their finances. It was possible, but unlikely, that she would be able to sell enough of them to raise the money she needed in the time she had.

Of the limited options available to her, however, that was the best one. She put a sign that read Used Boats For Sale in front of the marina and posted other notices in the area tackle stores. Even if she sold only one, that would lower the amount of money she would need to borrow.

Robert noticed the sign immediately. He walked in late that afternoon, removed his sunglasses and pinned her with a pale, oddly intense look. "That sign out front—which boats are for sale?"

"The rental boats," she calmly replied and returned her attention to waiting on a customer. Once she had made the decision to sell the boats, she hadn't allowed herself any regrets.

He moved behind the counter and stood in front of the window with his hands in his pockets, looking out at the marina. As she had known he would, he waited until the customer had left before turning to ask, "Why are you selling them?"

She hesitated for a moment. She hadn't told him anything about her financial worries and didn't intend to do so now, for a variety of reasons. One was simply that she was reticent about personal problems, disinclined to broadcast her woes to the world. Another was that she was fiercely possessive about the marina, and she didn't want word to get around that it was on shaky financial ground. Yet another was that she didn't want Robert to think she was obliquely asking for a loan, and she would be distressed if he offered one. He was obviously wealthy, but she didn't want the issue of money to become a part of their relationship. If it did, would he ever be certain, in his own mind, that her attraction to him wasn't based on his wealth? Still another reason was that she didn't want anyone else to have a share, and thus a say-so, in the marina. Banks were one thing, individuals another. The marina was *hers,* the base on which she had rebuilt the ruins of her life. She simply couldn't give up any part of it.

So when she answered, she merely said, "They're getting old, less reliable. I need to buy newer ones."

Robert regarded her silently. He didn't know whether to hug her or shake her, and in fact he could do neither. It was obvious that she was trying to raise money by any means available, and he wanted to put his arms around her and tell her it would be all right. But his instinct to protect his own had to be stifled, at least for now. Despite his decision that she was largely innocent in Mercer's espionage dealings, the small chance that he was wrong about her wouldn't let him relent. Soon he would know for certain, one way or the other. But if she sold the rental boats, what means would Mercer use to deliver the goods? Every one of those rental boats was now equipped with tiny electronic bugs that would allow them to be tracked; if Mercer was forced to use some other boat, or even change his method of delivery entirely, Robert would lose his control of the situation.

On the plus side, he was certain Mercer would act soon. They had intercepted a very suspicious phone call, putting them on the alert. It didn't matter if Evie managed to sell a couple of boats, or even most of them, so long as she had one remaining when Mercer made his move. He would simply have to monitor the situation and step in to prevent a sale if it looked as if she would manage to unload all of them.

Aloud he asked, "Have you had any offers yet?"

She shook her head, a wry smile curving her mouth. "I just put the sign up this morning."

"Have you put an ad in any of the newspapers?"

"Not yet, but I will."

That might bring in more customers than he could block, he thought with a sigh. The easiest way would be to stop the ads from being printed; there weren't that many area newspapers. The phones both here and at her house were being monitored, so he would know which papers she called. Somehow he hadn't expected to have so much trouble keeping abreast of her maneuvers. Evie was a surprisingly resourceful woman.

Five days later, Evie rushed in from overseeing a delivery of gas to answer the phone. She pushed a wisp of hair out of her face as she lifted the receiver. "Shaw's Marina."

"Evie? This is Tommy Fowler."

As soon as she heard his voice, she knew. Slowly she sank down onto the stool, her legs so weak that she needed the support. "What's the verdict?" she asked, though she knew the answer.

He sighed. "I'm sorry, hon. The board of directors says we already have too many real-estate loans. They won't okay the mortgage."

Her lips felt numb. "It isn't your fault," she said. "Thanks, anyway."

"It isn't a lost cause. Just because we aren't making that type of loan right now doesn't mean other banks aren't.''

"I know, but I have a deadline, and it's down to fourteen days. It's taken you longer than that to tell me no. How long would it take to process a loan at any other bank?''

"Well, we took longer than usual. I'm sorry as hell about it, Evie, but I had no idea the okay wouldn't go through. Go to another bank. Today, if possible. An appraiser will have to make an estimate of the house's value, but it's waterfront property and in good shape, so it's worth a lot more than the amount you want to mortgage. Getting an appraiser out there is what will take so much time, so get started as soon as you can.''

"I will," she said. "Thanks, Tommy.''

"Don't thank me," he said glumly. "I couldn't do anything. Bye, hon.''

She sat there on the stool for a long time after she hung up the phone, trying to deal with her disappointment and sense of impending disaster. Though she had been worried, the worry had been manageable, because even though she had been making contingency plans, she had been certain the mortgage would go through.

She hadn't sold a single boat.

Time was of the essence, and she didn't have a lot of faith in getting a loan through any other bank. It was as if an evil genie was suddenly in control of things, inflicting her with malfunctioning machinery and uncooperative banks.

Still, she had to try. She couldn't give up and perhaps lose the marina from lack of effort. She *wouldn't* lose the marina. No matter what, she simply refused to let it go. If she couldn't get a mortgage, if she couldn't sell the boats, she had one other option. It was strictly last-resort, but it was there.

She picked out a bank with a good reputation and called to make an appointment with a loan officer for the next morning.

The heat was already intense the next day when she was getting ready. Despite the ceiling fans, her skin was damp with perspiration, making her clothes cling to her. Robert hadn't asked why her house was so hot, but the past three nights he had insisted on taking her to his home and bringing her back after breakfast. This morning she had showered at his house as she usually did, then asked him to bring her home earlier than usual because she had a business appointment at nine. He hadn't asked any questions about that, either.

She retrieved her copy of the deed from the fire-proof security box under the bed and braced herself like a soldier going to war. If this bank wouldn't give her a loan, she wasn't going to waste any more time going to another one. Time was too short. She would rather be too hasty than take the chance of losing the marina.

She rolled the truck window down, and the wind blowing in her face cooled her as she drove to the bank. The heat was building every day, and soon it would be unbearable in the house if she didn't turn on the air-conditioning. She smiled grimly. She might as well turn it on; one way or the other, she would have the money to pay the power bill.

Her appointment was with a Mr. Waldrop, who turned out to be a stocky, sandy-haired man in his late forties. He gave her a strangely curious look as he led her into his small office. Evie took one of the two comfortable chairs arranged in front of the desk, and he settled into the big chair behind it.

"Now then, Mrs. Shaw, what can we do for you today?"

Concisely, Evie told him what she needed, then pulled the copy of the deed from her purse and placed it on his desk. He unfolded it and looked it over, pursing his lips as he read.

"It looks straightforward enough." He opened his desk and extracted a sheet of paper. "Fill out this financial statement, and we'll see what we can do."

Evie took the sheet of paper and went out to one of the small seating areas off the lobby. While she was answering the multitude of questions, her pen scratching across the paper, someone else came in to see Mr. Waldrop. She glanced up automatically, then realized she knew the newcomer, not an unusual occurrence in a small town like Guntersville. He was Kyle Brewster, a slightly shady businessman who owned a small discount store, dealing in seconds and salvage material. He was also known as a gambler and had been arrested once, several years back, when the back room of a pool hall had been raided on the information that an illegal game was being conducted there. Evie supposed that Kyle was fairly successful in his gambling; his style of living was considerably higher than the income from the discount store could provide.

The door to Mr. Waldrop's office was left open.

She couldn't hear what Kyle was saying, only the indistinct drawl of his voice, but Mr. Waldrop's voice was more carrying. "I have the check right here," he was saying cheerfully. "Do you want to cash it, or deposit it into your account?"

Evie returned her attention to the form, feeling slightly heartened. If the bank would lend money to Kyle Brewster, she saw no reason why it wouldn't lend money to her. Her business was more profitable, and her character was certainly better.

Kyle left a few minutes later. When Evie completed the form, someone else had come in and was with Mr. Waldrop. She sat patiently, watching the hour hand on the clock inch to ten o'clock, then beyond. At ten-thirty, the other customer left and she carried the form in to Mr. Waldrop.

"Have a seat," he invited as he looked over the information she had provided. "I'll be back in a few minutes." He carried the form out with him.

Evie crossed her fingers, hoping the loan would be okayed that morning, pending an appraisal of the property. She would get the bank's appraiser out to the house if she had to call him ten times a day and hound him until he appeared.

More time ticked by. She shifted restlessly in the chair, wondering what was taking so long. But the bank seemed busy this morning, so perhaps the person Mr. Waldrop had taken the form to was also tied up, and Mr. Waldrop was having to wait.

Forty-five minutes later Mr. Waldrop returned to his office. He settled into his chair and tapped his fingertips together. "I'm sorry, Mrs. Shaw," he said with real regret. "We simply aren't making this type of loan right now. With the economy the way it is..."

Evie sat up straight. She could feel the blood draining from her face, leaving the skin tight. Enough was enough. "The economy is fine," she interrupted sharply. "The recession didn't hit down here the way it did in other parts of the country. And your bank is one of the strongest in the country. There was an article in one of the Birmingham papers just last week about this bank buying another one in Florida. What I want to know is why you would lend money to someone like Kyle Brewster, a known gambler with a police record, but you won't make a loan on a property worth five or six times that amount."

Mr. Waldrop flushed guiltily. A distressed look came into his eyes. "I can't discuss Mr. Brewster's business, Mrs. Shaw. I'm sorry. I don't make the decisions on whether or not to okay a loan."

"I realize that, Mr. Waldrop." She also realized something else, something so farfetched she could hardly believe it, but it was the only thing that made any sense. "I didn't have a chance of getting the loan, did I? Having me fill out that form was just for show. Someone is stepping in to block the loan, someone with a lot of influence, and I want to know who it is."

His flush turned even darker. "I'm sorry," he mumbled. "There's nothing I can tell you."

She stood and retrieved the deed from his desk. "No, I don't suppose you can. It would mean your job, wouldn't it? Goodbye, Mr. Waldrop."

She was almost dizzy with fury as she went out to the truck. The heat slammed into her like a blow, but she ignored it, just as she ignored the scorching heat of the truck's upholstery. She sat in the parking lot, tapping her finger against the steering wheel as she stared unblinkingly at the traffic streaming by on U.S. 431.

Someone wanted the marina. No one had made an offer to buy it, so that meant whoever it was knew she wasn't likely to sell. This mysterious someone was powerful enough, well-connected enough with the local bankers, to block her attempts to get a loan. Not only that, the original transfer of the loan from her bank to the New York bank had probably been arranged by this person, though she couldn't think of anyone she knew with that kind of power.

She couldn't think why anyone would want her little marina enough to go to such an extreme. Granted, she had made a lot of improvements in it, and business was better every year. When she paid off the outstanding debt, the marina would turn a healthy profit, but it wouldn't be the kind of money that would warrant such actions from her unknown enemy.

Why didn't matter, she thought with the stark clarity that comes in moments of crisis. Neither did *who*. The only thing that mattered was that she kept the marina.

There was one move she could make that wouldn't be blocked, because she wouldn't be the one obtaining the loan. She wouldn't breathe a word about this to anyone, not even Becky, until it was a done deal.

Numbly she started the truck and pulled out into traffic, then almost immediately pulled off again when she spotted a pay phone outside a convenience store. Her heart was thudding with slow, sickening power against her ribs. If she let herself think about it, she might not have the nerve to do it. If she waited until she got back home, she might look around at the dear, familiar surroundings and not be able to make the call. She had to do it now. It was a simple choice. If she lost the marina, she stood to lose everything, but if she sacrificed the house now, she would be able to keep the marina.

She slid out of the truck and walked to the pay phone. Her legs seemed to be functioning without any direction from her brain. There was no phone book. She called Information and got the number she wanted, then fed in another quarter and punched the required numbers. Turning her back on the traffic, she put her finger in her other ear to block out noise as she listened to the ringing on the other end of the line.

"Walter, this is Evie. Do you and Helene still want to buy my place on the river?"

"She stopped at a convenience store immediately after leaving the bank and made a call from a pay phone," the deep voice reported to Robert.

"Could you tell what number she called?"

"No, sir. Her position blocked the numbers from view."

"Could you hear anything she was saying?"

"No, sir. I'm sorry. She kept her back turned, and the traffic was noisy."

Robert rubbed his jaw. "Have you checked to see if it was the marina she called?"

"First thing. No such luck. She didn't call Mercer, either."

"Okay. It worries me, but there isn't anything we can do about it. Where is she now?"

"She drove straight home from the convenience store."

"Let me know if she makes any more calls."

"Yes, sir."

Robert hung up and stared thoughtfully out at the lake as he tried to imagine who she had called, and why. He didn't like the angry little suspicion that was growing. Had she called the unknown third party to whom Mercer had been selling the stolen computer programs? Was she involved up to her pretty little neck after all? He had backed her up against a financial wall, just to find out for certain, but he had a sudden cold, furious feeling that he wasn't going to like the results worth a damn.

Chapter 15

"Would you like to go fishing this morning?" Robert asked lazily, his voice even deeper than usual. "We've never been out in a boat together."

It was six-thirty. The heat wave was continuing, each day seeing temperatures in the high nineties, and it was supposed to reach the hundred mark for the next few days, at least. Even at that early hour, Evie could feel the heat pressing against the windows.

It was difficult to think. Robert had just finished making love to her, and her mind was still sluggish with a surfeit of pleasure. He had awakened her before dawn and prolonged their loving even more than usual. Her entire body still throbbed from his touch, the echoes of pleasure still resounding in her flesh. The sensation of having him inside her lingered, though he had withdrawn and moved to lie beside her. Her head was cradled on one muscled arm, while his other arm lay heavily across her lower abdomen. She would have liked nothing better than to snuggle against him and doze for a while, then wake to even more lovemaking. It was only when she was sleeping, or when Robert was making love to her, that she was able to forget what she was doing.

But the throb of pleasure was lessening, and a dull ache resumed its normal place in her chest. "I can't," she said. "I have some errands to run." Errands such as finding a place to live. Walter and Helene Campbell had jumped at the chance to buy her house. They had wanted it for years and had decided to pay cash for it and worry about the financing later, afraid she would change her mind if she had a chance to think about it. Evie had promised she would be out within two weeks.

She couldn't bring herself to tell Robert, at least, not yet. She was afraid he would feel pressured to ask her to live with him, when he seemed perfectly satisfied with things the way they were now. It was difficult to think of anyone pressuring Robert to do anything he didn't want to do, and he might not offer, but neither did she want him to think she was hinting that he should. It would be best to find an apartment or house for rent first, then tell him about it.

For that matter, she hadn't told Becky, either. She hadn't told anyone. She had made her decision, but hadn't managed to come to terms with it yet. Every time she thought about moving, tears burned in her eyes. She couldn't bear to go into the explanations and listen to the arguments.

She didn't let herself think about who was behind all these financial maneuverings. First she had to concentrate on saving the marina and finding a place to live. After that was settled, she would try to find out who had been doing this to her.

"What kind of errands?" Robert asked, nuzzling her ear. His hand stroked warmly over her stomach, then covered her left breast. Her nipple, still sensitized from the strong suckling he had subjected it to a short while ago, twinged with a sharp sensation and immediately puckered against his palm. Her breathing deepened. Rather than becoming less intense with familiarity, his sensual power over her body seemed to increase each time he took her.

"I have to pay a few bills and do some shopping," she lied, and wondered why he'd asked. He had no compunction about taking over every facet of her private life but seldom inquired about what she did when they weren't together.

"Why not put it off until tomorrow?" His nuzzling was growing a bit more purposeful, and she closed her eyes as pleasure began to warm throughout her body again.

"I can't," she repeated regretfully. He rolled her nipple between this thumb and forefinger, making it even harder. She caught her breath at the tug of desire, as if the nerves of her nipples were directly connected to those in her loins.

"Are you certain?" he murmured, pressing his open mouth against the rapid pulse at the base of her throat.

Going fishing didn't tempt her, at least not in this heat. Lying in bed with him all morning, though, was so tempting it took all of her willpower to resist. "I'm certain," she forced herself to say. "It has to be done today."

Another man might have turned surly at having his advances refused, but Robert only sighed as he rested his head once again on the pillow. "I suppose we should get up, then."

"I suppose." She turned into him, pressing her face against his chest. "Hold me, just for a minute."

His arms tightened around her, satisfyingly tight. "What's wrong?"

"Nothing," she whispered. "I just like for you to hold me."

She felt his muscles tense. Abruptly he rolled on top of her, his hair-roughened thighs pushing hers apart. Startled, she looked up into slitted green eyes, glittering beneath those heavy black lashes. She couldn't read his expression but sensed his tightly contained violence.

"What—" she began to ask.

He thrust heavily into her, the power of his penetration making her body arch and shudder. He had had her only a little while before, but he was as hard as if that had never happened, so hard that she felt bruised by the impact of his flesh against hers. She gasped and clutched his shoulders for support. Not since the first time he'd taken her had he moved so powerfully. A primal feminine fear beat upward on tiny wings and mingled with an equally primitive sense of excitement. He wasn't hurting her, but the threat was there, and the challenge was whether she could handle him in this dangerous mood, all raw, demanding masculinity.

Desire flooded through her. She dug her nails into his muscular buttocks, pulling him deeper, arching her hips higher to take all of him. He grunted, his teeth clenched against the sound. Evie locked him to her, as fiercely female as he was dominatingly male, not only accepting his thrusts but demanding them. The sensation spiraled rapidly inside her, burning out of control, and she bit his shoulder. He cursed, the word low and hoarse, then slid his arms under her bottom to lift her even more tightly against him. All of his heavy weight bore her into the mattress as they strained together.

The sensation peaked, and Evie cried out as she shuddered wildly in the throes of pleasure. His hips hammered three more times; then he stiffened and began to shake as satisfaction took him, too. He ground his body against hers, as if he could meld their flesh.

The room slowly stopped spinning about her. She heard the twin rhythms of their panting breaths begin to calm. His heartbeat seemed to be thudding through her body, until it was in sync with her own. Their bodies were sealed together with sweat, heat rolling off them in waves.

Their first lovemaking of the morning had lasted an hour. This time, it hadn't taken even five minutes. The fury and speed of it, the raw power, left her even more exhausted than she'd been before.

What had aroused him so violently? After their first night Robert had been a slow, considerate lover, but he had just taken her like a marauder.

He was very heavy on top of her, making breathing difficult. She gasped, and he shifted his weight to the side. Pale green eyes opened, the expression still shuttered. His mouth had a ruthless line to it. "Stay with me today," he demanded.

Regret pierced her, sharp and poignant. "I can't," she said. "Not today."

For a split second something frightening flickered in his eyes, then was gone. "I tried," he said with rueful ease, rolling off her and sitting up. He stretched, rolling his shoulders and lifting his muscled arms over his head. Evie eyed his long, powerful back with pleasure and approval. The layered muscles were tight and hard, the deep hollow of his spine inviting kisses, or clutching hands. He was wide at the shoulders, his body tapering in a lean vee to his hips. She reached out and ran a lingering hand over the round curve of his buttocks, loving the cool resilience of his flesh.

He looked at her over his shoulder, and she saw a smile come into those green eyes. He leaned over to kiss her, his mouth lingering warmly for a moment; then with a yawn he was off the bed and heading toward the shower. She watched him until he closed the bathroom door behind him, drinking in his tall, naked body. She felt like smacking her lips, like a child drooling after a tasty treat. He was a fine figure of a man, all right. Sometimes, when she saw him sprawled naked and sleepy beside her, it was all she could do to keep from attacking him. She lay in bed for a while, listening to the shower run and entertaining a wicked, delicious fantasy in which he was tied to the bed and totally at her mercy.

But a glance at the clock told her that time was still ticking away. Sighing, she got out of bed and slipped into his shirt, then went to the kitchen to make coffee.

When she returned, he was just coming out of the bathroom, a towel draped around his neck but otherwise still completely naked. His skin was glowing from the shower, his black hair wet and slicked back.

"I put on the coffee," she said as she went to take her turn in the shower.

"I'll start breakfast. What do you want this morning?"

The thought of what she had to do that day killed her appetite. "I'm not hungry. I'll just have coffee."

But when she had showered and dressed, she went into the kitchen to find that he had his own ideas about what she was having for breakfast. A bowl of cereal, as well as a glass of orange juice and the requested coffee, was sitting at her customary place at the table. "I'm really not hungry," she repeated, lifting the coffee cup and inhaling the fragrant steam before sipping.

"Just a few bites," he cajoled, taking his own place beside her. "You need to keep up your strength for tonight."

She gave him a heated, slumberous look, remembering her fantasy. "Why? Are you planning something special?"

"I suppose I am," he said consideringly. "It's special every time we make love."

Her heart swelled in her chest, making it impossible for her to speak. She simply looked at him, her golden brown eyes glowing.

He picked up the spoon and put it into her hand.

"Eat. I've noticed you haven't been eating much while it's been so hot, and you're losing weight."

"Most people would consider that a good thing," she pointed out.

His black eyebrows lifted. "I happen to like your butt as round as it is now, and your breasts perfectly fit my hands. I don't want to sleep with a stick. Eat."

She laughed, amused by his description of her rear end, and dipped the spoon into the cereal. It was her favorite brand, of course; once he had seen the box in her cabinets, a box of the same cereal had taken up residence in his.

She managed to choke down a few bites, more than she wanted and not enough to satisfy him, which was a reasonable compromise. The cereal felt like a lump in her stomach.

Less than an hour later he kissed her goodbye at her door. "I'll see you tonight, sweetheart. Take care."

As she entered the house, she thought it a little odd for him to have added that last admonition. What on earth did he think she would be doing?

Sadly she dressed for work, so she wouldn't have to come back to the house before going to the marina. She wouldn't be braiding her hair in front of this mirror very many more times, she thought. After this afternoon, the house would no longer belong to her. Walter and Helene were getting a real estate agent, a friend of theirs, to handle the transaction immediately. They were supposed to bring all the paperwork to the marina this afternoon, along with a cashier's check in the specified amount. Evie was taking the deed to the property, the surveyor's report that she had had done when she inherited the house, as well as the certification of the title search that had also been done at that time. It was a measure of their trust in her that they were willing to forgo another title search, probably against their agent friend's advice.

She addressed an envelope to the bank in New York, stamped it and added it to her stack of papers. She would take the cashier's check immediately to her bank, desposit it and have another cashier's check made out in the amount of the outstanding loan against the marina. Then she would express-mail that check to New York, to Mr. Borowitz's attention. All her financial troubles would be over.

She wouldn't have her home any longer, but she could live anywhere, she told herself. The marina was more important, the means of her support. With it, she could someday buy another house. It wouldn't hold the memories this one did, but she would make it into a home.

She took a last look in the mirror. "Standing here won't get anything done," she said softly to herself and turned away.

She spent the morning driving around Guntersville. She had checked a few of the rental ads in the newspaper but didn't want to call them yet, preferring to see the houses and the neighborhoods before calling. She knew she was just stalling, despite the urgency of the situation, but somehow actually making contact was beyond her at the moment. She gave herself a stern talking-to, but it didn't help much. She didn't like any of the houses she saw.

It was almost noon when she came to a decision.

She made an abrupt turn, causing a car behind her to squeal its tires and the irate driver to lean on the horn. Muttering an apology, she cut through a shopping-center parking lot and back onto the highway, but in the opposite direction.

The apartment complex she had chosen was new, less than two years old, incongruously known as the Chalet Apartments. She stopped the truck outside the office and went inside. Twenty minutes later she was the new resident of apartment 17, which consisted of a living room and combination dining room/kitchen downstairs, along with a tiny laundry area just big enough to hold a washer and dryer, and two bedrooms upstairs. There were no one-bedroom apartments available. She paid a deposit, collected two sets of keys and went back out to the truck.

It was done. She doubted she would be happy there, but at least she would have a roof over her head while she took her time looking for a house.

The cellular phone beeped, and Robert answered it as he threaded his way through the traffic on Gunter Avenue, the one-way street that bisected Guntersville's downtown area and also ran through a neighborhood of grand old houses that looked turn-of-the-century.

"I think she spotted me."

"What happened?" he asked in a clipped tone.

"First she just drove around, all over town. I had to hang back so I wouldn't be as easy to spot. She slowed down several times but didn't stop anywhere. Maybe she was looking for something. Then she got on the highway, going south toward Albertville. She was on the inside lane, I was on the outside. All of a sudden, without a turn signal, she whipped the truck into a parking lot and nearly got hit doing it. I was in the wrong lane and couldn't follow her. By the time I got turned around, she'd vanished."

"Damn." Robert felt both tired and angry. Just when he'd been convinced of Evie's innocence, she was suddenly doing some very suspicious things. She was obviously worried about the marina, but there was something else on her mind, something she was trying to keep hidden. This morning, in bed, he had been seized by the urgent need to keep her with him all day, thereby preventing her from doing anything foolish. He wasn't used to women refusing any request he made, but Evie didn't appear to have any trouble doing it. She had said no with insulting ease.

Furious, he had even tried to seduce her into staying with him, only to lose his control, something he'd sworn wouldn't happen again. And afterward she'd still said no.

"I'll pick her up again when she comes to the marina," the man said in his ear. "I'm sorry, sir."

"It wasn't your fault. No tail's perfect."

"No, sir, but I should have been more careful about letting her see me."

"Have two cars next time, so you can swap."

"Yes, sir."

Robert ended the call and replaced the receiver. It took all his self-control to keep from driving to the marina to wait for her so he could shake some sense into her as soon as he saw her. But he had to play this through to the end.

As mundane as it was, he had his own errand to

run that day: grocery shopping. It wasn't something he normally did for himself, but it wasn't an onerous duty. Despite its strangeness, or perhaps because of it, he didn't mind doing it. Southerners imbued grocery shopping with the same casualness that characterized almost everything else they did. Shoppers ambled down the aisles, stopping to talk with chance-met acquaintances or to strike up conversations with strangers. The first time he had gone into the big grocery store, he had been amused by the thought that a New Yorker relaxed in the park with more energy than Southerners shopped. But when in Rome... He had learned to slow his own pace, to keep from smashing into old ladies who had stopped to pass the time of day.

Today, though, he wasn't in the mood to be amused. It went against his protective, controlling nature to leave Evie to hang herself with all the evidential rope he was feeding to both her and Mercer. He wanted to snatch her away from here, kidnap her if necessary. But if she *were* involved with Mercer, that would scare off the others and they might never be caught. Not knowing for certain, one way or the other, was driving him crazy with frustration.

Two more days. From the telephone calls they had intercepted, they knew that Mercer would transfer more stolen data the day after tomorrow. Evie hadn't been able to sell any of the rental boats, so that was one less problem for Robert. It didn't matter which boat Mercer took, since they were all wired. As a precaution, he had also had Evie's boat wired. In two days it would all be over except for the cleanup. In three days, if all went on schedule, he would be back in New York, and Evie would be with him.

He wouldn't need many groceries, just enough for three days, but he was completely out of coffee and almost out of food, and he didn't want to eat in restaurants for three days. He strode through the aisles of the grocery store, his expression remote as he planned the damage-control measures he would use. Operating with his usual efficiency, he was in and out of the store within fifteen minutes. As he walked out the automatic doors with a grocery bag in his arms, though, the woman just entering through the other set of doors stopped and stared at him.

"Robert."

He paused, immediately recognizing Evie's sister, Becky. Another shopper was exiting behind him, and he stepped out of the way. "Hello, Becky. How are you?" He smiled faintly. "And how's Jason? I haven't seem him at the marina again."

"Didn't Evie tell you? He can't come back to the marina for the rest of the summer. That's a real punishment to him," Becky said dryly. "The marina's one of his favorite places." She too, stepped away from the doors. "There's no sense standing here blocking traffic. I'll walk you to your car."

They strolled across the hot, sticky pavement. The heat was smothering, and sweat began to gather almost immediately on his skin. Wryly he waited, seeing Becky's determination plain on her face. The protective older sister wanted to have a heart-to-heart talk with him, to make certain he didn't hurt Evie.

They reached the Jeep, and he stored the groceries inside, leaving the door open so some of the heat inside could dissipate. He leaned against the vehicle and calmly eyed her. "You worried about Evie?" he prompted.

She flashed him a rueful look. "Am I that easy to read?"

"She mentioned that you're a bit protective," he murmured.

Becky laughed and pushed her hair out of her face. Her hair was darker than Evie's, but in that moment Robert saw a flash of resemblance, a similarity in expression and in the husky tone of their voices. "The big-sister syndrome," she said. "I didn't use to be this bad, only since—"

She stopped, and Robert felt his curiosity stir. "Since when?"

Becky didn't answer immediately, instead turning her gaze to the traffic on the highway. It was a delaying tactic, to give her time to think and organize her answer. He waited patiently.

"Are you serious about her?" she asked abruptly.

He wasn't accustomed to being interrogated about his intentions, serious or otherwise, but he quelled his surge of irritation. Becky was asking only out of concern for Evie, an emotion he shared. In a very level tone he said, "I intend to marry her."

Becky closed her eyes on a sigh of relief. "Thank God," she said.

"I didn't realize the state of our relationship was so critical," he said, still in that cool, dead-level tone.

Becky's eyes opened, and she gave him a considering look. "You can be very intimidating, can't you?"

He almost smiled. If he could, it obviously wasn't

working on her. He'd never managed to intimidate Evie, either.

Becky sighed and looked again at the traffic. "I was worried. I didn't know how important Evie is to you, and...well, the success of your relationship *is* critical to her."

His curiosity became intense. "In what way?"

Becky didn't answer that directly, either. Instead she asked, "Has she told you about Matt?"

Robert's eyes glittered suddenly. "Probably more than even you know," he said, his voice deepening as he remembered the first time he'd made love to Evie.

"About how he died?"

Sweat trickled down his back, but suddenly nothing could have moved him from the scorching asphalt parking lot. "He died in a car accident, didn't he?" He couldn't remember if Evie had told him that, or if it had been in the report he'd requested on Matt Shaw.

"Yes, the day after they married." She paused, organizing her thoughts, and again she made what appeared to be a shift in topic. "Our father died when Evie was fifteen. I was twenty, already married, already about to be a mother. A year later our mother died. Can you understand the difference in the way losing our parents affected us?" she asked, her voice strained. "I loved them both dearly, but I had built my home with Paul. I had him, I had my son, I had an entire life away from my parents. But losing Daddy shook Evie's foundations, and then when Mother died...Evie didn't just lose Mother, she lost her home, too. She came to live with Paul and me, and we loved having her, but it wasn't the same for her. She was still just a kid, and she had lost the basis of her life.''

Robert stood silently, all his attention on this insight into Evie's past life. She didn't talk about her childhood much, he realized. They had talked about a lot of things, sitting on the deck at night with all the lights off and the starry sky spread like a quilt overhead, but it was as if Evie had closed a mental door on her life before Matt's death.

''But she had Matt,'' Becky said softly. ''He was a great kid. We'd known him all his life, and I can't remember when they hadn't been inseparable, first as buddies, then as sweethearts. They were the same age, but even as young as he was, when Daddy died, Matt was right there beside Evie. He was there with her when Mother died. I think he was her one constant, the only person other than me who had been there for as long as she could remember. But I had my own family, and Evie had Matt. He put a smile back in her eyes, and because she had him, she weathered the loss of our parents. I remember what she was like back then, a giggling teenager as rowdy as Jason is now, and full of mischief.''

''I can't picture Evie as rowdy,'' he commented, because Becky's voice had become strained, and he wanted to give her a moment to compose herself. ''There's something so solemn about her.''

''Yes, there is,'' Becky agreed. ''Now.''

The jealousy he thought he had banished swelled to life again. ''Because of Matt's death.''

Becky nodded. ''She was in the car with him.'' Tears welled in her eyes. ''For the rest of my life,

I'll carry two pictures of Evie in my mind. One is of her on her wedding day. She was so young and beautiful—so *glowing*—that it hurt to look at her. Matt couldn't take his eyes off her. The next time I saw her, she was in a hospital bed, lying there like a broken doll, her eyes so empty that—'' She stopped, shuddering.

"They had spent the night in Montgomery and were going on to Panama City the next morning. It was raining. It was Sunday, and they were in a rural area. There wasn't much traffic. A dog ran out into the highway, and they hit it, and Matt lost control of the car. The car left the road and rolled at least twice, then came to a stop, on its right side, in a stand of trees. Evie was pinned on the bottom. Matt was hanging in his seat belt above her. She couldn't get out, couldn't get to him, and he b-bled to death in front of her, his blood dripping down on her. He was conscious, she said.'' Furiously Becky dashed the tears from her cheeks. "No one saw the car for a long time, what with the rain and the trees blocking the view. He knew he was dying. He told her he loved her. He told her goodbye. He'd been dead for over an hour before anyone saw the car and came to help.''

Robert turned to stone, his eyes burning as he pictured, far too clearly, what a young girl had gone through that rainy Sunday. Then he reached out automatically and took Becky in his arms, holding her head against his shoulder while she wept.

"I'm sorry,'' she finally managed, lifting her head and wiping her eyes yet again. "It's just that, when

I let myself think about it, it tears my heart out all over again.''

"Yes," he said. Still holding her with one arm, he fished his handkerchief out of his pocket and gently wiped her face.

"She's never let herself love anyone else," she said fiercely. "Do you understand? She hasn't risked letting anyone else get close to her. She's stuck with the people she already loved, before the accident— Paul and me, Jason and Paige, and a few, very few, special friends, but no one else. If you hadn't pulled her and Jason out of the river, she would have drowned rather than let him go, because she couldn't have stood to lose anyone else she loves. She's been so...so *solitary,* keeping everyone a safe distance from her heart.''

"Until me," he said.

Becky nodded and managed a wavery little smile. "Until you. I didn't know whether to be glad or terrified, so I've been both. I want her to have what I've got, a husband I love, kids I love, a family that will give her a reason to go on living when someone else dies.'' She saw the sudden flare in Robert's eyes and said quickly, "No, she never said anything about suicide, not even right after Matt died. That isn't what I meant. She recovered from her injuries—both legs were broken, some ribs, and she had a concussion— and did exactly what the doctors told her, but you could see that she wasn't interested. For *years,* life for her was just going through the motions, and every day was an effort. It took a long time, but finally she found a sort of peace. Evie's incredibly strong. In her place, I don't know if I could have managed it.''

Robert kissed Becky's forehead, touched and pleased by this fiercely competent woman's concern for her sister. He would, he realized, like having her for a sister-in-law. "You can put down your shield and sword, and rest," he said gently. "I'll take care of her now."

"You'd better," Becky said, her fierceness not one bit abated. "Because she's already paid too much for loving people. God only knows where she found the courage to love you. I've been terrified that you didn't care about her, because if you waltzed out of here at the end of the summer, it might well destroy her."

Robert's eyes glittered. "When I waltz out of here," he said, "I'm taking her with me."

Chapter 16

Walter and Helene Campbell were in their mid-sixties, retired, comfortable but not wealthy. Evie's house was just what they wanted, well-built and maintained, but old enough and small enough that her asking price was much less than what they would have paid for a new house on the lakefront. They were both thrilled to the point of giddiness at their unexpected good fortune, for though they had asked several times if she would sell, they had long since given up hope that she would.

They arrived at the marina over half an hour early, their estate agent in tow and bearing a huge sheaf of papers. Having never bought or sold a house before, Evie was struck by the amount of paperwork it evidently required and amazed that the agent had managed to get it all prepared in less than a day.

There weren't sufficient chairs for everyone to sit down, so they stood grouped around the counter. The agent explained the purpose of each document as he presented it first for her signature, then the Campbells'. After an hour of dedicated document-signing, it was finished. Evie had sold her house, and the check was in her hand.

She managed a smile to send the joyous Campbells on their way, but as soon as the door had closed behind them, her smile collapsed. She closed her eyes and shuddered in an effort to control the grief that had been growing since she had made the phone call the day before. No matter that she had told herself it was just a house and she could live anywhere, it was her *home,* and she had just lost part of herself. No, not lost it—sold it.

But the marina was a more important part of her foundation, and the green cashier's check in her hand had just saved it.

She wiped the betraying moisture from her eyes and braced her shoulders. She called Burt and told him she had to go to the bank and would be back in about half an hour. "Okay," he said, as laconic as ever, when she asked him to watch for customers.

The transaction at the bank took very little time. The Campbells' cashier's check was deposited and a new cashier's check cut in the amount she owed on the loan. Tommy Fowler saw her standing at the counter and came out to speak to her, his eyes anxious.

"How're you doing, Evie?"

She heard the worry in his tone and managed a

version of the same smile she had given the Campbells. "I'm okay. I have the money to pay the loan."

Relief flooded his face. "Great! That didn't take
long. So another bank gave you the mortgage?"

"No, I sold my house."

The relief faded, and he stared at her, aghast.
"Sold your house? But, Evie...God, why?"

She wasn't about to tell him, with the teller and
other customers listening, that she suspected someone of blocking the mortgage. "It was something I'd
been thinking about," she lied. "Now my bank account is healthy, the marina is out of debt and will
turn a pure profit, and I can take my time looking
for another house."

Varying expressions were flickering across
Tommy's face like slides. The final one, a rather uneasy relief, was testament to his belief in her pragmatic lie. "I guess it's worked out, then," he said.

She kept her smile intact with an effort. "Yeah, I
guess it has."

The teller handed the check over the counter to
her, and she slipped it into the envelope. "I'm getting this mailed today," she said to Tommy.
"Thanks for all you did."

"I didn't manage to do anything," he replied.

"Well, no, but you tried."

She left the bank and drove straight to the post
office, where the precious envelope was dispatched
by express mail. She felt a sense of finality. It was
done; she had gotten past this. It hadn't been easy,
but now she could move on.

Robert was waiting at the marina when she got

back. "Where have you been?" he demanded, striding up as she slid out of the truck.

She blinked at the unguarded fierceness of his tone. Robert was seldom overt in his reactions, except in bed. "The bank and the post office. Why?"

He didn't answer but caught her shoulders in a hard grasp and pulled her to him. His mouth was heavy and hungry, demanding rather than seducing a response from her. Evie made a muffled sound of surprise, her hands lifting to rest against his chest, but she gave him what he wanted, her mouth opening to admit the thrust of his tongue, her lips shaping to the pressure of his.

Passion rose sharply between them, strong and heady. She hadn't recovered her balance after the difficult events of the day and she melted against him, drawn irresistibly to the whipcord strength of his body. Although a whirlwind was tossing the rest of her life about, he wasn't swayed but remained solidly on his feet and in control. Though she had bitterly resisted—and feared—coming to depend on him, his very presence now made her feel better. She was both aroused and comforted by the familiarity of his body, his warm animal scent, all the subtle details by which she knew her mate.

He drew back, hampered by the public nature of the parking lot. Inside wouldn't be much better, with people coming and going. He threaded his hands through her hair, tilting her face back so he could read every nuance of her expression. He must have been pleased by the drowning look of desire he saw there, for his fingers tightened on her scalp. "Not here, damn it. But as soon as I get you home..." He didn't have to finish the sentence. Raw lust was on his face and in his voice, violent and intense.

Recalled to where she was, Evie cast a half-embarrassed look around and touched his hand as she slipped from his grasp. How many hours until they could go home? She didn't know if she could wait that long. Her body was throbbing.

The long afternoon was an exercise in self-control, and she wished the summer days weren't quite so long. She needed Robert, needed his driving presence within her, taking her into oblivion so she could forget everything but the almost narcotic pleasure of making love with him. She felt raw, her emotions sharp and too near the surface.

It was difficult, when she was finally able to close the marina that night, to hold to the schedule they had established. Robert wanted to take her straight to his house, but she resisted. "I don't want to leave my truck here overnight," she said. "You'd either have to bring me to pick it up in the morning or waste your morning hanging around so you could drive me to work."

"It wouldn't be a waste," he growled, his lean face taut, and she knew what he envisioned them doing to pass the time.

Temptation weakened her, but she shook her head again. "It would be so blatant, if my truck was still here and you brought me to work. Craig—"

"You're worried about Craig knowing that we sleep together?" he asked, amusement lighting his eyes. "He's seventeen, sweetheart, not seven."

"I know, but...this isn't New York. We're more conventional down here."

He was still smiling, but he gave in with good grace. "All right, protect his tender sensibilities, though I have to tell you that most teenage boys have the sensibility of a rhino in heat."

She laughed, and it felt good, her heart lightening. "Then let's just say that *I* wouldn't feel comfortable."

He kissed her forehead. "Then go home, sweetheart. I bought some fillets this afternoon, and I'll get them ready to grill before I pick you up."

"I have a better idea," she said. "You start grilling, and I'll drive over. That will save even more time."

He smiled again as he rubbed his thumb over her lower lip in a gentle caress. "You make me feel like a teenage rhino myself," he murmured, and she blushed.

Anticipation heated her blood as she drove home, preoccupying her so much that she showered and dressed without more than a twinge of sadness. Her heartbeat pounded in the rhythm of his name.

It was still hot, so hot that she couldn't bear the idea of encasing her legs in clothing, but she didn't want to wear shorts. She opted instead for a gauzy blue skirt and a sleeveless, scoop-necked chemise, with her breasts unconfined beneath. The floaty skirt was virtually transparent, clearly showing her legs, but allowed air to filter through the flimsy fabric and cool her skin. She would never have worn it out in public, but to Robert's house...yes, definitely.

He came to the door when he heard the truck in

his driveway. His face tightened as he watched her walk toward him. "God," he muttered. As soon as she was inside, he slammed the door and caught her arm, pulling her rapidly down the hall to the bedroom.

"What about the steaks?" she cried, startled by his haste despite the pleasant frustration of the afternoon.

"Screw the steaks," he said bluntly, wrapping his arms around her and falling across the bed. His heavy weight crushed her into the mattress. With a quick motion he flipped the skirt to her waist and caught the waistband of her panties, tugging them down her legs. When her feet were free, he tossed her underwear aside and pulled her thighs apart, kneeling between them.

Evie laughed, the sound low and provocative. He hadn't even kissed her, and her entire body was throbbing. He was tearing at his belt buckle with impatient fingers, and she added her hands to the confusion, trying to find the tab of his zipper and pull it down. She could feel the hard, swollen ridge of his sex, pushing at his clothing. He grunted as his length sprang free and lowered himself between her legs.

No matter how many times he took her, she always felt a small sense of surprise at his size and heat, and a flutter of uncertainty at the stretching sensation that followed the initial pressure as he sank deep within. She gasped, her entire body lifting to the impact. She was tender from the unbridled lovemaking of the morning, his thrusting sex rasping against inner tissues that were sensitive to the least touch. Intense pleasure rippled through her, tossing her unprepared into paroxysms of satisfaction. She cried out, her hands digging into his back as the shivery delight went on and on, past bearing, until she thought she would die if he didn't let the pleasure ebb. He was muttering hotly in her ear, sex words, the sound indistinct but the meaning clear.

And then he shuddered, too, holding himself deep as the spasms took him. Afterward, he lay heavily on her, both of them breathing deeply in the exhausted aftermath. Drowsily she let her eyes drift shut, only to open them again as he suddenly chuckled, the small movement shaking them both. "Definitely like a teenager," he murmured, nuzzling the lobe of her ear before taking it between his teeth and gently biting it. "No matter how often I have you, I want you again almost as soon as I move off you. The only time I'm satisfied is when we're like this." He thrust lazily, their bodies still linked.

"Then let's stay like this." She ran her hands down his muscular back, feeling the heat of him through the fabric of his shirt. "Someone will find us in a couple of weeks."

He laughed and kissed her. "They'd probably think, wow, what a way to go, but I'd prefer both of us being warm and pliable. If I want to keep you that way, I suppose I'd better feed you, hadn't I?" He kissed her again and rolled away to sit up.

She stretched, replete, the afternoon's aching frustration relieved. Even the hollowness in her chest had faded, though by no means vanished. She had never had this before, she thought dimly, this bone-deep sense of connection. And she wouldn't have it now if Robert had been less ruthlessly determined to have his way.

They spent the next couple of hours grilling the steaks, then sitting out on the deck after they had eaten and cleaned the kitchen. The night was thick and warm, the temperature still in the high eighties. Robert stretched out on a chaise longue and pulled Evie down on top of him. There were no lights on in the house, and the concealing darkness was like a blanket. They lay there in the heavy, peaceful silence, with his hand slowly moving over her back. Slowly his caresses grew more purposeful, and Evie melted against him. Her chemise top was lifted off over her head and dropped to the deck. She hadn't put her underwear back on, so when his hand moved under the gauzy skirt, he touched only the bare flesh of her thighs and buttocks. He cupped the twin mounds in his hands and held her hard against him, nestling his arousal in the soft junction of her thighs.

"You have on too many clothes," she murmured, kissing the underside of his jaw.

"You, on the other hand, hardly have on any."

"Whose fault is that?" Her wandering mouth nibbled down his neck. "I was completely dressed when I arrived here."

"I wouldn't say that, sweetheart. Even if your nipples hadn't been sticking out like little berries, the delicious jiggle of your breasts when you walked made it obvious you weren't wearing anything under your top. And this thing," he continued lazily, grasping a handful of material, "doesn't qualify as a skirt." Tiring of her mouth being on his throat rather than his own mouth, he pulled her up for a long kiss, during which his own clothing was opened and removed. Sighing with pleasure, she lifted the skirt out of the way and settled over him, gasping a little as he slid inside her.

Then they lay quietly again, bodies linked, content with the sensation as it was. The lights of a night fisherman drifted by on the lake, but they were shielded by the darkness. Sometime later it became difficult to lie still. Hidden impulses twinged deep inside, inviting undulating movement. She resisted, but knew he was feeling the same compulsion. He was growing even harder, reaching deeper into her, and a fine tension invaded his muscles as he lay motionless beneath her.

She pressed her forehead hard against his jaw, fighting not to move. He throbbed inside her, and she moaned softly. Her inner muscles clenched in helpless delight on his invading length, then did so again, and her soft cries floated in the night air as the moment took her. In an effort to control his own reaction, Robert gripped her bottom hard, his teeth clenched against the almost overwhelming need to give in. He won, but sweat beaded on his forehead from the struggle.

When she stilled, he lifted her from him and bent her over the end of the chaise. He knelt behind her, his thighs cupping hers, and thrust heavily into her moist, relaxed sheath. She clung to the chaise, unable to stifle her moans of pleasure as his rhythmic motion increased in speed and power. He convulsed, flooding her with warmth, and lay heavily over her for a long time, while his breathing slowed and his heartbeat returned to normal.

Recovered, he gathered their scattered clothing and pushed it into her arms, then lifted her and carried her inside, to the big bed that awaited them.

They slept late the next morning, until after nine o'clock. She yawned and stretched like a sleepy cat, and Robert held her close, stroking her tangled hair away from her face. As usual, he had awakened her at dawn with silent, drowsy lovemaking; then they had both gone back to sleep.

With a quick kiss and a lingering pat on her bare bottom, he left the bed and headed toward his shower. Evie yawned again and got up herself. She slipped into his shirt as she went to the kitchen to make coffee. "Robert, you need an automatic timer on your coffeemaker," she muttered to herself as she scooped the coffee into the round filter. Not that they would ever remember to prepare the coffee and set the timer before they went to bed.

Standing there in the sun-drenched kitchen, listening to the coffeemaker pop and hiss, she became aware that she felt strangely light, almost carefree. She hugged herself in an effort to contain the elusive feeling. She was happy, she thought with some surprise. Despite selling the house, she was happy. She had saved the marina, and she had Robert. Most of all, she had Robert.

Her love for him quietly grew each time she was with him. He was such a complicated, controlled, private man; no matter how often he made love to her, he still kept that inner core of himself inviolate, not allowing her or anyone else inside. Knowing that had no effect on the way she felt about him. He hadn't opened his heart to her, but that in no way made him less worthy of love. He might never love her, she realized. But if this was all he could give a woman, then she would take it.

A ringing interrupted the quiet. It sounded like a telephone, but the phone there in the kitchen definitely wasn't ringing, and this sound was muffled, as if it were in a different room. The line in Robert's office must be a different number, she realized. He was in the shower and wouldn't be able to hear it. It rang only once, though, and she realized that the answering machine there must have picked up the call.

She walked down the hall to the office and opened the door. The whirring sound of the fax machine greeted her. So it hadn't been a call, after all, but a fax.

The machine stopped whirring and lapsed into silence after having spat out only one sheet of paper. As she turned to go, her eye was caught by a name on the page, and curiously she turned back.

It was her name that had caught her attention.

The message was brief. "Mr. Borowitz just reported that a cashier's check from E. Shaw, in full payment of the outstanding amount, was delivered by express mail and received by him. His hands are tied. Further instructions?" The scrawled signature looked like "F. Koury."

Evie picked up the page and read it again. At first she was merely puzzled. Why would this F. Koury be telling Robert that she had paid the loan? And why would Mr. Borowitz be reporting it at all? Robert didn't even know about the loan, much less the threat of foreclosure.

Her mind stopped, along with her breathing. She hung there, paralyzed by a sickening realization. Robert knew all about it because he was the one who had been blocking her efforts to mortgage the house. He was also the reason why her loan had been bought, and why Mr. Borowitz had been so intractable in demanding full payment. He had been instructed to give her no cooperation at all, instructed by Robert Cannon. Her lover was her enemy.

Her chest was hurting. She gasped and resumed breathing, but the pain remained, a cold, heavy lump in her chest. The sense of betrayal was suffocating.

Obviously Robert was far wealthier and more powerful than she had imagined, to have this much influence, she thought with detached calm. She didn't know why he wanted her marina, but he obviously did. There were a lot of why's she couldn't comprehend, particularly right now. Maybe later, when she could think better, some of this would make sense.

Right now, all she could think was that Robert had tried to take over her marina and had cost her her home.

That distance she had sensed in him had been all too real. He hadn't committed his heart because, for him, it had all been business. Had he seduced her simply so he could stay close and keep tabs on what she was doing? Given what else he had done, that seemed to her like a reasonable assumption.

Her lips felt numb, and her legs moved like an automaton's as she left the office, carefully closing the door behind her. The damning fax was still in her hand as she returned to the kitchen.

The hopeless enormity of the situation overwhelmed her. How ironic that she had fallen in love with the man who was coolly trying to destroy her! Oh, she doubted he looked at it in such melodramatic terms, but then, he probably saw the whole thing as a successful business takeover, rather than a love affair.

She heard the shower cut off. With slow, achingly precise movements, she folded the fax and dropped it into the trash, then poured a cup of coffee. She desperately needed the caffeine, or anything, to bolster her. Her hands were shaking slightly as she lifted the cup to her lips.

She was standing in front of the window when Robert came into the kitchen a few moments later, wearing only a pair of jeans and still rubbing a towel across his chest. He stopped, his entire body clenching at the sight of her. God, she was breathtaking, with her mane of tawny gold hair loose and tousled. She was wearing only his shirt, and it was unbuttoned. There had never been another garment invented, he thought with a surge of desire, that looked better on a woman than a man's shirt. She was sipping coffee and looking out the window, lost in thought, her expression as calm and remote as a statue's.

He dropped the towel and went to her, sliding one arm around her as he took the cup and lifted it to his own lips. He imagined he could taste her on the rim, but then, his senses were so attuned to her that he could pick her out of a crowd blindfolded.

No woman had ever responded to him the way Evie did. She was pure fire in his arms, reveling in every thrust, tempting more from him. If he was gentle, she melted. If he was rough in his passion, she clung to him, clawed at him, her soaring desire feeding his own until they were both frenzied with need. He wanted her incessantly.

He smoothed his hand over the curve of her bottom, delighting in the silky texture of her flesh. "The shower's all yours, sweetheart."

"All right," she said automatically, but he had the impression she didn't really hear him. She was still looking out the window.

He tipped his head to see if he could tell what had her so interested. He saw only a wide expanse of lake, dotted with a few boats. "What are you looking at?"

"Nothing. Just the lake." She turned away from his embrace and left the kitchen.

Robert's brows briefly knit in puzzlement, but he was hungry, and breakfast took precedence at the moment. He had scarcely gotten the bacon started when Evie reappeared in the kitchen, fully dressed, and with her keys in her hand.

"A fax came in while you were in the shower," she said quietly.

He turned, going still at what he saw in her face—or rather, what he didn't see. She was pale and expressionless, her eyes empty. With a chill, he remembered how Becky had described the look in Evie's eyes after the accident and he knew it must have been something like this. She looked so terribly remote, as if she had somehow already left.

"Who was it from?" he asked, keeping his voice gentle while his mind raced, sorting through the possibilities, all of them damning. The worst-case scenario was if she was indeed working with Mercer and had found out that the trap was closing tight about them.

"An F. Koury."

"Ah." He nodded, concealing a sense of relief. "My secretary." Probably it had nothing to do with Mercer, then, but why was Evie looking so frozen?

"It's there in the trash, if you want to read it, but I can tell you what it said."

He leaned against the cabinet and crossed his arms, eyeing her carefully. "All right. Tell me."

"Mr. Borowitz notified your secretary that he'd received a cashier's check from E. Shaw for payment in full of the loan, and that his hands were tied. She asked for further instructions."

Robert's expression didn't change, but inwardly he was swearing viciously. Of all the things for Evie to stumble onto! It was less damaging, from a security standpoint, than anything connected with Mercer would have been, but a hell of a thing to try to explain to a lover. He'd never intended her to know about it. The pressure had been real, but he would never have let it go to foreclosure. He didn't rush into explanations but waited for her reaction so he could better gauge what to say to her. And how in hell had she managed to get the money to pay the loan?

"You're the reason I couldn't get a mortgage on my house," she said, her voice so strained it was almost soundless.

She'd put it together quickly, he thought. But then, from the beginning, she'd proven herself to be uncomfortably astute. "Yes," he said, disdaining to lie.

"You're behind the loan being sold to another bank in the first place."

He inclined his head and waited.

She was gripping the keys so tightly that her fingers were white. He noted that small giveaway of emotion held in check. She took several shallow breaths, then managed to speak again. "I want your boat gone from my marina by the end of the day. I'll refund the balance of the rent."

"No," he said gently, implacably. "I'm holding you to the agreement."

She didn't waste her breath on an argument she couldn't win. She had hoped he would have the decency to do as she asked, but given his ruthless streak, she hadn't really expected it.

"Then leave it there," she said, her voice as empty as her eyes. "But don't call me again, because I don't want to talk to you. Don't come by, because I don't want to see you."

Sharply he searched her expression, looking for a way to penetrate the wall she had thrown up between them. "You won't get rid of me that easily. I know you're angry, but—"

She laughed, but it was raw and hollow, not a sound of amusement. Robert winced. "Is that how you've decided to 'handle' me? I can see you watching me, trying to decide which angle to take to calm me down," she said. "You never just react, do you? You watch and weigh other people's reactions so you can manipulate them." She heard the strain in her voice and paused to regain control of it. "No, I'm not angry. Maybe in fifty years or so, it'll just be anger.'' She turned on her heel and started for the door.

''Evie!'' His voice cracked like a whiplash, and despite herself, she stopped, shivering at the force of will he commanded. This wasn't the cool strategist speaking but the ruthless conqueror.

''How did you pay off the loan?'' The words were still sharp.

Slowly she looked at him over her shoulder, her eyes dark and unguarded for a moment, stark with pain. ''I sold my house,'' she said, and walked out.

Chapter 17

Robert started to go after her, then stopped. Instead he swore and hit the countertop with his fist. He couldn't explain anything to her, not yet. Every instinct in his body screamed for him to stop her, but he forced himself to let her go. He stood rigidly, listening as the truck door slammed and the motor started. She didn't spin the wheels or anything like that; she simply backed out of the driveway and drove away without histrionics.

God! *She had sold her house.* The desperation of the action staggered him, and with sudden, blinding clarity he knew, beyond the faintest doubt, that she wasn't involved with Mercer in any way. A woman who could make money by espionage would never have sold her home to pay a debt. She had appeared to be leaving the marina and meeting with Mercer on the lake, but it must have been nothing more than damnable coincidence. Evie was totally innocent, and his machinations had cost her her home.

She wouldn't listen to anything he said right now, but after he had the espionage ring broken up and Mercer safely behind bars, he would force her to understand why he had threatened foreclosure on her loan. That he had suspected her of espionage was another rocky shoal he would have to navigate with care. He didn't imagine it would be easy to get back into her good graces, but in the end he would have her, because he didn't take no for an answer when he really wanted something. And he wanted Evie as he had never wanted anything or anyone else in his life.

He would have to make amends, of course, far beyond apologies and explanations. Evie was the least mercenary person he'd ever met, but she had a strong sense of justice, and an offer of reparation would strike a chord with her. He could buy her house from the new owners—they probably wouldn't be willing to sell at first, but he cynically suspected that doubling the price would change their minds— and present her with the deed, but he far preferred that she have a newer, bigger house. The simplest thing would be to deed over his own house to her. It meant nothing to him, he could buy a house anywhere he wanted, but Evie needed a base that was hers and hers alone. It would be a vacation home, a getaway when they needed a break from the hubbub of New York, a place for her to stay when she wanted to visit Becky.

He fished the damning fax out of the trash and

read it. Three concise sentences, Felice at her most efficient. There was nothing more he could do about the loan; realizing that, she had de-prioritized it and sent the information by fax so he could have it immediately but respond at his leisure, rather than calling and wasting both his time and hers. Felice was a genius at whittling precious seconds here and there so she would have more time to devote to the truly important matters. In this instance, however, her knack for superefficiency had worked against him and perhaps cost him Evie.

No. No matter what, he wouldn't let Evie go.

Evie drove automatically, holding herself together with desperate control. She tried to empty her mind, but it wasn't possible. How could she be so numb but hurt so much at the same time? She literally ached, as if she had been beaten, yet felt somehow divorced from her body. She had never felt as remote as she did now, or as cold and hollow. The heat of the sun washed over her, but it didn't touch her. Even her bones felt cold and empty.

Why? She hadn't asked him that and couldn't think of a reason that would matter. The why of it wasn't important. The hard fact was that he had sought her out for a reason that had nothing to do with love or even attraction, used the intimacy he had deliberately sought as a means to gather information that he wanted, and then turned that knowledge against her. How had he known about the loan in the first place? She supposed it was possible a credit report would have given him the information, but a far more likely explanation was that he had

GET 2

HOW TO GET YOUR
2 FREE BOOKS AND FREE GIFT!

1. Peel off the MIRA® sticker on the front cover. Place it in the space provided at right. This automatically entitles you to receive two free books and an exciting surprise gift.

2. Send back this card and you'll get 2 "The Best of the Best™" books. These books have a combined cover price of $11.98 or more in the U.S. and $13.98 or more in Canada, but they are yours to keep absolutely FREE!

3. There's <u>no</u> catch. You're under <u>no</u> obligation to buy anything. We charge nothing – ZERO – for your first shipment. And you don't have to make any minimum number of purchases – not even one!

4. We call this line "The Best of the Best" because each month you'll receive the best books by some of today's most popular authors. These authors show up time and time again on all the major bestseller lists and their books sell out as soon as they hit the stores. You'll like the convenience of getting them delivered to your home at our special discount prices . . . and you'll love your *Heart to Heart* subscriber newsletter featuring author news, horoscopes, recipes, book reviews and much more!

SPECIAL FREE GIFT!
We'll send you a fabulous surprise gift, absolutely FREE, simply for accepting our no-risk offer!

5. We hope that after receiving your free books you'll want to remain a subscriber. But the choice is yours – to continue or cancel, anytime at all! So why not take us up on our invitation, with no risk of any kind. You'll be glad you did!

6. And remember...we'll send you a surprise gift ABSOLUTELY FREE just for giving THE BEST OF THE BEST a try.

Visit us online at
www.mirabooks.com

® and TM are registered trademarks of Harlequin Enterprises Limited.

BOOKS FREE!

THE BEST OF THE BEST™ — Here's How it Works:

Accepting your 2 free books and gift places you under no obligation to buy anything. You may keep the books and gift and return the shipping statement marked "cancel." If you do not cancel, about a month later we will send you 4 additional books and bill you just $4.74 each in the U.S., or $5.24 each in Canada, plus 25¢ shipping & handling per book and applicable taxes if any.* That's the complete price and — compared to cover prices starting from $5.99 each in the U.S. and $6.99 each in Canada — it's quite a bargain! You may cancel at any time, but if you choose to continue, every month we'll send you 4 more books, which you may either purchase at the discount price or return to us and cancel your subscription.
*Terms and prices subject to change without notice. Sales tax applicable in N.Y. Canadian residents will be charged applicable provincial taxes and GST. Credit or Debit balances in a customer's account(s) may be offset by any other outstanding balance owed by or to the customer.

simply taken a look through the papers in her desk at home. There had been ample opportunity for him to do so; the very first time he had been in her house, she remembered, was when he had brought her home to change clothes after Jason had fallen in the water, and she had left him alone while she showered and changed.

She didn't know why he had targeted her marina, and she didn't care. She marked it down to simple avarice, the greedy impulse to take what belonged to others.

She hadn't known him at all.

She was still calm and dry-eyed when she reached her house. No—not her house any longer, but the Campbells'. Dazed, she unlocked the door and walked inside, looked at the familiar form and content of her home, and bolted for the bathroom. She hung over the toilet and vomited up the little coffee she had swallowed, but the dry, painful heaves continued long after her stomach was emptied.

When the spasms finally stopped, she slumped breathless to the floor. She had no idea how long she lay there, in a stupor of exhaustion and pain, but after a while she began to cry. She curled into a ball, tucking her legs up in an effort to make herself as small as possible, and shuddered with the violent, rasping sobs that tore through her. She cried until she made herself sick and vomited again.

It was a long time before she climbed shakily to her feet. Her eyelids were swollen and sore, but she was calm, so calm and remote that she wondered if she would ever be able to feel anything again. God, she hoped not!

She stripped, dropping her clothes to the floor. She would throw them out later; she never wanted to see that skirt again, or any other garment she had worn that night. She was shivering as she climbed into the shower, where she stood for a long time, letting the hot water beat down on her, but the heat sluiced off her skin just like the water, none of it soaking in to thaw the bone-deep cold that shook her.

She would have stood there all day, paralyzed by the mind-numbing pain, but at last the hot water began to go and the chill forced her out. She wanted nothing more than to crawl into bed, close her eyes and forget, but that wasn't an option. She wouldn't forget. She would never forget. She could stay in the shower forever, but it wouldn't wash his touch off her flesh or his image out of her mind.

He had never wanted her at all. He had wanted the marina.

The marina. Her mind fastened on it with desperate gratitude. She still had the marina, had salvaged something from the ruin Robert Cannon had made of her life. No matter how much damage he had done, he hadn't won.

The habits of years took over as she moved slowly about, getting ready to go to work. After towel-drying her hair, she stood in front of the bathroom mirror to brush out the tangles and braid it. Her own face looked back at her, white and blank, her eyes dark, empty pools. Losing Matt had been devastating, but she had carried the knowledge of his love deep inside. This time she had nothing. The care Robert had shown her had been an illusion, carefully fostered to deceive her. The passion between them, at least on his part, had been nothing more than a combination of mere sex and his own labyrinthine plotting. The man could give lessons to Machiavelli.

He had destroyed the protective shield that had encased her for so many years. She had thought she couldn't bear any more pain, but now she was learning that her capacity for pain went far beyond imagination. She wouldn't die from it, after all; she would simply rebuild the shield, stronger than before, so that it could never be penetrated again. It would take time, but she had time; she had the rest of her life to remember Robert Cannon and how he had used her.

She hid her sore, swollen eyes behind a pair of sunglasses and carefully drove to the marina, not wanting to have an accident because she wasn't paying attention. She refused to die in a car accident and give Cannon the satisfaction of winning.

When she drove up to the marina, everything looked strangely normal. She sat in the truck, staring at it for a few seconds, bewildered by the sameness of it. So much had happened in such a short time that it seemed as if she had been gone for weeks, rather than overnight.

No matter what, she still had this.

Robert prowled the house like a caged panther, enraged by the need to wait. Waiting was alien to him; his instinct was to make a cold, incisive decision and act on it. The knowledge of the pain Evie must be feeling, and what she must be thinking, ate at him like acid. He could make it up to her for the house, but could he heal the hurt? Every hour he was

away from her, every hour that passed with her thinking he had betrayed her, would deepen the wound.
Only the certainty that she would refuse to listen to
him now kept him from going after her. When Mercer was in jail, when he had the proof of what he'd
been doing and could tell her the why, then she
would listen to him. She might slap his face, but she
would listen.

It was almost three o'clock when the phone rang.
"Mercer's moving early," his operative barked. "He
panicked and called them from the office. No dead
drop this time. He told them that he needed the
money immediately. It's a live handoff, sir. We can
catch the bastards red-handed!"

"Where is he now?"

"About halfway to Guntersville, the way he was
driving. We have a tail on him. I'm on the way, but
it'll take me another twenty-five minutes to get
there."

"All right. Use the tracking device and get there
as fast as you can. I'll go to the marina now and get
ahead of him. He's never seen my boat, so he won't
spot me."

"Be careful, sir. You'll be outnumbered until we
can get there."

Robert smiled grimly as he hung up the phone.
Everything he needed was in the boat: weapons,
camera, binoculars and tape recorder. Mercer's ass
was in a sling now.

He drove to the marina, ignoring the speed laws.
He only hoped Evie wouldn't come out when she
saw him and do something foolish like cause a scene.
He didn't have time for it, and he sure as hell didn't

want to attract any attention. He tried to imagine Evie causing a scene, but the idea was incongruous. No, she wouldn't do that; it wasn't her style at all. She would simply look through him as if he didn't exist. But when he reached the marina, he didn't take any chances. He went straight to the dock where his boat was moored, not even glancing at the office.

Evie heard him drive up. She knew the sound of that Jeep as intimately as she knew her own heartbeat. She froze, trying to brace herself for the unbearable, but the seconds ticked past and the door didn't open. When she forced herself to turn and look out the window, she caught a glimpse of his tall, lean figure striding purposefully down the dock toward his boat. A minute later she heard the deep cough of the powerful motor, and the sleek black boat eased out of its slip. As soon as he was out of the Idle Speed Only zone, he shoved the throttle forward, and the nose of the boat rose like a rearing stallion as the craft shot over the water, gaining speed with every second.

She couldn't believe how much it hurt just to see him.

Landon Mercer walked in ten minutes later. Loathing rose in her throat, choking her, and it was all she could do to keep from screaming at him. Today, though, there was none of the slimy come-on attitude he thought was so irresistible; he was pale, his face strained. He was wearing slacks and a white dress shirt, the collar unbuttoned. Sweat beaded on his forehead and upper lip. He carried the same tackle box, but no rod and reel.

"Got a boat for me, Evie?" he asked, trying to smile, but it was little more than a grimace.

She chose a key and gave it to him. "Use the one on the end."

"Thanks. I'll pay you when I get back, okay?" He was already going out the door when he spoke.

Something in her snapped. It was a quiet snap, but suddenly she had had enough. Mercer was definitely up to no good, and today he hadn't even made the pretense of going fishing. The marina was all she had left, and if that bastard was dealing drugs and dragged her into it by using her boats, she might lose the marina after all.

Over her dead body.

It was too much, all the events of the day piling on top of her. She wasn't thinking when she strode out to the truck and retrieved her pistol from under the seat, then hurried to her own boat. If she had been thinking, she would have called the police or the water patrol, but none of that came to mind. Still reeling from shock, she could focus on only one thing—stopping Mercer.

Robert had positioned his boat where he could see Mercer leave the marina and fall in behind him without attracting his notice. The tracking device was working perfectly, the beeping increasing in speed as Mercer approached his position, then decreasing as the rental boat sped past. Not wanting to get too close and scare off the people Mercer was meeting, he started the motor and began idling forward, letting Mercer put more distance between them.

Another boat was coming up fast on the left, intersecting his path at a right angle. There was enough space that Robert didn't have to back off his speed, and he kept his eye on the diminishing dot on Mercer's boat. Then the other boat flashed across his line of vision, and he saw a long blond braid bouncing as the boat took the waves.

Evie! His heart leapt into his throat, almost choking him. Her appearance stunned him; then, suddenly, he knew. *She was following Mercer!* That was what she'd been doing all along. With that unsettling intuition of hers, she had known that Mercer was up to no good and had taken it upon herself to try to find out what it was. He even knew her reasoning: by using one of her boats, Mercer was involving her marina. Robert knew better than most to what lengths she would go to protect that place. She would give up her home, and she would risk her life.

Swearing savagely, he picked up the secure phone and punched in the number even as he pushed the throttle forward. "Evie is following Mercer," he snarled when the call was answered on half a ring. "She's on our side. Pass the word and make damn sure no one fires on her by mistake!"

His blood ran cold at the thought. None of his people would shoot at her, but what about the others?

* * *

Mercer was heading toward the islands again, as she had known he would. She kept about five hundred yards between them, enough distance that her presence wouldn't worry him, at least not yet. She would close the gap in a hurry when he reached the islands and slowed down.

The pistol lay in her lap. It was a long-barreled

.45 caliber, very accurate, and she not only had a license to carry it, she knew how to use it. Whatever Mercer was doing, it was going to stop today.

There was another boat anchored between two of the smaller islands, two men inside it. Mercer didn't take his usual circuitous route around and through the islands, but headed straight toward the other boat. Grimly Evie increased her speed and followed.

Mercer pulled up alongside the other boat and immediately passed the tackle box over. Evie saw one of the men point to her as she neared, and Mercer turned to look. She wasn't wearing a hat or sunglasses, and though her hair was braided, she knew she was easily recognizable as a woman. But she didn't care if Mercer recognized her, because the time for stealth was past.

The fact that she was a woman, and alone, made them less cautious than they should have been. Mercer was standing, his feet braced against the gentle rocking of the boat. Confident that they hadn't been caught doing anything suspicious, he said something in a low tone to the two other men, then raised his voice to call to her. "Evie, is something wrong?"

She waved to allay any suspicions. She was still twenty yards away. She eased the throttle into neutral, knowing that the boat would continue nosing forward for several yards even without power. Then, very calmly, she lifted the pistol and pointed it at the man holding the tackle box.

"Don't make me nervous," she said. "Put the tackle box down."

The man hesitated, darting a petrified look at his partner, who was still behind the wheel of the boat.

Mercer was frozen, staring at her and the huge pistol in her hand.

"Evie," he said, his voice shaking a little. "Listen, we'll cut you in. There's a hell of a lot of money—"

She ignored him. "I told you to put the box down," she said to the man who was holding it. Her mind still wasn't functioning clearly. All she could think was that if he dropped the tackle box into the river, the evidence would sink and there wouldn't be any way of proving what he was doing. She had no idea how she would manage to get three men and three different boats to the authorities, but there was a lot of boat traffic on the river this afternoon, and eventually someone would come over this way.

Another boat was coming up behind her already, way too fast. Mercer's attention switched to it, and a sick look spread over his face, but Evie didn't let her attention waver from the man holding the tackle box. A sleek black boat appeared in her peripheral vision, nosing up to the side of the boat holding the two men. Robert rose from the seat, holding the steering wheel steady with his knee as he leveled a pistol on the three men, his two-fisted grip holding the weapon dead level despite the rocking of the boat.

"Don't even twitch a muscle," he said, and the tone of his voice made Evie risk a quick glance at him. The facade of urbanity had fallen completely away, and he made no attempt now to disguise his true nature. The lethal pistol in his hand looked like a natural extension of his arm, as if he had handled weapons so often it was automatic to him now. His

face was hard and set, and his eyes held the cold
ferocity of a hunting panther.

The waves made by Robert's boat were washing
the others closer together, inexorably sweeping
Evie's boat forward to collide with them. "Look
out," she warned sharply, dropping one hand to the
throttle to put her motor into reverse, to counteract
the force of the waves. The two other boats bumped
together with staggering force, sending Mercer
plunging into the river. The man holding the tackle
box cursed and flailed his arms, fighting for balance,
and dropped the box. It fell into the bottom of the
boat. Robert's attention was splintered, and in that
instant the driver of the boat reached beneath the
console and pulled out his own weapon, firing as
soon as he had it clear. Evie screamed, her heart
stopping as she tried to bring her pistol around. Robert ducked to the side, and the bullet tore a long
gouge out of the fiberglass hull. Going down on one
knee, he fired once, and the driver fell back, screaming in pain.

The second man dived sideways into the rental
boat. Mercer was clinging to the side, screaming in
panic as the man hunched low in the boat and turned
the ignition key. The motor coughed into life, and
the boat leapt forward. Knowing she couldn't get a
good shot at a moving target, especially with her own
boat still rocking, Evie dropped the pistol and shoved
the throttle back into forward gear. The two boats
collided with a grinding force that splintered the fiberglass of both craft, her more powerful motor shoving her boat on top of the other. The impact tossed

her out of the seat, and she hit the water with a force
that knocked her senseless.

She recovered consciousness almost immediately
but was dazed by the shock. She was underwater, the
surface only a lighter shade of murky green. There
was a great roaring in her ears, and a vibration that
seemed to go straight through her. Boats, she thought
dimly, and terror shot through her as she realized
how much danger she was in. If the drivers couldn't
see her, they might drive right over her, and the pro-
peller would cut her to pieces.

She clawed desperately for the surface, kicking for
all she was worth. Her head cleared the water, and
she gulped in air, but there was a boat almost on top
of her, and she threw herself to the side. Someone in
the boat yelled, and she heard Robert's deep voice
roaring, but she couldn't understand his words. Her
ears were full of water, and dizziness made everything dim. If she passed out, she thought, she would
drown. She blinked the water out of her eyes and
saw the wreckage of the two boats, not five yards
away. She struggled toward it and shakily hooked
her arm over the side of the rental boat. It was very
low in the water and would probably sink within half
an hour, but for now it was afloat, and that was all
that mattered.

The boat that had almost hit her was idling closer.
Two men were in it, dressed in jeans and T-shirts.
The driver brought the boat around sideways to her,
and the other man leaned out, his arm outstretched
to her. The sunlight glinted off a badge pinned to the
waistband of his jeans. Evie released the rental boat
and swam the few feet to the other craft. The man

caught her arms, and she was hauled out of the water and into the boat.

She sank down onto the floor. The man knelt beside her. His voice was anxious. "Are you all right, Mrs. Shaw?"

She was panting from exertion, gulping air in huge quantities, so she merely nodded. She wasn't hurt, just dazed from the impact, so dazed that it was a minute before she could wonder how he knew her name.

"She's okay!" she heard him yell.

Gradually her confusion faded, and things began to sort themselves out. She remained quietly in the bottom of the boat, propped against one of the seats, and watched as the two men in the water were hauled out and roughly handcuffed, and the man Robert had shot was given medical aid. Though pale and hunched over, he was still upright and conscious, so Evie assumed he would live.

Four more boats had arrived, each of them carrying a team of two men, and all of those men wore badges, either pinned to their jeans or hung around their necks. She heard one of them briskly identify himself to Mercer as FBI and assumed that they all were.

Other boats who had seen the commotion on the water were approaching but stopped at a short distance when they noticed the badges. "Y'all need any help with those boats?" one fisherman called. "We can keep 'em afloat and haul 'em to a marina, if you want."

She saw one agent glance at Robert, as if for permission, then say, "Thanks, we'd appreciate your help.'' Several of the fishermen idled foward and added their boats to the snarl.

Evie resisted the urge to look at Robert, though she could feel his hard, glittering gaze on her several times. For the rest of her life she would remember the cold terror she'd felt when that man had shot at him and she had thought she would have to watch another man she loved die in front of her. The devastation she'd been feeling all day, bad as it was, paled in comparison to that horror. Robert didn't want her, had used her, but at least he was alive. Reaction was setting in, and fine tremors were starting to ripple through her body.

The mopping-up seemed to take forever, so long that her sopping clothes began to dry, as stiff as cardboard from the river water. The wounded man was placed in another boat and taken for further medical attention, with two agents in attendance. Mercer and the other man were taken away next, both of them handcuffed. There was a lot of maneuvering around the two wrecked boats as the salvaging continued. Gathering her strength, she took control of the boat she was in, while the driver added his efforts to the job. Finally, though, it all seemed to be winding down. Robert brought his boat alongside the one Evie was handling.

''Are you all right?'' he asked sharply.

She didn't look at him. ''I'm fine.''

He raised his voice. ''Lee, get this boat. I'm taking Evie back to the marina.''

Immediately the agent clambered back into the boat, and Evie relinquished her place behind the wheel. She didn't want to go anywhere with Robert, however, and looked around for anyone else she knew.

"Get in the boat," he said, his voice steely, and rather than make a fool of herself, she did. There was no way to avoid him, if he was determined to force the issue. If he wanted to discuss private matters, then she would prefer that they were private when he did.

Nothing was said on the ride back to the marina. The black boat moved like oiled silk over the choppy waves, but still every small bump jolted her head. She closed her eyes, trying to contain the nausea rising in her throat.

As Robert throttled down to enter the marina, he glanced over at her and swore as he took in her closed eyes and pale, strained face. "Damn it, you *are* hurt!"

Immediately she opened her eyes and stared resolutely ahead. "It's just reaction."

Coming down off an adrenaline high could leave a person feeling weak and sick, so he accepted the explanation for now but made a mental note to keep an eye on her for a while.

He idled the boat into his slip, and Evie climbed onto the dock before he could get out and assist her. True daughter of the river that she was, she automatically tied the lines to the hooks set in the wood, the habits of a lifetime taking precedence over her emotions. The boat secured, she turned without a word and headed toward the office.

Burt was behind the counter when she entered, and a look of intense relief crossed his lined face, followed by surprise and then concern when he saw her condition. It went against his grain to ask personal questions, so the words came reluctantly out of his throat, as if he were forcing them. "Did the boat flip? Are you all right?"

Two questions in a row from Burt? She needed to mark this date on her calendar. "I'm all right, just a little shaken up," she said, wondering how many more times that day she would have to say those words. "The boat's wrecked, though. Some guys are bringing it in."

Robert opened the door behind her, and Burt's expression went full cycle, back to relief. "I'll get back to the shop, then. How long do you reckon it'll take 'em to get the boat here?"

"About an hour," Robert answered for her. "They'll have to idle in." He went to the soft-drink machine and fed in quarters, then pushed the button. With a clatter, the bottle rolled down into the slot, and he deftly popped off the top.

"Well, don't make no difference. I reckon I'll stay until they get here." Burt left the unnatural surroundings of the office and headed back to where he felt most comfortable, leaving the oily smell of grease behind.

Evie walked behind the counter and sat down, wanting to put something between herself and Robert. It didn't work, of course; he knew all the moves, all the stratagems. He came behind the counter, too, and propped himself against it with his long legs outstretched and crossed at the ankle.

He held out the Coke. "Drink this. You're a little shocky and need the sugar."

He was probably right. She shrugged and took the

bottle, remembering another time when she'd been fished out of the water, and how he had insisted she drink very sweet coffee. The last thing she wanted to do was faint at his feet, so she tilted the bottle and drank.

He watched until he was satisfied that she was going to follow his orders, then said, "Mercer was manager of my computer programming firm in Huntsville. We've been working on programs for the space station, as well as other things, and the programs are classified. They began turning up where they shouldn't. We figured out that Mercer was the one who was stealing them, but we hadn't managed to catch him at it, so we didn't have any proof."

"So that's what was in the tackle box," she said, startled. "Not dope. Computer disks."

His dark eyebrows rose. "You thought he was a drug dealer?"

"That seemed as plausible as anything. You can't sneak up on anyone in the middle of the river. He must have been weighting the package and dropping it in a shallow spot between the islands, and the others were picking it up later."

"Exactly. But if you thought he was a drug dealer," he said, his voice going dangerously smooth, "why in hell did you follow him today?"

"The federal seizure law," she replied simply. "He was in my boat. I could have lost everything. At the very least, he could have given the marina a bad reputation and driven away business."

And she would do anything to protect the marina, he thought furiously, including sell her house. Of course she hadn't balked at following a man she sus-

pected of being a drug dealer! She had been armed,
but his blood ran cold at the thought of what could
have happened. She had been outnumbered three to
one. In all honesty, however, she had had the situation under control until the waves from his boat had
washed them all together.

"You could have killed yourself, deliberately ram-
ming the boat like that."

"There wasn't much speed involved," she said.
"And my boat was bigger. I was more afraid of the
gas tanks exploding, but they're in the rear, so I figured they'd be okay."

She hadn't had time to consider all that, he
thought; her reaction had been instantaneous and had
nearly given him a heart attack. But a lifetime spent
around boats had given her the knowledge needed to
make such a judgment call. She hadn't known that
reinforcements were almost there, she had simply
seen that one of them was about to escape, and she
had stopped him. Robert didn't know if she was cou-
rageous or foolhardy or both.

She still hadn't so much as glanced at him, and he
knew he had his work cut out for him. Carefully
choosing his words, he said, "I've been working
with the FBI and some of my own surveillance people to set a trap for Mercer. I soured some deals he
had made, put some financial pressure on him, to
force him to make a move."

It didn't take more explanation than that. Watching
her face, he saw her sort through the implications
and the nuances of what he had just said, and he
knew the exact moment when she realized he had
also suspected her. A blank shield descended over

her features. "Just like you did with me," she murmured. "You thought I was working with him, because he was using my boats, and because I'd been following him, trying to find out what he was doing."

"It didn't take me long to decide that if you were involved at all, you probably didn't realize what was going on. But you kept doing suspicious things, just enough that I didn't dare relax my pressure on you."

"What sort of suspicious things?" she asked, a note of disbelief entering her flat tone.

"Leaving the marina in the middle of the day to follow him. The day before yesterday, when you left the bank, you immediately stopped at a pay phone and made a call that we couldn't monitor. Yesterday you led the guy following you all over Guntersville, then ditched him by making an abrupt turn across traffic, and we weren't able to find you again until you came to work."

Evie laughed, but the sound was bitter and disbelieving. "All that! It's amazing how a suspicious mind can see suspicious actions everywhere. When the mortgage was turned down a second time, I realized there had to be someone behind it, someone who was blocking the loans. I couldn't lose the marina. The only thing left to do was sell the house, and I knew if I didn't make the call right then, I'd lose my nerve. So I stopped at the first pay phone I came to and called some people who have tried several times to buy the house, to see if they were still interested. They were so interested that they decided to pay me immediately rather than take a chance that I'd change my mind.

"Yesterday," she said softly, "I was looking for a place to live. But I knew I was just dithering, and that the longer I put it off, the worse it would be. So I made a quick turn, drove to an apartment complex and rented an apartment."

Yes, he thought, watching her colorless face. A quick, sharp pain was better than endless agony. Innocent actions based on desperate decisions.

She shrugged. "I thought you wanted the marina. I couldn't figure out why. It means a lot to me, but if you were looking for a business investment, there are bigger, more profitable ones around. Instead, you thought I was a traitor, and what better way to keep tabs on me than to start a bogus relationship and push it until we were practically living together?"

This was the tricky part, he thought. "It wasn't bogus."

"The moon isn't round, either," she replied, and turned to look out the windows at her kingdom, saved at such cost to herself.

"I wasn't going to go through with the foreclosure," he said. "It was just a means of pressure. Even if you'd been guilty, I'd already decided to prevent them from prosecuting you."

"How kind of you," she murmured.

He uncrossed his ankles and left the support of the counter, moving until he was directly in front of her. He put his hands on her shoulders, warmly squeezing. "I know you're hurt and angry, but until Mercer was caught, I didn't dare ease up on the pressure."

"I understand."

"Do you? Thank God," he said, closing his eyes in relief.

She shrugged, her shoulders moving under his hands. "National security is more important than hurt feelings. You couldn't have done anything else."

The flat note was still in her voice. He opened his eyes and saw that he hadn't cleared all the hurdles. The issue of the house was still between them.

"I'm sorry about your house," he said gently. "I would never have let you sell it if I'd known that was what you were planning." He cupped her cheek with one hand, feeling the warm silkiness of her skin under his fingers. "I can't get your house back, but I can give you mine. I'm having the deed made over in your name."

She stiffened and jerked her face away from his hand. "No, thank you," she said coldly, standing up and turning to stare out the window, her back to him.

Of course she had jumped to the wrong conclusion, he thought, annoyed with himself that he had brought up the house before settling the other issue. "It isn't charity," he said in a soothing tone, putting his hand on the nape of her neck and gently rubbing the tense muscles he found there. "It isn't even much of a gesture, come to that, since it will be staying in the family. Evie, sweetheart, will you marry me? I know you love it here, but we can compromise. I won't take you completely away from your family. We can use the house for vacations. We'll come down every summer for a long vacation, and of course we'll visit several times during the year."

She pulled away from him and turned to face him. If she had been white before, she was deathly pale now. Her golden brown eyes were flat and lusterless, and with a chill he remembered how Becky had said she'd looked after Matt had died. What he saw in Evie's eyes was an emotional wasteland, and it froze him to the bone.

"Just like everything else, your *compromises* are heavily in your favor," she said, a rawness in her voice that made him flinch. "I have a better one than that. Why don't you stay in New York, and I'll stay here, and that way we'll both be a lot happier."

"Evie..." He paused, forced himself to take a deep breath and reached for control. She was wildly off balance, of course, with everything that had happened today. She loved him, and he had hurt her. Somehow he had to convince her to trust him again.

"No!" she said violently. "Don't try to decide how you're going to manipulate me into doing what you want. You're too intelligent for your own good, and too damn subtle. Nothing really reaches you, does it?" She spread her hands far apart and gestured. "You're over here, and everyone else is way over here, and never the twain shall meet. Nobody and nothing gets close to you. You're willing to marry me, but nothing would change. You'd still keep yourself closed off, watching from the distance and pulling strings to make all the puppets do what you want. What I had with Matt was *real,* a relationship with a person instead of a facade! What makes you think I'd settle for what you're offering?" She stopped, shuddering, and it was a moment before she could speak again. "Go away, Robert."

Chapter 18

Evie's absence left a great, gaping hole in his life. Robert had never before in his life missed a woman or let one assume enough importance to him that he was lonely without her, but that was the predicament he found himself in now. After her flat rejection of his marriage proposal, he'd returned to New York the next day and immediately taken up the threads of his business concerns, but the social whirl he had enjoyed before seemed simultaneously too frantic and too boring. He didn't want to attend the opera or the endless parade of dinner parties; he wanted to sit out on the deck in the warm, fragrant night, listening to the murmur of the river and enjoying the array of stars scattered across the black sky. He wanted to lie naked on the chaise with Evie, motionless, their bodies linked, until their very stillness was unbearably erotic and they both shattered with pleasure.

Sex had always been a controlled but extremely important part of his life, but now he found himself unresponsive to the lures cast his way. His sex drive hadn't abated; it was driving him crazy. But he didn't want the controlled pleasure he'd known before, his mind staying remote from his body. He hadn't been remote when he'd made love with Evie, and several times he hadn't been controlled, either. Having her naked under him, thrusting into her tight, unbelievably hot sheath, and feeling her turn into pure flame in his arms…

The carnal image brought him to full arousal, and he lunged to his feet to prowl restlessly around the apartment, swearing between his teeth with every step. Nothing else made him hard these days, but just the thought of Evie could do it. He wanted her, and her absence was like acid, eating away at his soul.

He still couldn't decide what had gone wrong. He sensed the answer, but it was an ethereal thing, always floating just beyond his comprehension. His inability to understand the problem was as frustrating, in its own way, as his hunger for Evie. He had always been able to grasp nuances, see clearly to the crux of any problem, with a speed that left others in the dust. Now it was as if his brain had failed him, and the thought infuriated him.

It wasn't the house. As much as that had hurt her, she had understood his explanation; he had seen that in her eyes. Balanced against national security, her house was nothing, and she had believed him when he'd told her that he'd never intended to go through with the foreclosure. It was a dreadful miscalculation on his part, and though it chafed that he had made such a mistake, Evie had made a move that no one could have anticipated. Mortgage the house, yes, but not *sell* it. He was still stunned by the solution she had chosen.

But she had forgiven him for that, had even forgiven him for suspecting that she might be a traitor.

Why in hell, then, had she refused to marry him? The expression in her eyes still haunted him, and he lay awake nights aching with the need to put the glow back into her face. His golden, radiant Evie had looked like...ashes.

She loved him. He knew that as surely as he knew his heart beat in his chest. And still she had turned him down. "Go away, Robert," she'd said, and the finality in her voice had stunned him. So he had gone away, and he felt as if, every day away from her, he died a little more.

Madelyn had called several times, and she was becoming insistent that he come to Montana for a visit. Knowing his sister as he did, he was ruefully aware that he had maybe two more days to get out there before she turned up on his doorstep, holding one toddler by the hand and the other balanced on her hip, a ruthless expression in those lazy gray eyes. She knew him well enough to sense that something was wrong, and she wouldn't rest until she knew what it was. Her determination had been a fearsome thing when she'd been a child, and it had gotten worse as she'd grown older.

Robert swore in frustration, then made a swift decision. Other than Evie, Madelyn was the most astute woman he knew. Maybe, as a woman, she could put her finger on the reason that was eluding him. He called Madelyn to let her know he was coming.

With the time difference, it was still early the next morning when his plane landed in Billings. The ranch was another hundred and twenty miles, and had its own airstrip, so he had long since developed the habit of renting a small plane and flying the rest of the way, rather than making the long drive. As he banked to align the Cessna with the runway, he saw Madelyn's four-wheel drive Explorer below; she was leaning against the hood, her long hair lifting in the breeze. The color of her hair was lighter and cooler than Evie's tawny-blond mane, but still his heart squeezed at the similarity.

He landed the plane and taxied it close to the vehicle. As he cut the engine, he could see the two lively little boys bouncing in the cargo area, and a rueful smile touched his eyes. He had missed the little hooligans. He wanted some of his own.

As he crossed the pavement, Madelyn came to meet him, her lazy stroll fluid and provocative. "Thank God you're here," she said. "The imps of Satan have been driving me crazy since I told them you were coming. Did you know that when a one-year-old says Uncle Robert, it sounds remarkably like Ali Baba? I've heard it fifteen thousand times in the past hour, so I'm an expert."

"Dear God," he murmured, looking past her to where the two imps of Satan were shrieking what was undoubtedly their version of his name.

She went up on tiptoe to kiss his cheek and he hugged her to him. Something guarded inside him always relaxed when he set foot on the ranch. The sense of nature was much closer here, just as it had been in Alabama.

Madelyn waited until after lunch before broaching the subject he knew had been eating her alive with curiosity. The boys had been put down for their afternoon naps, and he and Reese were sitting at the table, relaxing over coffee. Madelyn came back into the dining room, sat down and said, "All right, what's wrong?"

He gave her a wry smile. "I knew you couldn't wait much longer. You've always been as curious as a cat."

"Agreed. Talk."

So he did. It felt strange. He couldn't remember ever needing help before in deciding what to do. He concisely outlined the situation with Mercer, explaining Evie's suspected involvement and the method he had used to force them into action. He described Evie, unaware of the aching hunger in his eyes as he did so. He told them everything—how Evie had sold her house to stop the foreclosure on the marina, how she had discovered that he was behind it all, and how Mercer had been caught. And how she had turned down his marriage proposal.

He was aware that Madelyn had stiffened during his recital of events, but she was looking down at the table, and he couldn't read her expression. When he finished, however, she lifted her head, and he was startled to see the molten fury in her eyes.

"Are you that dense?" she shouted, jumping to her feet with a force that overturned her chair. "I don't blame her for not marrying you! I wouldn't have, either!'' Infuriated, she stomped out of the dining room.

Bemused, Robert turned to stare after her. "I didn't know she could move that fast," he murmured.

Reese gave a startled shout of laughter. "I know. It took me by surprise the first time I made her lose her temper, too."

Robert turned back to his brother-in-law, a big, tough rancher as tall as himself, with dark hair and hazel-green eyes, coloring that he had passed on to his two sons.

"What set her off?"

"Probably the same thing that set her off when I was being that dense, too," Reese explained, amusement in his eyes.

"Would someone please explain it to me?" Robert asked with strained politeness. On the surface he was still in complete control, but inside he was dying by inches. He didn't know what to do, and that had never happened to him before. He was at a complete loss.

Reese leaned back in his chair, toying with the handle of his cup. "I almost lost Madelyn once," he said abruptly, looking down. "She probably never told you, but she left me. She didn't go far, just into town, but it might as well have been a million miles, the way I felt."

"When was this?" Robert asked, his eyes narrowing. He didn't like knowing that Madelyn had had problems and hadn't told him about them.

"When she was pregnant with Ty. I tried everything I could think of to convince her to come back, but I was too stupid to give her the one reason that mattered.''

Reese was going somewhere with this, Robert realized. He was a private man and not normally this talkative. ''Which reason was that?''

Reese lifted his gaze to meet Robert's, and hazel-green eyes met ice-green ones, both stark with emotion.

''It isn't easy to give someone else that kind of power over you,'' Reese said abruptly. ''Hell, it wasn't easy to even admit it to myself, and you're twice as bad as I ever was. You're a tough son of a bitch, more dangerous than you want people to know, so you keep it all under control. You're used to controlling everything around you, but you can't control this, can you? You probably don't even know what it is. I practically had to be hit in the head before I saw the light. You love her, don't you?''

Robert froze, and his eyes went blank with shock. Love? He'd never even thought the word. He wanted Evie, wanted to marry her, wanted to have children with her. God, he wanted all of that with a fierce passion that threatened to destory him if he didn't get it. But everything in him rebelled at the thought of being in *love*. It would mean a terrible helplessness; he wouldn't be able to hold himself apart from her, to keep uncompromised the basic invulnerability that was at the core of him. He was well aware of his true nature, knew the savage inside. He didn't want to unleash that kind of raw passion, didn't want anyone to even know it existed.

But Evie knew, anyway, he realized, and felt another shock. She had seen through him right from the beginning. With that maddening intuition of hers, she sometimes went straight into his thoughts. He could shut everyone else out, but he had never been able to shut out Evie, and he had spent the entire time they were together trying to regain control over himself, over the situation, over her. She knew him for what he was, and she loved him, anyway.

He swore, running a shaking hand over his face, blinding truth staring him in the eye. Evie wouldn't have loved him if that savage intensity hadn't been there. She had known real love with Matt, and lost it; only something incredibly powerful could take her beyond that. Loving Evangeline couldn't be a civilized, controlled affair; she would want him heart and soul, nothing held back.

The house hadn't been the issue. Neither had suspecting her of a crime. He could offer her a hundred houses, all the power his wealth could bring, and none of that would tempt her. What she wanted was the one thing he hadn't offered: his love.

"It was that simple," Reese said softly. "I told Maddie that I love her. More importantly, I admitted it to myself."

Robert was still stunned, still turned inward. "How do you know?" he murmured.

Reese made a low, harsh sound. "Do you feel as if you can never get enough of her? Do you want to make love to her so much that the ache never quite leaves your gut? Do you want to protect her, carry her around on a satin cushion, give her everything in the world? Are you content just being with her, listening to her, smelling her, touching her hand? Do you feel as if someone's torn your guts out, you miss her so much? When Maddie left me, it hurt so damn bad I could barely function. There was a big empty hole in me, and it ached so much I couldn't sleep, couldn't eat. The only thing that could make it better was seeing her. Is that the way it feels?''

Robert's green eyes were stark. ''Like I'm bleeding to death inside.''

''Yep, that's love,'' Reese said, shaking his head in sympathy.

Robert got to his feet, his lean face setting in lines of determination. ''Kiss Madelyn goodbye for me. Tell her I'll call her.''

''You can't wait for morning?''

''No,'' Robert said as he took the stairs two at a time. He couldn't wait another minute. He was on his way to Alabama.

Evie didn't like her new home. She felt hemmed in, though she had a corner apartment and neighbors on only one side. When she looked out the window, she saw another apartment building, rather than the river sweeping endlessly past. She could hear her neighbors through the thin walls, hear them arguing, hear their two small children whining and crying. They were out until all hours, children in tow, and came dragging the poor little tykes in at one or two in the morning. The commotion inevitably woke her, and she would lie in bed staring at the dark ceiling for hours.

She could look for another place, she knew, but she couldn't muster enough energy or interest to do it. She forced herself to go to the marina every day, and that was the limit of what she could do. She was going through the motions, but each day it took more and more effort, and soon she would collapse under the strain.

She felt cold, and she couldn't get warm. It was an internal cold, spreading out from the vast emptiness inside, and no amount of heat could get past it. Just thinking his name was like having a knife jabbed into her, shards of pain splintering in all directions, but she couldn't get him out of her mind. A glimpse of black hair brought her head snapping around; a certain deep tone of voice made her heart stop for an instant—a precious instant—as uncontrollable joy shot through her and she thought, *He's back!* But he never was, and the joy would turn to ashes, leaving her more desolate than before.

The sun burned down, the heat wave continuing, but she couldn't feel its heat or see its bright light. The world was colored in tones of cold gray.

I got through this before, she would think on those mornings when there didn't seem to be any reason to get out of bed. *I can do it again.* But the fact was, doing it before had nearly killed her, and the depression that sucked all the spirit out of her was getting deeper every day. She didn't know if she had the strength to fight it.

Becky had gone ballistic when she found out Robert had left town. "He told me he was going to ask you to marry him," she'd roared, so enraged her hair had practicallly been standing on end.

"He did," Evie had said listlessly. "I said no." And she had refused to answer any more questions; she hadn't even told Becky why she'd sold the house.

Summer was coming to an end, burning itself out.

It was almost time for school to start. The calendar said that fall was a month away, but the scent of it was in the air, crisp and fresh, without the redolent perfumes of summer. She was burning herself out, too, Evie thought, and didn't much care.

She went to bed as soon as it was dark, hoping to get a few hours' sleep before her noisy neighbors came home. It was usually a useless effort. Whenever she stopped, she couldn't keep the memories at bay; they swarmed at her from all the corners of her mind. Lying in bed, she would remember Robert's warm presence beside her, feel his weight compressing the mattress, and the memory was so real that it was almost as if she could reach out and touch him. Her body throbbed, needing his touch, the exquisite relief of having him inside her. She would relive every time he had made love to her, and her breasts would grow heavy with desire.

He was gone, but she wasn't free of him.

That night was no different; if anything, it was worse. She tossed about, trying to ignore the fever in her flesh and the misery in her heart. The T-shirt she wore rasped her aching nipples, tempting her to remove it, but she knew better. When she had tried to sleep nude, her skin had become even more sensitive.

Someone banged on the door, startling her so much that she bolted upright in bed. She glanced at the clock. It was after ten.

She got up and slipped on a robe. The banging came again, as thunderous as if someone was trying to beat down her door. She paused to turn on a lamp in the living room. "Who is it?"

"Robert. Open the door, Evie."

She froze, her hand on the knob, all the blood draining from her face. For a moment she thought she would faint. "What do you want?" she managed, the words so low that she wasn't sure he could hear them, but he did.

"I want to talk to you. Open the door."

The deep, rich voice was the same, the tone as controlled as ever. She leaned her head against the door facing, wondering if she had the strength to send him away again. What remained to be said? Was he going to try to make her accept the house? She couldn't live there; the memories of him were too strong.

"Evangeline, *open the door.*"

She fumbled with the lock and opened the door. He stepped in immediately, tall and overwhelming. She was swamped by her reactions as she fell back a pace. The scent of him was the same, the leashed vitality of his tall, lean body slamming against her like a blow. He closed the door and locked it, and when he turned back to her she saw that his black hair was tousled, and a dark shadow of beard covered his cheeks. His eyes were glittering like green fire as they fastened on her. He didn't give the apartment a glance.

"I'm only going to ask you once more," he said abruptly. "Will you marry me?"

Evie shuddered with the strain, but slowly shook her head. She could have married him before, when she'd thought he cared for her at least a little, but when she had realized he'd only been using her... No, she couldn't do it.

A muscle clenched in his jaw. She could feel the tension in him, like some great beast coiled to jump, and she took another step back. When he spoke, however, his voice was almost mild. "Why not?"

The contrast of his voice to the energy she could feel pulsing in him was maddening. All the misery of the past weeks congealed inside her, and she felt herself splintering inside. "Why not?" she cried incredulously, her voice shaking. "My God, look at yourself! Nothing touches you, does it? You'd take everything I have to give, but you'd never let me inside where you really live, where I could reach the real man. You keep yourself behind a cold wall, and I'm tired of bruising myself against it!"

His nostrils flared. "Do you love me?"

"Is that what you came for?" Tears welled in her eyes, rolled slowly down her cheeks. "A sop to your ego? Yes, I love you. Now *get out!*"

She saw his powerful muscles tense, saw his eyes flare with something savage. Her heart leapt, and too late she saw the danger. She turned to run, but Robert grabbed her, whirling her to face him. Confused, Evie thought at first it was one of his carefully gauged actions, designed to impress upon her how serious he was, but then she saw his eyes. The pupils were contracted to tiny black points, the irises huge and glittering like pale fire. His face was tight and pale, except for two spots of color high on the blades of his cheekbones. Not even Robert, she thought dazedly, could control those physical reactions.

His hands tightened on her waist until his fingers dug painfully into her soft flesh, a grip that she knew would leave bruises. "You're right," he said almost soundlessly. "I've never wanted anyone to get close to me. I've never wanted to care this much for anyone, to let you or anyone else have this kind of power over me." His lips drew back over his teeth, and he was breathing hard. "Shut you out? My God, I've tried to, but I can't. You want the real man, sweetheart? All right, I'm yours. I love you so much it's tearing me apart. But there's a flip side to it," he continued harshly. "I'll give you more than I've ever given any other human being, but by God, I'll take more, too. You don't get to pick and choose which qualities you like the best. It's a package deal. You get all the bad with the good, and I warn you now, I'm not a gentleman."

"No," she whispered, "you're not." She hung in his grip, her eyes fastened on his face, seeing the sheen of sweat on his forehead and the ferocity of his expression. Her heart thundered at what he had just said, her mind reeling with joy. He loved her? She almost couldn't take it in, couldn't believe he'd actually said it. She stared up into those fiery eyes, too dazed to say anything else.

"I'm jealous," he muttered, still in that tone of stifled violence. "I don't want you even looking at another man, and if any fool tries to come on to you, he'll be lucky if I only break his arm." He shook her with enough force to make her teeth snap together. "I want you all the time, and now, damn it, I'll take you. I'll be on you so often, four and five times a day, that you'll forget what it's like not to have me inside you. No more being a gentleman and restricting myself to twice a day."

Her golden brown eyes widened. "No," she said

faintly. "I wouldn't want you to restrict yourself."
There were no controls on him now; she could feel
the passion surging through him, a wild and savage
force that caught her up in its tide and swept her
along with him.

"I'll want you at my beck and call. I can't ignore
the business, so I'll expect you to fit your schedule
around mine, to be available whenever I'm home."
As he talked, he moved her backward and roughly
pushed her against the wall. His hands tugged at her
panties, stripping them down her legs. He leaned
against her, his heavy weight pinning her to the wall
as he tore his pants open. She gave a brief, incoherent
prayer of thanks that her neighbors were gone, then
clung to his shoulders as he hooked one arm under
her bottom and lifted her. Her heart pounding, her
blood rushing through her veins on a giddy tide of
joy, she parted her thighs, and he shoved himself
between them. His penetration was fast and rough.
She bit back a cry and buried her face against his
neck. She could feel his own heartbeat thudding
against her breast.

They were both motionless, overwhelmed by the
stunning relief and pleasure of their bodies being
joined once more, she trying to adjust to the hard
fullness of him, he groaning at the tightness of her
inner clasp on his sex. Then, still caught in the savage exaltation of emotional freedom, he drove mer-
cilessly into her.

"I don't want to wear a condom," he said fiercely,
his breath hot against her ear. "I don't want you to
take birth-control pills. I don't want you to act like
my semen is some hostile marauder that you have to

protect yourself against. I want to give it to you. I want you to want it. I want you to have my babies. I want a house full of kids.'' With each word he thrust, pushing himself deeper and deeper into her.

She moaned, shuddering around him with the force of her pleasure. ''Yes.'' She had unleashed a monster of passion, a total dictator, but she could meet his power with her own. This was the real man, the one who made her feel alive again, who sent heat throbbing through every cell of her body. She wasn't cold any longer, but radiant with vibrant life.

''I want marriage.'' His teeth were ground together, and a drop of sweat ran down his temple. ''I want you tied to me—legally, financially, every way I can devise. I want you to take my name, Evangeline, do you understand?''

''Yes,'' she said, and splintered with joy. ''Robert, *yes!*''

He bucked violently against her with his climax, flooding her with moisture and heat. Evie locked her legs around him and took him deep within, her senses whirling and fading, all consciousness gone except for the primal awareness of him inside her.

Some endless time later, she realized that she was on the bed and he was stretched out naked beside her. She hadn't fainted, but neither had she been aware of anything else but him. He hadn't released her during the entire time he had stripped both her and himself, struggling out of clothing while still keeping her in his grasp. She turned to snuggle closer, and the lure of his body, after the long deprivation, was too great. She found herself on top of him, wriggling to find the right contact and nestle his sex against the soft heat between her legs. He caught his breath, and she felt him begin to harden again.

"You might get started on that house full of kids sooner than you thought," she murmured, moving against him again in voluptuous delight. "I stopped taking the birth-control pills the day you left."

"Good." He caressed her bottom and hip, urging her closer to him. "I don't want to hurt you," he said even as he slipped inside her.

She heard the worry in his voice and knew that he was uneasy with releasing all the force he'd kept contained for so long. She kissed him and bit his lip as his subtle movements made her nerve endings riot with pleasure. "You can't hurt me by loving me," she said.

His eyes glittered in the faint light coming from the lamp in the living room. "That's good," he murmured. "Because God knows I do."

Epilogue

Evie heard the elevator arrive and crouched down beside the tiny, adorable creature who was clinging unsteadily to the chair in the entrance hall. "There's Daddy," she whispered, and watched her daughter's big eyes go round with delight. She barely restrained herself from gathering the baby into her arms; sometimes the surge of love was so strong that she thought she would burst from the force of it.

The elevator doors slid open, and Robert stepped out, an indescribable light flaring in his pale green eyes as he saw them waiting for him. With a joyous gurgle, the baby let go of the chair and hurled herself toward him, every toddling step teetering on the edge of disaster. Robert turned absolutely white, dropped his briefcase with a thud, and went down on one knee to swoop her into his arms. "My God," he said, shocked. "She's walking!"

"For a couple of hours now," Evie said, smiling as Angel caught her father's silk tie in one tiny, chubby hand and began babbling at him. "It makes my heart stop every time she lurches across the floor."

"She's too young to walk. She's only seven months old." Aghast, he stared down at the small head, covered with downy dark hair, that butted against his chest. He had been just as aghast when she had started crawling at five months. If he could, Robert would have kept his darling offspring as a babe in arms for the first five years of her life. She, however, was blissfully oblivious of his panic at her daring.

Still holding the baby, he hugged Evie close for a long kiss, one that quickly grew heated despite his squirming burden, who tried to poke her fingers between their mouths. They had named her Jennifer Angelina, intending to call her Jenna, but instead she had been Angel from the day she'd been born. She was angelic only when she was asleep, however; during waking hours, she had the fearless spirit of a daredevil.

Evie clung to his mouth for a long time, her hand clenching his hair to hold him in place. She had been waiting all day for him to come home, feeling shivery and excited and a little frightened.

"You were right," she murmured.

He lifted his head, and the green eyes gleamed. "I was, huh?"

She laughed and pinched him. "You knew you were." They had decided to have another baby as soon as possible. Both pregnancy and delivery had been easy for her, and though they had decided that two children would fill the house they were building just fine, they had both wanted to have them close together.

Three weeks ago, they had spent the night locked together, lost in the passion that hadn't faded during the sixteen months of their marriage. When they had awakened at dawn, for their ritual of morning love, Robert had looked down at her with his sleepy green eyes barely open and said, "We made a baby last night."

She had thought so, too, her instincts certain even before the early pregnancy test she'd taken just that morning had confirmed it. Already it was as if she could feel that hot, tiny weight in her womb, pulsing with life.

She leaned her head against his broad shoulder, remembering the sheer terror she'd felt when she had realized that she was pregnant the first time. Taking a chance on loving Robert had required all her courage, but now there was to be someone else to love, someone who was part of her, part of Robert. She would have no defense against this new little person, and she had thought she would shatter from the fear. But Robert had known how she was feeling, had seen the raw fear in her eyes and hadn't left her side all day. He had called Felice and announced that he wouldn't be in, cancel everything, and had spent the day holding Evie on his lap or making love to her. His solution, she thought wryly, had been to overwhelm her with what had gotten her in that condition to begin with; the tactic had been amazingly successful.

Angel was trying to throw herself bodily out of his arms. Sighing, he released Evie to bend down and set the baby on her chubby feet. As soon as he released her, she was off like a wobbly rocket. Evie went back into his arms, but they both kept a weather eye on their precocious daughter as she began investigating a fascinating crack in the hardwood floor.

Evie rested her head on his chest, reassured by the strong, steady thump of his heart beneath her ear. Far from losing himself in his work and demanding that she structure her time around him, as he'd said he would, Robert had instead ruthlessly reorganized his office schedule so he could spend every available moment with her and Angel. She had known that he was a man of alarming intensity, but instead of being frightened when he focused it on her, she had bloomed. Robert wasn't a man who loved lightly; when he loved, it was with every fiber of his being.

His hand moved to Evie's belly and pressed in gentle reassurance. "Are you all right?" he asked softly.

She lifted her head and gave him a luminous smile.

His love had renewed her strength, banished the shadows. "I've never been better."

Robert kissed her, savoring her sweet taste and the familiar, delicious tension of desire that quivered in their bodies. "I love you, Evangeline," he said, gathering her close to him. Loving her was the most joyous, satisfying thing he'd ever done. She demanded everything from him and gave him all of herself, and sometimes he was staggered by the richness of the bond between them. He'd been right; loving Evangeline took everything he had, heart and soul.

* * * * *

ONE MORE CHANCE
by Allison Leigh

To Dar, Susan, Linda and Deb.

Here's to many more pages, more laughs,
more learning and more successes.

Love, A.

Dear Reader,

Balmy breezes, sand as soft as powder, turquoise waters as far as the eye can see. Is it only these irresistible, physically enticing lures that draw people time and again to secluded islands, to other off-the-beaten-track lands? Or is it the discovery of a lifestyle that seems to progress at a different pace? And what is it in a person that seeks those things—a particular personality trait or event in their life? For me, it was wondering about these things that provided the "what if" kernel that grew into an island called Turnabout and the people whose lives are forever changed by their experiences there.

I don't know why I'm always surprised at the way the inhabitants of my stories become such a part of my life as I write. Yet they do. I laugh their laughter, cry their tears and triumph in their happily-ever-after. Mel and Luke were no different. I hope you'll enjoy their tale, and maybe—during the time it takes to turn these pages, at least—you'll share some of the magic of Turnabout.

Peace,

Allison

Chapter 1

She was crying.

Despite the low rush of the soft waves foaming up over the white sand, and despite the way she'd pressed her head against her drawn-up knees, Luke could hear her quiet sobs.

Not even sobs.

The woman was weeping.

He didn't really know why he considered there to be a difference. But there was. He'd seen it time and again in his line of work. Nervous tears. Choking sobs of despair. Weak sobs of disbelieving relief.

He recognized the difference, and the woman sitting on the sand, not even far enough up the beach to keep the folds of her ghostly pale dress from being soaked by the froth of water that advanced and retreated over her feet, was definitely weeping.

Luke's boots slowed, dragged to a stop in the sand and he shoved his hands into his pockets, turning his gaze from the huddled woman to the moon-gilded ocean.

Turnabout was the name of the island on which he stood. Doing a turnabout was pretty much what he wanted to do. A turnabout off this dinky island situated well off the coast of San Diego, and make tracks straight back to Phoenix. Even though his work there wasn't exactly a walk through the park these days, either, he could have climbed underneath the hood of the old Camaro he was restoring and used the smell of grease and the heft of heavy tools to forget the way he'd failed with a far more delicate task.

He blew out an impatient breath, glancing again at the woman.

She hadn't budged.

Which left him with few choices.

He hadn't really wanted to come to Turnabout in the first place. Hadn't wanted to do anything but keep going over the whole thing, endlessly trying to figure what he'd done wrong, wallowing in the guilt of it. But now he was here and the only thing he really wanted was a clean bed under him. In order to get that clean bed, he had to get the key to the cottage, and the key was with Maisy Fielding, the proprietress of the inn, who—according to the hand-lettered sign that had been taped to the door of the deserted inn—could be found at the community center. "The big building," the sign had further elaborated. "Straight up the road."

So what had Luke done? Headed straight up the road? Hell no.

He'd felt the call of the beach and, dumping his duffel bag on the inn porch, he'd walked, not up the road to the big building, but in the opposite direction.

He'd listened to enough of his boss's infernal stories about this place to know that there was only one town on Turnabout, with one main road crossing the length of the island. It didn't matter where you were, Jason Frame had said time and again, if you walked along the beach, sooner or later you'd end up at one or the other end of that road, which led to the town.

Luke glanced again at the woman. She wasn't curled in a ball anymore, but had propped her elbows on her bent knees. Her hands covered her face and her hair streamed back from her head on the breeze, looking like ribbons of silver in the moonlight.

Dammit.

He should have taken the short route and stuck to the road, because his choices now were limited to turning around and going back toward the inn or continuing on past the weeping woman.

The beach was a graceful curve of thick, fine sand, but it was increasingly narrow toward her and there was no way on God's windy shore that he could pass by her without disturbing her solitude. Walking all the way back to the inn to start over again held zero appeal. Walking all the way back to the inn to just wait until Maisy Fielding returned was even lower on the scale. According to the sign, the party at the "big building" that she was attending would probably last until dawn.

If Luke hadn't heard at least a dozen of Jason's stories, he'd have written off that particular nugget of information as pure exaggeration.

He started forward, staying close to the cliff wall and keeping his eyes straight ahead. Away from the hunched figure that sat on the wet sand, letting the edge of water flow up and over her.

Why didn't she move out of the water, at least?

Keep going, Luke.

He was almost even with her, now. She hadn't made a single movement betraying her awareness of him, yet she had to know he was there. Was the woman nuts? Completely unaware of her own safety? For all she knew he could be some scumbag, intent on harm.

Yet she just sat there. Getting soaked in the water. Weeping.

He couldn't do it. He wanted to. He tried to. But he couldn't do it. He couldn't just walk past the woman as if she weren't there.

He exhaled a long breath and veered toward her, shrugging out of his jacket.

"You must be cold," he said quietly as he approached her from the side, not particularly interested in scaring the tar out of her. He didn't want her mistaking him for some scumbag.

Her shoulders jerked a little, but she didn't look

at him. That was okay. He didn't intend to hang around long.

"Here." His fingers grazed her shoulders as he leaned over to drape his jacket around her, confirming the obvious. She *was* cold. It was the middle of January and she was wearing a white dress that didn't even cover her arms. "You should move back out of the water before you get even more wet."

She slowly tilted her head, the ripples of long, pale hair hiding her profile from him. She started to hand back his jacket.

"Keep it."

She hesitated and he took the matter out of her hands by simply dropping it once more around her shoulders.

Her slender fingers slowly closed around the lapels. She pulled them close. The jacket easily eclipsed her slender torso. The bottom of it folded over against the wet sand.

"You're very kind." Her voice was faint, husky.

He almost laughed. Most people would never associate him with that particular trait. He was good at what he did—at least he had been. But kind?

Not lately.

He shoved his hands into the pockets of his jeans and peered down the coastline. "Are you just visiting Turnabout?"

She silently shook her head.

"Then you'd know the community center. Is it far?"

She didn't answer immediately. When she did, it was hardly illuminating. "Not terribly," she said.

He looked at her down-turned head. The moonlight, what there was of it between the clouds striping the night sky, made her hair look white and he wondered, briefly, what color it would be in sunlight.

His boots were being baptized by salt water, same as the bottom of his jacket. His jaw felt tight. "You really should move back on the beach. You're getting soaked."

He heard her faint sigh. "I'm already soaked." But she rose to her feet and he automatically caught her arms when she swayed. She was taller than he'd expected.

The wind caught her long hair, blowing it across her face, blowing it against his arms, his chest. Her hair was silky. Soft. And something inside him warmed.

He brushed the strands away even as she caught at it with both hands, trying to tame it back.

His jacket started to slide from her shoulders and he caught it before it fell away completely. Hell, he grabbed it before the thing landed in the water that was currently ruining his boots. It helped a little with her long hair, when he pulled it back up on her shoulders, capturing some of the length beneath the collar before the wind could snatch at it again.

She didn't make a sound, but the waves of tension rolling off her were every bit as real as the ones pushing against the shore.

He didn't have time for this—to be waylaid by

some female who had desperation seeping from her pores. All he wanted was the damn key to his damn cottage. All he wanted was a clean bed, a decent night of sleep.

All he wanted was some peace.

So he'd keep walking and find that "big building."

Right.

He still hadn't seen her face. "Are you all right?"

"Please go. Here." She started to remove the jacket.

Annoyance rose swiftly inside him. Too swift.

Yeah. He needed peace.

He bracketed her hands with his, keeping the jacket in place. Her wrists were so slender, her hands so narrow, his hand easily encompassed both. "You're shivering." *Get going, Luke.* "I told you to keep it."

She said something, but the wind whipped her soft words into oblivion. Being able to hear her certainly wasn't helped by the way she kept her head lowered, her chin ducked. He bent his head closer. "What?"

"I said—" she finally lifted her head "—I can't." This time, her low voice was clear. He still barely heard.

The face she'd lifted was beautiful. The pain etched in it, though, was what stopped him cold.

He was acutely grateful for the less-than-brilliant moonlight, for the shadows. He wasn't sure he could stand to see this woman's sheer torment by the cold light of day.

He wasn't proud of it, but he still acknowledged the truth of it.

"It's just a jacket," he murmured. "I have others."

Her fingertips shifted, a small movement that he nevertheless noted. She was testing the feel of the leather with those narrow hands.

"I'm not the one shivering," he added quietly.

At that, her trembling increased. It was visible the way she shuddered and quaked. She drew her brows together. "I c-can't seem to s-stop."

"Your feet are bare and you're half-soaked." So why did he know that the shivers racking her body had little to do with external conditions and a lot more to do with whatever weight was crushing her heart? "Let me walk you home."

"That's not n-necessary."

His hand rasped over his jaw and he sighed, finally acknowledging another truth inside him. "I can't walk away from you like this."

She shook her hair out of her face, but it simply blew back across it. "Why not? You're a stranger to m-me."

He didn't even bother to answer that. "Do you have shoes somewhere?"

She was peering at him. "Why are you here?"

"Shoes?"

Her brows drew together again. "I don't know. I think they may have gone out on the tide."

He sighed. Then he put his arms around her and simply picked her up, right out of the water.

She went stiff as a board.

His hair was too long and he badly needed a shave, so he had no cause for offense. "If I were going to hurt you, I could have already done it," he said flatly, and carried her out of reach of the water. Then he set her down.

She shivered, but he could see some stiffening of her spine in the way her posture straightened and her head went back. "I'm not afraid of you."

"Well, if you had a lick of sense, you would be." The irritation in him came from nowhere. Again, it came too easily.

"You're on an island," she said. "A small one, with only one, tiny little port managed by Diego Montoya. If you want to get on or off the island, you're going to have to deal with him, a fact you surely know as...well—" she gestured "—here you are. Obviously, anyone coming to Turnabout to cause harm would be a fool as there is no place to run."

He ventured a guess that there were other ways a determined person could get around, but kept the thought to himself. He'd arrived by private charter and had not seen hide nor hair of anyone. Maybe Diego's diligence didn't extend to missing a party any more than Maisy's extended to making a key easily available for expected guests. "There you go, then. You're as safe as a babe in her mama's arms." *Get going, Luke.*

She shifted, not responding.

He studied her. She really was one tall drink of

water. The top of her head reached his jaw. "Do you want to talk about it?"

"No."

Fair enough. He didn't want to talk about his thoughts, either.

Silence twined between them. He needed to keep moving. Get the key. Get some sleep.

He needed to stop telling himself things like that, when it was obvious he was doing no such thing.

"I'm Luke," he finally said.

She didn't immediately respond. She adjusted her grip on the jacket, pulled it closer around her and cast him a quick glance that struck him as wary and longing all in one.

Maybe his sheer exhaustion had him hallucinating. *Longing?*

She shifted again and finally spoke. "I'm Mel."

A more feminine Mel he'd never before seen. "Well, Mel, you need to get dry before you end up sick."

She looked out over the water, her profile pure. "I've never been sick a day in my life," she said quietly. There was a wealth of sadness in her voice.

A tall drink of water, yeah. But more like a narrow crystal glass that would shatter if gripped too tightly. "Then you're luckier than most."

Her head slowly turned and she looked up at him, her eyes dark and unreadable. "Am I?"

He couldn't help himself. He brushed his thumb over her soft lips, tracing the frown that had drawn down the corners. Something dark and beckoning that had filled the air when he wasn't paying attention tugged at him again. "Lucky to have good health? Yeah. Don't wish away something that most people would consider a blessing."

He could feel those unreadable eyes studying him. Searching. "Why are you here?"

It was the second time she had asked and there was no point in pretending he thought she referred to his reasons for being on the island. "I don't know," he said. "To lend you my jacket, maybe."

"Please don't be kind," she whispered. "I don't think I can take it. Not...not tonight."

He exhaled a rough breath. "I'm not kind," he said flatly. Then he put his hands on her shoulders, which were buried under his pricey leather jacket, and gently pulled her against his chest.

He felt a sob work through her. Then another.

How many women had he held while they cried? Too many to count. None of them had ever made his throat tighten. None had made his head ache, deep, behind his eyes.

Then he felt her hands on his chest. Her fingers curling into his shirt. She was shaking like a leaf and, God, in that moment he wanted nothing more than to take away her pain, give her some peace, some respite from whatever plagued her soul.

Luke. The healer.

What a damned bloody joke.

His arms went around her back, one hand cupping the back of her silky head. He could feel the warmth of her tears against his neck, the desperation in her hands and the strength of her arms as they circled his waist.

His jaw ached and he swallowed. Hard.

"I don't want to hurt anymore." Her voice was broken, nearly inaudible against him.

Neither did he.

He held her closer. "It's okay."

Was he speaking to her, or to himself?

Did it even matter? He didn't know that anything would ever be okay again.

He closed his eyes, closed off the unbearable thought. But it kept sneaking back in, and he pressed his cheek to the top of her hair, inhaling the scent of the sea, the sand and her. It helped keep the yawning abyss at bay.

So he held her like that a while longer.

She thought he was kind.

Truth was, he was only being selfish.

He finally lifted his head and stared out at the dark water behind her. The clouds had covered the moon again. The wind was getting stronger. If it weren't for the warmth of her body pressed against him, he'd be cold, too.

He *was* cold, as he gently nudged a few inches of space between them. "Let me get you home."

"There's no one there." She spoke evenly, with no tears thickening her voice, no sobs breaking. The statement was all the more bereft because of it.

Though they were no longer standing in the water, he felt suddenly as if he were drowning in depths he should have been smart enough to avoid. Because she was warm against him, and very, very female. The face she turned up to him was vulnerable, and all he'd have to do would be tilt his head a few inches and his mouth would be on hers.

He thought about putting a little more distance between them. Thought about it, and did nothing to accomplish it. "Mel." Then he didn't know what to say.

Her hands slid up his back. Came around and glided up to his neck. Only his arms around her kept his jacket from falling away from her.

"Who is waiting at home for you, Luke?" Her words whispered over his jaw. "Who've you come to Turnabout to visit?"

He had no family left, anymore. And he'd just gotten rid of the last connection to the one piece of family who'd mattered. He realized he'd wrapped his fingers in her hair. "There's no one waiting for me."

She closed her eyes, pressed her temple briefly to his chin. "I'm sorry."

The throbbing was back again inside his head. "Why?"

She shook her head a little. "Maybe for the same reason you stopped to put your jacket around a stranger."

"Mel."

He saw her throat work. "Do you..." She stopped and moistened her lips. "Do you ever wonder if you'll make it through to morning, Luke?"

He couldn't take it. He ran his thumb down the trail left by her tears. Her cheek was cool, velvet over finely arched bones. He was barely aware that her hair was blowing around them again, like a curtain of silk.

Her lips parted softly and her lashes fell. She turned her cheek into his hand. "Warm." The word was more a sigh, and good sense, caution, and any claim to wisdom that he might have possessed scattered like dust thrown in the wind.

He tugged her head back and knew that it went willingly.

He lowered his mouth over hers, the briefest of tastes. And knew that her lips clung to his, silently asking for more.

When he lifted his head instead, searching her eyes for...what? Permission? Hesitation? All he saw was the same thing tightening his throat, exploding in his veins.

All he saw was need.

Chapter 2

Luke gathered her closer. Felt the quick breath she drew and the tightening of her fingers around his neck, in his hair.

He sucked in a sharp breath, his forehead touching hers. "Tell me to stop."

"Stop." She twisted her head around, pressing a quick kiss to his lips. "Stop." The tip of her tongue glided along his lower lip. "Stop."

Right. He stopped her tormenting little nibbles by kissing her. Flat out. His hands cradled her head, tilting it to suit him. Her lips parted and he tasted the low moan she gave as her tongue dueled, then danced, with his.

Heat blasted inside him, not at all cooled by the night wind. Sanity reared and he jerked back his head, stepping away, letting go of her. The cliff wall behind him stopped him short.

The jacket he'd worked so hard to keep around her slid off her shoulders. Her hands clasped together and she covered her mouth with them.

The gauzy white fabric of her damp dress blew around her legs, reaching toward him, fluttering over his jeans. Her hands slowly fell to her sides. "I'm sorry," she said, her voice raw. "I'm so sorry."

He needed to get out of there. Before he did something really stupid. "Mel—"

She shook her head. "I can't believe I threw myself at you like that, not when you're just being k—"

"Don't say it."

"—kind."

They stared at each other.

She moved first, reaching down to pick up the jacket that had fallen to the sand. She shook it a little and carefully smoothed her hand over it, brushing away the grains that stuck to it. "Here." She held it out to him. "The, um, the community center is about a mile up the beach, still. If you watch for it, you'll see a set of narrow steps in the cliff. They'll lead you right up to the building. You can't miss it. It's the biggest building on the island. And, um, well, everyone in town is there tonight."

"Except you."

Her hair was blowing madly, hiding her face again. "I was there. Earlier. I, uh, I didn't stay." She made a faint sound. "Obviously."

"I didn't kiss you out of kindness."

Her hand with the jacket dropped a little. "Oh." She stiffened her arm once more. "Well. Here."

He reached out, but closed his hand over hers instead of the jacket. His thumb traced her tightly clenched knuckles. "Yes. Sometimes I wonder if I'll make it to morning." He finally answered the question he'd avoided. "Kissing you wasn't being kind."

"Okay."

She made to pull her hand back from him and he knew she didn't believe what he'd said. He held on. "How old are you?" A damn sight younger than his own forty-one, he knew for a fact. The moonlight wasn't *that* faint.

"Old enough to know better," she said on a sigh. "I'm sorry."

"Dammit, stop apologizing. If you won't let me get you home, then at least go with me up to the community center. You said everyone in town is there."

She shook her head. "No."

"Did you have an argument with someone there? Your boyfriend? Is that why you're upset?"

She tugged her hair away from her face, holding it in a loose ponytail with her hand. "No. There's no boyfriend. There's nobody. Look, I'm so—" He saw the long, lovely line of her throat work. "You should go now. It's probably going to rain soon. You'll get wet if you linger."

"What about you?"

"I'm used to it."

Which made him wonder how many nights she sat,

alone on the beach, while she let the rain come down on her.

"I haven't sat in the rain since I was a kid." He hadn't enjoyed it then, mostly because it meant his mother had gone off and forgotten to leave a door open for him and his sister.

Her teeth caught her soft lip for a moment. "Stay out here much longer and you'll undoubtedly get a reminder of it," she said. "But I'm afraid it would probably ruin your jacket."

He didn't give a damn about the jacket. Staying on the beach—with her—held a much higher cost. "I want to kiss you again."

Her fist went slack, the jacket falling unheeded, and he turned her hand in his, pressing his palm to hers. It was oddly intimate, he realized, feeling her slender palm flush against his larger one. He heard her inhale sharply and wondered if it was because of his admission, or because of their hands.

"But I don't want to stop at a kiss," he continued evenly. "And I don't take what's not offered, so say the wo—"

"Then don't stop." Tension vibrated off her.

Heat collected at the base of his spine. *What the hell were they doing here?* "Mel."

She stepped forward, over the jacket that now lay in a heap on the sand, and pressed their joined hands over her heart. "Do you feel that?"

He felt her heartbeat charging against his palm. He felt the soft weight of her breast against his fingers.

"My heart," she said, her tone more than a little

ragged, "stopped hurting when you kissed me. I don't want you to stop. I don't care what you think of me, what it makes me. I just want—" she shook her head sharply, pressing her lips together "—to get through tonight. I want the pain to stop for just…one…night." Then her gaze met his. "Isn't that what you're looking for, too?"

He started to deny it. But what good would it do? She could have been describing him as easily as she described herself.

One night. Two strangers.

"I didn't come out here looking for an easy—"

"I know," she cut him off. "I know. Nor did I. Despite the way it probably appeared."

"I don't think that, Mel." He didn't. It hadn't even occurred to him. He'd had plenty of experience with women who had thrown themselves at him. He could recognize the difference.

She pressed her lips together for a moment. Her gaze dropped to their hands. She slowly slipped her fingers between his, curling them down. He curled his fingers, too, and she seemed to sigh a little as their hands linked even more firmly.

"I came out here looking for peace," she said softly. "Just…some peace." Her fingers tightened a little. "It wasn't working. The beach. The moonlight. It's always worked before. But not tonight." She moistened her lips and looked at him, and he felt the punch of it. It felt as if she were looking down inside him.

With recognition.

He searched her wide-eyed gaze for a long while. Then he tugged on her hand.

She came willingly.

The wind blew, and he turned his back to it, until he could protect her from the worst of it. He ran his hands down her back, slowly tracing the length of her spine. He thought about the rough, rocky wall behind her. The fact that he hadn't shaved in days, and the fact that her skin was soft. Tender.

"We should get in out of the cold."

Her mouth searched out his. "Now." Her lips moved against his. "I don't want to wait. I know if we have to walk you'll change your mind."

"You know that, do you? Know me so well?"

He felt her lips curve in the faintest of smiles. "Do you really want a mile-long walk, Luke?"

He liked hearing his name on her lips. He liked her lips, period.

Her fingers scrabbled at the sides of his shirt, tugging the tails loose. He sucked in a harsh breath when those fingers slid over his abdomen, slipping just inside the waist of his jeans. He caught her hand in his, halting the movement before she could go any further. "Maybe not," he allowed.

She made a soft sound, somewhere between a moan and a sob, and he swallowed it with his mouth, letting her hands go where they wanted.

His fingers, ordinarily known for their deftness, felt clumsy and thick as he worked a half-dozen buttons free. She was bare beneath the lightweight fabric.

Bare and warm and impossibly soft. Her head fell back as he kissed her jaw, her heart skittered when he slid his palm over her. She whispered his name, or maybe it was just wishful thinking on his part, when he tasted the long column of her throat, dawdled over her clavicle then slid down the valley between her breasts. She arched, making that low humming sound in her throat again, when he dragged his thumbs over her nipples, feeling them draw up even more tightly.

Her hands abandoned his strained fly and sank into his hair when he caught one crest between his lips. She tasted sweet, as warm and heady as the summer day on which she ought to have been wearing the fragile white dress. Then she twisted, pushing the thin straps of the dress from her shoulders, and he was vaguely aware of the fabric falling away from her slender torso, halting at her waist, her hips, where it fitted snug against her taut body.

He tore at the buttons of his shirt, then pulled her up, flush against him. Skin against skin. Curve against angle and felt satisfaction roar inside him at the contact.

Satisfaction that wasn't nearly satisfying enough.

He felt her knees go, and easily took her weight, glad to take it, because it brought her that much closer against him. Because his senses were consumed by her, because finally there was no room for thoughts, for regrets, for guilt.

There was only Mel.

Mel, who'd twined her long legs around his hips.

Mel, whose breath was as unsteady as his. Mel, who was prying open his button fly with neither elegance nor finesse. But he didn't care, because she managed to get the job done even as his fingers traced the path of the thin strip of soft fabric that stretched over her hip and found her beneath, even softer, even warmer.

She shuddered against him, humming, moaning his name, and somehow they ended up on the sand. The folds of her skirt fell over him as he pulled off her panties and she sank down on him, taking him in, bowing over him, all soft summer-sweet flesh and silken arms, rushing around him as surely as the surf rushed the sand.

Colors exploded in his head, fire exploded inside him. But he struggled for restraint, because, dammit, there was a piece of his brain still firing on more than half a cylinder and he knew there was something dangerous in this insanity. His hands tightened around her hips. Hips that were smooth and taut and unbelievably soft all at once. Hips that moved against his in a dance as old as time but just then felt as new as dawn. "Mel—"

Her lips covered his, her body tightening, beckoning.

He rolled over and caught her hands with one of his because her touch was going to be the death of him, and he hadn't had nearly enough.

She was shuddering wildly, and he heard a groan, vaguely aware it came from him, as he thrust deeper, wanting more, wanting to imprint himself on her the way she had on him. Wanting to hear the gasp in her voice as she cried his name, and feel every ripple work through her flesh that gloved him.

Then she cried out, and Luke felt her quake, deep inside where he couldn't tell where he ended and she began. Shocking pleasure ripped through him, splintered his gut, rocketed from the base of his skull to the depths of his soul.

And without another single coherent thought, he came, pouring hot and hard and fast, into Mel.

Chapter 3

Later, silent, Mel walked with him to the community center. The wind had died down until it was practically nonexistent. Without the wind, and with the clouds pressing down on the night, the temperature seemed to have actually risen. Still she wore his jacket.

She pointed out the steep stairs that had been carved by some ambitious soul into the cliff wall and tried to tell him that he ought to go first, as he wasn't familiar with the steps.

He just looked at her and, with a small sound in her throat, she climbed up before him, holding her long skirt gathered to one side of her thighs.

He shook his head as he wrapped his hand over the iron rail and began the ascent. His intention had been a simple matter of safety. If she fell on the dark, steep steps, he could catch her.

He looked up at her making her way.

Whatever his reasons, it was a helluva view.

It was also a helluva climb. And, by the time they made it to the top, the clouds had finally made good on their threat as it began to rain. A soft misting of water that was nothing at all like the sometimes vicious, generally brief, rainstorms he was used to in Phoenix.

Mel looked back down at him, and he could see the faint smile on her lips. "I warned you." Then she was climbing again. The flimsy sandals of hers that they'd finally found on the beach tangled in a hank of seaweed, made little squishing sounds with each step she took.

Maybe what they'd done out there on the beach had been as foolish as anything he'd ever done, but he'd be hanged if he could regret it.

Not when he thought about the way she'd giggled. Afterward.

He'd still been wearing his boots. They'd had sand everywhere.

She'd giggled.

And he'd laughed.

Then she'd pressed her soft lips to his, and they'd done it all, again.

Even now, he could feel the faint tug at his lips. He'd be lucky if he wasn't grinning like some damn fool teenager who'd just discovered that paradise wasn't a pretty Pacific island, but a warm place in one particular woman's arms.

He'd wanted some peace.

Well, he felt as peaceful now as he had in years. Maybe ever. There was also no more sign of Mel's tears.

He joined her at the top of the steps and frowned when she sidestepped the hand he held out. But maybe it was his imagination, because she'd turned and was pointing. "There's the community center."

Luke looked, nowhere near as interested in the place as he had been earlier. But even his humor was pricked at what he saw. The biggest building on the island wasn't really all that large. It was single storied, multiwindowed and shot off in wings from a central section in an assortment of directions. But the sign over the door that proclaimed it The Biggest Building On Turnabout was bold and unmistakable.

"People on Turnabout have a sense of humor," he said.

"A bit," she allowed blandly. She walked across the parking area—a wide pad of gravel, short-cropped grass, and an occasional patch of smooth cement that was covered with dozens of bicycles, a few Radio Flyers, and only three actual automobiles.

"There aren't very many cars on Turnabout," she told him, noting the focus of his attention.

He had to concentrate on not staring at her. In the moonlight she'd been beautiful. The closer they drew to the brightly lit community center, the more he realized just how exquisite her face really was. He scrambled for the thread of conversation.

So much for his supposed brilliance.

Cars. That was it. Not many cars on the island. "Too expensive to have them shipped here?"

She didn't seem to have noticed his conversational lapse. "That. But mostly because there isn't much that isn't just as easily reached by foot or bicycle."

"There's a road." He could see it. A thin ribbon of tarmac, admittedly, but still a road.

"Yes, but it's the only road and the Turns are perfectly happy with it that way."

"Turns?"

"The islanders who've been born and raised here call themselves Turns. You know. As in Turn—"

"—about." Luke stepped around a two-seater bicycle. "Yeah. I get it. So, do you call yourself a Turn, too?"

She smiled faintly, glancing very briefly up at him. "There is only one person on Turnabout who wasn't born here who is considered a Turn."

"Who's that?" He was more interested in knowing where *she* was from, though.

"Maisy Fielding."

The woman who had the key to his cottage.

Luke caught Mel's sidelong glance as they neared the entrance of the community center—two double doors that were propped wide-open despite the late hour and the misting rain. Music and laughter spilled from inside. "What?"

Her hand moved in a low, dismissive wave and

the sleeve that she'd pushed up above her wrist slid down over her fingers. "It's nothing," she dismissed. "None of my business."

He closed his hand over her elbow. It felt delicate beneath the leather. "Even after what just happened?"

She flushed. At least, he was fairly sure she flushed. It was hard to tell, given the number of colored lights strung around the exterior of the building. There were so many it was like some Christmas elf had run amok. They were all lit, blinking on and off in a crazed rhythm of blue, green, red and white.

Jason's wife, who could barely contain herself from decorating every inch of the clinic before December even began, would have loved it. Luke had little appreciation for Lydia's efforts, though. To him, Christmas—all holidays really—were just another day of the week. It wasn't as if those needing care at Sunquest took the day off every time a holiday rolled around.

Mel still hadn't answered. She brushed her hand over her hair, swiping at the damp tendrils clinging to her cheek, managing to look shy and sexy at the same time. It was a look that probably had every man who met her wanting to protect her as much as touch her.

She moistened her lips. "Luke, about…that." She dashed at her hair again. "I don't, um—"

"Don't?" He drew out the word and lifted an eyebrow. "Don't what? Spit it out, Mel, whatever it is." He already knew he wasn't going to like it.

"Don't think we should, well—"

"Talk about it? Refer to it? Remember it?" He eyed her. *"Repeat it?"*

She paled. Feeling like an ass, not liking it one bit, he let go of her arm, stepping back.

"You never said who it is you're visiting here." Her voice was careful. She'd folded her arms protectively across her chest.

"I'm not. I told you there was no one waiting for me."

"At least there's that," she said softly.

"Do you really think I'd have touched you if there were someone else in my life?"

Her lips pressed together for a moment. "I don't really know you well enough to say."

He put his hand under her chin, lifting it. "You say that to me? *Now?*"

Her lashes finally lifted, and he saw her eyes in the light. They were brown. Such a dark brown that he could barely distinguish the pupil from the iris. Her lashes were dark, too. All in all, she was mesmerizing. He'd have thought so, even if he hadn't just made love to her.

She turned her head away from his hand. "I say that because it is true." Her voice was husky. "I, um, I don't even know your last name. If you're on Turnabout for vacation or b-business."

"Business." It was true in a manner of speaking. "And I don't know your last name, either."

She seemed to absorb that. "Summerville," she

provided after a moment. "Will you be staying long?"

A part of him recognized the absurdity of their words. This situation. Her panties, torn from her by his hand, were stuffed in his front pocket, and here they were making small talk, near as he could tell. "A week."

"That long."

He laughed shortly, knowing it was only his dark humor rearing its ugly head. "Sorry to disappoint you."

Her cheeks colored again. "I didn't mean it that way."

"Are you certain?"

She didn't answer. Which pretty much *gave* him the answer.

Maybe the sudden hollowness in his stomach was just hunger. And maybe he really was the "kind" man she'd accused him of being.

Right.

Pigs had wings and he was actually entitled to the brief period of peace he'd been afforded.

He shoved his hand through his hair, raking back the too-long strands. "Mel—"

"I just meant that I hoped you had reservations somewhere. For a stay that long, I mean. There aren't that many guest facilities on the island." She spoke fast, her words nearly tumbling over each other.

"I do have reservations. Maisy's Place. That's why I was headed to the community center. There was a sign on the door that said to go there."

She gave a start. "Maisy's? But there was only one reservation for this week. I, um, I help manage the inn and guest cottages for Maisy Fielding," she explained, looking distinctly uncomfortable. "I have for the past few years."

"The reservation was for an associate of mine. Jason Frame. My coming here was a last-minute decision."

Her brows drew together. "You work with Dr. Frame?" Her voice was careful, making Luke wonder at the cause.

He nodded. Started to tell her, but a voice hailed Mel and she whirled around to face the diminutive woman who was hurrying out the double doors.

Short and skinny with a head of corkscrew red curls, the woman stopped, pressing her hand to her chest as she caught her breath. Luke realized she was older than her initial appearance suggested. "Chicken, I was beginning to wonder if I should send someone out for you!"

Mel cast him a quick look. "I didn't think you'd worry about me, Maisy. You know what tonight is."

The woman propped bony hands on her narrow hips and harrumphed. She cast a critical eye up and down Luke. "And who would you be?"

"Maisy," Mel shifted between them, making Luke wonder if she was trying to protect the scrawny little woman, or him. "This is Luke—"

"Trahern," he supplied when she looked to him.

"An associate of Dr. Frame's," Mel went on. "Luke, Maisy Fielding. Owner of Maisy's Place."

Luke nodded at the woman, but his mind was elsewhere. *What* was tonight to Mel? The thing that had caused her to sit on the beach, weeping her heart out. "Mrs. Fielding," he said. "Jason's often said how much he enjoys staying in your cottages."

Harrumphing again, Maisy looked at Mel. Her tart demeanor visibly softened. "Are you all right?"

Mel's cheeks reddened. Luke wasn't surprised when she didn't so much as breathe in his direction. "Of course. Just a little damp. From the rain." She moistened her lips. "Luke was kind enough to lend me his jacket."

Maisy's pointed little chin turned in his direction again. "Hmm. I see. Well, thank you, Mr. Trahern, for looking out for our Mel."

"It's doctor, actually. But Luke suits me better," he added slowly, watching Mel, who had stiffened at his words. "Jason assured me there would be no problem if I took over his reservation for the week."

"Dr. Frame and his wife have been visitors here for a long time. He's never mentioned you."

If Maisy Fielding thought he would be offended by her words, she was barking up the wrong tree. Nor was it his imagination that she was most definitely drawing an invisible line. With him on one side, and her and Mel on the other. "Lydia would have Jason's head if he talked shop on their vacations," Luke countered smoothly. "He's allowed to brag about their five grandchildren all he wants, but work is forbidden."

"Why didn't they come themselves?" The question came from Mel. She was still avoiding his eyes.

"A patient," he said abruptly. It was true enough, in a manner of speaking. Only it was his patient. *Had been* his patient. "He must have gotten sidetracked, or he'd have called ahead about the switch. If you can't accommodate me, say the word. I'll make other arrangements."

"Good idea—"

"Oh, no, that won't be —"

Luke watched the two women stare at each other and wondered grimly what was behind the undercurrents running thick and heavy between them. Wondered, too, just what his boss had tossed him into, because there was little that Jason didn't do without very specific reasons.

Luke might admire the hell out of his boss, but that didn't mean he was ignorant of the man's penchant for manipulating people to suit his purposes.

"Maisy," Mel was saying softly, "the only other empty rooms are at the Seaspray Inn, and you know he can't possibly stay there. Of course he should use Dr. Frame's reservation."

Red curls positively vibrating with displeasure, Maisy shoved her hands into the patch pockets of her green and purple dress. "Dr. Frame or his wife should have called about the change. I was expecting *them*." She huffed again, then pulled out one of her hands and extended a large key. "I serve breakfast in the dining room between eight and nine o'clock. Don't expect room service, because we don't give it.

If you miss the meal, you miss it. Whether you do or not, the rest of the day you're on your own.''

Luke took the key. He wasn't interested in food, simply a clean, dry bed. ''Thank you.''

He wouldn't have thought it possible for Maisy's eyes to narrow even more, but they did. As if she didn't quite trust his polite expression. ''The Blue Cottage,'' she finally added. ''The last one on the path from the main building. You ought to be able to find it, even in the dark.''

''Mel can show me the way.''

Mel, however, looked as if she wanted to do anything but that. ''A-all right. Yes. Of course.'' She leaned over and bussed Maisy's cheek. He overheard her soft murmur to the woman that she was ''tired anyway.''

''Between eight and nine,'' Maisy reminded, as he and Mel started off again.

If he *did* sleep, he hoped like hell it would be for about twenty-four hours straight, and Maisy's breakfast hour be hanged. As for Maisy herself, he'd be dealing with her soon enough, since that was Jason's only charge in suggesting Luke take advantage of his reservation and regroup.

Regroup. As if he'd had some small setback.

He followed Mel as they left the noise of the party behind. He watched her hair drifting around her shoulders. Moonbeams, he thought again, then shoved his hands into his pockets as he walked along, cutting off that entire area of thought. The thought embargo lasted all of fifteen minutes. He figured he'd done well, at that, considering the fingertips of one hand were tangled in the delicate hank of silky fabric in his pocket.

He pulled his hands free. "What's wrong with the Seaspray Inn?" He wasn't dying of curiosity, but at least it was a safe topic.

"Excuse me?"

"The Seaspray. You said I couldn't possibly stay there."

She looked away from him again. "It's on the other side of the island. Near Castillo Cove."

"So? Too pricey for the likes of me?"

She made a soft sound. "The fees at Seaspray are perfectly reasonable. It's just not a very popular place with visitors."

"Why not?"

She looked uncomfortable. "It's kind of barren over there," she finally said. "The people who go there are usually locals and there are only a few rooms. Even if they have a vacancy, you'd have probably been turned away. Nothing personal. But you're not a Turn." They walked a while longer in silence.

"Were they celebrating something in particular back there?"

"A birthday."

"Full of information, aren't you."

The rhythmic squishing of her sandals hesitated. "You didn't say you were a doctor."

"We didn't exactly exchange résumés down there

on the sand.'' Full body contact, yeah. Talk, details of their respective lives—no.

''Do you specialize?''

''Yes.''

When he said no more than that, she looked over her shoulder at him, never slowing her pace. ''Now who is being reticent?''

''Pediatric neurosurgery.''

She stumbled a little. He shot out an arm, steadying her. ''A surgeon,'' she murmured. ''Naturally.''

''Something wrong with that?''

''Not if you're a child requiring neurosurgery,'' she said, and began walking again. ''We're almost there.''

Luke tilted his head back, feeling the mist on his face. The moisture didn't so much rain on him as enclose him. He blew out a long breath and cursed Jason, even though he knew his friend's motives in sending him to this place had been more altruistic than not.

''Luke? Are you coming or planning to stand in the rain until dawn?''

He slicked his hand down his face and caught up to her with two long strides. ''Are you planning to stay with me until dawn?'' So much for safe topics.

He heard her quick inhalation and that betraying hesitation in her squishing steps as they walked up the stone path to the inn. ''You shouldn't say things like that.''

''I should pretend that nothing happened.''

"Isn't that the way men like it? A...good time, with no strings attached?"

"That's it." He closed his hands over her shoulders, stopping her progress, making her stand there and face him. "I don't know what the hell kind of game you're playing." It infuriated him that he'd believed she hadn't been playing anything. "And right now, I'm too far beyond pissed to care. You don't want anything more to transpire between us, fine. I'm reasonably intelligent. I get it. But don't make it sound as if all I was out for was a *good* time. Don't forget, baby, you kissed me."

Disgusted with himself, with everything, he let go of her and stomped up the porch steps to grab his duffel, which he'd dumped there earlier. He unzipped the side and pulled out a cheerfully wrapped package that he tossed to her as he went back down the steps. She caught it, surprised.

"That's from Jason and Lydia for Maisy's granddaughter," he said flatly. "I suspect if I give it to Maisy directly, she'll toss it in a tub of water first just to see if it explodes."

"You're exaggerating."

"Don't think so. Suspicion reached new heights with Maisy Fielding. Where is her granddaughter anyway?"

"At the party, of course. It's for her and she does have a name. April."

"Isn't it a little late for a seven-year-old to be at a party?" Much less a girl who was as ill as Jason had indicated.

"She wanted a grown-up party," Mel said. Her voice was thin. "It's not so much to ask. There are places she can rest at the community center. Lily Villanova is there. She's a relative of sorts to Maisy. She helps look after April."

From Jason, Luke knew that Maisy had been raising April since she was a baby, after April's mother, Tessa, left the island, only to never return. There had been an exhaustive search, but she'd seemed to disappear right from the planet.

"Well, the gift is for her, April. Jase and Lydia would undoubtedly appreciate it if she actually received it." He stepped past Mel, heading around the side of the inn. Jason's incessant descriptions were at least proving useful now. Luke figured he could find the last cottage on the lane with no assistance. And the sooner he got away from Mel, the better.

He didn't like being an idiot any more than he liked being a failure.

"It's not you." Mel was following him. He looked back, just to be sure he wasn't imagining it. There she was, trotting after him, clutching the wrapped present with hands that were nearly swallowed by long leather sleeves. "Maisy's behavior. She doesn't open up easily to outsiders."

He stopped in front of the last cottage. Lacy Queen palms bracketed the door that even in the dim light he could tell was painted a bright blue. "But she'll run guest cottages for those outsiders."

"It's her livelihood."

He refrained from belaboring the irony. "So that's Maisy's excuse. What's yours?"

She didn't look at him. "I don't know what you mean."

"Bull."

"You're not at all like Dr. Frame."

"No kidding." He smiled humorlessly. Luke knew for a fact that, before he'd turned to administration, Jason had possessed one of the most spectacular success records of any surgeon in the field. Until recently, Luke had been hard on Jason's heels in that regard. He doubted that Mel knew that, though. More likely, she'd taken one look at him and, without a suit and tie or scrubs, decided he didn't look the part. It wouldn't be the first time he'd been judged that way, but it had long ago ceased to matter to him. He was what he was. A rancher's grandson who'd been encouraged to follow his call.

Only now he wasn't sure about that calling at all.

He headed to the blue door and fit the old-fashioned, oversize key into the lock. The door swung inward.

"Luke."

Don't be even more monumentally stupid than you've already been, he told himself. Go inside. Shut the bloody door and go to bed. *Alone.* He dumped his duffel inside the doorway. Exhaling a long breath, he turned around to face her. She was holding out his jacket, her expression torn. "I'm sorry."

Feeling even wearier than he had been before he'd encountered Mel, he took the jacket from her. The slick lining of it was warm from her body. "For what?"

She closed her arms over her chest. "For everything." Then she turned on her heel.

Luke didn't go inside until he could no longer see the glint of her pale hair and the ghostly drift of her dress through the mist.

By the time morning came, he was almost convinced he'd imagined the entire episode. But the silky strand of white-blond hair caught on the collar of his sand-encrusted jacket told him otherwise.

He took the jacket and opened the rear door of the small cottage. Outside, the morning sun was brilliant, the sky an endless blanket of brilliant blue. The air was cool and clean, and the view of the ocean spectacular.

"Paradise," Jason had told him.

Luke sighed. He held out the jacket and shook it hard. Sand rained down on the dry stone patio.

"I'm sorry, too," he murmured.

He was. He just wasn't quite sure what exactly he was the most sorry about.

Chapter 4

The light shining behind Mel's eyelids told her it was morning. Well past time to get her lethargic bones out of the cocoon offered by her bed.

She opened her eyes. They felt dry and scratchy. Probably because she'd not given them any true rest until nearly dawn. She rolled on her side, cushioning her head on her folded arm, and stared past the empty half of the bed to the alarm clock on the opposite nightstand.

Of course, her mother wouldn't call the little three-legged turquoise-painted table a nightstand. But it was enough to hold Mel's clock and a small lamp. The clock told her it was most definitely time to get herself going. Past time.

She pushed up on her elbows, wrinkling her nose at the abrasive feel of the white sheet. Even though she had showered when she'd come in, there were still a few grains of sand in her sheets. "Cracker crumbs are nothing compared to a little piece of the beach," she murmured as she pushed back the bedding and padded to the small bathroom attached to her room. She'd shower again, change the sheets, then go over to the inn and the small room there that served as an office for Maisy's Place.

If she was lucky, she'd be able to avoid Dr. Luke Trahern altogether.

The pipes rattled when she flipped on the shower. But the water came out in a strong enough spray, rapidly filling the dinky bathroom with steam. Mel only wished she could blot out the memory of the previous night as easily as the fog blotted out the mirror above the sink.

She tugged off the faded T-shirt she'd worn to sleep in and stepped under the shower. The heat slowly worked its way into her sore muscles. Mel didn't want to remember just exactly why she felt tender and tired, but the reason still sat there in her mind, large as life. How could it not? She hadn't been with a man since Jonathan.

Mel ignored the whispered thought and blindly snatched up the bottle of shampoo. It was handmade on the island, but just then she had no appreciation whatsoever for the calming scent. Ten minutes later, her wet hair woven back into a French braid that reached halfway down her back, she was on her way to her office.

Of course, the first person she encountered was the

one individual she'd hoped to avoid. Her footsteps faltered as she turned the corner and saw Luke leaning against the wall next to her office door. She didn't even have an opportunity to turn tail and run because he immediately spotted her and straightened from his indolent slouch.

There was nothing indolent about his hooded gaze, however, when he focused on her and she felt the sting of color heat her cheeks. She fell back on her role as manager with no small amount of desperation. "Is the cottage to your satisfaction?"

"There's no phone."

"I'm sorry, I thought you knew. None of the cottages are wired for phones. But there is always someone on hand to answer the main line in the inn, in case you're expecting a call. And of course it's available for your use whenever you need. Unfortunately cell phones are useless out here. No signal. Is, um, everything else to your comfort?"

"Yes."

When it became apparent that he wasn't going to add anything else, that he wasn't going to ease the awkwardness between them with some sort of idle chitchat about the weather or the incredible color of the ocean, she stepped past him and entered the office, harboring a fantasy that he'd go along his way.

But she knew he wouldn't. For why else would he have been standing outside her office if not to see her?

She moved behind her desk, setting aside the small basket filled with two enormous apricot-walnut muffins. Every morning, before the crack of dawn, Maisy prepared the fresh muffins for the guests, saving two for Mel to begin her day. If April was feeling up to it, she was charged with the task of sneaking into the office to set the basket front and center on Mel's whitewashed oak desk.

The apricot-walnut muffin fairies. April always giggled over the "mystery" of how the muffins came to appear on Mel's desk each morning. Mel would swallow glass before she'd unveil her knowledge of that particular pleasure for the child.

Sitting down was not an option. Being seated with Luke looming tall and brooding over her desk was definitely *not* the way to go. So she stood, and tried not to fidget with the stapler or the muffin basket.

"Are you all right?"

"Of course."

"Are you sure?"

"Why wouldn't I be?" She cringed at her sharp tone.

He looked at her and her cheeks went even hotter. She wished he would get to the point of his visit and be on his way. He was tall and masculine and filling up her small office in a way that made her feel vaguely panicked. As if she might do something stupid again. Like baldly throwing herself at him one more time.

His lips twisted, and she wondered if he'd read her mind, or if his thoughts were as unwanted as her own.

"We didn't use anything," he said.

Mel nearly choked. She couldn't even pretend she didn't know of what he spoke, because the way they'd behaved was, well, too...large...in her thoughts to ignore. "It's okay." Her voice was faint.

"You're on the Pill, then."

"Well, no, but—"

His eyebrow lifted. "No?"

She wanted him out of her office. She wanted him off the island. Then, maybe, she could stop the unfamiliar sensations that curled inside her. "You needn't worry," she assured flatly.

He was still, his attention never wavering from her face. "I'm a doctor," he said. "I made one mistake already with you, having unprotected sex."

"Please, don't—"

"I'm not likely to make another mistake and act as if it didn't happen." He rolled right over her embarrassed protests. "There are health issues at stake, not just the matter of pregnancy."

Forget the home-court advantage. She needed to sit, after all. "I can't get pregnant." Not only was the notion terrifying, it was really impossible. "The past had proven that. I don't have any dreaded diseases. So can we please end this conversation now?"

He looked as if he had plenty more to say on the matter. She nearly oozed off her chair in relief when he didn't speak.

He reached out and plucked one of the muffins from the basket. "Do you mind?"

As long as he took it and went, she'd gladly give him both muffins. "Help yourself."

He didn't go, however. He leisurely consumed half the muffin, looking perfectly at home. "I need a favor," he finally said.

"What kind of favor?" With any other guest, she'd have immediately offered whatever assistance she could provide. With Luke, however, she couldn't seem to find her way back from the person who'd buried her grief with him on a windswept beach, to the manager of Maisy's Place. He wasn't just a guest and she couldn't pretend otherwise. Though she was certainly going to try.

"So suspicious." Another bite and the muffin was gone. "Dr. Frame seems to think that Maisy's granddaughter should be evaluated."

Mel's heart squeezed. April Fielding was a joy in all of their lives. But April was dying. "You'll have to talk to Maisy about that."

"I have."

"When? It's still early."

"In the kitchen. She was baking." His gaze drifted to the other muffin. As far as Mel could tell, there was no dissatisfaction in his expression. But she didn't need there to be any to know how that particular conversation must have turned out.

"Maisy won't allow it," she predicted flatly. "I could have told you that before you bothered her." A part of her mind wondered if he'd gotten any sleep at all if he'd been bothering Maisy during her preferred baking time.

"Which is where the favor comes in," he said

mildly. "Everyone around here I've talked to this morning says you and Maisy are close, that you're very fond of April. Talk Maisy into it. I can't get near the girl without Maisy's consent. Without her cooperation."

No matter what Mel's personal feelings were, she respected Maisy's position. She might not agree, but she certainly did understand. She knew, only too well, how much the little girl had already endured at the hands of the medical profession. "Maisy is April's legal guardian. She's devoted to her."

"So devoted she won't let the girl be seen by anyone but the doctor who's here on the island."

He couldn't have been more wrong, but it wasn't Mel's place to divulge Maisy's business. "Maisy trusts Dr. Hugo. He's served the Turns for decades."

"There's no hospital here. Dr. Frame said the clinic isn't remotely equipped to handle a case like April's. And regardless of equipment or lack of it, no matter the longevity of a doctor-patient relationship, any medical professional will tell you that second opinions are never unwarranted."

Unless that medical professional believes he's the next thing to God. Mel stifled the bitter thought. "If Dr. Frame has such a strong conviction on this, he could have spoken to Maisy himself, on any number of occasions."

"He's not actively practicing."

"I know that. But Maisy has known the Frames for many years. She does respect him."

"And she neither knows nor respects me."

"Don't put words in my mouth."

"Even if they're true."

She felt rather like a child summoned to the principal's office. The fact that he was right made it no more palatable. "Maisy doesn't know you," she allowed.

His expression didn't change. But the air between them was suddenly charged and she felt the impact of his deep blue gaze. Her spine straightened in defense against the ripples that skittered along it.

"Not like you do," he said.

Denial leaped to her lips, but the words stalled. Did she know him? At all? Had she imagined the connection she'd felt last night on the beach? Was it merely wishful thinking that what had occurred had had nothing to do with sex and everything to do with one despairing human reaching out for another?

Or was she merely trying to justify her positively outrageous behavior?

A pain set up a lively beat in her temple. "If Maisy had wanted Dr. Frame's medical opinion, she'd have asked for it."

"That's your answer. You're not going to help April."

"I'm not going to help manipulate my friend just so you can feel the high-and-mighty surgeon," she said flatly. "Dr. Frame surely knew better than to interfere."

"Dr. Frame has April's best interests in mind."

"Meaning that April's grandmother doesn't?" She struggled against her rising temper.

"Now who's putting words in someone's mouth?" He flattened his palms on the edge of her desk and leaned forward. "I don't know what you've got against surgeons or if it's just something about last night and me that you don't want to face. But I came here because Jason asked me to see what I could do. I specialize in pediatric cases. Maybe he considers April worth the interference."

"So, you're looking to win brownie points with him. What's at stake? A promotion of some sort? A partnership with Dr. Frame?" She knew the moment the words found life that she'd gone too far. Disagreeing with him was one thing, deliberately insulting him another. "I'm sorry."

He'd straightened from the desk, his eyes unreadable. "The person you should be apologizing to is April Fielding." Then he turned on his heel and walked away.

Mel sagged back against her chair, swiveling around to face the window behind her desk. The view beyond was the type that sold glossy travel magazines by the thousands—vivid green palms swaying in a balmy breeze, ripples of pristine white sand disappearing into a calm azure ocean. In her mind's eye, however, all she saw was the gleam of a small casket draped in tulips being slowly lowered into the cold, hard ground.

Sighing, she left her office and went in search of Maisy.

* * *

Luke found the office of Dr. Hugo easily enough. He'd headed up the only road and stopped when he came to the pink-and-blue square house with a weather-beaten wooden sign hanging from a rusty metal hook that read Doctor.

The front door was wide-open, obviously taking advantage of the morning breeze that had the collection of wind chimes hanging over the porch jangling in cheerful harmony. He ducked his head under the chimes and went inside. There was no receptionist, no patients sitting in the cluster of chairs situated around an oval coffee table. The surface of the table was almost obscured by outdated entertainment magazines.

If not for the wind chimes, the place would have been as silent as a tomb. He walked down the central hallway of the clinic. It was obvious that, at one point, the place had been a residence. The doors that opened off either side of the hallway had undoubtedly been bedrooms. Now they were small exam rooms that were more on the barren side than the well equipped.

He continued down the short hall to the door at the end of it, and knocked. There was no answer, and he opened it. Instead of an interior office, however, the door opened to the outside again. He focused on the white-haired man sitting before an upturned barrel covered with cards in a game of solitaire. ''Dr. Hugo?''

The other man barely gave him a glance. The unlit cigar in his mouth slid from one corner to the other as he frowned at his display of cards. "You sick?"

"No."

The answer earned him another glance. "I don't got none of that Viagra stuff."

For the first time that morning, Luke felt a stab of humor. "I'm not looking for any."

"Tourists," the other man said, flipping up another three cards and shaking his head critically, whether for the tourists or the cards, Luke couldn't tell.

"Every week one of you comes looking for Viagra," the man went on. "There isn't a single dose on Turnabout."

"Only thing I'm looking for is April Fielding's history," Luke said, and stuck out his hand. "Luke Trahern. I'm an associate of Jason Frame. He spoke with you the last time he visited Turnabout."

The old man adjusted his cigar again, took another considering look at Luke, then brusquely returned the handshake. "Maisy doesn't like strangers poking into her granddaughter's business."

"She's protective of her grandchild. It's understandable. But you shared April's prognosis with Dr. Frame."

"Professional courtesy. And Maisy about boiled my head for chowder when she found out," he added with a grimace. He chewed his cigar a moment, looking Luke up and down. "April has a brain tumor. Nobody on this isle wants that child to die. But it is gonna happen."

"It could happen later rather than sooner," Luke said. "There are some techniques we've developed that—"

"There's always some new technique. Some new drug protocol, some new miracle. April is seven years old now. She's had her condition since she was a toddler. She's already outlived everyone's expectations by several years."

Frustration tangoed with anger. "That's defeatist. All I want is to look over her history. She's very young for atypical meningioma."

The other man's eyes were a pale, faded green. His years were mapped in the wrinkles on his weathered face. "You get Maisy to agree, and my files are your files." His expression was clear. He knew that Maisy wouldn't acquiesce.

"I'll hold you to that," Luke said evenly. He wasn't used to failing, and he'd had too bitter a taste of it lately. His skills were in the O.R. At least they had been. Given his go-round with Maisy Fielding that morning, he seriously doubted his ability to change Maisy's mind, and wondered why in hell Jason had thought he could.

The cigar shifted corners again. "Should've asked for Viagra. Would have been easier to produce." The old doctor turned back to his solitaire game.

Luke could see the other man had said all he intended to. He left and walked back down the long road, past several flower fields that undulated in waves of vibrant colors. He slowed and watched. It was idyllic, he thought.

Idyllic and impossible to enjoy. Because once again, he was failing those who needed him the most.

April Fielding was only the latest name on a list that had grown too long.

Chapter 5

Six months later

Mel stood on the beach, watching the setting sun. In the four years since she'd come to Turnabout, she'd never tired of the sight. Today, though, she was even more grateful than usual for the descent of evening because it meant the air would finally start to cool. The summer heat had never bothered her as much as it did this year.

She tilted back her head, letting the breeze blow her hair away from her face. The air whispered along her neck, sliding up her nape. She sighed. Closed her eyes. Red orbs shone against the inside of her eyelids but all her mind saw was a cloudy, moonlit night.

She opened her eyes. Thinking about Luke Trahern—*Dr.* Luke Trahern—served no useful purpose.

He'd left the island six months ago, after staying only a few days. There was no reason to think she'd see him again. There was no reason he'd want to see her. She sighed again.

No reason.

She'd been telling herself that for several months now. She still believed it. Didn't she? She was only thinking about him now, because she was out here on the beach where they'd...they'd...

What they'd done had been madness. Aside from marrying Jonathan when she'd been a silly young college student with stars in her eyes and romance clouding her good sense, what she'd done with Luke had been the single most foolish action in all the thirty-one years of her life.

Her legs ached. She'd been on her feet too long. She sat down, tucking her skirt around her knees. But even her seated position reminded her of that night. Because she'd been seated just like this when Luke had come across her.

Why had *this* year been so different than the previous ones? Maisy gave a birthday party for April every year on that day, after all, though this was the first time it had been held in the evening. Mel had left the celebration because she hadn't been able to bear the festivity one moment longer. And she'd sought solitude on the beach as she did every year on that particular night, hoping for the peace to get her through to the next morning. To survive yet another year.

Another year without Nicky.

She swallowed and covered her face with her hands. Nicky's loss was a constant ache inside her. One that had become more bearable as the weeks, months, passed. But on that particular night, each year, the ache couldn't be contained. It continued to find its way, front and center, until it threatened to consume her sanity, her soul.

But this year, there had been someone *else* on her beach with her. Someone who hadn't let her cry alone.

Mel pressed a fist to her lips, the memory far too vivid for her peace of mind. He'd been a stranger, and she'd known it immediately. If he weren't, he'd have been back in the community center, raising the roof with music and voice, food and drink, along with every other resident of Turnabout—most of whom she knew at least by sight if not by name. He wouldn't have been out there walking along what she'd come to consider *her* patch of ivory white sand, where she could let the wind blow around her, through her, soothing away the pain that writhed inside her.

There was no way to soften the truth. Regardless of the circumstances, of her state of mind that night, she'd thrown herself at Luke Trahern, and he'd well and truly caught her. At least for a few hours.

Then he was gone, and she could hardly blame him. Neither she nor Maisy had gone out of their way to make him feel welcome. Regret was a familiar taste for Mel, though she'd worked hard over the past few years to keep from having a steady diet of it. But she did regret treating Luke the way she had. Before they'd slept together on the beach, and afterward.

Pushing those thoughts away, her gaze slid along the horizon. There was old Diego and his ugly but sturdy craft, heading back out to the mainland for his last run of the day.

Her legs were beginning to cramp. She pushed to her feet, wincing a little. It was time she got started on dinner for Maisy and April. And these days, the walk from her favorite beach perch back to the inn took a bit longer than it used to.

She tugged a little on her dress and turned to head back. All thoughts of cold soups, chicken salad or sliced turkey wrap, went right out of her head, though, at the man standing several yards off.

For a moment she actually believed her thoughts had conjured his image, as adrenaline, elation, and plain old shock swept through her.

But the screech of a seagull behind her, the drone of an engine somewhere up on the road, the soft hiss of water sliding over sand told her she was quite lucid.

Luke was definitely there.

His tall body seemed intensely still. There was no pretending that he hadn't seen her. She was the only one on the beach. Except for him. "Luke."

Sunlight glinted on his blinding white polo shirt. She couldn't see his expression. But she could imagine it. There was no reason for her to stand there like a guilty criminal in the eye of her executioner. Yet she couldn't make her feet move one inch in the soft sand beneath her.

She watched him push his hands into the front pockets of his baggy khaki-colored shorts. Evidently his feet didn't suffer the same lack of superiority over the sand as hers, because he slowly closed the distance between them.

Then Mel could see his expression all too clearly.

She swallowed. Feeling nervous, foolish, damnably *caught.* Jonathan had often stared at her in the same way. As if he could intimidate her into speaking first whenever they were at an impasse of one sort or another. Which, admittedly, had been most of the time.

The one who speaks first loses. The thought hovered in her mind. With Jonathan, she'd known exactly what was at stake. With Luke? She wasn't at all sure she could bear to find out.

His lips were tight, rimmed by a thin line of white. A muscle jerked in his jaw. She had the brief notion again of walking away, but dismissed it immediately.

"What are you doing here?" Lose or not, she couldn't bear the silence another moment.

"Is it mine?"

She tightened her knees, painfully aware that she might have swayed. She almost pressed her hand protectively to her abdomen, and only sheer willpower kept her hands at her sides. "I don't know what you mean."

His laugh was short and totally devoid of humor. He stepped forward and, before she could finish drawing in a shocked breath, wrapped his hand in the loose, gauzy folds of her dress, tightening it against her obviously pregnant body. "Is that baby mine?" The words were slow. Torturous. Furious.

She yanked back from him, uncaring that he still held her dress, that if he hadn't suddenly let go, she'd have torn the delicate fabric beyond repair. Then she did cross her arms over herself, and if it betrayed defensiveness or protectiveness, that was too bad. "This baby is mine," she said flatly. And God help her, she was barely able to cope with that fact, much less this man appearing again.

Luke's fingers curled as he studied Mel's fierce expression. He wanted to reach for her again. To do what? Shake her? Kiss her? He wanted a reaction from her. Anything other than the pale, shocked stare she'd had since she spotted him. "And a convenient way to get yourself a doctor for a husband," he goaded.

She gaped. "What?"

"It's hardly an original method, but it's effective enough. That baby is mine. I won't let it be born a bastard." *Not like I was,* he thought, wondering where his famed patience had gone.

"The last thing I want is a husband who's a doctor." Her voice was sharp. "And if I'd known *that* about you before, I'd never have—"

"Tussled in the sand with the likes of me?" He deliberately unlocked his jaw. She was right, of course, and he'd known it even as the accusation came out of his mouth. He hadn't told her what he was any more than she'd given him her life history before they'd climbed inside each other's skin that night. "You told me pregnancy wasn't possible." Information that should have been discussed *before* they burned sand into glass.

"I thought it wasn't."

Which told him exactly nothing and made him want to know everything. "You should have contacted me," he said.

Her expression didn't change. Or course, she hadn't admitted to anything, either.

Didn't matter. The moment Luke had seen the swirling blue fabric of Mel's dress blow against her otherwise slender silhouette, he'd known. She was pregnant. The baby was his. He knew it with every breath in his body. Yet she hadn't bothered with the tiny detail of letting him know. The betrayal of it bit hard. But he'd deal with that later.

She was still silent. Her eyes wouldn't meet his and he stifled a sigh, anger a hard knot deep down inside him. She looked like another gust of wind might just blow her over. And it was patently obvious that she hadn't expected him. He supposed he could thank Maisy for that, because the ornery woman had expected him. He'd spoken to her himself. Hell, she'd directed him to Mel's whereabouts when he'd checked in.

He put his hands back in his pockets again. "You should get off your feet."

Her eyebrows shot up. "I beg your pardon?"

"Beg all you want," he said evenly. "Your ankles are swelling. You need to get your feet elevated."

Her cheeks went red. "Well, I don't *need* anyone telling me what I need. I'm perfectly capable of watching out for myself."

Definitely a sore point. "Like you clearly felt no *need* to contact me with the happy news."

Her brown eyes flickered. "Luke, what are you...why are you here?"

"Mel!"

They both jerked at the hail, and Luke swallowed his response. What he was doing on Turnabout had nothing to do with the shock of finding her pregnant and everything to do with the mess he'd created.

A golden-skinned young man skidded in the sand as he stopped next to Mel. "Maisy's been looking for you." His words were for Mel, but his frankly suspicious gaze was all for Luke. Mel had captured her hair again in one hand and Luke felt another shaft of hot remembrance.

"Thanks, Tomas."

"I brought a cart."

Sure enough, there was a lime-green golf cart parked some distance away. Luke was more interested, though, in the flicker of relief that crossed Mel's drawn features.

Without looking Luke's way, she mumbled an excuse and began walking toward the cart. Tomas Duran looked half Luke's age. He was definitely younger than Mel, but the protective stance the man took as he walked beside Mel was loud and clear.

As clear as the unhappy look he gave her when she stopped halfway to the cart and looked back at Luke.

"Coming?"

A smart man would sit back, let his emotions cool and examine the situation with tactical precision. A smart man wouldn't have been allowing his life to slip through his fingers for the past half year. "Yeah," he said. "I'm coming."

The fact that he took some satisfaction from the flare of panic in her eyes told him how much better it would have been to take the smart route. But he'd apparently given up that path when he'd taken Mel into his arms with no concern or thought to consequences until it was too late.

He stepped up and sat on the rear-facing bench, well aware of the worried looks Mel surreptitiously sent him as Tomas took the wheel and the cart lurched over the sand. When the tires hit the sun-baked tarmac, though, they made short work of the distance back to the inn.

A small crowd had gathered on the neatly trimmed grass in front of the main building and Luke swallowed an oath when Mel jumped from the cart before it had even come to a stop. He caught up to her as she crouched down beside a young man, and Luke silently absorbed the way she pressed her hand comfortingly to the guy's brown-skinned shoulder.

"What happened?"

Dr. Hugo looked up at Luke over the prone man. "Ah, Leo Vega here thought he'd work on the roof without benefit of a ladder. Don't think whoever he was trying to impress saw fit to hang around when he fell on his butt.'' He waved his hand over Leo's swollen ankle. "Got a healthy sprain and a bruised ego, but he'll live.''

Leo groaned and folded his arm over his eyes as a chuckle worked through the small crowd. Mel's head was bent close to Leo's as she murmured something.

Leo didn't look quite as young as Tomas and the instinct to pull her away from the guy was a foreign and unwelcome one. Luke studied Leo's ankle until the urge passed. "He needs an X ray," he told Hugo.

''Think so, eh?'' Hugo's cigar—unlit as always—rolled from one corner of his mouth to the other. He looked back down at Leo. "Guess you know what to do, son.''

Leo groaned, nodded. Somebody produced an ancient wood-and-canvas stretcher, Leo was loaded up by his friends, and they trotted off down the road, laughing and poking fun at Leo's clumsiness.

''That boy's gotten into more fixes from pulling some stunt to impress a pretty girl,'' Hugo said, shaking his head as he pushed to his feet. "But he's been a handyman for Maisy since he was a schoolboy, and she doesn't seem to mind the eye he casts over the guests as long as he keeps his hands to himself. Mel, I'll get the info for the insurance to you later.''

Luke rose too and, ignoring the tight-lipped look she cast him, helped Mel to her feet. "Are they taking him to your clinic?''

Hugo shook his head. "No point.''

"Leo lives with his sister, Jane." Mel put in, moving her arm away from his hand. "She'll take care of him until he's ready to come back to work."

"You look like you swallowed something still wriggling," Hugo said, and there was only one word Luke could think of to describe the man's expression as he looked from Luke to Mel—*crafty*.

For a moment, just a brief moment, Hugo reminded Luke of his grandfather. But it was enough to let a swell of undefined emotion join the flood already filling him every time he looked at Mel.

Every time he looked at the swell of the child growing inside her. His child.

Mel must have seen that look of Hugo's, too, because she suddenly cleared her throat and spoke. "I have to get Maisy and April's dinner," she announced, and turned on her heel and hurried away. Her dress fluttered like a song around her slender legs and her hair danced around her shoulders as she moved. Lithe. Graceful.

But there was no mistaking what she was doing. Fleeing.

Chapter 6

"You knew Luke Trahern was coming, I take it," Mel said as she slid the heavy tray she'd carried from the inn's kitchen onto the table in Maisy's cottage.

Maisy's thin fingers toyed with her narrow glass of fresh lemonade. "His money is as green as anyone else's."

"You've turned away other guests with plenty of green stuff," Mel said as she laid out the meal for her friends, then sat down in the third chair to join them for dinner. Tonight her appetite was nil. "You weren't at all pleased when he showed up instead of Dr. Frame earlier this year. I thought you'd dance a jig when he left only a few days after he'd arrived."

Maisy's lips tightened. "Maybe I can't afford to do that anymore—turn away paying customers."

"What are you talking about? Maisy's Place is

doing very well. Occupancy is the highest it's ever been.''

''What's 'occupancy'?'' April's green eyes were bright and curious, completely belying the fact that she was nearly blind.

Maisy reached over and gently brushed April's dark blond curls away from her ivory forehead. The ringlets promptly sprang back into place. April was having a good day today, which tended to put everything else into perspective. The annoyance that had been budding inside Mel since Luke had found her on the beach trickled away, leaving her feeling tired, and mostly confused.

''It's how many beds we've got filled at the inn, chicken.''

''How come you call me 'n' Mel 'chicken'?''

''How come you're so full of questions today?''

April shrugged. Then she forked another chunk of mango into her little bowlike mouth. ''I wanna learn everything in the whole world,'' she said around her food.

Maisy's smile looked a little strained at the edges. Mel leaned across the table, studying April seriously. She'd learned early on to not act as if April's sight was impaired, for the child had an uncanny sense of being able to decipher expressions despite her challenge. ''*Everything?* That's a whole lot. Then there'd be no surprises left.''

April seemed to consider that as she plowed her way hungrily through her meal. At that moment, nobody would ever imagine the child was seriously, desperately ill. "I like surprises," the little girl said after a while. "Good surprises, I mean. Bad surprises are just yucky."

Mel smiled then pointedly looked over at Maisy. "I hear you on that one, pumpkin."

Maisy raised her chin, looking not the least bit defensive. Mel didn't know what she'd expected. It wasn't as if she and Maisy had ever sat down and discussed how Mel came to be pregnant. She owed her sanity to Maisy, but even with *her* Mel hadn't been able to discuss what had happened on the beach. But that didn't mean Maisy couldn't have her suspicions.

"When did he make his reservation?"

"Two weeks ago."

Mel absorbed that. "You put him in the Blue Cottage." The cottage that Maisy had abruptly "closed" for renovations two weeks earlier. Renovations that hadn't yet begun, a fact that Mel had blamed on the sometimes fluid definition of time the Turns exhibited. Now she realized there were no renovations to be done, at all.

"Grammy, can I be excused?"

Maisy gave her permission and April scrambled off the chair, took a moment to find her balance, then scampered out the door into the enclosed garden and play area where she plopped down on the grass with her collection of toys.

Mel watched Maisy watch April and her heart squeezed in empathy. She didn't know what Maisy was up to, but she knew she didn't have the heart to probe. Not when Maisy looked every bit as tired as Mel felt, and certainly not when Maisy only wanted to share every precious moment she and her grand-daughter had together.

"Go on out with her," Mel said gently. "I'll clean up here."

"You do too much, chicken." Maisy sighed and patted Mel's hand before standing. "You're like my daughter was when she was pregnant with April. Always doing, doing. Going, going. She should've had someone taking care of her when she was big with a baby, too." Not giving Mel a chance to respond to that, she slipped out the door and joined April.

Mel leaned back in the chair, her hand resting on the restless movements of the baby. A vision of an auburn-headed boy swam into her thoughts and she banished it before the wave of pain could accompany it. Pushing to her feet, she returned the dishes to the tray and propped one edge of it on her hip to carry back to the main building where the kitchen was located.

She could hear April's chatter and giggles and Maisy's lower voice as she let herself out of their home and headed to the path, turning left. She didn't dare look down the path the other way to the blue-doored cottage that lay at the end of it.

"Are you done avoiding me?"

Mel quailed inwardly at the hard look in Luke's eyes when she stopped beside the small table he was occupying in the sun-drenched dining room the next morning. The fact that she *had* been avoiding him made her cowardice even more abhorrent. She wasn't a doormat, she reminded herself firmly. Not anymore. It had taken her years to work the footprints out of her spine.

"I want an apology." She got out the words she'd rehearsed half the sleepless night before.

His slashing eyebrows skyrocketed. "What? You're the one who—"

"You accused me of angling for a husband. I wasn't. I'm *not*. The last thing I want is a husband—trust me. And I want an apology."

A muscle in his jaw ticked. But his voice was smooth. "All right. I apologize."

Surprise hit her. She hadn't truly expected him to do anything of the sort. Neither Jonathan nor her father would have.

"Now, would you sit down? Please?"

She swallowed and slipped into the waiting chair. "Is breakfast to your satisfaction?"

His lips twisted. "We're going to discuss scrambled eggs and fresh fruit?"

"The, um, the food is all from local sources. Eggs are from a small farm here that provides most of our dairy. And you've undoubtedly seen the citrus grove beyond the Blue Cottage. And of course, the mango and papaya—I see you tried those already. We offer lunch and dinner now, too, during the busier summer season. George Glass is a great chef. Maisy hired him a few months ago. If you join us, the seafood salad is very popular—"

"I can read the menu myself." He rested his arms on the small circular table and leaned forward. "And I don't want to talk about food unless it pertains to whether or not you've been eating properly."

She pressed her lips together, her heartbeat skittering around. She had no intention of telling him that ordinarily her appetite rivaled a horse's. At least it had until the previous day when he'd shockingly turned up on the beach. Dr. Hugo had warned her that she needed to watch her eating because she was gaining so quickly.

When she thought her voice might be remotely steady, she finally spoke. "My diet is none of your concern."

"Really. And that baby is none of my concern, either, I suppose."

A knot formed in her throat. So much for thinking he'd be put off by her demand for an apology. "No."

His hair was even longer than it had been six months earlier. Even more shaggy and more…inviting to her traitorous fingers. But when he lifted one eyebrow at her statement, he looked like a dark angel, come to punish her for her sins.

"No what? It's none of my concern, or no, it is of my concern."

His small table had originally been set for two. She focused on straightening the unused knife with the unused fork and ignored his tight question. She'd have to talk with the wait staff. The unused setting should have been removed. "I'm not going to intercede with Maisy for you about April."

"Did I ask you to?"

"You did before."

"And it didn't work," he said.

Mel chewed the inside of her lower lip. She *had* gone to Maisy that morning after he'd showed up in her office. And Maisy had done exactly what Mel had expected her to do. Refused to put her granddaughter through yet another grueling round of tests that had a ninety-nine-point-nine percent chance of giving the same exact results as all the others.

"If not about April, then why *are* you here?"

"For a vacation, of course. Isn't that what most everyone is here for when they visit Turnabout?"

Something in his tone made her look at him. He wasn't conventionally handsome. He was simply too intense. And the kindness he'd exhibited that night six months earlier seemed long gone. Still, looking at him made her stomach hollow out, reminding her that his touch had been like none other. "You're missing the carefree look of our usual tourists," she countered.

His glance dropped to her basketball-size tummy. The grooves in his hard cheek deepened. "Imagine that."

She didn't for a moment believe that she had anything to do with his purpose for coming to Turnabout. He hadn't notified her that he was coming, after all. His communication had been strictly with Maisy. And Maisy—for reasons that thoroughly escaped Mel—had chosen to keep it to herself. Unless Maisy really did suspect he'd had something to do with Mel's current state.

"Turnabout is pretty quiet for a vacation destination," she said. "There are more sights and activities on Catalina Island. And it's closer to the mainland. It's far easier to reach, more shuttle services. There's even a helicopter shuttle."

"Better not let the tourist board of Turnabout hear you." His voice was bland. "One would think you're trying to send customers to the competition."

"Catalina is hardly the competition. It's easily twice the size of Turnabout. It's a beautiful island. Avalon—"

"I've been there," he cut her off. "Two months ago, in fact. I took a weekend there."

Mel swallowed. Somehow she had the distinct impression that he hadn't gone alone. And the thought of that was rather more disturbing than she wanted to acknowledge. Just because she and Luke had done something foolishly dangerous together didn't mean she had any right whatsoever to be interested in how he conducted his life. Or with whom.

The baby fluttered inside her and she shifted in the iron chair. Her back was hurting. She was hardly comfortable anymore, and she still had three months to go. "H-how are Dr. Frame and his wife?"

Luke eyed the antsy woman across from him and wondered what she'd say if he told her the answer that sprang to mind. *Thoroughly disgusted with me.* "They're fine." He smiled, though he felt no humor.

"They're expecting another grandchild in a few months."

Mel's smoky lashes fell, hiding her eyes. Dark eyes, as soft and engulfing as velvet, which had haunted his thoughts for months no matter how many other women he'd seen. There'd been plenty, too. One had accompanied him on that abysmal Santa Catalina weekend. And, despite them all, he hadn't been able to keep his thoughts off this much more obscure island where a young woman with sad eyes had touched something inside him.

Belinda had stomped out on him after Catalina when it became apparent that he had no intention of taking their casual relationship to another level, calling him more names than he'd heard in years.

He should never have gotten involved with her in the first place. Even though she was a successful woman in her own right, she was still a member of the Conroy family—one of Sunquest's most generous benefactors. And the whole lot of them were more than a little disenchanted with Luke.

He didn't much care what anybody thought of him, but he did know their money was sorely needed to continue the work at Sunquest. Children from the world over depended on the clinic's services. And with Luke out of the way for a while, maybe Jason could repair the damage and coax more money from the Conroys' coffers.

"How nice for the Frames," Mel was saying. "I know they're thoroughly devoted to their grandchildren. They talk about them a lot whenever they visit

Turnabout. Mrs. Frame carries around dozens of pictures of them in her purse. She's obviously very proud of them.''

"What about *your*—" the word sat bitter on his tongue "—baby's grandparents? Is this their first grandchild? Their tenth? Or are you pretending that *your* baby doesn't have grandparents any more than it has a father?"

She looked as if he'd slapped her. He let out a rough breath, but couldn't bring himself to apologize. She was the one who'd kept silent about her pregnancy.

"I haven't talked to my parents in four years," she said after a moment. Her voice was brittle and her movements stiff as she pushed back the chair. She hurried away from the table as if the devil were biting at the hem of her pale green dress twining around her slender ankles.

Luke looked around the open patio that served as a dining room.

Get out of here and don't come back until you've got your head together, Luke. Jason's words swam in his thoughts.

His "vacation" was enforced. Luke could be irritated about it, aggravated and thoroughly, royally pissed. But the truth of it was Luke hadn't been doing anything good at home. He hadn't been for months. Not since before he'd visited Turnabout the first time and found Mel.

After all, what good was a surgeon who couldn't bring himself to pick up a scalpel for fear of killing another patient?

Chapter 7

Mel might have walked off on him, but Luke considered their conversation far from over. His career might be on the skids, but he wasn't going to let his personal life head any further south than it already had.

He found her in her office, looking uncommonly still where she sat in the chair behind the plain desk, gazing out the window behind it. "There was nowhere else I wanted to go," he said quietly.

Her sixties-era swivel desk chair squeaked when she slowly turned to face him. Her expression was wary. And he felt like a devil because he'd caused it.

"I beg your pardon?"

"You asked why I was here."

The corners of her lips lifted in a forced smile. "I

help run Maisy's Place," she reminded. "More or less. I merely wanted to know so I could assist in arranging activities for you. If you wanted to scuba dive, or sail. Fish. Horseback ride. That sort of thing."

He sat in the lone straight chair in front of her desk. "Liar."

Color bloomed in her cheeks and her eyes sparked. "I don't make a habit of lying."

He nodded. "I believe you. You're not very good at it."

Her lips tightened. "I think you should go."

"And if I don't?"

"Then *I'll* leave."

"And I'll come after you."

She blinked. "Is...that some sort of threat?"

"A promise."

"Why does that not comfort me?"

He leaned forward, resting his elbows on her desk. "I couldn't forget you."

She pressed back against her chair, her eyes widening. "I—what? Don't say things like that."

"Why not? It's true. I couldn't sleep at night without thinking about you." He watched her face flush. "I couldn't wake up without thinking about you."

"So, we had...great sex," she blurted out in a low voice, pushing to her feet, looking as if she was ready to run for the mainland. "*That* is what you thought about, and we both know it."

"It wasn't sex."

Her lips parted. "Oh, please. How did I get like

this then?" Her mouth snapped shut and she stared at him.

Silence filled the room.

Even though he'd already been sure of it, her admission still rocked through him. His throat tightened. "It was more than sex," he said. Great sex. Phenomenal sex. "We both needed something that night. Something we wouldn't have found with anyone else."

She looked panicked, now, color riding high on her cheeks. "You're romanticizing."

"You're telling me you haven't thought something similar? Not once during all the nights since?"

"No."

"I told you that you weren't a good liar."

"This must be quite a disappointment to you," she said, angling her body to move through the narrow space between her desk and the wall.

When she got bigger—and she would over the course of the next several weeks—she wouldn't even be able to fit through there, he thought.

"After my behavior last time, you probably expected a far more…entertaining…vacation. How disappointing for you. Instead of an easy lay, you found a thoroughly unattractive pregnant woman."

The tip of her nose was pink and her eyes were wet. He tamped down the anger that coursed through him and caught her wrist as she tried to step by him. He knew what was bugging him, but he was damned to figure out what was tormenting her. Other than the obvious, that was. "Stop."

She didn't look at him and he stood, very aware of the swell of their child beneath the soft fabric of her thin dress. He was also painfully aware of the thrust of her breasts and the scent of her barely golden skin, her sunshine-kissed hair.

"First of all, I didn't come to Turnabout *expecting* anything. I didn't have anywhere else to go. Secondly, there's nothing in the least bit easy about you. I never thought there was and I still don't." Even if he was struggling with the fact that if he hadn't come back to Turnabout, he was pretty certain she'd have kept him in the dark about her pregnancy. "And lastly, you need to look in a mirror, honey, 'cause there's nothing unattractive about you."

His voice was low, his words all the more fierce because of it. But one statement struck Mel far more than the others. And she trembled, because no matter how badly she wanted to pretend she had no involvement with this man, part of her silently screamed otherwise. "What do you mean you didn't have anywhere else to go?"

His dark brows drew together. "Marry me."

Mel stared at him, her question lost in the gale of shock at his. "What?"

"We're having a baby together. What do you plan to do when the baby comes? Have it here on the island? Go to a hospital in San Diego—make the crossing while you're in labor? What about after? You want to raise him or her alone? Join the ranks of single parenthood? You don't have to do any of that. Marry me."

She clamped a hand over her mouth, pushing his hand away, vaguely aware of his dark expression as she darted from her office and raced for the small bathroom nearby.

He was waiting, leaning against the wall outside the door, when she finally emerged. She'd expected no less, but she hadn't expected to see Maisy standing there with him. Still shaky, Mel strongly considered closing herself back in the bathroom.

"You didn't eat any breakfast this morning, did you," Maisy said, her arms crossed. "You only get sick when you don't eat."

"I'm fine," she assured. She ignored Luke. "Now, I've got to get started on the inventory."

"No. You're going to take the day off and rest."

Mel saw past Maisy's tart tone to her concern. "I don't need the day off. I just need to get back to work." Which she couldn't do as long as they blocked her way.

Maisy's eyes narrowed. "Don't go back to your office today, chicken. Inventory can wait." She looked up at Luke and sniffed. "Be of some use and make sure she does as I say. And here." She stuck a pink message slip into his hand. "Dr. Frame called looking for you. He said to call him back pronto." She strode down the wood-floored hallway, her heels clacking in tempo to the curls vibrating on her head.

"Does she know?" The message slip disappeared into his pocket.

"That I'm pregnant?" She smiled falsely. "It's become hard to disguise."

His jaw tightened. "Does she know that I'm the father?"

Her burst of sarcasm dwindled. She shook her head. "Nobody knows."

He seemed to think about that. "Well, I don't know about you, but I don't have the nerve to ignore her. So, come on."

Mel glared at Luke. "Very funny."

He didn't look particularly humorous. "At least Maisy figures it's your lack of food that had you tossing your cookies in there. Wonder what she'd think if she knew the real reason. Marriage proposals always make you nauseous or is it just mine in particular?"

Her stomach gave a dangerous lurch. "That wasn't a proposal. That was a demand." She brushed past him, heading back to her office. "I told you before that I wasn't husband hunting."

She had long legs, but his were longer. He blocked her office doorway. "Is Maisy right? Have you eaten?"

"Move aside, please."

"Answer the question."

"Stop treating me as if I cannot think for myself!"

"I'm only asking if you've eaten. I'm—"

"High-handed." And she'd had enough of that to last her a lifetime.

"—concerned." His lips were tight. "That's my baby you're carrying. Have you even had proper care?"

"Dr. Hugo is—"

"Lackadaisical at best."

Mel caught her breath. "You are unbelievable. How dare you cast aspersions on Dr. Hugo. He's delivered countless children."

"The man doesn't even order X rays when he should. And he hasn't delivered any kids of mine."

"Knock up a lot of women, do you?" Mel sucked in her breath, wishing the words back.

"Only you, sweetheart. Only you."

Her heart was racing, her breath short. She felt dizzy suddenly, and saw the shadows in Luke's blue eyes clear as he swore under his breath and caught her about the waist just as her knees gave way.

"Don't." She closed her eyes, willing away the whirling sensation as he swept her up in his arms as if she were no bigger than April.

"Shut up." He turned away from her office, striding down the hall. "Do you have a room here in the inn, or someplace else of your own?"

Her eyes prickled. She did *not* want to cry. "Put me down. Go call Dr. Frame back. If I'm lucky, he's calling your vacation short because they can't manage without you."

He stopped at an intersection of hallways. "I guarantee you that isn't it," he said shortly. "Which way, Mel? Or should I just find Maisy and ask her?" He looked toward the lobby where Maisy's voice could be heard as she spoke to someone.

"You play dirty."

"All's fair in love and war."

"We're not in love," she said sharply.

He looked down at her, his eyes unreadable. "Which way am I going, Mel?"

He needed a shave. His lean cheeks were shadowed, but she could still detect the muscle twitching in his tight jaw. Were they at war, then? She didn't want that any more than she wanted to lose herself in another impossible relationship. A hot tear slipped from the corner of her eye. "I have my own cottage," she whispered.

"Where?"

"Out back. There's a turnoff on the path right before the Blue Cottage." She swiped at her damp cheek. If he said one single thing about their cottages being in such close proximity, she wasn't sure what she'd do. Kicking him was out of the question considering the way he held her.

His gaze captured hers. For once, there was nothing angry, demanding or patronizing there. Only simple reassurance. "It'll be okay, Mel."

She felt her mulishness fade. The foolish thing was that she wanted to believe him. She swallowed the knot in her throat and blinked back more of the stupid, weak tears that wanted to break free. "Would you put me down, please? Before someone sees us."

"Are you going to run away from me again?"

"I'm hardly in shape to run these days."

He let her legs go slowly to the floor, which left him standing so close to her she could feel the heat off his body. Her swollen abdomen was pressed against him.

The baby kicked.

Hard.

His gaze dropped, looking at that spot, focusing so intently that Mel felt weak from it.

Time shrank down to a limitless pinpoint as his hand lifted. His fingers were long, sturdy and strong looking. Veins defined the back of his hand. It was a thoroughly, utterly masculine hand. One that held a fine tremble as he slowly pressed his palm, fingers widespread, against the swell of her child. His child. *Their* child.

She felt the warmth of his touch through her thin cotton dress. Felt the warmth and that tremor, almost like a vibration, right through her. For an odd moment, she found herself thinking about the tuning fork her music teacher had loved to wave about during the private lessons her parents had insisted upon. Mel still couldn't play the piano or the harp or the violin to save her soul.

But the tuning fork had always fascinated her. Her teacher had given it to her when she finally retired from the job. It was one of the few items Mel had taken with her when she'd walked away from the shambles of her life four years earlier.

In that moment Mel knew what she'd done about Luke had been wrong. All the months of justifying her silence over the matter were for naught.

"I'm sorry." Her voice was husky. "I should have notified you."

She heard him slowly exhale, as if he'd been waiting for that admission for a lifetime. "Yeah." He didn't cut her any slack. "And I should have called."

Her disquiet deepened. "Why? You couldn't have known this happened." On cue, the baby bumped against his hand.

A ghost of a smile played about his lips. "I told you, Mel. I couldn't stop thinking about you."

Before she could defuse that particularly explosive nugget, he ushered her through the rear of the inn, out the open dining area that had now been cleared of food and guests and down the stone steps to the path.

He kept steady hold of her arm as they walked to her cottage. Inside, his gaze traveled over the interior of her cottage. It was almost identical to the Blue Cottage. Except her bedroom was half the size of the one in Luke's cottage; the bed half the size of the ocean-wide thing there.

She lifted her arm out of his hold and moved away from him as surely as she moved away from thoughts of him and the size of the bed in his cottage.

Her kitchen was little more than a row of cupboards, a small refrigerator and a cooktop against the far wall. Ordinarily Mel would have bristled at the sight of Luke "entering" her kitchen area, where he began rummaging around in the cupboard and refrigerator without one word to her.

But she felt so tired that she didn't utter a single protest. She sank down on the oversize chair that had seen her through countless sleepless nights when she'd first come to Turnabout. With fat arms, a deep seat and a thickly pillowed back, the chair almost seemed to wrap around her with comforting familiarity.

She leaned her head back, watching Luke beneath her lowered lids. He was wearing shorts again. Slouchy, baggy things that didn't detract at all from the strength and shape of his long legs. And he moved easily. Confidently. As casually as if he'd rummaged through her cupboards a hundred times before, as if there was nothing more important or momentous on his mind beyond fixing some food.

It was almost possible to convince herself that she'd imagined his marriage proposal. *Almost.*

She prayed he didn't bring it up again. She wasn't sure her nerves could take it.

In minutes, he handed her a plate filled with a fluffy egg concoction, sliced cantaloupe and two slices of toast.

She slowly took the plate. ''You cut the crusts off the toast.''

He turned back to the kitchen. ''Habit.''

Frowning a little, she picked up the perfectly golden toast and took a bite. Her parents' cook had trimmed crusts from the bread. Somehow, it was hard to visualize Luke—dangerous looking with his untamed hair and whisker-roughened cheeks—doing the same task that fussbudget Reeves had performed in the pristine kitchen he'd claimed as his domain.

At least Luke hadn't skimmed a thin coating of marmalade on the toast before presenting it to her. Not that she had marmalade in her cupboards since she hated the stuff. ''Habit from what?'' *From whom?*

At her question, she sensed more than saw his shoulders stiffen and she realized she'd swum into sensitive waters.

Her gaze shifted from the set of Luke's broad shoulders beneath his loose tan shirt to a small, framed photo sitting on the mosaic-tiled end table beside her chair. Understanding someone else's need for privacy was second nature to her now.

Biting her lip, she drew her fingertip along the frame. Then she quietly slipped the frame into the table's narrow drawer alongside that small tuning fork from her music lesson days before picking up the fork he'd provided. She lifted a bite of the eggs to her mouth.

Demanding, intense and a surgeon, for God's sake. Could she possibly have found a more impossible man to complicate her life?

But oh, he could cook. And she was suddenly ravenous.

Too bad that once she got her shakes out of the way, she was definitely going to make sure he left her alone.

She'd come too far in her life since her arrival on Turnabout. She'd put the pieces of herself back together in a shape that was far more satisfying than the weak, submissive soul she'd once been as the pretty little trophy of the powerful Dr. Jonathan Deerfield.

No matter *what* Luke said, there was no way that Mel could go back to that kind of life.

No way, at all.

Chapter 8

"How come you are watching me this afternoon instead of Grandma or Lily?"

Mel smiled into April's inquisitive face. "Because Lily had an appointment and your grandma went with her. So I get to stay with you, instead."

Though she'd heard the explanation that day already, April nodded with satisfaction. "This was a good surprise," she decided.

Mel laughed softly. "Yes." She kissed April's nose, then leaned back on her hands, looking at the laden bushes surrounding their grassy picnic spot. "I need daisies," she said. "Which ones are the daisies?"

April rolled her eyes and pointed with uncanny accuracy. "Those ones. How come you don't know your flowers, Mel? Grammy says you're supersmart but I keep having to *teach* you 'bout the flowers.''

Mel shrugged, making her eyes wide. A master's in language studies did not a botanist make. "I guess I'm not as smart as you, kiddo.''

April giggled and rolled onto her back as Mel leaned over and plucked a half-dozen stems from the bush next to them. She stared up at the blue sky. "Grammy says my mom's in heaven.''

Mel sat back down, automatically weaving the flower stems together. Maisy was convinced that her daughter was dead. For Maisy believed that nothing would have kept Tessa Fielding from returning to her baby. "Yes. I know.''

"Do you s'pose she'll like me?''

"Who?''

"My mom. When I go to heaven.''

Mel's heart squeezed. How badly she wanted to assure the girl that was something that wouldn't happen anytime soon. "Of course. Everybody likes you, but your mother does most of all.''

"I can't remember her.''

Mel's fingers fumbled. She picked up the flower she had dropped and fit it into place. "I know.''

"I wish I had friends.''

Mel frowned. "Of course you have friends, pumpkin.''

"Not like the other kids do. They get to spend the night at each other's houses, and go to parties—''

"Your grandmother threw you a huge party for your birthday.''

April's narrow shoulders moved. "I know. It was fun." She blew out a little breath. "I just wish Grammy would let me spend the night at Lani's." Lani was Lily's little sister and the friend closest to April's age.

"Have you asked her?"

April nodded. "She's afraid to let me go, though. In case o' something happening." She turned her head and peered at Mel through eyes as wise as time. "I think it'll be soon. You know. Grammy doesn't want me to say that. It upsets her. She thinks I don't understand what all the doctors told her."

Her throat felt tight. "I know, baby."

"I do understand, though. And Grammy will be all alone when I go. Except for you and Lily and Dr. Hugo."

"And Tomas and Leo and everybody else on this island who loves your grandmother," Mel assured gently.

"And your baby when he's born. Grammy says she doesn't want you to do the same thing my mom did."

Mel's fingers paused over the flowers. "Oh?"

"She went off the island when I was a baby to look for my dad, but she never came back."

Mel didn't see how her situation could at all be compared to that of Maisy's daughter, who'd desperately loved the man with whom she'd conceived her child. Definitely not the same as Mel's case at all.

She handed April the daisies she'd woven together into a wreath. "There you go."

Older than her years, April was nevertheless still a delighted child. She sat up and plopped the wreath on her blond curls, her face breaking into a grin as her fingers nimbly felt out the details of the flowers atop her curls. "I'm a marrying girl, now!"

Mel couldn't help but smile at the child's glee, even though she wanted to rail at the hand April had been dealt.

April pushed to her feet, her arms held out wide. She slowly twirled, then stopped and took the wreath from her own head to drop it unerringly on Mel's. "Did Dr. Luke put the baby in you?"

Standing on the path, not ten feet from the patch of grass surrounded by gloriously blooming plants, Luke heard the piping of the child's question.

Eavesdroppers never hear good of themselves. The remembered words of his grandfather swam in Luke's head. He'd had a sleepless night followed by a restless morning. So restless that he'd gone to see Hugo, if only to keep his mind occupied on anything other than the twists life had thrown him. He stopped cold on the opposite side of the bushes, and waited.

He could see the top of Mel's gilded head. Could see, too, the child that Jason had wanted him to evaluate the first time he'd come to Turnabout. It was the closest he'd ever been to April.

And she was looking straight at him with the most vivid green eyes he'd ever seen. He knew from Hugo that her vision was seriously deteriorating because of the tumor. But he would have sworn in that moment that she was looking right into his eyes, seeing everything—good and bad and worse—that was hidden there.

"Did he, Mel?" the child prompted.

"Where did you get that idea, April?"

"From Grammy."

Luke had the strangest sense that April's gaze was filled with sympathy as she eyed him over the bushes. Which was impossible on so many levels it was laughable. She was only curious about the suspicion her grandmother must have voiced. And sympathy? He was probably only a sizable blob of shadow in her vision.

"Yes." Mel's voice was soft. Even. Giving little clue to the child what her feelings were on that reality. Still Luke felt tension leak out of him as surely as a spent balloon when Mel freely admitted the truth.

April's head tilted and her curls danced in the faint breeze, reminding him uncannily of her grandmother. "Is it fun to be in love?"

"I...beg your pardon?"

"Grammy says that's how you get a baby. By loving someone. But Dr. Hugo loves Grandma and she doesn't have a baby. She won't even kiss him 'cause of the curse."

Luke raised his eyebrows. *Hugo and Maisy? Curse?*

Mel suddenly turned, her eyes widening with

shock at the sight of him across the blossoms. "How long have you been standing there?"

Luke stepped through one of the breaks in the row of plants. She started to get up and he touched her shoulder, staying her. "Not long."

He looked at the little girl. She was petite, appeared to be underweight, with translucent skin as pale as snow. "You must be April. I've heard a lot about you. I'm Luke."

The girl preened and, despite her delicacy, her smile was wide and thoroughly engaging, full of spirit and life. Luke's stomach felt hollow. Damn Jason and his bloody interfering ways! Had he known all along that one look at the girl would be enough to fell Luke at the knees?

Of course he had. Jason was no fool. That was probably the reason for the phone message Luke still hadn't returned. Jason probably wanted to reel them all in, satisfied that he was solving two problems in one. Getting April the help she needed, and getting Luke back in a saddle he wasn't certain fit him anymore.

Then Luke felt small fingers close around his hand and April was tugging him down to the red-and-white-checkered cloth spread across the grass. "You sit next to Mel," she ordered. "You can have my sandwich and we'll all have a picnic together."

From the corner of his eye, Luke watched Mel, waited for her protest. "I think *you* should eat your sandwich, April," was all she said.

April wrinkled her nose. "I don't want it. My head

hurts today. But Luke can have it!'' With hardly a fumble, she rummaged in the basket beside her and pulled out a wrapped sandwich that she stuck out for him to take.

Mel nibbled the inside of her lip, watching Luke. He'd shaved and his dark hair was pulled back in a leather thong. Why it didn't make him look less dangerous, she didn't know. His jaw was a sharp blade, his lips tightly held. As he reached over and took the offered sandwich from April, she saw the muscle twitching in his jaw.

But his voice was that same, kind tone it had been the night on the beach, as he thanked April for the sandwich and unwrapped it when April told him to do so.

When he took a bite of the peanut butter, tuna and banana concoction that April loved, and even managed to smile and swallow it, Mel felt something inside her soften.

She stared down at her own sandwich. A thankfully ordinary peanut butter and honey mixture. The baby kicked. She looked up and realized Luke was watching her. He'd taken another bite.

Her eyes burned. Why did he have to be *kind?* She could withstand most anything except that.

''Eat your sandwich, Mel,'' April ordered, sounding so much like Maisy that she couldn't help smiling again. Judging by Luke's expression, he'd thought the same thing.

Feeling that odd disquiet again, Mel silently consumed the sandwich. She knew that April's spurt of energy would soon wane. On other afternoons they'd spent together, the girl would take a nap, after which they'd walk back to Maisy's cottage. But that afternoon, instead of curling up next to Mel on the checkered cloth, the child plopped down on Luke's lap and slipped her fingers through his, giggling a little over the way his dwarfed hers.

Mel saw him close his eyes for a moment, his face suddenly pale. She was on her knees, automatically reaching out to touch his arm, when he looked at her. His expression was so harsh, so darkly wounded, that she froze in place.

Beneath his chin, April hummed off-key as she played with his long fingers. Around them was the heady scent of lavender, daisies, gardenia, all carried on the gentle, constant breeze.

And Luke looked at her with a world of pain in his eyes that she recognized only too well.

Grief. Guilt. Despair.

Her heart ached. Her fingers stretched toward his arm, almost grazing his bronzed skin.

Then he blinked, and it was as if Mel had never seen a single thing out of the ordinary in his sapphire eyes.

Feeling off balance, she sat back, her hand slowly falling to her side.

Eventually April dozed off. And still they sat there on the patch of grass. Silent. Luke looking lost in his thoughts. Mel wondering who this man was who'd eat an inedible sandwich in order to please a child whose presence seemed to cause him pain.

The baby kicked again and she shifted, absently trying to find a comfortable position. She finally lay back, flat, keeping her knees bent. A vision of a beached whale hovered on the edge of her thoughts.

"What curse was April talking about?"

"How long were you standing there eavesdropping?" One glance at him told her he wouldn't be answering that question. "Turns believe it is bad luck to fall in love with an outsider." It was the short explanation.

"What makes them believe that?"

"Because tragedy always follows." She looked at April sleeping in his arms. The beautiful child was a result of one such union that had ended in disaster. "There's a hundred-year-old curse that promises it. But don't ask me the origin of the curse, because as long as I've lived here, nobody has ever told me. Being an outsider, and all."

"Do you believe the curse yourself?"

"I'm not a Turn."

"Where *are* you from?"

"Is this *Twenty Questions?*"

"Are you hiding out here, Mel?"

"Yes. From the Feds. I'm wanted in twenty states." She made a face. "Born and raised most properly in Northern California and not hiding in the least." At least not from anything but her own emotions.

She bent her arm over her eyes, shading them from the sun. "What about you? Have you always been in Arizona?" She asked only out of politeness, she assured herself, not because there was an insatiable curiosity burning inside her.

"No. She's had surgery already, hasn't she."

Mel sighed faintly. She turned her head to find Luke watching her. April was sound asleep in his arms, so trusting that it broke Mel's heart a little. *I'm sorry, Maisy.* "Yes."

His fingers smoothed over the girl's head. "There was recurrence."

"Yes."

"Jason didn't know about the previous surgery."

"Maisy doesn't talk about it much. Certainly not with her guests, even if they are regulars. Maisy doesn't trust outsiders easily and she's very protective when it comes to April."

"I noticed." His voice was dry as dust. "Yet she trusts you. An outsider."

"She's my boss and my friend." The urge to make him understand Maisy was swift and compelling, if confusing. She'd never before felt a need to defend Maisy to anyone. "She came to this island as a girl and later married a local man. He died shortly after their only child—April's mother—was born. Nearly everyone she's loved has been lost because of someone or something from off-island. Her husband. Her daughter."

"Proving the curse, I suppose."

"You don't have to believe it, Luke. The point is that Maisy does. There was a, um, a surgeon who heard about April's condition when she was a toddler. He convinced Maisy that he could help. So

Maisy took April off Turnabout for treatment. It was two years of misery. And still the tumor returned less than twelve months later. So there was another battery of exams, consultants, therapies. Nothing changed. Even the original surgeon had to admit defeat. There just aren't cases like hers. Maisy refuses to put April through more than she's already had to endure. She wants her to have some enjoyment in her young life.''

"Who was the surgeon?"

Mel frowned. "Why?"

He smoothed his hand through April's curls. They sprang back, coiled around his fingers. "Maybe I know of him."

Mel swallowed. Why had she gotten into this? "Deerfield. Something like that." She rolled onto her side and began pushing herself to her feet. "Would you mind staying here with her?"

"What's wrong?"

"Nothing. Just—" her cheeks felt warm "—you know. Nothing."

"Too much water in too little space," he deduced, his lips twitching. "Why don't I carry April, and you ladies can finish the afternoon out of the sun. You're starting to get sunburned."

Before she could protest, he'd risen with nary a jiggle to disturb April, who slept on.

Since it *was* hot and bright, Mel didn't feel compelled to argue the point. She also didn't want to continue wading in the conversation that she'd gotten involved in through nobody's fault but her own. She quickly shook out the cloth and folded it inside the picnic basket, gathered up April's collection of toys and slipped through the bushes to the path that led back to the cottages.

She knew that Maisy and Lily would be some time, yet. But she also knew that Maisy's cottage was unlocked, so she led the way there. It was a little closer than her own, and April could finish her nap in her own bed.

Her urgency lending a little speed to her steps, they made short work of the walk and, leaving Luke to take care of April, Mel hastily visited the bathroom. When she came out, the faint hope that he might have gone on his way was quickly dashed, for he sat on the rattan love seat in Maisy's living room, looking very much like a man who'd come to stay.

"There's some ice water for you," he said when he saw her. And sure enough, two glasses were sitting on the coffee table right there among Maisy's magazines and April's fat crayons.

"What? No milk?" Mel regretted the peevish question as soon as it emerged.

"Buttermilk," he said. "Somehow I didn't figure you'd welcome that."

She shuddered. The truth was, she didn't like drinking any kind of milk. She'd already choked down her daily quota of the stuff, and unless it came in the welcome form of a thick chocolate milkshake, she was free from milk for another day. "No."

There was a pile of clean, folded towels on the

chair, leaving Mel no place to sit but beside him. She picked up the glass of water. Put it back down.

"I've met Deerfield. At a symposium," Luke said. "Brilliant surgeon. If it was John Deerfield, that is. Folks called him 'the great knife.'"

Mel shot to her feet.

"You okay?"

She nodded. "Yes. Of course. My, um, my back hurts some. I'm more comfortable moving around." Her hand rubbed absently over the hard thump the baby gave her at the lie. She looked out the window at the ocean view. "Is the Blue Cottage still comfortable for you?"

"It was, last I checked." His voice was dry. "I'm not going to shackle you off to the preacher, Mel, so relax."

"I don't know why you said that in the first place." It was proof that her hormones were wreaking havoc with her common sense, for why should she feel irked that he so easily backed off his marriage demand-proposal when she didn't want to marry him or anyone else, anyway?

"Because I want my child to know I exist."

"Marriage is no guarantee of that. I know people who've been married decades who don't know their children."

"Is that why you haven't talked to your parents in four years? Because they didn't understand you?"

Mel lifted one shoulder. Admitting the truth seemed easier than trying to come up with some other plausible excuse. "What I wanted from my life and what they wanted for my life were two very different things." They'd been horrified, for one thing, when she walked away from her hollow marriage.

"At least they cared enough to *have* something in mind that they wanted for you."

She turned from the ocean view. "Your parents didn't?"

His lips twisted. "Not even close. My grandfather raised us."

"Us?"

"My sister and me."

"I always wanted a brother or a sister. Where is she now? Your sister. Does she live in Arizona, too?"

"She died when she was fourteen."

Sympathy settled inside her. "I'm sorry."

"So am I." He looked at his hands. "It's the reason I decided to go to med school. She shouldn't have died. I've done countless procedures for neurological conditions exactly like hers. Successfully." He flexed his fingers once then closed them in fists that belied the calm expression on his face. "Her doctors gave up on her too soon. Just like April."

Mel flinched. "Luke, you don't know what it's been like for them." She started toward him, but a crippling pain in her leg stopped her cold.

Luke was on his feet like a shot when she involuntarily cried out. "What is it?"

Feeling stupid, she couldn't help wincing again.

"Charley horse," she muttered. "I keep getting them in my—oh!—leg."

She heard him exhale. "Damn, woman, you about gave me a heart attack, you know that?" Without waiting for a response, he swept her over to the love seat, settling her on one end, him on the other, facing her. "You probably need more calcium," he said. His hand was gentle as he lifted her leg in his hands.

He slid off her sandal, tossed it onto the floor and brushed the long folds of her dress aside. Then his palms circled her ankle and slid up over the knot in her cramping calf. "There?"

Mel swallowed, words strangling in her throat. "It's fine, Luke, really."

"Right." He was looking at her leg as if he could see through to the knotted muscle. His hands were warm, his fingers gentle. He slid one hand behind her knee, lifting a little as he kneaded with the other hand. "Relax," he said quietly. "I can make it better."

"That sounds a little too close to 'trust me, little girl, this won't hurt.'" She jerked when his touch honed in with painful accuracy.

That same ghost of a smile haunted his lips. "Don't you trust me?"

A tart retort died on her lips, to be replaced by painful honesty. "It's not necessarily you I don't trust."

Chapter 9

Mel's words hung in the air. Luke kept working on her muscle spasm and tried not to notice how smooth and supple her skin felt beneath his fingers.

"What's not to trust?" He asked the question even though he wasn't sure it would be good to hear the answer. Particularly when he had his hands on her naked leg and his curiosity about what she might or might not have on underneath the airy dress was heading right off the scale.

She shifted, winced a little. "Luke…" Then she didn't say anything more. She just looked at him, with eyes that were so wide and so brown.

His touch slowed. Became less therapeutic and a lot more tactile. He was too damned old to have his hormones jumping through hoops the way they were.

But he was hanged if he could make himself take his hands off her sweet, smooth leg.

Beneath her knee, his fingers drifted back and forth, and he felt a fine shiver work through her. Saw the way her hands moved just slightly, the way her head lifted infinitesimally, her lips drawing in, then softening as she exhaled a soft whisper of sound that raised every nerve in his body.

"Stop," she whispered.

"Charley horse gone?"

"You know it is."

So why didn't he stop touching her? Why did he keep running his hand over her calf? Curving up over her knee, grazing the velvety skin of her taut thigh.

Folds of yellow fabric pooled against her thighs. How many times had he used the memory of their shared time to get him through another nightmare-studded night? And on those rare occasions when he hadn't been plagued by the nightmare, he had awakened in the morning, aching for the feel of her silky hair slipping through his fingers, the press of her soft lips against his.

He ran his hands all the way up her thighs, only some deeply ingrained common sense making him keep to the outside of her dress, and he curved his hands up over the firm jut of her belly. "It wasn't just sex," he muttered. Then he lowered his head, pressing his mouth against the swell of their child.

She sucked in her breath, her hands closing over his shoulders, sinking into his hair. He expected her to protest, to pull at his head, but she did none of those things. She trembled wildly and smoothed her hand over his hair down to the band he'd restrained it in.

"Don't do this to me." Her voice was low, shaking. "It's too easy. Too easy to lose myself. I can't do that again."

"Nobody has to lose anything." He braced one hand against the back of the love seat and the other on the edge beneath the cushion under them, and levered himself up, keeping his weight off her. He brushed his mouth over hers. "Our baby won't be losing anything. Marry me."

She pushed against his chest so abruptly that he nearly fell off the small sofa. He caught himself and ended up on the coffee table where the glasses of ice water promptly tipped over, dousing him but good.

He swore under his breath and jumped up.

She clapped her hands over her mouth. Luke had the momentary thought that she was going to be sick again, but then her shoulders shook and he heard her laughter.

His shorts were soaked. Maybe it was a good thing. He heard himself laugh, too. It felt a little rusty, but it was a laugh.

And it felt good.

"You look like you had too much water in too little space." Mel's eyes danced. "That'll teach you to mess with a pregnant lady."

That's all it took for Luke to go from ice-water cold right back to hot. Still smiling, he studied her lips longer than was wise or polite. Long enough for her to know exactly where his thoughts had returned.

"Don't look at me that way."

"What way?"

She swallowed, hard. He saw it in the movement of her long, lovely neck. She moistened her lips. "Like, like—"

"I want to make love to you right here, right now?" Her nipples were rigid, pushing impudently against the modest lines of her yellow dress. She was ripe with his child and he'd never been more aroused in his life.

She swallowed again, groaning a little. "Luke—"

"But we won't. Not here. Not now." It was Maisy's cottage, after all, and the child napping in the other room could awaken at any time.

Desire swept through Mel like wildfire, dizzying her with it. But it didn't matter. Because further involvement with Luke Trahern was out of the question. "Not...ever." Oh, why was it so hard to push that word past her lips? And why did he have to just stand there, his hands propped on his hips, his eyes too wise, too knowing, looking dark and dangerous and like every good little girl's fantasy come to life? "I m-mean it, Luke. Not ever. We're not going to do that. Once was quite enough. Obviously."

"It was twice," he reminded softly. "And who are you trying to convince with your protests? Agree to marry me or don't agree, yet. I'm not going to stop pushing for what I know is right, so you might as well get used to it. Regardless, you and I are going to end up in bed together, Mel. It's a matter of time, and you know it.''

Then she could only sit there, speechless, when he leaned down. Her hands clutched at the cushion under her, but the onslaught of his mouth on hers never came. He looked at her, then pressed a soft kiss to her forehead, ran his finger down her cheek and left.

Well after the click of the screen door sounded, Mel finally remembered to breathe. She let out her air in a whoosh, and just sat there, her heart thundering as his words circled in her mind and his baby kicked in her womb.

Mel didn't see Luke again that day. April eventually woke from her nap, but she had such a violent headache that Mel gave her a dose of her medication and she went right back to sleep. Maisy returned, took one look at the prescription bottle that Mel had left on the coffee table and paled.

Mel fixed her friend some tea and a sandwich and quietly left. She'd learned long ago that there were times when Maisy was up for company, and times when she wasn't.

Tomas handled most of the duties on the weekend, and Mel usually caught up on her own laundry and personal matters during that time. But once she had hurried to her cottage, half afraid she'd see Luke on the way and half afraid she wouldn't, she couldn't seem to concentrate on even the most mundane tasks. When night fell with no sign of Luke, she convinced herself she was grateful.

The next morning, after an impossibly restless night, she was doubly convinced that his absence was for the best. Maybe he'd reconsidered his crazy words, his impossible proposal.

By the time that afternoon rolled around, Mel felt as if she were going crazy herself. Her laundry was still undone, her small refrigerator still unstocked. Rattling around her cottage with Luke's only a few dozen steps away was making her nuts and she finally took refuge in her office at the inn. But even there she felt disjointed.

It was proof of her own madness when she found herself holding the phone in her hand, dialing her parents' number. It was further proof of her cowardice when, at the sound of Reeves's ponderous voice answering the phone, she quickly pressed her finger over the disconnect button.

"I thought you didn't work on Sundays."

She sat back in her chair, so startled by the voice at her doorway that she fumbled and the phone clattered noisily as she replaced the receiver. "Luke."

"Well?" He leaned his shoulder against the door-jamb. "It's Sunday. What are you doing here in the office?"

Trying to pretend none of this—you, me, the baby—is happening. She didn't voice the thought. "Playing catch-up." It wasn't quite a lie. She did have some paperwork to take care of.

He lifted one eyebrow and she had the insane thought that maybe he'd read her mind. Which was nonsense, of course. "Important stuff?" he asked.

"Very." Seeing as how it had waited two weeks and could easily wait two more. "Where have you been, anyway?" She wanted to kick herself for voicing the question.

"I was talking to Hugo."

"The man you think is incompetent."

"I never said that."

"No. *Lackadaisical* was your word of choice, as I recall."

"Well, he was right about Leo's ankle, as it happens. There was no fracture."

For a moment she was surprised that he'd so easily admit it. "How do you know that?"

"I found out where Leo lived and went there myself."

"Double-checking Hugo's work."

"Am I supposed to apologize?"

"Maybe to Dr. Hugo."

"Maybe I did," he said evenly.

She wasn't certain if he was serious, or not. In her personal experience, apologies weren't in a surgeon's vocabulary. But more than once, now, Luke had offered one when due. "Why does any of this matter to you, anyway? Turnabout needs one doctor, but it doesn't have a large enough population to support two."

He watched her. "Afraid I'm looking to relocate here, Mel?"

Her stomach dropped. "You're a pediatric neurosurgeon."

"Who'd likely only have one patient on the island—a girl whose grandmother won't let her be examined.''

''I told you all that they'd been through—''

He shook his head, cutting her off. ''So you did.'' He came into her office and sat on the corner of her desk, bringing with him the warmth of the day, the scent of the ocean. ''I've spent some time with Hugo lately. Maybe I'm considering a switch to general practice.''

Her jaw loosened as she actually considered the statement as truth. It took only a moment, however, for the ridiculousness of it to penetrate. ''No, you're not. You'd be bored stiff inside a week. People go into surgical specialties for the demand of it, the adrenal high, the power. You'd never find that in general—'' His eyebrow had risen again and she realized her mouth was seriously running away with her.

''And you consider yourself an expert on that because...why?'' He waited.

His attitude smacked of superiority. She'd left behind that sort of attitude from her father, from Jonathan, but she still saw red. ''Because I was born and raised by Daddy the surgeon, and his good little wife,'' she snapped. ''Now, would you please go?'' She lifted several reservation forms and shook them. ''I have work to do.''

''I never was good at listening to orders,'' he said mildly. ''So, your dad was a surgeon. Does he still practice?''

She wished she'd kept her mouth shut. She'd never had trouble with that before. What *was* it about

this man that got under her nerves so thoroughly?
"He...teaches."

"No kidding?" He inexorably tugged the forms
from her and set them aside, but he didn't release
her hand. His thumb smoothed over the backs of her
knuckles, setting all manner of sensation skittering
through her. "Where?"

"At a university." Where he was dean of the college of medicine.

"Full of more details, Mel?"

She couldn't think straight when he touched her.
That *had* to be the answer. He touched her, and her
brain short-circuited. What other explanation could
there be? "Please let go of my hand."

A whisper of a smile entered his eyes. "Something
wrong?" He placed her hand between both of his,
looking at her palm, smoothing his fingers slowly
over it in a manner reminiscent of the palm readers
who'd set up shop on Fisherman's Wharf, catering
to the tourists.

"Luke, really, I have work to do." It was a blatant
lie, but she was getting desperate.

"I'll let you go for a price."

Her lips parted. "I *beg* your pardon?"

The smile spread to his lips. "Where is your mind
at, Melanie? Mel is short for Melanie, isn't it?"

She nodded, feeling flushed. "I prefer Mel."

"What's wrong with your full name?"

It belongs to the woman I used to be. "Too...frilly."
She expected him to be amused, and he was.

He turned her hand over, looking at her short, unpolished nails. "You don't have to be wearing ruffles and have paint on your face to be thoroughly female." His gaze met hers. "Believe me, you are *thoroughly* feminine. And Mel suits you."

Her thoroughly feminine hormones were shifting into overdrive. "All right, so let go of my hand now."

He tsked softly. "Impatient, Mel. I might think you're a little unnerved, here."

"Well why not? You're the one who goes around promising bed bouncing."

"Promising?"

"Threatening."

His smile widened. But he did let go of her hand. "Don't you want to know the price?"

"My hand is free." She wiggled her fingers.

In a smooth movement that abruptly reminded her just how quickly the man could move when he felt like it, he'd rolled her chair out and was leaning over her, his hands on either side of her shoulders, effectively trapping her. Her heart skittered and her bravado breathed its last.

"The price is answering one question."

His lips were only inches from hers. She caught herself, barely, from tilting her head, closing the gap. "What?"

"When's your next appointment with Hugo?"

It was the last thing she'd expected. "In a few days."

"Good." He straightened, giving her space to pretend she wasn't reeling from the kiss that *hadn't* come. "I'll go with you."

"I don't—"

"Do you really want to argue with me about this? The baby is mine, too."

And she'd already kept him "out of the loop" long enough. He didn't have to voice the thought; her twanging conscience heard it all the same. Which didn't mean it was all that easy to swallow her objections, even knowing they were unreasonable. "Don't you have to go back to Arizona soon? You can't stay on Turnabout indefinitely." She'd already checked the schedule, but the Blue Cottage still reflected Maisy's supposed renovations and not Luke's presence at all. "Didn't Dr. Frame call to summon you back? You must have patients."

"You think my going home will get me out of your hair?"

"I can hope."

He laughed softly, but his eyes were dark, serious. "Sorry to disappoint you, honey, but Jase most definitely does not need me. You've got *all* my attention."

For Mel, who'd spent her entire life wishing fruitlessly for the attention of the men she'd loved, his words ought to have been a dream come true.

Somehow, coming from Luke, they felt more like a threat to the semblance of contentment she'd finally managed to obtain. If she lost herself in a relationship with *him,* she wasn't sure she could ever recover.

Chapter 10

"So, you're the mystery father after all."

Mel flushed as Dr. Hugo eyed Luke speculatively.

"Maisy was right, then," he continued. "At least you're both from off-island, so we don't have to worry about the curse. What do you intend to do about our Mel, here?"

"Dr. Hugo!" Mel wanted to sink through the floor of the examining room. "I hardly think that's any—"

"Marry her, only she won't have me. Little does she know just how smart she might be."

Beneath the thin cotton smock with the pale blue flowers that Dr. Hugo's sometime nurse had provided her for the exam, Mel's shoulders stiffened. "Stop talking about me as if I'm not here."

Luke's hand closed over the back of her neck and

she caught the seriousness underlying the amusement in his gaze. Her annoyance stuttered. "Can we just get on with this? I've got things to do."

"Haven't you learned anything since you came to Turnabout, Mel?" Hugo washed his hands and pulled out his stethoscope. "Time has a different meaning here. Priorities aren't the same as they are on the mainland."

"Well, if time is different, maybe that's why I'm getting *huge*." Mel was determined to ignore Luke, standing beside her where she sat on the examining table.

"Good thing you showed early," Hugo muttered, "considering how long it took you to finally admit that you were pregnant and not just suffering some flu bug you couldn't shake."

Mel flushed, feeling Luke's quick look at that.

Obviously seeing no reason for discretion, Hugo looked at Luke. "She was nearly four months gone before she came to me, but anybody with a lick of sense could *see* she was expecting."

"I took vitamins before I came to you," Mel said defensively. "Ate right, did everything a person is supposed to do."

"Good thing," Hugo grunted. He listened to her heart, checked her blood pressure, made some notes on his chart, eyed his cigar on the counter but managed to refrain. "Fortunately, you're healthy as a horse, so the baby didn't seem to take any harm from his mama's refusal to see the light of day. All right, let's see how things are going."

"His?"

Hugo grinned. "Manner of speaking, Luke. Don't go getting excited that you're gonna have a son."

"A girl as beautiful as Mel would do just fine."

Mel closed her eyes against Luke's quiet words. "Can we get on with this, please?"

"Only people who make worse patients than doctors themselves are children of doctors." Hugo shook his head. "I oughta know. My daughter won't go near a white coat." He brushed aside the gown, discreetly revealing the bulge of Mel's abdomen. He squirted gel over it then pressed the Doppler against her through the gel, listening closely to the watery rush of sound that came through the amplified device.

Mel saw him frown in the same moment that Luke did. Unease sliced through her way too easily. Without thought, she reached for Luke's hand. "What? What's wrong?"

Hugo waved her silent. He turned and rummaged through his cabinet of tricks and came out with another stethoscope. "Wish we had an ultrasound," he muttered as he pressed the instrument to Mel's belly, his head close as he listened. "I'll be damned," he muttered.

Mel struggled to sit up. "What is it? I can't lose—"

"Twins." Dr. Hugo looked up, grinning. "I'd bet my favorite humidor you've got twins kicking around in there."

All the anxiety racing inside her screeched to a

screaming halt. She could hear her heartbeat thumping in her ears. "I...what?"

"Twins, Mel." Luke looked stunned. "Do they run in your family?"

She blinked and shook her head. Turned from Luke to Dr. Hugo. "How can this be?"

Dr. Hugo pulled her gown over her belly and dumped his equipment on the counter behind him. "Well, now, see there's this thing called an egg. Sometimes two. Meets up with sp—"

"Very funny." Mel huffed and fell back against the inclined table.

"Hey," Luke murmured. "Look at it this way." He was still holding her hand, and he kissed her knuckles, looking as pleased as if they'd been planning to have children together for years. "Double the fun."

Mel folded her arm across her eyes. Tears burned behind her eyelids. Two babies. Dear Lord, she could barely face one baby for fear of the past repeating itself. Now there were two? She swallowed. "Maybe you're mistaken. Maybe—"

"Possibly," Dr. Hugo agreed. "If you want to know for certain, you'll have to go off-island. Have an ultrasound. Although they've been fooled by twins now and then, you're far enough along now to get a good look-see at what's happening in there. I can refer you to an OB in San Diego. You two better hold off on, uh, having relations for a while. Least until we have a better picture of your progress."

Mel refused to look at Luke. Relations? That

would only happen if they *had* a relationship. Which they most certainly did not.

"I'll make arrangements for the trip immediately," Luke said.

"No. I don't want to go anywhere." She ignored Luke's immediate protest and focused on Dr. Hugo. "There's no real need for an ultrasound, is there? Twins explains the fact that I'm a little bigger than normal. All my other tests have come back with good results, my blood pressure is within normal—"

"Relax, Mel," Luke said. "Ultrasound is perfectly routine."

She knew that. How well she knew that. "If I had wanted one," she told him, wanting to tear out her hair in the face of his perfectly smooth bedside-manner voice. Jonathan had used that type of voice too many times on her to count, and she still hated it. "I am perfectly capable of having it arranged."

Silence filled the tiny exam room, finally broken by Dr. Hugo, who told her she could get dressed again, and left them alone quite without his usual, characteristically colorful comments.

Mel turned her back on Luke, swinging her legs down from the table, and reached for her dress.

Luke's hand was there first, handing it to her.

"You can forget trying to dress me, too. I'm not entirely inept." She snatched the dress from him and stepped behind the screen in the corner of the room.

"Nobody said you were. And I wouldn't mind dressing you, but first I'd rather *un*dress you." His voice was smooth. "Seeing how we never really got to that part. It was too cold that night on the beach."

Mel closed her eyes, telling herself that the idea held no appeal, that her hormones weren't leapfrogging all over themselves at the mere thought of Luke and the presence or lack of her clothing.

She was almost getting used to lying to herself.

"Very funny." Dressed, she stuffed the gown in the basket left there for used ones, and stepped from behind the screen.

"Do I look like I'm joking?"

She decided against answering. It just seemed wiser. She picked up her wallet, wrote out a check for Dr. Hugo and left it sitting on the counter where he'd be sure to see it. "I need to get back to Maisy's Place."

She saw him look at the check. "I need to add you to my health insurance," he murmured.

Mel headed for the door. "I'm capable of paying my own bills."

"I didn't say you weren't. But the bills relate to my baby—babies."

"Are you coming, or not?"

He left the check where it lay. "I'm the one who rented the Jeep that we drove here, remember?"

"If you weren't coming, I'd just walk."

"You take this independence thing a step too far, you know."

"Well, maybe it's about time," she said, feeling near tears all over again and not really knowing why.

Maybe it was the result of having her life turned topsy-turvy *twice*…in the form of twins. Twins!

She stopped next to the Jeep. Despite her bravado, she didn't feel up to the task of walking all the way back to the inn.

He opened her door and helped her up. "You know, Mel, you're going to have to deal with what's going on."

"Who says I'm not?"

He snorted softly. "Anybody with two eyes in their head." He rounded the Jeep and climbed behind the wheel. He started the engine and drove out from behind Dr. Hugo's rainbow-hued building. They passed the fields, vibrant with blooms of every shade. He slowed to let a trio of children cross the road, which they did, smiling gap-toothed grins, the kites they held rippling as they ran. Then he was driving again, heading over the highest point of the road, where a person could see all the way to Catalina and beyond if the weather was clear.

She wondered if Luke had really meant it when he'd said she was the only woman to carry his child. Found herself wondering how old he was, if he'd been married, if he had family other than the sister he'd lost. And if he did, why he'd felt that he'd had nowhere else to go when he'd returned to Turnabout.

Thinking about any and all of them was easier than contemplating the news Dr. Hugo had delivered.

"How early did you know?"

She closed her eyes against the incredibly beautiful view. "Pretty early." The honesty was nearly as painful as remembering the unadulterated shock, panic, that she'd lived with during those early days when she'd suspected the impossible had occurred.

"Earlier than four months."

She swallowed. Nodded.

"You told me pregnancy wasn't possible."

"Obviously I was wrong."

He turned the wheel, veering off the road, spewing gravel as they rocked to a halt near the guardrail. "Could you turn off the sarcasm for twenty seconds?"

"No." She fumbled with the door latch.

He caught her arm before she could escape. "Dammit, Mel, what is your problem? If you didn't want the baby—*babies*—so much, you could have done something about it months ago."

Nausea accosted her. "Stop. Please, Luke, I can't…just…stop."

His eyes, so dark they looked nearly black, searched her face. "I can't stop, Mel. Those are *my* children you're carrying. We made them together. Maybe you don't want them, hell, I don't know what's—"

"I *do* want them! That's why I couldn't see Dr. Hugo too early!" She yanked free and pushed out of the vehicle, sliding awkwardly from the seat.

Luke was taller and moved a lot faster. He was around the Jeep in a flash, catching up to her before she made it to the guardrail overlooking the cliff. He grabbed her wrists, making her face him. "Every time you walk away, I'm going to be right behind you.''

She cast him a look that could have broken the heart of a granite statue. He gentled his grip, moving his hands from shackling her wrists to cupping her shoulders. He could feel her trembling. Without another thought, he pulled her into his arms, shushing her protest, holding her close, cushioning the unnamed emotion that racked her.

Maybe it wasn't the wisest course. Following his instincts lately had mostly been disastrous. But after a long while, after he'd held her, smoothed his hand over her slender back, brushed his hand again and again down her thick, silky hair, he felt her shift.

Then he felt her arms sliding around his waist, fingers clutching the back of his shirt. A long shudder rippled through her. Between them, the babies bumped. He pressed his cheek to the top of her head, breathing in the clean scent of her hair, feeling the wash of an ocean breeze drift over, coil around them.

The tension seemed to slowly fade, and as it did, the utter silence of the island seemed to penetrate Luke's senses.

His life had changed on this island. Regardless of the circumstances, he was going to be a father. And there wasn't a cell in him that didn't want to howl at the moon in satisfaction. He wanted the babies.

He wanted Mel.

And for some reason, this woman was afraid of being pregnant, afraid of having a baby, afraid of being involved.

He slid his fingers through her hair again, finding the action as soothing to him as it might be to her. "I know pregnancy is scary, Mel—" He felt her start to stiffen up all over again, but held her snug against him, willing her to stay calm. If ever there was a person who cried out for connection with another human being, it was this prickly, intensely private woman. "Particularly the first time around, but I'm going to be with you every step of the way. You're not in this alone."

She pressed her forehead to his shoulder. "This isn't my first pregnancy." Her voice was muffled.

Luke's hand hesitated as he made another pass through the hair lying across her shoulders. A dozen questions, theories, flew through his thoughts, but he voiced none of them. The fact that she did not have a child with her on Turnabout spoke volumes. "It's my first," he said.

She laughed brokenly, then slid her arm around his neck. "I wondered if you'd meant that."

"I did."

Her fingers tightened, her face turning against his neck. "I'm scared, Luke."

Her voice was barely audible, and the admission rocked him. He'd known she was frightened; he hadn't exaggerated when he'd made that comment about anyone being able to see that. Mel's emotions showed so clearly on her beautiful face. But to hear her admit it, the words raw on her voice, made something inside him ache. "Of what?"

Her shoulders moved. He felt her soft breath on his jaw. "Everything."

God, he couldn't take it. Knowing she was scared, hurting, and there wasn't a damned thing he could do about it—particularly when she wouldn't tell him any reason why. "It'll be okay," he murmured, thinking they were some of the most useless words in the English vocabulary.

She looked up at him, her eyes even darker against her pale skin. "You don't know that. Nobody ever knows that."

"Then you've gotta have faith."

"Faith didn't work before."

He absorbed that. "Then have faith in me," he said. "Have faith in this." He covered her mouth with his.

He felt the wave of shock bolt through her. The hint of stiffening that never really formed into resistance. Then her lips softened, and she made a soft sound that was like manna for his starved senses. Her arms closed around his shoulders.

He groaned, took her mouth more fully, absorbing the taste of her. His hands swept down her spine, caught her hips. She arched against him, her breath nearly a sob as she tore her mouth from his, pressing her lips against his neck.

Mel struggled for sanity. "I can't think when you touch me."

His chest rumbled. "Maybe we do better when we don't think." He stepped backward, coming up against the side of the Jeep, pulling her easily with him. The ocean swept in and out far below them, the Jeep shading them from the road, and his hand covered her breast.

Mel gasped, moaned, felt fire streak through her as his thumb roved over, around her tight nipple. "Luke—"

"Shh." His lips burned down her throat. He flipped open the top button on her dress. His arm around her waist urged her closer, his hard thigh slipping between hers as he took more of her weight. His hand moved against her breast. Another button escaped.

And, oh, she wanted his hands on her. It was insane, it was foolish, it was—

He slid his hand inside her dress, tipping the cup of her bra down, finding her bare flesh.

It was perfect.

Her heart raced, need twining deep inside her with every brush of his fingers. And it wasn't enough. She knew it.

He knew it.

His mouth found hers, both hands working on the buttons that stretched from the modest scooped neck to her waist, and freed them all. He pushed it from her shoulders, his eyes burning over her. Her skin tightened, seemed fit to burst from the way her breasts swelled under his gaze. "Beautiful," he murmured.

The dress dipped to her waist, caught by the press of their bodies against each other. He lowered his head, caught one peak between his lips, and Mel's head fell back, staring unseeingly at the pure blue overhead, wildness sliding into her bloodstream, expanding, bubbling.

She arched against him, mindless with need, and heard the rough caress of his breath, felt the strength of his hands cradling her against him, the hard press of his body in return. "Luke…I…Dr. Hugo said—"

"It's okay," he promised, seeming to know what she wanted, what she needed, without words. "Forget Hugo." His thigh was hard against her, notched high between her thighs. His hand slid over her breasts, over the hard swell of her abdomen, the panties that clung to her moist flesh. Then he kissed her, slid his fingers over her, inside her.

Her mind screamed his name, and she convulsed against him, endless pleasure streaking from nerve ending to nerve ending, from the ends of her waist-length hair to the toes curling against her leather sandals.

And when her strength gave out, he was there, holding her, taking all of her weight, soothing in the wake of exciting, calming in the path of inflaming. She could feel his arousal, felt fire in her cheeks in the face of her utterly wanton behavior. "I'm sorry."

His chest rumbled again. "You're kidding, right?" He tilted back her head, looking at her. His eyes narrowed. "You're not."

She blushed even harder.

A strange look crossed his face. He touched the corner of her lips, then pressed a gentle kiss to her forehead. "You're so damned sexy you kill me, Mel."

"But I...you didn't—"

His lips tilted crookedly. "So? You did, and that's enough for me."

He adjusted her clothing, started doing up her buttons and laughed softly when she sank her teeth into her lip, hauling in her breath on a hiss as his knuckles brushed her hypersensitive breasts.

"Enough for now. Until next time," he amended.

Then he helped her back into the Jeep, leaving her to silently wonder if she was more comforted or frightened by his seeming certainty that there *would* be a next time.

Chapter 11

Mel stared at the notation she'd made on the appointment calendar spread out in front of her on the desk. Only a day had passed since she'd seen Dr. Hugo.

Since her madness at the hands of Luke Trahern.

She'd done it. Made the appointment for the ultrasound with Dr. Hugo's contact in San Diego. Now she just needed to have the courage to tell Luke, knowing that he'd fully, rightfully, expect to accompany her.

She tossed aside the pen she held when she realized she was chewing on the plastic end of it. It rolled, coming to a stop against her daily muffin basket.

Since their picnic the past weekend when Luke came upon them, Mel hadn't been over to visit April.

It was only a few days, of course, but for April, each day counted. She sighed, turning her chair until she could see out the window. It had been the same way with Nicky. Every day was more precious than the last, a gift in a life that was destined to be far too brief.

In Nicky's case there'd been no choice, no miracle surgery that could come along and save the day. She'd known that early on when the results of the oh-so-standard, thoroughly innocuous prenatal tests started coming back with disturbing results. Then had come the early ultrasound, followed by the damning amnio, and Jonathan's flat insistence that she get rid of the baby that would be born nowhere near perfect.

A sharp nudge from a little foot or a head or a hand caught her attention and she rubbed her hand gently over the spot, soothing the babies even as she pushed away the memories of her pregnancy with Nicky.

It seemed her life was filled with areas about which she didn't want to think too deeply. Nicky. Her parents.

Luke.

His name sighed through her thoughts. She still couldn't believe what had occurred between them on the road outside of town. Traffic was nearly nil on the road, but that didn't mean that someone might not have passed by, wondered, speculated over what the two people on the far side of the Jeep were doing.

Her cheeks ran hot. If only *she* could forget what

they'd done. Forget the feel of his hands on her. Forget the feel of her hands on *him*.

"Chicken, what's got your mind in a twist?"

Mel whirled around in her chair, facing the door and Maisy, who stood there. Guilt suffused her, as if her friend had divined her unwholesome thoughts. "Excuse me?"

"You ordered seventy-two pounds of horseradish and one pound of laundry soap on your monthly order with Nielsen's."

"I did?"

Maisy nodded. "Don't worry. I fixed the numbers. Nielsen called me, seeing how we don't use seventy-two pounds of horseradish in a year, much less a month."

"Sorry."

Maisy came into the office and sat down. "You want to tell me what's got you so dithered? Or do I even need to ask?"

Mel studied Maisy for a moment, and then simply took the bull by the horns. "Why didn't you warn me that Luke was coming back to the island?"

"And give you a chance to run away again?"

"I wouldn't have."

"Chicken," Maisy said, and sighed, "don't kid a kidder. I love you dearly, but you've been running since you left San Francisco. I understand why, I do. But it's time you started living life again. Those babies you're carrying deserve a mama who is living in the present with them, not in the past with a sad memory."

"You don't even like Luke."

Maisy didn't jump up and deny it. "I don't like arrogant doctors butting into my business."

"That's what Jonathan did."

Maisy nodded. "And I let him use April like some great pincushion for way too long. A thing to be studied, experimented on, rather than a child to be cherished. It's what Jason Frame tried to do, too, but I think his motives were truer than your ex-husband's. Even though he sent Luke initially to do the hard work of getting around me, I think he has April's welfare at heart, while Dr. Deerfield considered her a specimen."

"Maisy," Mel sat forward, clasping her suddenly unsteady hands together atop the desk. She looked at her friend. "Are you considering it? Allowing Luke to evaluate April's condition?"

Maisy didn't answer for a long while. "Maybe," she finally allowed. "Well, that's not what I'm here to yammer about, anyway. I want to know if you've told Luke about all that? About your life with that man?"

Mel's heart charged with hope at Maisy's admission. But she knew better than to run with the issue, force the woman to make her choices at anyone's pace other than her own. Though she wanted to. Badly. "*That man* presumably being Jonathan. And no, I haven't. I can't."

Maisy's eyes were kind behind the impatience. "Why not?"

"I don't want his pity, Maisy."

"Good grief, chicken, who says you'll have it? You think he hasn't had his share of loss, of grief? You can see it in the man's eyes. All you have to do is look. Even faded old peepers like mine could see it."

Mel had looked. But every time she did, something about the man drew her, and she couldn't afford to be *drawn*. "He lost his little sister when they were young," she admitted.

"There you go, then. Tell the man, Mel. He might surprise you."

"And what good would that do me? He lives in Arizona, for heaven's sake. And I—"

"Have been hiding out on Turnabout for too long, now."

Mel went stiff with shock.

"Oh, relax, chicken. I've gotten as much out of your being here as you have. Probably more. There's nobody on this island that I'd have trusted Maisy's Place to more than you, and it's let me spend far more time with April. I've been entirely selfish in that regard. You remind me so much of Tessa, and I really made a mess with her. I don't want the same thing happening with you."

Mel's thoughts were reeling. "You're one of the least selfish people I know. Where is all this coming from?"

"I had breakfast with Luke today."

Mel gaped. "You…what?"

"Actually," Maisy looked a tad defiant, "if I'm gonna be strictly honest, and it seems I'm feeling like it this morning, April and I had breakfast with him. I invited him. And I think you might be confusing Jonathan's behavior with Luke's. Maybe we both have been.''

"Who's Jonathan?"

Mel nearly jumped out of her skin. She went from staring at Maisy to staring at Luke, who'd appeared out of nowhere in her doorway. Her mouth worked but no sound emerged. "Nobody" finally came out. And it was true. Jonathan *was* nobody to her now. She was barely the same person she'd been when they'd been married. She owed most of the credit for *that* to the red-haired woman sitting across her desk who was giving her a disgusted look.

Well, just because she owed Maisy her very sanity for providing a place for her on Turnabout when Mel hadn't been sure whether living was preferable to dying didn't mean that she now had to bare all to Luke Trahern.

She'd bared plenty already, thank you very much.

The man in question was studying her as if he didn't believe the answer, either.

"I made the ultrasound appointment," she said, certain that it would be more than enough to distract him.

"When?"

"Tomorrow at four. They're fitting me in at the end of the appointment schedule."

"You'll have to take Diego's early run, otherwise you might be late," Maisy said. She pushed out of the chair and sidled past Luke, giving him a sniff.

"Make sure she eats before you make the crossing, or she'll probably make a mess of those expensive shoes you wear."

He watched Maisy depart then entered the office on his "expensive" shoes—a thoroughly dilapidated pair of athletic shoes. "Your eating habits are a frequent tune of hers. Who's Jonathan?"

"Don't you have something to do other than disturb my workday?"

"Why?" A whisper of a smile crossed his lips. "When this is such a fun way to spend a vacation."

Mel frowned at the reminder of Luke's seeming reason for coming to Turnabout. Jonathan had never wanted to take vacations. Unless it combined business and pleasure, with an emphasis on business, he had no time for it. "Tomas takes divers out several times a week. You should go with him. The water is great this time of year."

"I'm not interested in strapping a tank on my back and disappearing under a ton of water. Thanks anyway."

Amusement was unexpected but undeniable. He looked as if he'd rather have his toenails peeled off than go scuba diving. "Not your idea of fun. Then what is?"

"Working on the '69 Camaro I'm restoring," he said easily.

She narrowed her eyes, visualizing. "I can almost picture you playing grease monkey." With his lean, bristled cheeks, too-long hair and his clothes that suited him but were hardly *GQ*-worthy, he looked big and tough and just a little bit rough. Wrenches sticking out his back pocket didn't seem too far a visual stretch.

"There's no play about it," he assured. "You're talking about a man and his car. Serious matter."

"Well, as long as you don't crush your fingers under an engine block and end the career that probably pays for your little hobby, I say go for it."

One moment there was laughter in his sapphire eyes and the next there was nothing. His expression closed, utterly and completely. "What time does Diego make his run in the morning?"

Feeling rather like the rug had been pulled out from under her, Mel wavered a moment. "Um, around ten, usually." She didn't bring up the subject that they'd probably be stuck in San Diego overnight, as Diego's last run was shortly after the time of her scheduled appointment.

"Okay." He nodded. "I'll meet you at the dock in the morning."

Then he disappeared as silently as he'd appeared.

"Well," Mel said to the plant growing on the window ledge behind her. "Well."

There was no real reason to feel piqued at his abrupt departure, yet she did. But she also couldn't deny the curiosity that swelled inside her. Curiosity and…concern.

And beneath it all, a stone-cold fear of what the ultrasound might reveal.

Her anxieties were alive and well when Tomas dropped Mel off at the dock the next morning. The sight of Luke already there surprised her. He and Diego were bent over the mechanical workings of Diego's ugly boat and neither man made so much as an acknowledgment of her presence when she walked up behind them.

"Ahem." Her eyes drifted over the boat. Over the sight of Luke. He wore a plain white shirt tucked into faded blue jeans. She swallowed and focused on Diego, who was probably fifty but looked eighty and provided a much safer view. "Is there a problem with the motor?"

Both men straightened and turned to her. "No," Luke said. He picked up a faded red rag and began wiping black goop from his hands. "Not a thing." He'd shaved, revealing a slash of a dimple that showed when his lips tilted. "So if you were hoping you could still get out of this, you're wrong."

"I made the appointment, didn't I?"

At her defensive answer, Luke just gave her a knowing look and finished leisurely wiping the grease from his hands. It'd felt good to mess with an engine again. Even though the '69 was sitting in his garage waiting for him whenever he wanted to tinker, he hadn't done even much of that over the past half year.

He finished with the red cloth and tossed it on top of one of the heavy wooden crates that were lined up on the dock, then helped Mel onto the craft. The boat looked as if it could transport a few dozen people at best. Today, half the space was filled with cargo.

Mel stepped around an oversize box fastened shut with twine and tape, and chose a single seat among the unpadded benches marching across the forward section. She plopped her large purse on the deck near her feet.

After retrieving his small gym bag from the dock, Luke sat across from her and stretched out his legs. "I like the dress. You look good in white." Truth was, Melanie Summerville looked good in just about anything. Particularly her honey-tinted skin.

She smoothed her hand over the dress, only to cut the gesture short. "Thank you."

"Reminds me of the dress you wore on the beach. Why *were* you wearing that kind of dress on that night? It was cold out." And he'd warmed her. And had wondered ever since what had been so significant about that night to her. The desire to know had long outgrown simple curiosity.

"Too bad I hadn't chosen woolens to wear," she said. "Then you'd have been able to walk right by me with no qualms whatsoever."

The deck vibrated underneath their feet, and with a slight lurch, the boat began moving. He focused on her pregnant belly. "And miss this?"

"As if you wouldn't jump at the chance for *this* to have never occurred."

He watched her for a long moment. Then he sat forward, resting his arms on his legs, his loosely clasped hands belying his complete urge to shake her. "I don't know who set that standard for you," he said quietly. "The guy who was responsible for your other pregnancy, I imagine. But don't compare the two of us. I stand by my responsibilities."

"And every woman just loves to hear that she's a *responsibility*."

"I'd stand by you even without the babies." He meant it, too. Sooner or later she'd understand that when he'd said she was his focus now, he'd meant it.

She looked startled. And impossibly yearning, though he knew she'd spit nails before admitting it.

Then, as he could have predicted, her lips tightened and she looked away. "Easy enough for you to say given the situation."

The boat picked up speed, and she was facing the wind head-on. It blew her hair away from her fine features, her long, lovely neck. Want, never far, was a steadily tightening fist inside him. "What's it gonna take for you to trust me, Mel?"

Her lashes swept down, hiding her dark eyes. "I don't know," she finally admitted in a voice so low he had to work hard to hear.

But he did hear. "Well. At least that's honest." Then he sat back again, stretching his arms across the empty bench on either side of him.

They were silent the entire rest of the trip. By the time they made port, Mel seemed glad to escape as he settled up their fares with Diego. When he joined her, she'd signaled for one of the cabs that were parked nearby. He helped her into the rear of the vehicle, then pleased himself by sitting closer to her than she wanted him to.

They still had a few hours before her appointment. "Do you have a place you like to go for lunch?"

She lifted a shoulder and shook her head.

"Nowhere?"

"I come from San Francisco, not San Diego."

"Yeah, but when you come to the mainland, you must—"

"I don't."

"No favorite places?"

"Don't come to the mainland."

Luke looked at her. She was staring out the side window and had inched closer to the opposite side of the car, in fact, as if she needed to put as much space between them as humanly possible.

One step forward, twenty steps back, he thought, and struggled for patience until he had a good, tight grip on it. "You've stayed on Turnabout the entire time you've lived there?"

"Yes."

"Why?"

She finally moved her shoulders in irritation. "Because I felt like it, okay?"

"Hey, pal, the meter's running whether we're moving or not." The cabby's rusty voice interrupted them.

Luke sighed and gave the address of the medical center. Once they got there, he figured it was a good bet there would be eateries within easy distance.

Whether she liked it or not, he was going to take care of her, and their babies.

Then he reached over and gently but insistently loosened the white-knuckled fist she'd made around the strap of her leather bag and took her hand in his.

He felt as if he'd scored a winning touchdown when she slowly relaxed and curled her fingers around his.

Chapter 12

Mel's tension grew with every minute that ticked by. Though she tried to hide it from Luke, she knew she was doing a miserable job of it.

She'd choked down some of the lunch he'd ordered for her in a cute little café down the block from the medical center only because she hadn't wanted him to make a federal case out of it had she refused.

But now, as they sat in the cool white-tiled room and waited for the technician to come in and run the ultrasound, Mel felt as if her nerve endings were slowly but surely eating right through her skin.

"Couldn't they at least try to stay on time?" She looked at the clock for the umpteenth time. It was half past the hour of her appointment. "What is it with you medical people that you think your time is more valuable than anybody else's?"

Slouched on a metal stool, Luke looked thoroughly relaxed and at home in the sterile environment. She realized that he generally looked at home wherever he was, and envied him the ability.

"Because we *are* better than anybody else," he answered smoothly.

Her jaw loosened. She shot him a look, only to see the amusement in his face. "Hilarious," she grumbled.

He slid the rolling stool over to the side of the inclined table where she sat, a ubiquitous paper gown and sheet covering her more than adequately. Still she felt practically naked with Luke there, and it was just one more reason her nerves were spiking.

She nearly jumped out of her skin when he grabbed her hand, much as he had in the cab. "Appointments get off track," he said calmly. "It's what happens when you're dealing with people. Some patients take longer than others. It has nothing to do with establishing some supposed superiority over the lesser mortals."

"Even though we *are* lesser mortals," she added.

His lips tilted. "Smart aleck."

Her stomach dipped, hollowed out. He was far easier to resist when he was…oh, who was she kidding? He was *never* easy to resist. That was the whole problem.

Fortunately, the technician arrived then—a harried-looking young woman who perked up almost immediately when she laid eyes on Luke. One lazy half smile from him and the girl was all sweetness and light.

Mel was so annoyed that she forgot to be nervous, and before she knew it, the ultrasound was well underway, images of her babies—yes, there were two— on the screen that the technician rolled close for viewing.

"These little ones like to have their picture taken," the girl said, and within minutes it seemed, the process was complete, and Mel was holding a snapshot of the black-and-white images. "Everything looks good."

Mel stared at the photograph, studying every line, every curve. Bone-deep relief numbed her. She was vaguely aware of the technician exchanging a bunch of medical jargon with Luke before departing, and highly aware of the warmth of Luke's body next to her as he sat on the table beside her.

"A boy and a girl," he said. He leaned forward, peering at the photo. "Or so it appears. Have any names in mind?"

She was shaking. "I didn't let myself think about names."

He looked at her, and she realized how closely they sat. She could see the fine web of lines arrowing out from the corners of his eyes and the thin, dark ring of near black that surrounded his sapphire irises. There were even a few strands of silver hair at his temples, barely noticeable among the thick, dark waves of hair.

"Why not?" he asked.

Would their daughter and son have his coloring? Or would they be fair like she was? Or maybe they would have combined traits—fair hair and blue eyes or rich brown hair and equally dark brown eyes. "What?"

A faint smile played about his lips. "You're looking a little glazed, Mel."

Her cheeks warmed, yet she felt powerless to find her equilibrium. "The babies looked fine."

His expression gentled. "Yes." He brushed his fingers through her hair, then tucked his knuckles under her chin. "You want to tell me why you were afraid they wouldn't?"

It was that kindness in him again. She shook her head, blinking back tears, and slipped off the table, paper gown and sheet rustling. "I need to dress."

"And I guess that's my cue to step outside." He stood but didn't head for the door. "It'd help to talk about it, Mel."

"Counseling 101?"

"Grandfather 101. A burden shared is a burden lessened."

Mel's teeth worried the inside of her lip. Her head knew the truth of his words, but a lifetime of living the opposite seemed impossible to overcome. Even after Nicky's death, Jonathan hadn't shared his thoughts or his grief with Mel, and he'd made it clear he hadn't wanted to hear hers, either.

"Is that what you tell all your patients when you're saving them?"

A shadow came and went in his eyes. "Maybe."

He finally reached for the door. ''I'll be in the waiting room.'' He left, closing the door quietly after him.

Mel picked up the photograph and studied it for a moment. Then she smoothed her hand over her belly and dressed.

On her way out, she learned that Luke had already taken care of the bill. But he was in the waiting room when she made her way through the maze of corridors the large office possessed.

He stood as soon as she entered the room and tucked his hand under her elbow as if he'd been doing it all their lives, walking with her from the office and out into a lovely California sunset. ''I called for a cab. It should be here any minute.''

They stopped on the sidewalk outside the gleaming glass doorway. Palm trees lined the exterior of the building and lush plants with vivid scarlet flowers filled brick planters nearly to overflowing. As far as medical complexes went, it seemed particularly welcoming. Too bad the exam rooms were almost cold in comparison. ''What's your clinic like in Arizona?''

The look he shot her was indecipherable. ''Sunquest?''

''It's in Phoenix, isn't it?''

''North of it a little. But, yeah, still part of the metro area.''

''What's it like there?''

''This time of year? Hotter 'n hell.''

''I meant the clinic.''

"It's well cooled by the best AC money can buy."

"And you call me a smart aleck."

"Birds of a feather."

A cab pulled smoothly to the curb in front of them. "Another truism from Grandfather 101?"

He smiled faintly and opened the taxi door for her. "Sunquest sits on about five square miles overlooking the city. The property was deeded over to the clinic nearly fifty years ago by a grateful family. Jason is the third—and best—administrator the place has had." He followed her into the cab and pulled the door shut.

"And you?"

"Have no interest in administration." His faint smile took the sting from the flat statement before he leaned forward and spoke quietly to the driver.

Mel shifted, trying to get more comfortable with two babies jockeying for position. Given Luke's seeming dedication to force food upon her at every possible juncture, she was surprised when the cab did not deposit them at a restaurant. And she was struck silent when it did deposit them at the posh entrance of a resort hotel.

"No comments?" Luke paid the driver.

"We have to stay somewhere. Unless we were able to find a charter to take us up to Turnabout, Diego's last run was an hour ago." She was almost proud of the nonchalance in her tone. The hotel she'd thought to stay at was in her budget, while this place most certainly was not. Though she was hungry, she was also exhausted. Asserting her independence just then seemed more than she could manage.

And she was very much aware that she had deliberately chosen not to discuss the need for overnight accommodations with him. He'd obviously known, though, given the small bag he'd brought.

Would he expect to share a room with her?

Did she have the strength to resist him if he did?

He took her big leather purse from her and handed it, along with his small gym bag, to the bellman. Then he ushered her through the entry into what seemed more like a beautiful tropical forest than a hotel lobby.

Jonathan would have sailed straight to the concierge, fully expecting his every wish to be catered to and never giving Mel a second thought. He would have his needs attended to and, in Jonathan's mind, that meant that Mel was supposed to be satisfied, as well.

Luke, however, found a nicely cushioned chair and nudged Mel into it. He even scared up a little decorative pillow that he tucked at the small of her back, alleviating some of the pressure that seemed her constant companion these days. Then he ambled in that loose-jointed way of his over to registration, and managed to look just as purposeful in his movements as Jonathan ever had when he was striding the halls of the hospital, his half-dozen sycophants trotting dutifully along.

Mel closed her eyes. Why was she having so much trouble keeping thoughts of the past out of her mind?

Thinking about Jonathan wasn't so awful; she'd long ago come to terms with the fact that he'd married her without loving her. But thoughts of her marriage invariably turned to thoughts of Nicky, and she could hardly bear to go there.

A fine shiver of recognition had her opening her eyes in time to see Luke approach.

All her anxiety, curiosity, anticipation of what room arrangement he would expect coalesced into a ticking bomb. One that exploded when he stopped in front of her chair and held out his hand to help her stand. "I'm not sleeping with you," she blurted. Fire spread through her face right up to the roots of her hair.

"At least you didn't say 'never.'" He handed her a little envelope that contained a keycard. "Relax. It's a suite."

The wind went right out of her sails. She saw his lips tilt and knew he was amused. With no alternative, however, Mel accompanied him to the suite.

And what a suite it was. Every bit as fine as anything Jonathan or her father would have demanded. She barely had time to see that her leather bag had already been placed in one of the enormous bedrooms when there was a discreet knock at the door. She went out to find Luke directing two young men from room service who were bearing a linen-covered table.

Luke must have spotted her hovering in the doorway of her bedroom. "Outside or in?"

"Out," she said faintly.

He nodded, and the tray was set up on the palm-shaded terrace. She watched him sign the check and accompany the two waiters back to the door. Whatever he was saying to them had both young men chuckling as they left.

Then he closed the wide door and looked at her. She still hadn't moved.

"Something wrong?"

"Why did you arrange room service?"

"Because you're exhausted and I'm starved. Now, are we going to go out and enjoy the meal and the sunset or do we have to debate it?" His gaze didn't leave her face as he unbuttoned the cuffs of his shirt and folded them up his arms.

"Is that what I do?"

"What you do is make sure both of us know that you make your own decisions."

She absorbed that. He said no more but merely waited, as if it *were* completely up to her whether or not she went out onto the terrace that was fairly steeped in a romantic setting. He didn't grow impatient and tell her she was behaving like a fool, even though she knew she was more than halfway there.

He was kind and he was patient, and in that moment, that very moment, she felt that same awesomely intimate connection as she had that night on the beach. As if he had looked into her soul and recognized something familiar there.

"Mel?" He held out his hand.

She swallowed, following her instinct rather than her fear, and put her hand in his. And out to the terrace they went. He made sure she was comfortably seated in the cushioned iron chair—even going inside to find another small round pillow that would help her back—before sitting himself, and her throat tightened.

He began removing silver domes, setting them aside, and she bit her lip. All of her favorites. From a sliced avocado and shrimp salad to strawberries and whipped cream. There was even a frosty chocolate milkshake. "You've been talking to Maisy."

"Does that bother you?" He uncovered his own plate, which contained a mammoth-size hamburger and fragrant, golden French fries.

Was she bothered that he'd been interested enough to not only find out what her preferences were but to indulge her? It was the first time in her life that a man had done such a thing.

Willing herself not to bawl like a baby, she busied herself by smoothing the linen napkin on what little lap she still possessed. "No," she said huskily. "It was very—" she remembered just in time that he never appreciated the word *kind* being applied to him "—thoughtful of you. Thank you."

He studied her for a moment. "You're welcome." Then he reached for a fancy little bottle of ketchup and dumped it over his fries.

Her heart continued skipping every few beats, but she finally managed to follow his lead and begin eating. The food was as delicious as it appeared, but by the time she made it to the silver bowl of plump strawberries, she was positively replete.

The sun was a brilliant orange disk as it sank toward the sea. The breeze was balmy, and from somewhere nearby they could hear the faint strains of music and laughter. All in all, it was a nearly perfect evening. When he suggested a walk on the beach, she mindlessly agreed.

So they headed down the three steps to the smooth beach. Mel slipped off her shoes and felt her stomach dip a little when he took them from her. "Easier than having to find them later," he said.

Which naturally reminded her of the night on the beach when they'd searched for her sandals. After they'd made love.

They walked near the water's edge, where the wet sand was cool and packed. Somewhere along the way, he looped his fingers through hers. When his steps slowed and finally stopped, she stopped, too, and they watched the sun give its last gasp of daylight and finally disappear.

"Hard to get tired of watching that." His voice was quiet.

"What kind of sunsets do you have in Arizona?" How often did he take time from his schedule to stop and watch one?

"Spectacular ones. Sometimes the entire sky looks like it's been set on fire. Then the fire goes out and the city lights go on for as far as you can see."

She wondered if he was even aware of the arm he'd slipped around her shoulder. *She* was excruciatingly aware of the weight of it, the warmth of it. The fact that his fingertips grazed her upper arm, the fact that his scent was consuming her senses. "Sounds like you miss it. You've been away for a few weeks, now. Are you anxious to get back?"

He made a low sound. Of assent, dissent, she wasn't sure.

She swallowed. "Most people find vacations thoroughly enjoyable, but toward the end, returning home has a particular lure, also."

"Vacations." He let out a short breath, not quite a laugh. "Is that how you discovered Turnabout? Headed there on vacation and decided to stay?" His fingers drifted up her shoulder, sliding through her hair.

Shivers danced down her spine. "No, I knew of Turnabout long before I went there."

Chapter 13

Luke shot her a quick look. "How's that?"

Mel realized too late what she'd admitted. It was because he was touching her, she thought somewhat desperately. He touched her, and her brain shut off. "Turnabout isn't well-known, of course. The Turns prefer it that way. There always seems to be enough tourism to keep the local economy moving along, but not enough to—"

"Ruin it."

She nodded. "Yes."

"That still doesn't tell me how you learned about it."

She should have known he wouldn't be derailed from the question. "I, um, I met Maisy when she took April to San Francisco for treatment. I lived there."

"Right. One of the few things you've almost told me."

"Luke—"

"I don't need to know all the details of your past," he said abruptly. "Unless they affect the here and now, your past is your business."

Unfortunately, they both knew her past was most definitely affecting the here and now.

"But I still want you to marry me. I still want to be there for our children."

Her knees felt weak. "That doesn't require marriage."

"It does in my book." He caught her head in his big hand and pressed a kiss to her temple. "Grandfather 101."

Then, just when she was a mental mess at the proof that he hadn't given up the marriage business, he slid his hand down from her shoulder, caught up her hand in his, and turned back toward the hotel. "Let's get you back inside before you get chilled. I don't have a jacket with me to keep you warm."

She didn't need his jacket to be warm. She only needed him. The disturbing thought settled in her mind for the walk back and stayed there even after she excused herself for the night and closed herself into the bedroom.

It was still a little early, but remaining in the living room with him represented more danger than she could handle. So she showered and partly dried her hair, using the blow dryer provided in the well-appointed bathroom. She wouldn't have minded a soak in the enormous tub, but was afraid that once she got in, she'd be unable to get back out.

Her nightgown was short and lightweight and had taken up little room in her oversize purse along with her change of clothes for the next day. Luke had been right that the evening would be cool. But she didn't want to shut out the fresh air drifting through the terrace door, so she wrapped herself in one of the plush robes that hung in the closet, again courtesy of the hotel.

With nothing left to do, though, Mel still felt no real inclination to go to bed. She tried the television, but it failed to hold her interest. She called the inn and reached Tomas, who assured her that all was well. As usual, Maisy had spent the day with April.

She even went so far as to listen against the door, trying to hear whether or not Luke had retired for the night. But the door was too solid.

Disgusted with herself, she yanked open the door and sagged a little at finding the living area empty. The door across from her bedroom was closed. Luke had obviously done just what she had. She only hoped he was having better luck settling in for the night.

While they'd been out on the beach, room service had cleared away the remains of their dinner. But they'd left behind the bowl of strawberries and the whipped cream. They were nicely nestled in a crystal bowl of melting ice on the gleaming granite bar, and Mel took both the berries and the cream and carried them over to the deep sofa.

She stretched out, her back propped up against the arm of the sofa, and began nibbling away. Luke had left the ultrasound photograph on the cocktail table and she leaned over and picked it up, studying it.

And that's how Luke found her when he opened his door a few minutes later. He'd been intent on finding a cold beer somewhere. 'Cause God knows he was having a helluva time overlooking the fact that Mel was only a handful of steps and a door away.

But the sight of her told him that it wasn't beer he really wanted. It was her.

Her robe had parted where her long legs were crossed one over the other, and for a long while, he let himself look at the shapely limbs. High on her creamy thighs he could see the gleaming edge of dark blue fabric and tortured himself with the immediate vision of satin sliding over her soft skin.

His hands curled.

He didn't doubt that he could get her into his bed. He knew that his touch was as potent for her as hers was for him. But somewhere along the way—maybe from the very first—he'd begun to want more.

So he sucked in a long breath, yanked the tails of his shirt loose from his jeans to hide the predictable effect she had on him, and cleared his throat as he walked into the salon. "Can't sleep?"

She sat bolt upright, the two bowls tumbling out of her grasp. She grabbed for them quickly, only to end up with a hand doused in whipped cream. The bowls hit the floor, and strawberries bounced across the thick ivory carpet. "Great," she grumbled. "Stop sneaking around."

He smiled faintly, conscious of the awareness in her eyes and the pink color riding her cheeks. They were having babies together, they were adults, and they were alone in a hotel suite that seemed fit for honeymooners.

If he were a nicer man he would have arranged for completely separate rooms. Instead, he was wondering how he could get into her head and keep outta her bed. And wondering why he was bothering. Making love with her was something they both wanted, whether or not they chose to admit it.

"Stay put," he said. "I'll clean up."

She leaned back once more, watching as he hunted down strawberries and tossed them back into the silver bowl. He found the last just under the edge of the cocktail table and straightened, on his knees next to the sofa and the hand she was holding aloft, being careful not to smear any of the whipped cream onto the sofa. It was already covering her fingertips, and there was a white smear on her knee and the hem of her nightgown that was even more visible, thanks to the way she'd jumped when he'd startled her.

Hell. "Go to bed *now,* Mel."

Her eyes widened, her lips looking soft and probably tasting sweeter than the cream. "Or what?"

"Or come to bed in mine."

She hesitated. He could see her pulse beating in her throat. It took every inch of willpower he possessed to keep his hands where they were. *Off* her.

Her legs moved, slipping from the couch and her knee—the one with the tiny smear of whipped cream—brushed against his elbow.

Good, he thought. Go, and go fast. Because he was at the edge of sanity.

Her hair slid forward over her shoulder, slightly damp, utterly touchable, grazing his wrist.

"The dress," she said softly. "The white one. From that night on the beach. It was my son's favorite. I wore it for his last birthday." She hesitated, her gaze on her whipped-creamed fingers.

Last birthday.

She hadn't had a pregnancy that hadn't made it to term.

She'd had a child who hadn't lived to adulthood.

Luke damned the volatile situation. He gently took her hand, wiping it clean on his shirt before he did something really stupid, like lick it off. Then he put his arms around her and carried her to her bed.

He settled her, robe and all, in the middle of the wide bed that showed signs of her having tried to occupy it earlier. He pulled the soft blanket over her then sat on the side of the bed. She didn't seem to want to let go of his hand, and that was okay, too. "How old was he?"

"Nearly five. His name was Dominic." She was looking at their linked hands. "I called him Nicky and he was everything to me. I saw in a baby-name book once that it meant 'belonging to the Lord.' I figure it must be true, because according to all the doctors, it was a miracle he was ever born." She turned on her side, away from him, but she still held his hand. "Much less that he lived past his first year."

"What happened?"

"He died."

The scientist in him demanded details.

The man in him wanted to protect her from them.

The father he was going to be fell somewhere in between, but for now, the man won out.

She'd finally shared. And he finally understood·the fears she must have had as a constant companion since discovering he'd left her pregnant on that fateful night.

"This is why you were hesitant to see Hugo. Because you were afraid what the prenatal tests might show."

"Yes." Her voice was barely a whisper.

"What if they hadn't been in normal ranges? What would you have done?"

"The same thing I did before. Have the baby."

He let out a long breath and studied the slender line of her back. He wondered if there had been somebody beside her while she'd dealt with those decisions the first time. And if there had been, whether she'd been supported. But wondering was all he'd do, just then. If she wanted to tell him about the father, she would.

Maybe she still loved him. The thought was dismal.

"Try to get some sleep," he said after a moment.

"We'll catch Diego's first run in the morning." He started to rise, but she tightened her hold on his hand.

"Don't go."

He looked at her. "I don't think my staying is a good idea."

She pushed up on her elbow. "Are you angry with me?"

"No."

She let go of his hand and sat up even more, and her robe parted completely, displaying a satin nightgown every bit as appealing as he'd feared. And it clung lovingly to curves that appealed most of all.

"Then why are you leaving me?"

"Because you don't need a guy like me right now."

"What's that supposed to mean?"

"You're still grieving your son."

"It was four years ago."

"Yeah, and you haven't even come close to accepting it."

Her lashes swept down, hiding her expression. "You don't know that."

"You obviously left San Francisco when it happened. You've admitted you haven't been off Turnabout since you went there. You haven't spoken with your parents. You've barely been able to acknowledge your pregnancy. Are you telling me all that is a sign of a woman who's come to terms with a horrible loss?"

She looked wounded. He ran his hand down his face. No matter what he wanted from her, he knew

he wasn't good at this. Matters of the heart, matters
of the mind. But he wasn't heartless, either, and he
didn't know how to help her when he could barely
keep his hands off her. "Look. I'm sorry. It's late.
And we're both tired."

Her lips compressed. "Of course," she finally said
quietly. "You're right."

She looked to the side of the bed, spotted the light
switch and snapped it off. Then she lay back down
and pulled the blanket over her shoulders.

He watched her in the dim room.

She'd shared a huge piece of herself with him. But
instead of feeling good about it, he felt as if he'd
failed.

Again.

He turned and left, pulling the door closed with a
click.

Inside, in the darkness, Mel wiped away a tear.
She knew she wouldn't sleep that night.

By morning, the proof of that was apparent in the
drawn features that looked back at her from the bathroom mirror as she dressed in the peach-colored crin-
kly dress she'd brought with her.

It was no comfort, whatsoever, that Luke appeared
just as weary as she felt when she left the loneliness
of her bedroom behind. He was obviously waiting
for her, standing at the granite bar, paging through a
newspaper. The lines around his eyes seemed deeper,
the set of his mouth tighter. He still wore jeans, but
he'd traded the white shirt for a black polo. He was

gorgeous, and he was about as distant as a person could seem.

''Ready?''

She nodded and he picked up his small bag and headed for the door. Mel tucked the ultrasound photo inside her purse and followed. They stopped off at the casually chic coffee shop located near the lobby, and shared a silent breakfast.

Then it was back down to the port where Mel bought a magazine in a crowded little shop, and Luke seemed lost in his own thoughts while they waited for Diego. Once his boat came into view, and he'd unloaded and they'd boarded, the crossing passed just as silently.

Tomas was waiting with a motor cart when they arrived over an hour later on Turnabout. Mel looked from Tomas to Luke's Jeep that was still parked where he'd left it. But before she could head toward it, Luke had already climbed in and started the engine. Without another look her way, he slowly drove away.

If she'd thought that telling Luke about Nicky would bring them closer, it seemed she'd failed miserably.

The realization that she wanted to be closer to Luke, though, was as much of a shock as anything. It was a distinct problem considering that, sooner or later, he *would* return to Arizona. Whether or not she agreed to be his wife.

Chapter 14

The first thing Mel did when Tomas stopped the cart was go in search of Maisy. She found her at her cottage. As soon as April heard Mel's voice, she tossed off her blanket and hopped up from the rattan couch. She bounded across the room, throwing her arms around Mel's expanded waist.

"Hello, babies," she greeted. "Hello, Mel! Do you really got two babies in there?"

Some of Mel's tension slid away and she laughed. "I really do." She wished she could show April the ultrasound photo and had to content herself with handing it over to Maisy. "A boy and a girl, so I'm told."

April pulled her head back, staring at Mel's belly as if she could see right through to the babies. "Cool."

Mel smiled and ruffled April's curls. "Yeah. Cool."

"So," Maisy set down the photo and propped her hands on her hips, "I don't suppose you and Dr. Daddy got hitched overnight."

Mel's jaw loosened. "Of course not."

Maisy made a face. "In my day, people who made babies got married. Usually beforehand."

Mel's eyebrows rose. "Is something bothering you?" Maisy had never before made such comments.

"Dr. Hugo wants to marry Grammy," April said into the silence. "I heard him talking to her last night."

"When you were supposed to be sleeping," Maisy pointed out. Her cheeks were almost as red as her hair. "Now, go in and finish the lunch Tomas brought over for you and let Mel and me catch up."

April grinned up at Mel, then walked unerringly over to the table where a sandwich and glass of milk sat waiting.

Mel sat down. "Well? What'd you say to him?"

Maisy waved her hand. "Please. That old coot? He was just trying to get my goat."

"Maisy, Dr. Hugo has loved you ever since I've lived here."

"And he's a Turn."

"So are you."

"In most people's minds, but not for a fact," Maisy corrected. She shook her head. "He shouldn't have asked me. He was just feeling cocky and full of himself, and, well, he just shouldn't have done it, that's all. He knew I'd never agree."

"Just because of that old curse?"

"Don't go sniffing at it, missy."

Mel sighed. She'd defended Maisy's right to believe in a curse to Luke, but now she was pulling the same disbelieving note that he had. "I'm sorry."

Maisy huffed. But she softened quickly enough. "And you? The test went well?"

She nodded. "There were no abnormalities noted at all." She knew an ultrasound couldn't detect many things, but if this pregnancy had been similar to her first, she would have known it once the ultrasound was complete. "Two babies, two healthy-looking hearts, four active little legs and arms, twenty toes." And the relief of it still made her weak.

"Grammy," April called from the dining table. "Can I spend the night with Lani?"

Maisy frowned. "She's been asking that every night for two weeks," she said in a low voice.

"Maybe you should let her," Mel replied in an equally low voice. They'd had the discussion more than once.

"Maybe you should," April piped in, giggling.

Mel laughed and pushed to her feet. "I'm going to see what kind of mess the office is in."

"No mess, missy. You've only been gone a day. You think this place won't run without you?"

Mel kept her smile in place. The truth was, however, that she knew the inn could run perfectly well without her. It had before she'd arrived. It would, even if she left. That was part of the nature of Turnabout. The nature of life.

Things went on.

Proof of that fact was more than apparent later that evening, as well, as she and Maisy stood in the doorway of the open-air dining area and watched.

Luke and Dr. Hugo were there, looking as if they'd been friends forever. The other guests—two middle-aged married couples and a trio of young women lawyers— were crowded around them. Waving his unlit cigar around expansively, Dr Hugo seemed to have them in stitches of laughter. Luke seemed to have the unattached females eating from the palm of his hand.

"Well," Maisy muttered, next to her. "They've been at it for two hours, now."

"Tomas said they've gone through several bottles of wine."

"If those fool men want to get snockered, it's no business of mine."

"Right," Mel echoed. She rubbed her hand over a particularly hard kick from one of the babies. "No business."

Maisy huffed yet again. "I'm going to bed," she finally announced. And stomped straight through the dining area where she gave Dr. Hugo an evil eye as she passed.

"Stubborn old woman," he called after her.

"Stubborn old man," she called back just as loudly. The gate that closed off the area from the paths leading to the cottages crashed behind her.

Mel realized Luke was watching her. He raised his wineglass toward her. "Want to join us?"

She eyed the lawyer-ettes clinging to him. "I don't think so."

His lips twisted and when one of the girls—titian-haired and large-breasted—leaned against his shoulder, he turned his attention to her.

Mel spun on her heel and headed toward her office, slamming the door shut so hard it bounced right back open. Yeah, right, the man wanted to marry her.

He only wanted to do what some pea-brained piece of conscience, drilled into him by an old-fashioned grandfather, told him was right. Marry out of duty?

Well, not her.

No way.

He could sit there with a *dozen* chesty ladies climbing all over him and she didn't care. She didn't!

"Jealous?"

She gasped, turning to see the man in question standing in the doorway. "Hardly," she snapped. "And you're drunk."

"Not anywhere near drunk enough," he said, and came into the office, closing the door far more quietly than she'd done. "Still standing, aren't I? Still awake. Always awake and when I'm not, I wish I was."

She held out a stiff arm. "Just stay over there."

He leaned back against the door and crossed his arms. "Afraid of what'll happen if I get any closer?"

"Your ego is astounding."

"Even if I am right," he nodded, his eyes heavy

lidded. It was the only evidence of the wine he'd apparently consumed. "Why are you in your office at this hour? You should be resting somewhere."

"Gestating like the good little woman while you're out carousing?"

His lips tilted. "You won't carouse with me, rightfully so, and you probably don't want me rubbing your feet anymore, 'cause that'll lead to rubbing your calves and your thighs and—"

"Stop."

He did, his expression knowing. "You're thirty-one, with your whole life ahead of you."

"Go back to Dr. Hugo, Luke." Mel sat behind her desk. "You're making no sense whatsoever."

He stepped forward and leaned over her desk. "Maisy's going to change her mind about April, you know. She's almost there."

The possibility sent hope streaking through Mel, even as she cautioned herself against it. "I thought you didn't come to the island this time to talk to Maisy about April."

His sapphire eyes narrowed. "I didn't. I told you. I came 'cause—" he frowned "—'cause Jase said I needed a vacation."

"And how long is that vacation supposed to last?"

"Can't wait to get rid of me?"

She didn't dare tell him how badly she feared the opposite. "You've got work waiting for you at Sunquest. Patients."

His lips twisted. "You'd think so, wouldn't you. Fortunately for them, I'm here. With you."

"Please. A surgeon doesn't exist who doesn't put his patients ahead of everything else in his life."

"You really have it in for us, don't you. All 'cause of your dear ol' daddy."

"I don't want to hear this."

"Why not? The truth hurts, doesn't it."

"What about your truths, Luke? You're not full of life stories that you're dying to share with me. You only want to climb inside *my* head. And the only reason for that is because you think it'll get me to agree to marry you, so that your infernal sense of *duty* is satisfied."

"You wouldn't want to see what's inside my head, Mel."

"Well, you never give me a chance, now do you."

He watched her for a long while. Long enough for her to doubt that he was as inebriated as Tomas had warned. He reached across the desk and drew his fingers down her cheek. Caught her chin when she tried to move away. "Some nightmares are better left unshared." Then he smiled humorlessly and straightened.

"Why are you acting like this?" She never would have pegged him to have even an ounce too much alcohol.

"Maybe I'm celebrating."

"Celebrating what?"

"Fatherhood."

"You have to single-handedly drink several bottles of wine to do that?"

"Considering the alternative? Yeah, maybe so."

"What alternative?"

"Making love to my babies' mother." He waited a beat. "Nothing to say, Mel?"

She moistened her lips, suddenly feeling very unsure of her footing. "You were the one who wouldn't stay with me last night."

"My one good deed lately, and now I get to be punished for it." He shook his head. "Well, that's life."

"Luke—"

"G'night, Mel. Sleep sweet dreams for us both, why don't you?" He opened the door and was gone.

For a long while, she sat there, wondering what on earth had just transpired, feeling it was important, only she couldn't quite figure out why. Eventually, however, she left her office and took the long route back to her cottage.

She could still hear Dr. Hugo's booming laugh and assumed that Luke had returned to the "party" as well.

It wasn't until she was lying in her bed, staring up at the dark ceiling, that it finally came to her.

Still awake. And when I'm not, I wish I was. Luke's words.

She knew why her sleep was often fitful.

But why was Luke's?

"Luke, please. Wake up." Mel tugged at the sheet, pressing her hand to his darkly bronzed shoulder, shaking him. "Come on, Luke, how much did you and Dr. Hugo drink last night?" She shook him again. Harder. Her throat was tight, tears thickening her voice. "Dammit, wake up!"

He opened one eye. Then the other. Propped himself up on his elbows and gave a slow, feral smile. "Finally."

"Oh! Get your mind out of your pants." She slid off the bed, yanking at the sheet that was tangled around hips that definitely wore no pants of *any* type at that moment. "Come on. Wake up. Maisy needs you."

He fell back against the flat mattress, wincing at the movement. When he opened his eyes next, they were somewhat more clear. "April?"

Mel shook her head. "No, Maisy. She's hurt, Luke. Come on!" She jerked at him, at the sheet, and nearly lost her footing when he sat bolt upright and the sheet flew free from him. He was one-hundred-percent naked.

She gasped, closed her eyes, turned on her heel, looking anywhere but at him.

He made an impatient sound as she heard him moving. "Stop acting like a maiden aunt," he muttered. "You've seen it before."

By moonlight, when she was half-crazed with grief. Not in the cold light of day, when all that gloriously bronzed male flesh was exquisitely revealed. She closed her eyes, but the impression seemed permanently imprinted. She was hardly a prude, but didn't the man know what a swimsuit was? He was tanned…all over.

"Silly girl," he chided softly after a moment, and

she felt his hands on her shoulders, turning her to face him. She flushed furiously when her eyes automatically dipped, only to find he'd pulled on a pair of jeans. His eyes were amused when she looked up at him, but at least they looked clear and sober. "Now, what's wrong with Maisy?" He tugged a Hawaiian-print shirt over his shoulders.

Mel gulped, guilt spurring her into motion. "She fell off her stepladder. I'm afraid she might have broken something."

"Did you call Hugo?"

"I...no, I...you were closer." She hurried out the door. "She's in her cottage."

Luke dragged her to a halt when she reached the uneven path. "You walk," he ordered. Then he jogged down the path, turning out of sight as he headed for Maisy's cottage.

She tried. She really did. But she ended up doing more of a hop-skip-walk, and when she arrived, Luke was already ministering to Maisy, who was muttering and cursing colorfully under her breath at her own clumsiness.

"Dratted step stool," she said, and glared at the old metal contraption that lay on its side nearby. As if the thing had deliberately failed in order to cause her problems. "Hugo keeps telling me to stay off the thing. I should have him pitch it off the cliff! Where is that infernal man, anyway? Doesn't he know there're people around who need him? Suppose he's away somewhere sleeping it off."

Mel sank down beside Maisy, taking her hand,

making soothing noises. But over the woman's orange corkscrews, she glared at Luke. He ignored her, continuing to carefully examine Maisy's left leg.

"I need something to splint it," he murmured, glancing around. "And ice. Then we need to get her to Hugo's clinic. How'd it happen?"

"I found her lying on the floor when I brought by some papers for her to sign."

"Conscious?"

Mel nodded.

"Darn it all, boy, don't talk like I'm not here," Maisy snapped, but her cheeks were pale and Mel knew she was in terrible pain.

The corner of Luke's lips tilted. "You know you can't be too badly off if you can still give me what-for, Maisy."

Mel nearly choked when Maisy flushed and huffed but calmed right down. Luke pushed to his feet and disappeared into Maisy's kitchen—she had a real one even though it was rarely used—and returned a few moments later carrying several flour-sack dish towels that he ripped into strips with fast movements. Then he flipped two movie magazines off a shelf and rolled them into tubes, which he used to brace Maisy's leg before fastening it all up with the cloth strips.

"I know, honey," he murmured, when Maisy groaned as he worked. "It's not a perfect solution, but it'll get you to the clinic."

"Call Lily." Maisy's hand gripped Mel's. "April spent the night with her last night."

Mel looked toward the hall that led to April's room, surprise working through her. Had her conversation with Maisy actually had some effect?

"Get some ice first," Luke suggested as he checked the splint for excessive pressure, then touched Maisy's toes.

Mel knew he was looking for signs of good circulation. She nodded and pushed up on her knees, then to her feet, and hurried into the kitchen. She dumped out a loaf of bread and filled the long bag with ice, then slammed it against the floor a few times until the ice broke up. She also grabbed a bag of frozen peas and carried them back with her. Luke had wrapped a blanket around Maisy's shoulders and elevated her feet. He took the ice and frozen peas and packed them carefully around the splint. Then he took Mel aside and told her to get Tomas quickly, with the stretcher.

"And don't forget to call Lily!" Maisy's voice was shaky as Mel dashed out the door.

The next hour was a blur as they transported Maisy, alternately bickering then tearful, to the clinic where Dr. Hugo—thoroughly sober—took one look at Maisy and turned grim. Between Luke and the older doctor, they got Maisy's fracture set. When Mel phoned Lily, April had insisted on coming to the clinic, too, and before long, it seemed the entire population of Turnabout was crowded into the little building.

It didn't seem to matter to anyone that Maisy had finally dropped into a sedated sleep. They still had to come by and check on her, fuss and tsk and gossip, and generally exclaim what a handy thing it was that Dr. Luke had been so nearby to render immediate aid.

Eventually, however, Dr. Hugo shooed the visitors away, leaving only Mel sitting in the waiting room, wondering what was taking Luke and Dr. Hugo so long back there with a sleeping Maisy. Finally she could wait no longer and went in search of them, only to have Luke appear in the short hallway.

One glance at his face told her more than she wanted to know. "Something *is* wrong. That's why it's been taking you so long."

He rolled his head around, loosening up his neck. "Yeah, but you can consider Maisy's tussle with the stepladder a blessing in disguise."

"What do you mean?"

He was looking at her feet. "Your ankles are swelling."

"I'm carrying twins, remember? They're *always* swollen."

He smiled faintly and took her arm. "Come on. Let's get you settled somewhere other than one of those hard chairs in the waiting room."

"Luke—"

"Let me take care of you first, okay?"

He looked weary, beyond what tying one on the night before should cause, and she wondered again about his sleeping.

Her protests died. And her usual spurt of defensiveness, whenever he tried to tell her what to do, didn't rear its ugly head, either. She just nodded in agreement and saw the flare of surprise in his eyes at her acquiescence.

They were more than halfway to Maisy's Place in the Jeep he'd rented before he spoke again, and then it was only to ask if she'd eaten breakfast that morning.

"Bananas and tuna."

"Well, at least you didn't add peanut butter to it," he said, amused. "Does April eat anything that doesn't have peanut butter on it?"

"Not if she can help it." Mel looked away as remembrance swept through her, sweet and aching. "Nicky loved peanut butter, too."

She felt the weight of his gaze, but he said nothing as he parked the vehicle on a patch of grass at the side of the inn.

Before Mel could even maneuver from the passenger seat, he was there, helping her. "How do you do that?" She felt like a slow-moving blimp, and he was faster than the proverbial speeding bullet.

"I'm not carrying around twins," he said. "Tomas is handling things, I assume."

She nodded. He immediately took her arm and started for the rear of the inn where the paths led off to the private cottages. In her cottage, he nudged her down into her favorite chair, disappeared into her bedroom and returned moments later with two pillows in hand that he tucked under her feet to elevate them even more on the ottoman. Then he moved over to her kitchen area and started rummaging.

His hands on her legs had been brief, but enough to needlessly remind her just how effectively he could use his touch.

She swallowed, willing away the prickles of awareness that plucked at her nerves. "Now, tell me why Maisy's fall is a blessing in disguise."

He turned, a soda in his hand, and popped the top. "You're not drinking these, are you? They're loaded with caffeine." He lifted the can, tilting his head back, and drank deeply.

Her little prickles bloomed into a full-scale body flush. She folded her hands together, looking at her nails. Anything was safer than looking at him. He was better than that old soda-pop commercial during which office workers ogled the hunky laborer during his break.

After a moment, she heard the distinctive crumple of the can, and looked up to see him tossing it into her trash. He raked his hands through his hair and, nudging her legs a bit, sat on the ottoman facing her.

And still he didn't speak. He just looked at her. And dread sliced through her. "Luke?"

Chapter 15

Luke scrubbed his hands down his face, wishing he'd had more than an hour of sleep, wishing he didn't want this woman as much as he did. He knew he'd made an ass of himself the night before, and he wished that hadn't happened, either.

Mostly he wished for a lot of things, none of which were likely to happen.

"We think Maisy has hypertension," he told her. "Hugo's been concerned for a while, trying to monitor her, but—" he spread his hands "—Maisy can be difficult."

"What with April she's had more than enough doctors in her life."

"She said something to that effect," he agreed mildly.

Mel frowned. "I can only imagine what Maisy

536 One More Chance

might have *really* said.'' She sighed, then nodded. ''Okay, she has high blood pressure. She needs to adjust her diet, get more exercise or something.''

''If Hugo's suspicions bear out, she'll need more than that. Her pressure was so high back there we think she might have had some sort of episode before her fall. You said she *was* conscious when you discovered her.''

Her expression fell. ''Yes, but she never really said how long she'd been lying there. She's...she's going to be all right, isn't she? April needs Maisy, Luke. If anything happened to her—''

He leaned forward, catching her head between his hands. ''Don't borrow trouble. As long as Hugo's got her under his wing for a while, he'll get her stabilized. She'll probably be on meds from now on, but that's hardly catastrophic. The point is that she's going to get the treatment she needs for certain, now. There's no reason to think anything worse will happen.''

''And her leg?''

''It will heal.'' He smoothed his fingers through her silky hair and felt something inside him tighten warningly when her cheek pressed, so briefly, against his palm.

''Thanks for helping her.'' Her voice was husky.

''Why wouldn't I have?'' Setting a fracture was a light-year away from picking up a scalpel. He rubbed his thumb slowly over the fine cheekbone, his gaze on Mel's soft lips. She was maddening, this woman who carried his children. ''You didn't call Hugo.''

Her lashes drifted downward. "You were closer."

"You trusted me. Even after I made an ass of myself last night."

"Luke—"

He shook his head once. "Admit it, Mel. You came to me because you trusted me."

Her lips pressed together. She looked up at him, mute, her eyes soft. Heat blasted through him.

"So why won't you trust me about everything else?" He could feel her drawing away from him then, mentally if not physically, and damned his tongue. "I haven't told you much about my grandfather."

Though she was still, he could feel the struggle inside her. Whether to stay. Whether to run. He waited, impatience rife within. And finally she gave a faint shake of her head. Apparently *stay* had won out. At least momentarily.

"No," she said. "Obviously he had a large impact on you, though. Grandfather 101 and all. You said he raised you and your sister."

"Bethany. Yeah. She's the one who liked the crusts cut off her toast."

"Where were your parents?"

He *wanted* her curiosity, he reminded himself when a flip dismissal automatically rose in him. "I never knew my dad. Mom never saw a need to marry Bethany's dad, either. Eventually, she didn't see a need for her kids, either, and dumped us off at her dad's ranch in Wyoming."

"I'm sorry."

His hand slid down where her pulse beat like a trapped bird against the smooth column of her throat. "Don't be. We were better off with my grandfather."

Her pupils dilated. "You loved him."

"Does that surprise you?" He smiled ruefully. "Yeah. Mac Trahern was his name and he was a tobacco-chewing, bowlegged son of a gun who loved only one woman in his life."

"Your grandmother?"

He nodded. "She died long before Bethany and I went to live with him, though. When Beth died, he was devastated."

Her hand fluttered upward, as if she would have touched him. He very nearly lost his sense when her cool fingertips grazed his jaw then fell away. "You, too," she murmured.

There was no point in denying the obvious. "Mac gave everything he had to put me through medical school. Sold off half his land, his stock. Most people go into debt with student loans for years, but he wouldn't have it. Said I could take care of him in his old age in return."

"Did you?"

"Until he died. Almost a year ago now. I...finally sold his ranch in January."

Her lips sounded out the month.

"The same week I came to Turnabout," he added at the question in her eyes.

"Selling must have been difficult."

"Yeah." He stared at his hands. He'd tried to keep

the place going, feeling torn between what little was left of his grandfather's legacy and his own career. The career had won. Only Luke had failed that, too. "Leaving the land there with nobody to care for it was worse," he finally said. "Mac would have hated that. I took a few things from the old house, and sold everything else, lock, stock, and barrel to a neighboring outfit—a huge ranching operation. They'll take care of it the way Mac would have wanted." The way he hadn't.

"What things did you take?"

He shook his head. "His old desk. A clock. Nothing important."

"Important enough for you to keep them. Why the clock?"

"He made it. Sat on his mantel. He had to wind it every day. Took this big old key. Even kept track of the month and day."

Her eyes held a suspicious gleam. "I'm sure your grandfather would have understood your selling, Luke. You just said how he sacrificed for your medical career. Why on earth would he have done that if he'd expected you to follow in his footsteps?"

It was a valid point. One he'd told himself more than once. And he still had a hard time accepting what he'd done. But they were getting off track. He was trying to impress on her that he was a determined man, a focused man. And she *was* his focus.

"People always said how much like my grandfather I was."

"Bowlegged, with chew tucked in your cheek?" She waited a beat. "I don't think so."

"Maybe not in looks or habit, but definitely in temperament. He only loved one woman his entire life. He told me once that he knew the first time he saw my grandmother—even though she was spitting mad at him for letting his prize-winning goat eat its way through her prize-winning county fair brownies—that she was the one for him. It took him a while to convince her of it, but he did. He was a determined man, my grandfather. And so am I. I want you to come back with me to Arizona."

"So, now you're finally acknowledging the fact that you'll be going back? That your vacation isn't indefinite?"

"You're avoiding an answer, Mel."

She let out a harried breath. "You know I can't."

"You mean you won't."

"Luke—"

"Mel, just *trust* me. I won't hurt you."

"Nobody ever *tries* to hurt me, it just ends up happening."

"Is this about losing your son? About his father?" He knew he was right when her face went white. "What'd he do? Leave you hanging when he found out you were pregnant? I'm not doing that, Mel. I want you to marry me. I want to be there when the babies are born. When they take their first steps, say their first words."

"Jonathan didn't leave me! I left him." She covered her face with her hands. "After Nicky died, I left him. I walked away from our sham of a marriage and I kept walking until I ended up here. On Turnabout with Maisy. She gave me a place to stay, gave me a job to do.''

Luke sat back. He didn't know why it hadn't occurred to him that Mel had been married to Nicky's father. It should have. She was so clear in her position against marriage that he should have realized it came from experience. An experience she flatly refused to repeat.

''How long were you with him?''

''Seven years.''

Which meant she'd been hardly more than a teenager. ''You were young.''

''And he was older,'' she said tiredly, ''and I was besotted and more than happy to be his lovely little trophy.''

''Honey, you're far too much your own person to be any man's trophy.'' He'd seen her in action around the inn. She had a keen eye for organization and an even better gift for making everyone around her feel welcomed, and he'd yet to see her really be pushed around by anyone, even Maisy.

''Well, you must not know me as well as you think you do.'' She dropped her hands. ''I was twenty. And I was thrilled at his attentions. Even my parents respected him. I was going to have exactly the kind of life I'd been raised to believe every good girl wanted. He wanted children. Right away. Though it took several years for me to conceive. So long that I thought there was something wrong with me. By then I knew what my place was supposed to be. He wanted the properly bred, proper-looking wife and mother in his house. But he didn't really want *me*. Having my life managed by him didn't mean I was adored by him.''

"I'm ten years older than you. Is that what you think I want? That any beautiful young woman would do? Dammit, Mel, if that's what I wanted, I could have had my pick of women long ago.''

She glared at him and he sighed roughly. "That didn't sound right.''

"No kidding.''

"I don't want a trophy wife, Mel. We both have a chance, here. I want a marriage. With you.''

She moved, dislodging the pillows, and pushed to her feet. "You don't love me, and I refuse to lose myself in that world all over again! I'm not strong enough, Luke, don't you see that?''

"*What* world?''

"*Your* world.'' She waved her hand, encompassing him. "You're a surgeon, too. I know how it is. I grew up in that world, and I married into that world. The family comes second to the patients, always.''

"Mel—''

But she wasn't finished. "I'm not begrudging that. Truly. If it weren't for surgeons, Nicky wouldn't have lived as long as he did. But it's all the rest. The dinners. The benefits. The committees. I had a degree in foreign languages, but the only thing I was allowed to do with it was emcee a fund-raiser fashion show put on by a French designer!''

A bark of laughter escaped him. He wasn't even sure he'd be welcomed back at the clinic even if he *could* go back into the O.R. without puking. Sunquest's budget was tight enough without carrying a surgeon who couldn't cut it. "You're kidding me. I hate that stuff. Jason could quote you chapter and verse on just how bad at it I am. It's one of the reasons he wanted me out of the way. So I wouldn't screw up a fund-raiser that he has scheduled."

She whirled around, her eyes glistening. "Well, I hated it, too. But I did it all, Luke. I fit right in just the way my mother taught me. But none of it was compensation for a husband who only cared that I stayed because of appearances. I was the mother of his child—even though he couldn't even admit to loving Nicky—and he didn't want his associates thinking he couldn't keep his personal life under control.

"I won't try to keep you out of the babies' lives, Luke. But I won't marry you. And I won't go with you to Arizona."

"You want to stay here on this little island, hiding out for fear that the past might repeat itself."

"It nearly finished me, Luke. Leaving behind everything that was familiar, even if it was slowly choking the life out of me. My mother—" She pressed her lips together for a moment. "I went to my mother and told her I wanted to leave Jonathan, thinking that maybe she'd understand. But I was a fool. She was sad about Nicky's death, but she said I was just being ungrateful. That I had a husband with a prestigious career and a beautiful home. She said I was obviously unbalanced because of Nicky and that I should turn around and go right back to my husband. A husband who never once shed a tear over losing our son; who never gave away any of his feelings or his emotions. Everything was always on his terms.'' Her voice was raw.

''You still love him.''

She shook her head. ''I stopped loving Jonathan Deerfield the day he wanted me to have an abortion because the prenatal tests showed Nicky wasn't perfect.''

Luke closed his eyes, seeing the full circle of it all. Deerfield had been the first surgeon to treat April. That's how Mel had met Maisy. And she'd come to Turnabout where she'd done a partial job of burying her grief, only to meet *him.* When Mel had gotten pregnant, she'd avoided acknowledging it as long as possible so that if the results weren't perfect, she wouldn't have to relive the kind of choice her ex-husband had tried to force on her.

And now here they were.

Mel and Luke.

On opposite sides of a fence that she'd built, while he had no idea how to tear it down.

He could force the issue when it came to their babies. Paternal rights were alive and well and gaining popularity by the day with the courts. But Luke refused to go that route. Maybe it was pride, maybe it was something else. He wanted Mel and their children, but not by legal maneuvering.

Regardless of the past, he knew she wasn't the type of woman she described. "You're wrong, you know," he said. "You are strong. Everything about you, what you've lived through, what you've changed, proves it."

She was stronger than he was, when it came down to it. Because he just kept avoiding the problem that kept him awake at nights.

Her lips pressed together, her entire being seeming to reject his words, and frustration coursed through him.

"I don't care if you paint your face blue and twist balloons for a living, if you attend one single dinner or committee or benefit. The only one who thinks she's got to force herself into some mold of your so-called appropriate doctor's wife is you. I know half a dozen women—wives—who could show you that mold doesn't exist. Maybe it used to. Hell, it probably did. But not anymore. And not with me. I want you to think about one thing, though. And think about it well, Mel, because it's the future of our babies that we're talking about. What are you really afraid of? Taking one more chance or letting go of the past?"

Then, before he did something really stupid, like tell her he loved her when it was so bloody damned clear that she did not love him, he strode from the cottage, the wooden screen door banging after him.

Chapter 16

"Hey, there." Mel poked her head in the room at the clinic that Hugo had outfitted for Maisy. "How are you feeling?"

Maisy, sitting up in the hospital bed that someone had managed to procure, shrugged. Her face was wan, her vibrant hair without its usual spark. "Like I've been pulled backward through a knothole. Plus Hugo's got me on some new thing to keep my blood pressure down."

Mel scooted the plastic side chair that was against the wall closer to the bed. "You never indicated that you weren't feeling well. Why didn't you say something?"

Maisy huffed. "You're a fine one to talk."

That was true enough. Mel sighed. "How long will the cast be on?"

"Weeks." Maisy's thin fingers plucked at the light blanket covering her. "Everything okay at the inn? That couple from Alaska arrive okay?"

"Everything's fine." She'd checked on all the guests that day herself, except one. Mel wasn't prepared to face Luke just yet. She'd refused him; she didn't have the strength to do it again. If that meant avoiding him, then that's what she'd do. Cowardly or not, it was the only way she could get through the day. "Tomas met the new people at the dock this afternoon. They're all settled. Has Lily brought April by to see you yet today?"

"No. She…she had another episode last night. Hugo had to go over. He gave her a shot for the pain."

Mel's mouth dried. April had been doing so well, managing the pain with only an occasional pill. "Lily didn't tell me that."

"I didn't want her upsetting you and the babies." Maisy's eyes grew red. "She's needed her pills every day, Mel. The pain just gets worse. I can't bear for her to have more pain. I've just been a selfish old woman and enough is enough. I see that now."

Mel shook her head, pressing her forehead for a moment to Maisy's hand. "Oh, Maisy. You should have said something. Told me. Do I really seem so fragile to everyone? As if I can't take care of myself? You know how I feel about April. You could have told me."

Maisy cleared her throat and tsked. "Hardly fragile, chicken. Hardly that. But you do have a tendency to hold everything inside you.''

Mel didn't know what to say to that.

''Chicken, you trust Luke. Don't you?''

Mel's lips parted. ''Maisy, I—''

''Don't you?''

It wasn't Luke she didn't trust, but herself. After all, he hadn't let her down once since he'd returned to Turnabout only to discover she'd kept an enormous secret from him. ''Yes. I trust him.''

''And when it comes to April?''

Mel hesitated, immediately wondering where Maisy was heading. She easily remembered the day that April had fallen asleep in Luke's lap. ''I don't believe he'd use her to glorify his own work.''

''You think I should let her go to that clinic. To Sunquest. Let them examine her. Run their tests and God knows what else.''

''Yes,'' Mel said gently. She rubbed her hand over her forehead, barely noticing that she was trembling. ''Agreeing to an evaluation doesn't necessarily mean that April will have to have surgery again. Maybe she only needs a change in meds. Maybe there's something other than surgery.''

''That's what Hugo's been saying. Man never shuts up. He tells me Dr. Frame considers Luke the best. Well, all right then. Go get the man. I want to see his face when I talk to him.''

Mel scooted the chair back against the wall and headed back to the inn. It seemed no matter what she did, avoiding Luke was impossible.

When she got there, though, he wasn't in his cottage. Her heart jumped up in her throat and stayed there until she peered through the window and saw that his belongings were still inside—a shirt tossed over a chair, his boots lying on their sides on the floor.

"You're a lunatic, Melanie Summerville," she muttered, and turned back to the inn. Lunch was long over, and neither Tomas nor Leo, who was hobbling around with a cane even as he did his job making small repairs around the place, had seen him.

Luke wasn't at the clinic, and he wasn't at Maisy's Place. So where was he?

Their beach.

The thought had barely whispered into her mind when she slid into the golf cart and started driving down toward the beach.

He was there. Sitting on the sand, staring out at the jeweled glitter of the water.

Battling down her nerves, she climbed from the cart, slipped off her shoes and made her way across the powdery sand.

He didn't turn his head as she approached, but he obviously knew she was there, for he spoke as she neared. "Makes a person's life and all their problems seem small in comparison."

"Watching the ocean? Yes." Goodness knows she'd lost her painful thoughts in the mesmerizing magnificence of it all more than once. "What problems are you and the water working out?"

He looked at her.

She flushed. "Well. I, um, was looking for you."

He lifted his eyebrows.

"Maisy sent me to find you, actually. She wants to see you."

His lips twisted. "Of course. You wouldn't come of your own accord, would you."

She paused at that. But her assigned task waited. "She wants to talk to you about April. She's willing to have her evaluated."

He absorbed that. "Jason'll be pleased."

"And you?"

"The girl needs treatment. Yeah. I'm pleased."

"You don't look it."

He rolled to his feet, the open lapels of his blue shirt rippling in the breeze. His chest was broad, hard and dusted with hair. She curled her fingers against the tingle that shivered across her palms.

His lips stretched into a smile that seemed macabre given the dark shadows in his eyes. "Better?"

"No. You haven't slept, have you? I can tell just by looking at you. You look—"

"What?"

"Terrible," she said on a faint sigh. "I'm sorry. I didn't want things to be like this."

He made a rough sound then put his hands on her shoulders. "What is it that you *do* want, Mel?"

There were shadows under his eyes, as well as in them, and she was distinctly aware that she was not necessarily the cause of them. Feeling impotent to change anything, she shook her head. "I don't know what you want me to say."

He exhaled slowly. "Why does it even matter to you what I want?"

"Of *course* it matters. Everything about you matters."

"But not enough to marry me." He let go of her shoulders and shoved his hands in his pockets. "Maisy's waiting, I assume."

Feeling unsteady and not liking it one bit, Mel nodded. He watched her for a moment longer, then turned and headed toward the cart parked on the sand.

She slowly followed, wondering why it felt as if something precious was slipping through her grasp.

Luke took the wheel and he drove the cart straight back to the clinic. He didn't speak. Neither did she. And when they arrived, she hurriedly climbed from the cart before he could do his usual thing of coming around and helping her from it as if she were made of crystal.

Maisy was awake and waiting when they stepped into the room. Hugo sat on the chair beside her, the cigar clenched between his teeth. The air seemed thick with tension.

"About time," Maisy said tartly when they stepped into the small room.

"Calm your jets, woman."

"Choke on your cigar."

Hugo glared at her. Maisy glared back.

Mel cleared her throat. "Maisy, I told Luke about April."

"Good. Then you can get right on it. I talked with

Dr. Frame while you were lollygagging. Mel, you can go with Luke back to Arizona and take care of April.''

''What?''

Maisy had the grace to appear contrite as she looked up at Mel. ''If you're with April then she'll be all right. At least until I get out of this contraption and can join you.''

Mel was excruciatingly aware of the steadying hand Luke had settled at the small of her back. ''Why not wait until you're on your feet again and then make the trip together?''

''Because April's condition is worsening,'' Luke said quietly. ''Isn't it?''

Maisy glanced up at Luke. ''I can't wait until Hugo here gives me the clear to get on my feet again. Darned man seems to think I'm gonna keel over with a stroke or something—'' Her voice choked and she hauled in a breath.

''Easy, girl,'' Hugo muttered, ''or I'll call off this little tea party.''

Maisy's lips tightened. ''I can't send Lily with April—she has to take care of her little sister.'' Her voice was calmer. ''But I can send you, Mel. And I know what I'm asking, but—''

Mel wanted to weep for the impossible situation. ''Of course I'll go with April. You don't have to ask twice. I love her.''

''I know you do.'' Maisy looked at Luke. ''She visited every day we were at the hospital in San Francisco. She was there because Nicky was there, too, but she always took time to look in on us, on all the pediatric wing's patients for that matter. She was always kind that way.''

Kind. Mel watched Luke, afraid of what she'd see in his face. But his expression showed nothing at all. "And you've already spoken with Jason," he said.

"He said to tell you he's sending the plane. It'll be here by nightfall.''

Mel started. "So quickly?"

"Jason's not one for sitting on his thumbs," Luke said flatly. "It's one of the reasons he's the best at what he does.''

"And he says you're the best at what you do. That if anyone can help my granddaughter, it's you.''

Luke's eyes narrowed. "He did.''

Maisy nodded. "And I know April trusts you. She may not see, but she *sees*.''

"And what do *you* see?" Luke asked, his voice low.

"I see you standing beside Mel," Maisy said after a moment. "So, I know that she's in the best hands. Yours and Mel's.''

Luke didn't answer that. His jaw was tight and Mel felt nervousness bubble in her stomach as he looked at her. "Then I'd better grab my gear," he said simply before he strode from the room.

Maisy didn't look at Mel. "I know it's a huge favor, chicken.''

Mel watched down the hall until she couldn't see Luke any longer. "Anything that helps April isn't too huge.''

"She's still at Lily's. She's bringing April here in a little while. I haven't told them what I've decided."

"You're doing the right thing, Maisy," Hugo said gruffly. "April's going to be happy to do anything you say is best. She'll probably look on it as some great adventure. Now, I oughta make sure everybody stays off the road or that plane isn't going to have any place to land."

Maisy's gaze tracked Hugo's progress. When he was gone, she looked at Mel, all business. "You'd better go pack, too. Goodness only knows how long you'll be there with Luke."

"I'm going with April," Mel said quickly. "I won't be staying with Luke."

"Oh, don't talk nonsense, girl. Of course you'll stay with him. He's the father of those babies of yours. You think he's going to allow you to be anywhere other than with him?"

"Maisy, you know how I feel about—"

"About marriage and surgeons and losing yourself somewhere in the mix. I know, I know. Just give the man a chance, Mel. Give love one more chance."

"I don't love—"

"Bah." Maisy waved her hand. "Chicken, you are so in love with that man that even April could see it on your face. Now, go on. Get yourself ready. Tell Tomas he's in charge and that he'd better not mess up the reservations like he did that one time, or I'll have his hide. He should see if little Janie Vega can come in and help out with breakfasts like she did last year when I had the flu. George can manage the rest of the cooking like he usually does.''

Still Mel hesitated. ''I don't want to leave you, either, Maisy.''

The other woman's expression softened. ''I'm going to be fine, chicken. Hugo will see to that. He's a pain in my side, but he'll do that. I'll be fine. And so will you.''

Mel's eyes burned. ''It's only for a week or two,'' she reasoned, knowing it was only her own self that needed reasoning. ''Probably. Then—''

''You can always come back here, Mel. You know that. But it's time to put the past to rest. Nicky's gone. You loved him enough for both you and his father. But let him go. And look to the future. You all deserve it.''

Mel swallowed the knot in her throat and quickly hugged Maisy. The woman had been more of a mother to Mel in the years she'd known her than Mel's own mother. ''I know, Maisy. I just can't chance raising my children in the same way that I was raised.''

Maisy cupped Mel's cheeks and clucked her tongue. ''I've met your mama, Mel. Just one time in passing at the hospital in San Francisco, but it was enough. You're nothing like her and no amount of yammering will convince me otherwise. Trust yourself for once. You've been doing all right, but you won't even let yourself take credit for it. Now, go on with you. You've got some packing to do.''

Since there seemed nothing else to say, Mel left.

Luke hadn't taken the cart with him and she drove back to Maisy's Place, her emotions spiraling.

She stopped by the inn to tell Tomas he was in charge and then went to her cottage. But once there, she could only stand in the center of the living room, not knowing where to start.

"Mel? Are you packed?"

She whirled around. Luke stood behind her. She hadn't even heard the squeak of the door, she'd been so lost in thought. "What?"

"Are you packed?" His gaze took in the room. "Where's your suitcase?"

"I don't have one. I'll have to use a box or a plastic bag or something." She shook her head, feeling tears threaten again. Maybe it was hormones or maybe she was really as ridiculous as she feared. What kind of a nut cried over whether or not she had a suitcase? "When I came to Turnabout, I didn't have anything with me. Only what I'd stuffed in my purse. Some cash." She slid open the drawer next to the sofa and withdrew the photograph of her sweet son and the tuning fork. "And these."

He took the small frame and looked at the photo. "Why the tuning fork?"

"Nicky liked to play with it."

"When you said you walked away from it all, you weren't exaggerating." He handed her the frame. "Pull out whatever you want to take. Your clothes, anything else you've collected since you came to Turnabout. I'll go find you a suitcase."

"You don't need to keep taking care of me, Luke."

"Yeah," he said evenly, "I do. Because taking care of you is all I have left."

Chapter 17

"Is she settled?"

"Yes." Mel smoothed her hand over April's curls where they lay against a soft yellow pillowcase. "She was thrilled with the plane ride. But it exhausted her."

Luke nodded. He silently rounded the bed and pulled out the metal chart that hung on the side of a whitewashed wooden dresser. This private room that April had been settled in minutes after a car had whisked them from a small airfield to Sunquest looked far more like a lovely bedroom than a hospital room.

"I've assigned a private duty nurse for her," he said. Mel could hear the faint scratch of his pen as he made notations on the chart. "Denise Blankenship is young and extremely capable. I think April will like her. All of our kids do. She'll probably be here any minute now.''

''Oh, but I—''

''I'm not saying you can't stay with April anytime you want. But you're not a nurse, Mel.''

She subsided, knowing he was right. ''Will she be with her all night? I wouldn't want April to wake alone.''

''She'll be at the nurses' station.''

''Then I'm going to stay here.'' She looked around the comfortably appointed room. ''I can sleep in that chair.''

He rubbed the bridge of his nose, looking weary and beautiful and completely removed. ''You're six and a half months pregnant, Mel.''

Her spine stiffened, though it was an effort considering that she felt fairly exhausted herself. Riding an emotional roller coaster had that effect. Pile on a couple hours on a small plane that could have doubled for an airborne emergency room, and she wanted only to sit down and put up her feet. ''Yes,'' she said, smoothing her hand over the inordinately active babies. ''I sort of noticed.''

His lips tightened. ''Fine. Suit yourself.''

She frowned, put off balance by his seeming agreement. ''That's all you have to say?''

''You're a grown woman, Mel. As you've ably argued, you can decide what is best for you.'' His gaze skipped over her. ''You don't need me to tell you that your ankles are swollen. You already know. Feel better?''

It was foolish. "Yes."

His lips twisted. "I'll be in my office. The driver who met us at the airport took your stuff to my place. If you need anything, check with the nurses."

"Aren't you going home? You need some sleep, too."

"I'll go when you'll go with me." He went out the door. "Don't forget. You need something, you ask."

And just like that, she was alone in the silent room with the sleeping April.

Mel blinked. "Well." She rubbed her hands down her arms and adjusted the sheet covering April's thin shoulders. Then she maneuvered the chair around—it was far easier than she'd expected because there were casters hidden beneath the upholstered skirt—until it was closer to the bed. She sat down, kicked off her shoes and propped her feet on the end of April's bed. It wasn't the most comfortable she'd ever been, but it would do for now.

The babies bumped and rolled inside her and she smoothed her hand over them, willing them to be calm. If they were, then two out of three wouldn't be bad.

Luke went to his office after he left Mel and April. It seemed stale and musty inside, though, as if it hadn't been used in months. Considering how little time he'd been there since January, it was no wonder. And in those few days a week that he'd forced himself to attend to his work—if only to consult—he'd hardly been the model of organization. Jason should have fired him, he thought grimly. Only years of non-stop work had earned him a *lot* of vacation time. There was a pile of files covering one side of his rough-hewn desk. Covering the other side were stacks of correspondence. Notes from the other doctors on staff. Letters from doctors the world over regarding patients, invitations to speak, teach, attend.

He sighed and picked up one invitation in particular. Ivory parchment and sedate black ink.

"The prodigal son returns."

Luke dropped the invite back on the pile and glanced over at Jason. "Hardly prodigal," he said flatly. He rounded the desk and sat down. "You look like you just walked off a golf course."

Jason, silver-haired and bronze-skinned, chuckled. "Lydia dragged me out for an evening round. Too hot to golf otherwise."

Luke eyed his boss. Jason Frame had been his mentor and his friend. "You hate golfing."

"Yeah, but my wife loves it," Jason countered. He entered the office and sat on the long butter-soft couch that had seen Luke through more nights than his own bed had. He stretched out his legs. "And I love my wife, so there you go. You look like hell. The vacation was supposed to do you some good, Luke."

Luke spread his fingers, staring at his hands. As long as he'd known Jason, Lydia had been by his side. Forty-one years of devotion, of support. "Do you have the Conroys appeased?"

Jason made an impatient sound. "Hell, son, you know that's not the only reason I kicked your tail out of here for a while. The Conroys are fine, and the fund-raiser is on course. It took some doing to convince them that you hadn't trifled with their darling daughter's affections. But Belinda's already moved on to her next quarry and now we've very nearly got the rest of the funding we need for the new wing. Did you ever doubt it?"

"Doubt you?" Luke smiled faintly and shook his head. "No."

"You're too busy doubting yourself. It's not going to get better until you get back in the O.R., Luke. You know that as well as I do. You get kicked off the horse, you climb back on."

"If I'd stuck with horses, Jennifer Melendez would still be alive."

Jason sat forward. "How many cases have you treated, Luke? Too many to count. And you never lost one on your table."

"Not until Jennifer." She'd been fourteen years old. The same age as Bethany when she'd died. Jennifer could have been her twin, with wavy black hair and snapping brown eyes. Bethany's death had been out of Luke's hands.

Jennifer's had not.

"The review board was conclusive. You did everything right."

"But she still died, didn't she." Luke slammed his hand on the desk, pushing to his feet. "I signed the papers on my grandfather's ranch one day and walked into that O.R. the next and killed that girl.''

''Dammit to hell, Luke. I know you weren't happy about selling the ranch. You were upset. But that didn't affect your performance. Jennifer Melendez had about a five percent chance of surviving no matter *what* you did or did not do in that O.R. You did everything humanly possible to prolong her life, even if only for a matter of weeks. I've seen you in action, Luke, too many times to worry that your concentration isn't exactly where it needs to be. On your patient. But even with you, sometimes skill isn't enough.''

''The surgery was successful but the patient died,'' Luke repeated the old humorless joke.

''That's pretty much it,'' Jason said flatly. ''You've never been the kind of man who believed that your skills with the scalpel superseded a patient's will to live or die. You believed that it was the combination of the two that meant success.''

''So you sent me to Turnabout in January after it happened 'cause you knew there was no way I could turn my back on that little girl sleeping down the hall.''

''Well.'' Jason shrugged. ''It took you longer than I figured it would. And I'd pretty much given up hope until I found out you headed back there again. You're the best surgeon Sunquest has, Luke. If April gets you back in the saddle, then we've two victories to celebrate.''

Luke knew, though, that it was the memory of Mel

that had lured him back to Turnabout the second time. He'd spent six months trying to erase thoughts of her through every means possible—including Belinda Conroy's inventive charms. He'd been no more successful at forgetting Mel than he was at accepting what had happened in his O.R. It was only a matter of time before Jason had to cut him loose. A surgeon who couldn't operate was nothing but a liability.

"I had nothing to do with changing Maisy Fielding's mind about April," he said. "She did that all on her own."

"Maybe. Maybe not. Who's to say what all conditions are present to make a person do one thing or another. The point is, April's here. We'll see if we can do anything about her situation, and go from there."

"And if somebody's gotta scrub, you think it'll be me." Even though there were other perfectly able surgeons on staff, who had been picking up his slack for months now.

"From what I saw of April's history in Dr. Hugo's charts, I know that, even scared spitless, you're that child's best hope."

Pain throbbed in his temples as Luke told Jason about April's previous treatment. "What makes you think I can accomplish what a guy like Jonathan Deerfield couldn't?"

"Because Jonathan is a coldhearted son of a bitch," Mel's voice came from the doorway. "And you're not."

Luke stared.

Mel's dark gaze flickered over Jason, who'd risen. "Hello, Dr. Frame. It's good to see you again," she greeted. "I assume Maisy informed you that I was accompanying April?"

"Yes." His gaze was on her obviously pregnant form. "She didn't mention anything about this, however. Congratulations."

Luke caught the quick glance Mel sent his way. "Thank you" was all she said, though. She tucked her silky hair behind one ear. "April's still sleeping. Denise is there. You were right, Luke. She's very nice. I...decided that it probably isn't necessary for me to stay in April's room."

"Of course we've got accommodations here at Sunquest for family members," Jason said immediately. "You're all set up—"

"I'm sorry." Mel's cheeks were red. "Thank you for the offer, but I'll be staying with Luke."

Silence settled on the room. A portion of Luke's mind was aware of the considering look Jason sent from Mel to him. Mostly he was aware that, given a choice, Mel had chosen him.

"Well," Jason finally said. "That seems all taken care of then, so I'll get out of your hair and see you in the morning." He smiled at Mel as he passed her for the door. "Lydia will be delighted to see you, Mel, when she learns you're visiting." He patted her arm as he left.

Luke leaned back in his chair and looked at Mel. "How much did you hear?"

"Enough." Her eyes were soft and she slowly

closed the office door before walking over to the desk. She did the same thing he had; ran her fingers over the pile of correspondence. "I wish you'd told me."

"So you could talk Maisy out of trusting me?"

She made a sound. "Of course not." The line on his desk buzzed, and she pressed her lips together.

He exhaled and grabbed the phone. "Trahern." His gaze didn't leave Mel as he listened for a moment. "Yeah. Five minutes." He dropped the phone on the cradle. "I've—"

"Got to go. I know. I recognize the drill. Go."

She recognized it and was probably already finding him wanting, he thought blackly. "I'll have a driver take you to my place. It's only ten minutes from here."

"No. I'll go when you go."

"Turning my words around on me, Mel?"

"Maybe." She eyed his couch. "That looks more comfortable than the chair in April's room. I'll just stretch out here and wait." To prove it, she glided past him, her arm brushing against his, and settled on the couch, turning on her side and tucking her arm beneath her head. Her hair flowed around her and her eyes looked like black opals. "Go on, then. Someone needs you."

"But not you."

"I'm here, aren't I?"

"Not by choice."

"There's always a choice," she whispered, her gaze following him to the door. "A lot of things happen that are out of our control. But how we deal with it? There's the choice.''

"Grandfather 101."

"Maisy Fielding." Her lips curved faintly. "Graduate course."

Luke watched her for a long moment. Then he turned and went to deal with the nurse who needed help with an unruly patient.

Mel's eyes came open with a start. It only took a moment to remember where she was.

Sleeping on the couch in Luke's office.

Her gaze drifted over the painfully silent room. There was a clock on the credenza behind Luke's desk. An old-fashioned mantel clock. The kind that had to be wound with a key. It was undoubtedly the clock Luke had taken from his grandfather's ranch. Along with the desk, before he'd signed away the property.

The clock was silent and it struck her as inordinately sad. She sat up, pushing aside the soft butterscotch throw that had been covering her legs, and swung her bare feet to the floor. Someone had covered her. Had placed her shoes beside the couch where they'd be easily found.

Not someone.

Luke.

Ignoring the shoes, she walked over to the clock and studied it for a moment. She ran her fingertip along the gold circle framing the round glass plate, felt the invisible latch. The glass swung open. The key—oversize just as Luke had mentioned—sat beside it and she picked it up. She'd seen clocks like it before, of course. But never one that she knew to be handmade. Never one that had a small window indicating the month and day. She leaned closer, reading the faded gold engraving. The fifth of January.

Her throat closed and she sat down in Luke's big desk chair, closing the key in her fist. Luke had taken the clock from his grandfather's house. But he obviously hadn't wound it once, since.

"We're a pair, Luke Trahern," she whispered.

She wound the clock, set the time and, after some effort, figured out how to adjust the date, as well. Then she gently pushed the glass front closed. It snapped into place. The quiet, soothingly rhythmic ticking of the clock sounded throughout the silent office.

She set the key back in the same spot beside the clock and left the office.

She certainly didn't expect to find Luke in April's room. But not only was he there, he was sleeping.

He'd pulled up that same chair and propped his feet on the end of the bed, just the way she'd done.

Mel realized she'd never watched him sleep. His lashes were thick smudges against the bronzy olive cast of his face. His lips were more relaxed. Softer. Kissable.

She pressed her fingertips to her temples, willing away the jolting ache that warmed her insides and made her want to brush her mouth across his. She put April's bed between her and Luke, and sat in the other, smaller side chair.

"I thought you'd sleep until morning." Luke's eyes were heavy lidded, and impossibly intense as he watched her across the small mound of child sleeping on the bed.

She pressed her hand to her heart. "I didn't mean to disturb you."

"You've been disturbing me for months now."

Mel's gaze flicked to April. If she'd thought to find some protection from that quarter, she was sorely mistaken. The little girl's lips were parted, so deeply asleep she was very nearly snoring.

She moistened her lips. "You'll be starting her tests right away in the morning, I assume."

He gave a barely perceptible nod. The weight of his gaze was like a physical caress. She swallowed and cleared her throat. "And if you decide s-surgery is the way to—"

"I'm ready to go home," he said.

Her mouth dried. Her heart stuttered, then charged. She opened her mouth to speak but found she had no words.

The corners of his lips lifted and if she'd thought he looked dangerously sexy while dozing, it was nothing compared to the way he looked now. Like a languorous big cat that had spotted his quarry and was slowly circling it. "You do get silent at the most interesting times, Mel." He waited a beat. "Remember that night?"

As if she could forget.

"There was one thing we were both looking for."

Her paralyzed tongue finally broke loose. "Peace."

"Yeah." He pulled his legs from the bed and stood. "Only time I get close to that feeling is when I'm with you. Now I have one question before I go home and take you with me."

She rose, also, too agitated to sit. "What?"

"Which room are you gonna sleep in? The guest room? Or mine."

Chapter 18

In the shadowed light of the room, Luke watched Mel's face as he waited for her answer. Her lashes slowly lowered, and she caught her lip between her teeth.

"We've done everything backward."

It was hardly either response he might have expected.

She tucked her hair behind her ear, took a few steps along the bed, then hesitated. If she knew how she drove him mad, he'd never have a moment's freedom for the rest of his days. "How so?"

Another step took her to the end of the bed. She smoothed her hand over the swell of their babies. "We started here. And have gotten to know each other...some...after the fact."

"Nobody said it was the perfect situation. But I'm not complaining."

"No. You're not." Her slender hand drifted along the hospital-cornered bedding. "I'm sorry I didn't contact you right away. It was wrong, cowardly, of me."

"Mel, it's over. We're here, now."

She moistened her lips. Took another inching step around the bed. "Yes, but I think it's only fair...right...that I should tell you that, had we not done things backward, had you and I gotten to know each other some, properly, you know—"

"Get to the point, Mel."

"I'd still choose you to be the father of my children." She stopped in front of him.

She was killing him. Slowly but surely, degree by painful degree. "Which room, Mel."

"Yours."

He let out a long breath. Slid his hand down her arm and caught her hand in his. He stopped at the nurses' station to let Denise know they were leaving. Then, out of necessity, they stopped by his office so he could retrieve the keys to his car, which had been parked in the covered lot since he'd been banished by Jason. They were in the drawer inside his credenza. He bent over, closed his hands on the keys and straightened.

Then he noticed the soft tick-tick-tick. He looked at Mel. "You set the clock."

"It seemed a shame to leave it there. It was all

alone, stuck in the past." Her cheeks colored. "You probably think that sounds ridiculous."

"I think it sounds familiar."

She finally nodded, set her shoulders and held out her hand. "Can we go, now?"

He took her hand and led her from the office, out of the building and into the quiet night. Their footsteps sounded loud across the pavement to his car. "The city lights do go on forever, don't they," she murmured, looking out beyond the edges of Sunquest. "What kind of cactus is that? The one with the arms?"

"Saguaro."

"They appear to be standing guard."

Luke stopped and looked where she was focusing. Sunquest was slightly higher in elevation, giving the impression of surveying the valley below. Against the glow of distant lights, the cacti nearby stood tall, proud, the way they had for decades. "They do," he agreed. It had been a long time since he'd bothered to appreciate the stark, distinct beauty the desert had to offer. And while it *was* beautiful, it was steadily creeping toward dawn.

He steered her toward his car, and she went willingly. The drive, ten minutes on any other day, was made in seven. Later, when there was more time, he'd slow down, giving her time to absorb the scenic setting. He punched the button and drove straight into the garage the moment the doors swung wide enough and parked next to the '69.

The inner door from the garage led through the

laundry room. The light went on automatically when they entered.

"Nice setup," Mel said, blinking against the sudden light. "There's as much room in here as there was in my house growing—"

He pulled her close and kissed her.

"—up," she finished faintly when he lifted his head a long while later. Her breath was unsteady, her hair tumbled, her dress already falling from her beautiful shoulders.

He considered it fair, given the state she'd had him in for months.

"This isn't your room, though."

He smiled slowly. He took her hand and led her through the house. There was a vase of fresh flowers on the dining room table. Lydia Frame, he thought. She'd be the only one to think of that particular touch, and she and Jason were the only ones Luke had given a key to while he'd been gone.

His room was on the far side. It took up the entire east side of the house, to be exact. It had a wall of windows that overlooked the city at night and welcomed the sun at dawn. "This one is," he said gruffly, and tugged Mel back into his arms.

The land surrounding his house went far and wide. Luke had never considered it before, but he was grateful then, for the complete privacy, as he stood with Mel in front of those windows, in the wash of moonlight, and slowly unwrapped her. Like a gift. Contents fragile, precious and incredibly beautiful.

"Your dresses always have so many buttons," he

murmured, finishing the job he'd begun in the laundry room. "I've dreamed about your buttons. Undoing them." He slid the loosened bodice from her shoulders. It fell all the way to the carpet, pooling around her feet. Next went her bra, and her breasts, fuller and crested with velvety nubs taunted the palms of his hand, tempted his lips. He slid his hands over them, heard her breathe in sharply when he couldn't help but tarry there before running his touch over the warm, taut heat of her abdomen.

"H-hardly the pair I wore in January," she whispered, when he slid his fingers under her panties and drew them inexorably down her thighs.

He wondered if it was a woman thing. She was carrying twins. Wearing maternity clothes. Did she think he expected bikini panties? He was more interested in getting her naked. Fast. "You're beautiful." He rose, letting his eyes take his fill. "Do you doubt it?"

"I'm huge." Her words ended on a squeak when he tore off his shirt.

He felt her gaze rove over him. "You're carrying my children. You think that isn't appealing to me? Physically?" He saw her struggle, instinctively knew the cause of it and damned the man who had put insecurities into her lovely head. "We don't need a threesome," he said evenly. "It's only you and me, here, Mel. And I like what I see just fine." He popped open his strained fly. "Obviously."

Her lips parted, her gaze dropping. Staring. And he felt a faint laugh strangle in his throat.

"Well," she said huskily, "at least I'm not the only one who's huge."

He laughed, groaned, cursed, when her touch, too fleeting, too maddening, grazed him. "Wait. Can you do this?"

She made a soft sound. "You're the doctor."

"I'm not *your* doctor."

She touched him again. "Hugo gave the 'all clear,'" she whispered. "Before we left Turnabout."

Luke silently blessed Hugo. "The bed," he muttered. "Let's be novel. Try a bed finally." More specifically, *his* bed.

Graceful, womanhood personified, she stepped out of the clothing piled around her feet and turned to the bed.

Even that small distance between them was too much. He caught up to her, sliding his arm around her, cupping her breast, kissing the curve of her shoulder. Tall enough to fit him. His other hand smoothed over her belly, brushed through the downy triangle between her thighs. He could feel her trembling. Or maybe that was him. She was so responsive, so magical. A sound rose in her throat, that same sound, that hum of hers that had lived in his mind for more than six months now.

Her hands caught his, stilling him. "Not again," she whispered hoarsely, turning in his arms. "I want you with me this time." Her mouth sought his, her breath warm, sweet, arousing. Her hand reached for him, encircled him.

He groaned, and pulled her down onto the bed,

settling her beside him. He'd let her set the pace. Go as slow as she wanted, as slow as she needed.

Mel couldn't touch enough of him, couldn't get enough. "I've heard about women having, heightened, uh—"

"Libidos," he provided, looking thoroughly content at the notion.

"Yes, but I never really had that trouble before you." Mel dragged his hands back to her breasts, nearly whimpering with delight, relief, want. "It's embarrassing," she whispered, "but I look at you and I...want you." She sucked in her breath, then sighed out a moan when he plumped her breasts together. Tasted one, then the other. Her fingers slid through his hair. Her legs moved restlessly.

"Does it seem like I'm complaining?" He guided her thigh over his hip and slowly thrust against her, sliding through her slick folds, not entering, but nearly blinding her with sensation anyway.

She sighed his name and pressed her mouth against his throat, tasting his pulse, his skin. She arched against him, twined her leg higher, but even then it wasn't enough, and with an impatient sound that shocked her, she pushed him back on the wide bed and slid over him, taking him.

He shuddered and groaned, bowed upward until they were breast to breast. Then he kissed her, and she felt him grow even harder inside her as she melted over him. His hands swept down her back, caught her hips, pulled her tight. "One of these days," he growled, "I'm going to get the top." He thrust slowly, deeply.

Her breath stuttered, pleasure spiking so fiercely she gasped. "Are you complaining *now?*"

"No," his voice was rough. "Only promising that when I do, I'm going to take my time."

Her breathless laugh was cut to the quick when he kissed her and the coiling pleasure inside her unfurled in that blaze of ecstasy that only he could create. And in the dim reaches of her mind, as pleasure racked through them both, tearing her apart only to put her back together again more complete than ever before, she was aware of his arms holding her safe, her name on his lips.

Luke woke to the smell of coffee and the sight of Mel silhouetted against the golden dawn. She wore one of his shirts and the rising sunlight shone through the white fabric. "No wonder cultures as old as time have worshipped feminine images," he said.

She turned when he spoke. "Because we bring male images coffee in bed?"

His laughter was short. He threw back the sheets and climbed from the bed, heading toward her, ignoring the mug of coffee sitting on the nightstand. "It's not the coffee that's spurring me on at the moment."

Her smile was half shy, half lazy satisfaction. "I think, somewhere along the way in that very bed over there, you said we should get to Sunquest first thing this morning."

He swept her up in his arms, laughing softly when she gasped and insisted he put her right back down. He did. Inside the shower. Which they shared. And Luke took his time.

Chapter 19

Once April's tests were underway at the clinic, Mel was surprised at how quickly the time passed. She called Maisy around lunchtime, and April chattered for a few minutes before handing the phone over to Mel and tucking her head into her pillow, sleepy yet again. Mel had barely finished talking to Maisy herself when Denise came into the room bearing a wheelchair. Luke followed on her heels.

Mel swallowed, feeling heat in her cheeks. She hadn't seen him since that morning. Then he'd been wearing jeans and a Diamondbacks T-shirt. Now, he wore soft green scrubs that only defined his impressive body even more. When he leaned over to lift April's slight weight into the wheelchair, she found herself actually staring at his behind, completely inappropriate and thoroughly lascivious thoughts circling her mind.

Denise caught the direction of her gaze and grinned sympathetically.

Mel flushed even harder. Then Luke straightened, caught Mel's eye and heat streaked through more than her face. "We're going to do her MRI," he said. "Do you want to come, or wait here?"

"I'll come with you."

April grabbed Mel's hand. "What's an MRI? Is it gonna hurt?"

"Not a bit," Mel assured.

They headed down the hall and Luke explained what April could expect.

"Too bad we don't have an open MRI," Denise said beside her. "I know Dr. Frame has been trying to get the funding for it. As it is now, if patients have any sort of claustrophobia, we have to send them down to Phoenix."

April had let go of Mel's hand and was practicing wheeling the chair herself. Luke let her, only adjusting now and then to keep her from running right into the walls. "There's a new wing being built, I understand."

"A pediatric wing. Right now, we have to mainstream peds in with the adults. Dr. Trahern doesn't advertise it, but he was the one who spearheaded the effort. He's a special man. But I don't suppose I need to tell you that."

"Mel—" Luke looked back at her "—you can wait in there. You'll be able to see everything, and talk to April, as well." He gestured to a glass door and headed April through another set of double doors.

Denise pushed open the door and went inside, holding it for Mel. "We're all glad that Dr. Trahern came back," she said, as they watched Luke and April enter the room on the other side of the thick glass panels. "He's one of a kind."

"He's been spending a lot of time with April," Mel murmured. "He got to know her and her grandmother on Turnabout—during his vacation, otherwise I'm sure he'd..." Her words trailed off. She didn't know how to put it. Luke was spending much more time with April than was usual.

But Denise didn't seem to notice anything amiss. "He's obviously fond of her," she agreed. "But he's this way with all of his patients. Definitely not one of those types that sails into the O.R. at the last minute, seeing only the sterile field to apply his skills, and none of the individual beyond the drape." She laughed slightly, flushing. "And yes, I'll admit, I'm one of the rest of the hoards around here who are crazy for the man. And not just 'cause he has a world-class hiney in his scrubs." She grinned, too engaging for anyone to take offense.

"If you're through admiring the scenery," the technician sitting at a complicated console spoke, "maybe we could get on with this?"

Denise giggled and left the room, going into the other room to sit beside April, who was now lying on the narrow table that would slowly move into the machine. She'd sit with April during the test. Mel would have, but given her pregnancy, Luke had already cautioned her against it.

She drew in a deep breath, not entirely sure what kind of results for which to pray—that April's tumor would be deemed operable, or that they'd choose to treat it by some other means. Luke left the room and joined the technician at the console. And the test began.

And so it went.

During the day, Mel stayed at Sunquest, keeping April's flagging spirits occupied as she underwent test after test so Luke and his associates could determine their best course of action, finding herself the center of a good deal of attention by the nurses, and hearing again and again how well liked Luke was. During the night, she rested in Luke's arms. On the third night, she accused him of leaving the clinic before ten o'clock only because of her. He grinned, and asked if she was complaining.

Since she was presently enjoying the fruits of his labors, she assured him that she most definitely was not.

But underneath it all, Mel was excruciatingly aware of Luke's increasing tension and his flat refusal to discuss the matter when she broached the subject.

On Friday, she saw Dr. Frame for the first time since their arrival at Sunquest. He had stopped in, his wife with him, to visit April and drop off the gift of a stuffed animal that had a tape player built into its stomach, along with several tapes of children's stories. April was delighted and promptly began experimenting with the tapes and the headphones that were also provided.

Lydia Frame hung back in the room when her husband headed for his office, exclaiming over how well Mel looked. "I hope you've had a chance to find an appropriate dress for the benefit tomorrow night what with all the time you've spent here."

Mel felt her neck tighten warningly. "Well, I wasn't really—"

"Darling, you *have* to go. Luke is receiving an award from the governor. Hasn't he told you?"

Since it was obvious to them both that Mel knew nothing, she shook her head. Lydia chattered on about the distinguished award for outstanding service in the community. "Luke hates all that fuss, of course. Doesn't seem to realize the ripple effect he has on those around him. At first we thought he wouldn't be back from his vacation for the benefit, but then when you both returned, I juggled things around so he could receive the award that night. I know someone in the Governor's office."

"Mrs. Frame—"

"Oh, darling, Lydia. Please. Mrs. Frame makes me sound positively ancient." She smiled, a friendly, thoroughly comfortable middle-aged woman with an avid passion for golf. A passion only slightly surpassed by her interest in meddling, Mel suspected.

"Lydia," she began again, "whether or not Luke attends really has nothing to do with me."

Lydia blinked. "But…you're his fiancée."

"Did he tell you that?"

"Well, no, but I assumed…well, darling you are pregnant." She waved her hand, her expression falling. "I'm sorry. That's so old-fashioned of me, I know. People have babies all the time today without marriage. I just thought Luke would want—"

"He does. Don't think less of Luke, Lydia. I'm the one who's been…hesitant." It seemed a puny word.

"Hesitant over marrying Luke Trahern?" Lydia's eyebrows skyrocketed. "Darling, he's probably the most elusive, eligible bachelor in this state. Whether you intended to or not, you've landed yourself quite a catch."

Mel felt her facial muscles freezing. The words were eerily similar to what her mother had said when she'd told her parents that Jonathan had proposed.

"All of that is only so much nonsense, of course," Lydia continued. "The only thing that matters is how you both feel. And Luke looks at you the same way my Jason looked at me way back when." She laughed. "Still does, now and then, come to think of it. See what you can do to drag his ornery hide to the benefit. It may not be important to Luke to receive thanks, but sometimes it is important for those who need to express it to have an opportunity to do so."

Mel felt panicked at the very thought of it. "I don't have a dress," she said, seizing on the very excuse that Lydia had already provided.

Lydia waved her hand. "Nonsense. We'll go shopping. Tomorrow morning. I'll pick you up at ten. We'll hit the shops and be done in a few hours, and you can get back to see this little doll-baby here." Before Mel had a chance to argue, she lifted April's earphone and told her goodbye, and strode out the door.

"I like her," April announced after Lydia's departure. "She has a nice laugh."

"Yes, she does," Mel agreed. Lydia's laughter was completely without falseness. And it very nearly disguised the steamroller she wielded.

"Are you gonna go to that thing she was talking about?"

"I don't know." Luke hadn't asked her to accompany him to the benefit. She wasn't sure how she'd react if he did.

"I miss Grammy."

Mel ruffled April's curls. "I know, pumpkin. Why don't we call her right now and you can talk?"

April nodded and Mel immediately reached for the phone, putting through the call. April's mood brightened considerably, and Mel whispered that she would come back in a while after the two had a chance to chatter to their heart's content.

In the hall, she nearly ran right into Luke. He caught her arms in his, steadying her. "Hey. You look like you're in a hurry somewhere."

Thoughts of special fund-raising benefits that he wanted to avoid—at least with her—dissipated the moment his thumbs rubbed over her shoulders. She swallowed, feeling her cheeks warm. "No hurry," she managed. "April's talking to Maisy on the phone."

The corners of his lips tilted slightly. His thumbs continued rubbing. In a slow circle across her arm, up over the curve of her shoulder. He was doing it deliberately, she knew. The dark gleam in his eyes told her so. She could hardly breathe. She moistened her lips.

The rattle of a cart broke through the heady spell he cast and Mel practically jumped back a half foot when it came into view, a white-haired volunteer wielding the heavy book cart. She passed by them with a smile.

Mel crossed her arms, avoiding the amusement in Luke's expression. "Saved by the books," he murmured. Then he drew his finger down her cheek and his amusement died. "Actually, I need to talk to Maisy, myself."

Mel went still. "You've made your decision about April."

He didn't deny it.

"She needs the surgery."

"I've already told Hugo," he said instead of answering. "He thinks Maisy is up to making the trip here."

"Right away?"

"This weekend would be good."

He didn't need to elaborate. Mel had known all along that he would probably act very quickly once a plan of treatment was determined. "When do you want to schedule it?"

"Monday morning."

"Maisy will want to tell April herself."

"I know."

Mel glanced up and down the corridor that was, once again, mercifully empty. "Mrs. Frame told me about the award you're getting at the benefit tomorrow night."

"Lydia has a really big mouth."

"Why hide it?"

"Why advertise it?" He grimaced. "We're not going, anyway."

"Why not?"

He just looked at her.

"Okay, so I said I hated those kinds of events. But this is important. They want to honor you, Luke." It wasn't Luke seizing an opportunity to bandy about his greatness. Maybe it was splitting hairs, but Mel saw a distinct difference. "What's so wrong with that?"

He pinched the bridge of his nose between his fingers. "Because I don't deserve it," he gritted. He dropped his hand. "Now, go back in there and get off your feet. I'll have somebody drive you home later today. Once Maisy gets here, there will be no reason for you to spend every minute with April."

He didn't wait for Mel to protest. He simply turned and strode off down the hall. She wanted to go after him, but he disappeared into another patient's room.

Sighing, she slowly turned back to April's room.

"Grammy wants to talk to you." She held out the phone to Mel.

"Well," Maisy said as soon as Mel said hello. "Are you two still dancing around each other, instead of with each other?"

Mel flushed. But how could she deny it? She and Luke might have found complete accord in the bedroom. But outside of it, she wasn't anywhere near as confident. "Nice to hear your voice, too," she said instead.

Mel didn't see Luke again that afternoon. He was as good as his word though when it came to Maisy. She arrived shortly after dinnertime, much to April's delight. Someone even moved another bed into April's room so that Maisy could sleep there at night. Mel knew it had to have been Luke. The bed also gave Maisy a comfortable way of coddling her broken leg. She also knew he hadn't made the offer so that Mel could stay with April around the clock. What had he said before they'd left Turnabout?

Taking care of you is all I have left.

So when a young man stopped by April's room, announcing that he was there to take Mel back to Luke's, she went without debate. She spent the rest of the evening wandering through his spacious home. She fixed dinner, aware of the faint hope inside her that he would appear to join her. But he didn't. She showered in his shower, wrapped herself in his robe and propped herself in the center of his bed.

And wondered what she was doing with her life

and whether she was destined to spend it, yet again, with a man who couldn't share his emotions with her.

Only her heart knew what her head refused to recognize. That Luke actually *possessed* emotions, while Jonathan had not. Jonathan had never had any family he'd tried to live up to. His mother had died after Mel had married him, but she'd lived in Florida and Jonathan's schedule had been full. Mel had flown to Florida alone, attending the funeral of a woman she'd never met. Nor had Jonathan ever torn himself up over a patient. And if he'd ever grieved over Nicky, he'd never grieved with Mel.

She'd tried. So many times, she'd tried to reach Jonathan. After one too many puzzled looks, one too many suggestions that she go shopping or go to a spa, she'd finally realized that Jonathan just hadn't possessed any kind of emotional depth. Or at least, the depth that she'd needed. And she'd stopped trying.

And what are you doing to reach Luke? The small, silent voice inside Mel haunted her as she lay sideways on the bed and hugged his pillow to her cheek.

Despite finally opening up about her marriage and her son, was she still keeping Luke at bay just as surely as he was her? Is that why he hadn't explained about the poor patient he'd lost even after he'd realized she'd overheard him and Jason discussing her? Why he'd kept silent about the benefit? The award?

She was sharing his bed. His house.

Her abdomen shifted and she smoothed her hand over the restless babies.

She was sharing his children.

And she was glad. If nothing else, Mel knew that she was glad that Luke had found her that night on the beach.

Sleep continued to elude her, and she finally reached for the cordless phone on his nightstand. It wasn't particularly late. She called Maisy to check on April, who'd eaten only a little for dinner and was sleeping again, under the effects of the powerful pain medication she'd been administered. Before she'd gone to sleep, Maisy had told April that she was going to have surgery on Monday morning. In typical April fashion, she'd accepted the decision with a barrage of questions that Luke had come in and patiently answered.

Mel had barely disconnected the call when the phone rang in her hand, and she was so startled, she answered it. It was Lydia, reminding her that she'd be by to pick her up at ten the next morning.

Though she knew it would be smarter to beg off, she surprised herself by not doing so.

For some reason, that small action was enough to dissipate some of the fog that clouded her thoughts. And when she settled again in Luke's bed, tugging his pillow against her cheek, she finally slept.

It was completely dark when she awoke later. The soft lamp she'd left turned on had been turned off. But she didn't need to sweep her arm across the wide expanse of bed beside her to know that Luke wasn't there.

She tilted her head, listening, but all she heard

were the now-familiar sounds of the silent house. The low hum of the central air-conditioning. The occasional call of an owl outside the windows. Maybe Luke had come and gone.

She lay there, fully awake now, feeling the babies bump and roll inside her, and with a huff of impatience, she climbed out of bed. She was beginning to have fantasies of a night slept all the way through without needing to visit the bathroom every few hours.

Not that Luke's bathroom was any hardship. It, alone, was larger than the bedroom she'd had at the cottage at Maisy's Place. Rather than the ornate gold and marble fussiness she'd been used to from her parents' house and then her husband's house, however, Luke's was warm, streamlined. Had she had an opportunity to choose fixtures, fittings, colors herself, she wouldn't change a thing. It was made for comfort, from the massive whirlpool tub to the stone-floored separate shower.

She dragged her attention from the shower and looked in the mirror, to see if she was actually drooling. Assured she was not, she flipped off the light and padded back through the bedroom.

A particularly hard little kick under her ribs made her wince, and she rubbed her hand over her expanding belly. "Come on, guys, give your mom a break, okay?" The twins just kept flip-flopping, and Mel knew there was no hope of getting back to sleep just yet.

She went into the kitchen, and was perched on the

bar stool at the mottled black-and-brown granite countertop, forcing down a glass of milk, when she heard a muffled sound.

Relief swept through her. Luke hadn't gone back to Sunquest after all. She followed the sound through the laundry room, to the garage.

And he was there, all right. She could see him around the edge of his sleek BMW. He was sitting on an overturned five-gallon drum, his dark head bent over whatever piece of his '69 he was currently coaxing back into life. "I thought I heard you," she said, and stepped down into the garage, rounding the cars. The floor was cement and warm beneath her bare feet. "I'm glad you came home."

He didn't look up.

She stepped closer and barely refrained from touching his hunched shoulder, running her fingers through the silky weight of his thick hair. "Luke, I know you're irritated with me about the benefit tomorrow night, but I—" Her gaze drifted past his body to the greasy engine part sitting on a spread of newspapers between his feet. Only it wasn't just covered in grease. It gleamed, wet and shiny.

She swallowed, dismay washing through her as her gaze slowly slid from the part to the hand he held oddly, stiffly, over it.

A hand covered in blood. She sucked in a harsh breath. All thoughts of a logical, sensible discussion about their future went flying right out the window.

"I think—" his voice was emotionless "—I might have cut myself."

"Might?" Her voice went up half an octave. "Are you kidding me? You're bleeding all over the floor! You're supposed to cut open other people. Not yourself."

His lips twisted and his eyes went dark. "Maybe this way is safer."

Chapter 20

Safer.

Right before Mel's eyes, blood flowed from a deep gash on the palm of his hand down his fingers. It gathered at the end of his middle finger, pooled, formed a fat drop and fell to the darkening puddle soaking into the newsprint. "Don't be ridiculous," she said as she ran to the built-in cupboards lining one wall. They were filled with tools, all things macho, as she'd teased him just the other day. She grabbed the roll of paper towels, uncaring that she'd dislodged a row of tools that clattered to the floor. She hurried back to him, yanking off a hank that she crumpled into a ball and pressed against his palm. "Hold that," her voice shook.

He sighed, slowly curling his fingers. "Don't upset yourself. Or the babies. It's not as bad as it looks."

She tore off another long strip, wrapping it around his entire fist. "Sure, not bad at all," she agreed hoarsely. "I just come out to the garage to find you bleeding to death all over the garage floor." She swiped her eyes when her vision blurred. "You need stitches."

His dark blue gaze drifted over her and she realized she was still only wearing her short blue nightgown. With an oath, she ran back into the house, pulling off the nightie and dragging a denim dress over her head. She pushed her feet into her sandals, grabbed her purse and darted back to the garage.

The paper towels were soaked through. "God," she cried. "You're a surgeon, Luke, what were you thinking?" She pulled the towels away, replaced them with more, wrapped his hand again. "Come on. We have to get you help."

"I *was* a surgeon," he said flatly.

She was looking around for his car keys. "Don't say that. It's a cut. You'll get stitches. You'll be fine." She prayed. Her own father had turned to academics when he'd broken his hand in a skiing accident because the fine mobility had been irreparably damaged. "Dammit, where are your keys?" She finally saw them still in the ignition. "Luke, come on. I'll drive. Sunquest is closest, right?" She rounded the car, opening the passenger door, tossing her purse inside.

Luke still hadn't moved.

Her heart was in her throat. She went back over to him and tucked her hands beneath his arm. "Come on."

He yanked out of her hold, his expression suddenly angry. "It's just a cut, Mel. Leave it alone. Leave me alone."

She blinked, stared. "Like you left *me* alone? Pushing and poking and prodding until you know everything that's in my head, my heart." She huffed impatiently, yanking more towels off the spool, tucking them around the last batch that was already starting to redden.

"I don't know what's in your heart."

"Love, you stubborn fool. Love!" She pulled at his other arm. "Now would you please come on! How do you think you're going to be able to help April if half your hand is missing 'cause you cut it off fixing some bloody carburetor!"

"I didn't cut off my hand." He rose but didn't take any steps away from the '69. "And it doesn't matter anyway, because my career has been shot since January!"

"This is about that patient of yours who died, isn't it. Because you're blaming yourself."

"What do you know about it, other than what you overheard that night from Jason?"

"I know plenty," she said evenly. "Though, goodness knows it hasn't come from you. Honestly, Luke, what do you think your staff talks about all day long but everybody else's business, particularly the exalted surgeons? You think I haven't heard, chapter and verse, about that poor girl you tried to save? Or about the hundreds that you *have?*''

''It's not Jennifer Melendez.'' His voice was tight. ''It's the fact that I can't pick up a goddamned scalpel without wanting to puke. The fact that I can't sleep at night for seeing patient after patient on my table, only they're not alive and breathing—they're corpses, cold and beyond breath, expressions etched in eternity that damn me for my failures. And it only gets worse every day that goes on.''

She swallowed the sudden knot of tears that seemed large enough to choke her. She touched his chest. Felt the unsteady pulse of his heart against her palm. She'd wanted emotion. Only now it was enough to break her heart. ''You're only a man, Luke. With an incredible talent. And there is a little girl named April who trusts you to take care of her. It's not the rest of your staff, the other surgeons, not even Dr. Frame who convinced Maisy to take another chance. It was *you.*''

''I hardly talked to her about it!''

''You didn't have to. Maisy trusts you, Luke. April trusts you, and so do I. But unless we get your hand taken care of the point will be moot, because you won't be in any shape to do *anything!*''

''You haven't been listening to me,'' he said slowly, distinctly. ''My hand is not the problem. My head is.''

''Then shut off your head and follow your heart,'' Mel said huskily. ''That's the only reason I'm here with you. Because if I listened to my head, I'd have run far and fast the second you put your leather coat over my shoulders that night on the beach. Instead, I looked up at you, and all the kindness that is inside you, and…here we are.''

''Mel—''

''You sleep fine when you're with me,'' she whispered. ''I know, because sometimes, I'll lie there awake with these two dancing a midnight merengue inside me, and watch you sleep.''

''It's the only time I sleep fine,'' he said flatly. ''With you.''

''Well.'' She blinked. ''I'm not going anywhere.'' The pink seeping through his paper towels was darkening. ''Now, could we please go and have your hand taken care of? Because, you know, I've got to drive you, and I'll tell you here and now that despite being a surgeon's daughter, I never really enjoyed the sight of blood.''

He snatched up the paper towels, bunching more around his hand. ''Dammit, I'll drive.''

''My name is Melanie,'' she said huskily, slipping into the driver's seat before he could. ''Not 'dammit.'''

He rounded the car and climbed in. Mel reached over him, tugging his seat belt into place. Her forehead brushed his chin and she looked up into his dark eyes. ''I love you, Luke,'' she whispered. ''We'll get through this all, okay? April's surgery. The babies. Just don't shut me out. Because I can take just about anything but that.''

A muscle in his jaw flexed. He caught her head

with his uninjured hand and pressed his lips to hers for a long, aching moment. "Just tell me one thing," he said when their lips finally parted.

"Anything."

"You *do* have a legal driver's license, don't you? You were on Turnabout a long time."

She breathed out, groaning. Started the car, and whipped it out of the garage and down the winding road, heading straight to Sunquest. "I'm born and bred Californian," she said. "On my sixteenth birthday, my parents gave me a cute little Benz."

"That's not an answer," he muttered, bracing his good hand against the dash as she rocketed down the road and pulled up in front of the clinic in less time than he'd ever made it.

In the end, it turned out that Luke's hand wasn't as badly slashed as Mel had feared. It took stitches, certainly. But he hadn't damaged any tendons or nerves. After he was stitched up, bandaged, and shot full of antibiotic, it was well past midnight. By unspoken agreement, they went by to look in on April. Luke checked her chart. Mel pulled up her covers.

Maisy, leg propped on a mountain of pillows, slept soundly.

They drove home, Mel at the wheel again after proving that she did possess a license after all. Instead of tumbling exhausted into bed, however, they both seemed wakeful. Mel finally opened the glass doors leading out to the stone terrace that led down to the pool. "Come on."

She selected one of the chaise longues that was

positioned to look out over the glowing lights of the city. "Sit there."

He eyed her but sat. She kicked off her sandals and sat down in front of him, pulling his hands around to rest with hers on the bulge of her stomach, careful of the thick bandage cushioning his injured hand. "There," she murmured. "Still hot outside, but bearable. And it's sort of like looking out at the ocean."

"An ocean of light."

"Are you making fun of me?"

"Not in this lifetime."

She smiled faintly and rested her head back against his chest, her temple right beside his chin in the spot that seemed made for her. But her smile faded as the worry bottled inside her crept back to the surface. "You didn't deliberately cut yourself, did you?"

He exhaled roughly. "No. I'm not that self-destructive, thanks."

She believed him. "Good. I'm glad."

"If I'd wanted to immobilize my hands, I'd have done a better job of it," he said evenly, "instead of just bleeding a mess over the carburetor that's going to have to be cleaned all over again now."

She closed her eyes, an unwilling smile tugging at her lips. "You're worried about the car part."

"Man and his engine, Mel. Serious stuff."

She watched a pinpoint of light moving across the inky sky. Wondered if it was a shooting star. Figured it was more likely an airplane. Phoenix had an incredibly busy airport. "How'd you end up working at Sunquest, anyway?"

"You're as full of questions as April."

"Well, I think that if I ask a dozen, you might conceivably respond to fifty percent."

She felt the long breath he drew in and let out. "I was on staff in Cheyenne," he said eventually. "I had a young patient that everybody else had written off as untreatable. But I'd read about Sunquest, about Jason's progressive efforts in treating neurological conditions. I contacted him."

"And the patient?"

Luke leaned his head back against the soft cushion. "I got a wedding invitation from her a few years ago."

"Did you go?"

"No."

"Why not?"

He thought back. "Wall-to-wall surgeries," he finally said. "I sent a gift."

She laughed softly. "I think you'd already given the bride the gift that mattered."

"Anyway, that's how I met Jason. That was nearly ten years ago. Our interests kept converging. Then he offered me the spot at Sunquest about eight years ago and I took it. I was at UCLA Medical Center then. Ever since we've been haranguing people to open up their checkbooks, making Sunquest even better. Jason's good at fund-raising, but it's not his favorite. I'm miserable at it, so I generally keep my focus on what we can achieve if we have better funding. It's a constant battle, though. And critical if we're to keep our fees sliding. If a patient has insurance, great. If they don't, we foot the costs ourselves. Nobody'll lose their life savings at Sunquest to save the life of someone they love. But we can't save the world, so we select our patients pretty carefully.''

"Then Maisy doesn't have to worry about the money.''

"It's taken care of.''

"What did your grandfather think when you joined Sunquest?''

"Mac? He bragged to all his cronies. Made noises about moving out here to Arizona. Retirement capital of the western U.S. But he never did. He was too tied to the ranch.''

"And your mother? Did you see much of her after she left you with your grandfather?'' She caught his hand as it ventured over the curve of her breast, and dragged it down to safer zones.

"She sent cards at Christmas for a while, then even that petered out. Mac tried to locate her when Bethany died, but he never found her. I tried too, the year I graduated from med school. No luck.''

"What would you have done if you'd been successful?''

He found himself missing her button-down dresses. The one she wore now was like a shield of denim across her front, no hope of sneaking in a fingertip. "I don't know,'' he said. "Made sure she was okay, I guess.''

"But why? She abandoned you and your sister.''

"She made sure we were somewhere safe, first," Luke said. "I told you. We were better off with Mac. But," he sighed, "she was my mother."

Mel didn't say anything after that. He almost thought she might have fallen asleep, she was so still against him. When she did speak, it wasn't another question.

"I want to see you accept that award, Luke. People want to thank you, and you never let them. I want to go to the benefit."

"Mel, you don't have to prove anything to me."

"I have something to prove to myself," she said quietly.

And what could he say to that? "Okay."

They stayed on that chaise all night. Finally dropping off to sleep only to awaken with the warmth of the sun shining over them. Luke rose and took Mel by the hand and led her inside, where he slowly pulled her denim dress over her head. When she lifted her hands, reaching for his shirt, he caught them, kissed her knuckles. "Let me."

"But your bandage, your hand—"

"Let me."

Her lips parted. She slowly straightened her fingers, then relaxed them, curling them softly, trustingly over his. "All right." Her voice was barely a whisper.

He kissed her knuckles again. Released her only long enough to tear off his shirt, then turned her palms upward and kissed the vulnerable pulse throbbing on her smooth inner wrists. She made a soft sound, that little hum, and he clamped down on his sudden urge to rush. To devour.

Her fingers flexed again, brushing against his face. His throat. He tasted the inside of her elbow. She murmured his name. He tucked his fingers under the straps of her bra and steadily drew them down her shoulders. Her breasts, full, velvety, rose above the soft, white cups, filling his hands. The early sun shone through the windows, golden and warm on her flesh, his hands. She felt soft yet strong, but it was her eyes that held him captive. They looked heavy, dark, full of want.

He dragged his thumbs around, over her tight nipples. Her eyelashes dipped. He repeated the motion, and she pressed her lips softly together. Her throat worked as she swallowed. His jaw felt locked with need and he deliberately unclasped her bra, letting it fall where it may. Her white slip felt slippery under his fingers as he knelt and pulled it down, taking her panties along with it.

He straightened and slid his palm over the thrust of her belly that nestled against him. She sucked in her breath, audibly. Her hands covered his. She was trembling.

He was a doctor. There were no secrets the body possessed that he hadn't studied or examined. But the feeling running through him now had only one name. Wonder.

A single, glistening tear stood out on her lashes.

Patience gone, Luke lifted her in his arms and carried her to his bed. Her arms lifted toward him and as he went down beside her, he thought maybe, just maybe, he must have done something right along the way to deserve her, after all.

Lydia Frame picked up Mel on the dot of ten o'clock, and they drove into old town Scottsdale where little shops and boutiques lined the narrow streets. "We have more malls than Carter's has pills," Lydia said, "but I think the most interesting things can be found down here."

"Well," Mel said as she stood on the sidewalk and felt heat radiate back at her from the cement, "as long as the shops are cool. I always thought stories of the Arizona heat had to be exaggerated. But it's like the inside of an overheated Laundromat dryer, here."

Lydia laughed and led her into the first of many perfectly lovely, perfectly cooled shops. By noon, Mel had found a dress. Lydia's running commentary on everything from her grandchildren to Sunquest's funding challenges to how much she enjoyed her visits to Turnabout ceased only when they stopped for a quick lunch. But it started up again as soon as they were inside Lydia's long Lincoln with the air-conditioning blasting over them.

"It'll be good to have this benefit tonight out of our hair," she said. "Then I can concentrate on my next project."

"You do a lot for Dr. Frame's career, I suppose."

"Well, I support Jason, of course." She drove through the busy weekend traffic with ease. "When

I can. It was just handy that I could help with the benefit. Ordinarily I'm busy enough with my own dog and pony shows for the school where I teach. It's appalling how badly budgets have been cut lately. To the point we have to raise our own money to support the music and arts programs. Disgraceful.''

Mel stared at Lydia. ''I didn't know you were a teacher.''

''Oh, heavens, yes. Twenty-five years now. I hope to retire next year.'' She grinned. ''More time for golf and grandbabies. Not necessarily in that order.''

''You never mentioned it.''

''Well, darling, it's not as if you and I ever really had a chance to sit down and chat much when Jason and I visited Turnabout. You were always the soul of discretion and hospitality, going about your job there. And while I'm proud of my career, I have to say I tend to brag far more about my grandchildren when given an opportunity. We'll have great fun, Mel. Assuming you do stay here with Luke, of course, I mean.'' She flushed a little. ''There's a group of women, most of them wives from Sunquest in fact, and we get together once a week for breakfast.''

''And plan fund-raisers,'' Mel presumed weakly.

''Good God, no.'' The notion seemed to truly horrify Lydia. ''We kibitz and laugh and complain and do whatever suits our fancy. Some of us are grandmothers, some, like you are just starting out with their families. We all know it's not always easy being

involved with a man with a calling, whether it's as
a doctor or a minister or what have you. But it's not
as if their life is our only life. Now, do you want me
to drop you off at Sunquest, since I know that's
where Luke is, or do you want me to drop you at his
place?''

"Sunquest," Mel said faintly.

Lydia just smiled brilliantly and headed up the
driveway to the clinic. "Do you like golf, Mel?"

"Never tried it."

"Ha." She parked in front of the main door.
"Fresh blood." She laughed and waved as she drove
off, leaving Mel standing there holding her shopping
bags and a wealth of unsettlingly new perspective. It
took only a moment for the baking heat to drive her
inside, and she dumped her purchases in Luke's office then headed down to visit with Maisy and April.
After a few hours with them, she went back to Luke's
office. She knew he was doing consultations most of
the day, but he'd expected to be through early
enough so they could get ready for that evening.

He wasn't there, yet, though.

Before she could think better of it, she sat down
at his desk and picked up the phone, dialing quickly.
It was answered on the second ring, as it had always
been.

"Hello, Reeves," she greeted. She nervously
wound the coiled phone cord around her finger. "It's
Melanie. I'd like to speak to Mother."

"Have I told you that you're beautiful?"

Mel smiled and tilted her head back to look at

Luke. The benefit had been underway for two hours. Luke had received his award, they'd shaken dozens of hands, posed for dozens of photos, met dozens of people. Now they were dancing and Luke had made it plain that as far as he was concerned, their time was officially their own.

"I believe you might have mentioned it," Mel said. She felt beautiful. Her soft brown dress bared her shoulders, a good portion of her back, and a hint of cleavage, didn't exaggerate just how pregnant she was, and ended at the floor, hiding ankles that, for once, weren't even puffy. But the most glorious part of it was dancing with Luke. He'd shaved. He'd even gone so far as to cut his hair. And as much as she had fancied his mane of wild waves, she personally found his close-cropped do particularly mouthwatering. Maybe because it didn't distract from his thoroughly masculine features. "You look swell, yourself," she said. In a conservative tux that made her fingers itch to delve beneath.

His lips tilted, as if he'd divined her thoughts. "You dance pretty well for a pregnant lady."

"I can do other things pretty well, also."

His eyes darkened. "Ms. Summerville, are you threatening me with—what did you call it—bed bouncing?"

She slid her arm around his neck and lifted her mouth close to his ear. "Promising. But first, I have something I want to give you. I was saving it for the right moment."

Luke's eyes drifted downward. "There's nothing else you can give me that matters more than this."

"All right, so it's a gift for Sunquest." She slid out of his arms and headed back to the table they'd shared with the Frames and some members of the governor's staff. Her heart pounded, not just from Luke's proximity, but because she wasn't entirely certain how he would react to what she'd done. She lifted her little crocheted purse that went with the dress and plucked the check from inside. "Here," she blurted, handing it to him. "I don't want you to think that I'm doing this for any reason other than that I believe in what Sunquest does."

He looked from her to the check. "What are you talking about?"

"It's a donation." She nibbled her lip. "I, um, I talked to my parents today, Luke. And told them that I finally had a use for the trust fund I've tried to ignore most of my life. My father had the funds wired this afternoon. Figures that he'd be able to get around little details like banks being closed on Saturday afternoons."

He didn't even glance at the writing. "You talked to them? When? Why?"

"Because of you." She realized that it might have been better to wait until they were home before announcing things this way. They were in the grand ballroom of the famed Arizona Biltmore, surrounded by hundreds of guests, though mostly nobody was paying them any heed at the moment. "Because you tried to find your mother, despite all that happened.

Because you're decent and kind and you don't deserve a wife who's afraid to face up to the disappointments of her past.''

"Wife?"

She swallowed. "Luke, the check is a gift, no matter what. No strings, no expectations. It's just that I can finally put the money somewhere that I believe in.''

"Wife?"

"No matter what happens Monday morning, with April, I know you'll do your best for her. Whether or not that means you'll scrub, or oversee or what—''

Luke covered her mouth with his bandaged hand and watched her eyes go wide. *"Wife?"*

She blinked. Nodded jerkily. Carefully lifted his hand away from her mouth. "And I think we should probably do it soon, 'cause you know twins sometimes have a tendency to come early. And my parents will probably want to come, too, so it's only right to give you fair warning. As long as it's before fall session begins at the university. He's the dean, you see, and—''

"Mel.''

"—what?''

"Shut up.''

Her mouth snapped closed.

"I'm going to say this once and you listen well. I'm glad you called your parents. For your sake. But you never, *ever*, have to do something because you think I expect it. I don't give a flying flip who or what your parents are, except that they did something right in creating you. I love you. I want a life with you. With our children. I want a partner, not a pretty prop. I want—what are you crying for?''

She dashed away a tear. ''You haven't said that before.''

''Said what?''

''That you love me.''

He gave her a long look. ''What do you think the past month has been about, Mel? I love you. I've loved you from the night you seduced me on the beach.''

''I didn't—''

''You did. We did. And it's been my sanity when there wasn't anything sane left about me. The sooner you're my wife, the happier I'll be.''

''It's not just about the babies?''

''It's never been just about the babies,'' he said, his voice raw. If he started kissing her, he wasn't going to stop. Which meant he needed to get her alone. ''I suppose you're gonna want a wedding, all the trimmings and fuss.''

''I've done all that, Luke. And none of it matters. What matters is the man who shares the vows. I don't care if we have a hundred guests or a mere handful. As long as my parents and Maisy and April are there, and Jason and Lydia, too, I think, we'll have everyone who truly matters.''

''And if April—''

''Shh. I don't even want to hear it. I have faith in you, Luke. In you. In us. In the incredible fact that we ever met at all that night. And I have faith that April will come through this, healthier and better than ever before because of you and everyone else at Sunquest.''

''Mel, my hand is able, but that doesn't necessarily mean I'll be—''

''You will.'' Her lips softened, pressed against his. ''Have faith, Luke. You're the one who told me that. Trust your heart. Have faith. We have one more chance. The rest will come.''

He cupped her face in his palm and ran his thumb down the fine line of her jaw. Stared into the depths of her mesmerizing eyes and saw the truth there. The truth and the peace that had bound him to her from the very start. ''You really believe that.''

Her cheek pressed into his hand, her eyes never straying from his. ''I believe in you, Luke. I believe in us,'' she said.

And that was all they needed.

Epilogue

Mel hugged her arms against her body and stared out the window to the desert landscape beyond. It seemed as if days had passed since Luke had disappeared behind the double doors of O.R. 2. In truth, it had only been a few hours.

But with each minute that ticked by, the atmosphere in the small waiting area seemed to grow ever more silent. More tense. Mel looked over at Maisy, who sat still as a statue, on the upholstered couch. She hadn't moved once since Luke went in to scrub.

"She's going to make it," Mel said quietly.

Maisy swallowed and nodded. Even her red curls looked subdued today. "I'll never forget the day Tessa told me she was pregnant." Her hands lifted then fell back to her lap, twisting together. "I was…horrified. She hadn't been seeing anyone that

I knew of. She never once told me who he was. April's father. But she loved him, I never doubted that. I could see it in her face. Then April came along.'' Her throat worked. ''Losing Tessa was bad enough,'' she said unsteadily. ''April has to come through.''

Mel sat down beside Maisy and closed her hand over the other woman's. If she was nervous, she knew Maisy's nerves were stretched far more thinly. ''Luke told us the surgery would take—'' She broke off at the hushed whoosh of the double doors opening.

Maisy sat forward in her seat, her grip on Mel's hand tight.

Jason Frame stepped into view. He looked tired, but as his gaze fell on the women, a small smile stretched his lips. ''She's being moved to recovery,'' he said without preamble. ''If you want to come with me, Maisy, you can sit with her for a few minutes. Luke will be out soon.''

Maisy nodded, her eyes red-rimmed. She squeezed Mel's hand and rose, looking shaky on her cumbersome cast. Jason tucked his hand under her arm and gently helped her through the double doors.

Mel pressed her hand to her heart and sank back against the couch. She closed her eyes, thanks coursing through her mind. Then she heard that whoosh again, and she opened her eyes to see Luke.

Luke, wearing pale green scrubs with a white hand towel slung around his neck, his hair sticking up in damp spikes. She pushed to her feet. "You look like you've just gone ten rounds."

"With a seven-year-old prizefighter," he said, his lips tilting. "You, on the other hand, look beautiful." He stepped close and hooked his hands over her shoulders, pulling her against him. He lowered his head, resting it on her shoulders, and let out a long breath.

Mel wrapped her arms around him, loving him so much it felt as if she'd always loved him. "Are you okay?"

"Should be asking that about April."

Mel tilted her head against his, pressing her lips against his temple. She slid her fingers through his sweat-damp hair. "I know April is okay."

Luke breathed in the sweet, clean scent of her. He'd spend a lifetime earning the faith she had in him. He lifted his head until he could see into her eyes. And he felt the jolt he always did when she looked at him, inside him, and soul recognized soul. "She's got weeks of recovery ahead of her. We won't know conclusively until—"

"Shh." She pressed her lips against his. "How are *you* doing?"

His hand hurt like hell. And it was true that he felt as if he'd just fought his way out of a boxing ring. "Never better. Do you want to go back and see April? I have an in with the nurses back there."

"I'll bet you do," said Mel wryly. "Half the nurses here want to marry you and the other half want to adopt you."

"What do you want?"

"To marry you. To have our babies. Maybe more."

He raised his eyebrows. "More?"

"Well, it's fun to try," Mel pointed out sedately.

Only the fact that they were in the waiting room where any member of the staff could find them kept him from kissing her the way he wanted. "How about you? Are you okay?"

"Why wouldn't I be? I have everything I ever wanted in the palm of my hands."

"Your concern for April goes deeper than simple friendship," Luke said quietly. It was inextricably linked with memories of her son.

Mel studied him for a moment. How had it happened that he knew her so well? Or that she could read his thoughts, his emotions, as easily, maybe better, than her own?

"Dominic will always be with me, a beautiful little boy," she said. "If it weren't for him, for the short life he had, I wouldn't have met Maisy and found Turnabout. Or you. It's all a path. Our lives. The people we've known, and loved, let go and found." She slid her palms against his, linking their hands. "Now I'm on the path with you. And our family. I have more happiness than I'd ever thought I could find and I know that no matter what turns our path might have, we'll walk them together."

"Turnabout is quite a place," he said.

"A little sand, a little surf and a little magic." She leaned against him and he could feel the uneven movements of the babies inside her. "But the magic we keep with us wherever we go."

He decided he didn't give a flip if a staff member strolled in and found him kissing his fiancée. "I love you, Melanie Summerville."

Her lips curved against his. "I love you, too, Dr. Trahern."

* * * * *

*Be sure to watch for more stories
set on Turnabout, coming only to
Silhouette Special Edition in Fall 2003.*

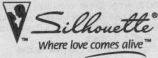

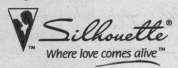

CLAIMING HIS OWN

These men use charm, sex appeal and sheer determination to get what they want—so these women had better be very careful if they have things to hide....

RAGGED RAINBOWS

by *New York Times* bestselling author

LINDA LAEL MILLER

Would Mitch Prescott's reporter instincts uncover *all* of Shay Kendall's painful secrets?

SOMETHING TO HIDE

an original story by

LAURIE PAIGE

Only rancher Travis Dalton could help Alison Harvey— but dare she risk telling him the truth?

Available March 2003 at your favorite retail outlet.

Where love comes alive™

This February—2003—
Silhouette Books cordially invites you
to the arranged marriages
of two of our favorite brides, in

The *Wedding* ARRANGEMENT

A man fulfilling his civic duty finds himself irresistibly drawn to his sexy, single, *pregnant* fellow juror. Might they soon be sharing more than courtroom banter? Such as happily ever after? Find out in **Barbara Boswell's** *Irresistible You.*

She *thought* she was his mail-order bride, but it turned out she had the wrong groom. Or did she? The feisty beauty had set her eyes on him—and wasn't likely to let go anytime soon, in **Raye Morgan's** *Wife by Contract.*

Look for **The Wedding Arrangement** *in February 2003 at your favorite retail outlet.*

Silhouette®
Where love comes alive™